Advance Praise for
The Haight Mystery Series

"*The Haight* is a fabulous book!"

—Pamela Callow, author of
The Kate Lange Thriller Series

⎯⎯•⎯⎯•⎯⎯

"Highly recommended."

—Ken McGoogan, author and adventurer

ALSO BY PETER MOREIRA

The Haight

A HITMAN
ON HAIGHT STREET

BOOK 2 OF THE HAIGHT MYSTERY SERIES

BY PETER MOREIRA

PERMUTED
PRESS

A PERMUTED PRESS BOOK
ISBN: 978-1-68261-963-6
ISBN (eBook): 978-1-68261-964-3

A Hitman on Haight Street
© 2020 by Peter Moreira
All Rights Reserved

Cover Design by Teddy Lapierre

PERMUTED
PRESS

Permuted Press, LLC
New York • Nashville
permutedpress.com

Published in the United States of America

For Carol
With love

CHAPTER 1

MONDAY
JUNE 17, 1968

He felt rejuvenated that morning. It was more than just a sense of accomplishment. He woke without dreading ridicule. He woke without fearing he might fail. His mission had been the transcendent moment of his life. He felt…fully formed. Still, he longed to linger in bed, he'd had so little sleep. But there was more work to do. He shoved back the covers, stood, and stretched. A morning breeze billowed the threadbare curtains, filling his little room with sunlight and chilling his naked body. He smiled—the breeze was refreshing and heightened the zest he felt. It would have been a perfect start to the day if not for the dreadful noise from across the alleyway.

"Yummy, Yummy, Yummy." It was a radio in the next building blasting the chart-topper that had been everywhere the previous summer. He strode to the window and yanked it shut. Relieved, he stretched again, linking his hands, and lifting his arms up. He felt taller, lighter. Release. He padded across the linoleum floor to his bedside table and pressed the play button on his cassette recorder. The room filled with a strumming guitar then the loon-like call of Jasmine's voice.

I'm listening for Jackie. She is watching me
Plucking plump suspicions from my paranoia tree

He smiled and let the glorious noise pulse through him. It was hard to believe his neighbor across the alley had come to Haight-Ashbury to listen to Ohio Express. You come to Haight-Ashbury for the Dead and Jefferson Airplane and Moby Grape and Janis and

1

Jimi, and now—Jasmine. All the world was listening to the music from this little corner of San Francisco, and Jasmine was the latest star in the constellation. He felt his body warm at the thought of her. He'd felt close to Jasmine the moment he heard that soaring voice, saw her beautiful body—the cascading hair, her sweet face, glorious mouth....

It amused him to hear her described as "the new Joni Mitchell." That wasn't right. Jasmine was better than Joni, she was so much more...fascinating. He picked up the little case of the cassette and studied her photo. Long blonde hair flowing over her bare shoulder. It excited him to think such a beautiful creature could write and sing the song he was listening to.

> Jackie's green with envy, Mary's red with rage
> I'm lavender with ennui, Jane's blue without her sage
> They prowl about and whisper with efficiency and stealth
> Words almost as harsh as what I think about myself

He listened motionless, rapt. When the song finished, he rewound the tape and turned up the volume as loud as it would go without distorting the sound. Once he finished this mission, he'd buy himself a component stereo so he could listen to the Haight-Ashbury sound properly.

He thought about getting dressed but the excitement of the previous night lingered. It had been a glorious experience, like sex, but even more exhilarating, consuming. His nakedness seemed to prolong the carnal glory. He took a vial of hash oil from the little table by his bed and prepared a spliff. He thought how hash had become his drug of choice since arriving in Haight-Ashbury. He'd avoided LSD after having a bad trip in New York the year before. He never touched heroin—he'd seen what it does. Hash offered a mellow high and was easy to hide. And he'd recently learned that the word "assassin" was derived from the word "hashish," so it had special meaning for him. Especially today.

He took a long, long toke and held it. His throat burned and the rush surged up his spine. He exhaled slowly. He took another drag and relived the wonders of the previous night. He had only been in Golden Gate Park twelve minutes, but it was twelve minutes of ecstasy. During his third toke he thought of how he'd arched his back, pulling her feet from the ground. She was squirming, her back against his stomach, her ass against his crotch. She tried to claw him but couldn't reach round. She weakened quickly and went limp. He'd always loved it when his partners climaxed, but no orgasm could compare with the thrill of feeling her life leave her body.

He held the smoke in his lungs as he walked to the corner and picked up a metal wastepaper basket. He tossed in the stained jeans and sweatshirt he'd worn the night before then got a canister of lighter fluid from the pile of equipment on his bureau and soaked the clothes. He took one last hit from the spliff and tossed it into the metal container.

As the blue flame enveloped his clothes, he wondered if he should open the window to let the fumes out, but it would let his neighbor's music in. He decided to take his chance with the fumes.

He replaced the lighter fluid on his dresser along with the other equipment: Mr. Clean, wash cloths, rubber gloves, Clorox bleach. He even had something that was new to him—big plastic bags called Glad. He donned a pair of rubber gloves and filled the sink in his washroom with warm water and Mr. Clean. He wiped down the spot where he'd tossed the jeans and sweatshirt hours earlier then felt under the bed until he found the bulky garbage bag that he'd stashed there.

He pulled out the bag and glanced at the window again. The curtain was drawn, no one could see in. He untied it and reached inside to find his rucksack. It was sticky. Blood had begun to drip from the rucksack by the time he got back to his room, so he'd had to stash it in a garbage bag. Now, the blood had oozed through the knapsack and he had difficulty unbuckling and opening it. But he got it opened and felt around in the tangle of blood-clotted hair and around the ears, chin, nose, nose stud. Finally, his fingers found it— his knife. It was still entangled in her hair. Her hair had been so lovely. As she struggled, it had filled his face and he'd inhaled the strawberry scent of her shampoo. He was tempted to smell her hair again now, but he was sure the blood and gore must have obliterated that delicate scent.

He drew the knife out and eased the bloody strands from around the hilt. Her blood covered every inch of the blade. He was surprised how much there was, how it blackened and crusted the steel. In the bathroom, he washed the knife at the sink, ensuring all the blood went down the drain. Then he flushed the ashes from the wastepaper basket into the toilet. He was stoned, but he paid attention to detail. Once he'd cleansed the knife, he could focus on the next assignment.

He returned to the bed, tucked her fine hair back in the rucksack, and re-tied the garbage bag. He made sure there was no blood on the outside of the bag and shoved the bulky package under the bed. He felt a twinge of resentment twist his gut. He knew what they'd say. It was only a girl. He hadn't really been challenged. But it had been a successful mission. It had been perfect—almost. The import- ant thing was he'd held his nerve, even when things went wrong. He was an assassin, a hit man, a made man—he'd proven it. When he'd encountered a minor problem in the dark on Hippie Hill, he'd swiftly found a solution and executed it. No one had any reason to laugh at him, to belittle his achievement.

CHAPTER 2

It was Armageddon at the breakfast table—protests, yelling, fussing, and tears. Jimmy Spracklin had hoped to get into the Hall of Justice early to check up on his detectives and initiate some inquiries before going to court. As the head of the Bureau of Inspectors, he had to oversee the entire homicide squad for the San Francisco Police Department, as well as handling his own cases. Today, Spracklin had to be in court because Andrew Fox—a man he despised—was finally out of hospital and would be arraigned. Spracklin could not be late, but first he had to help his wife, Valerie, with Sam.

"My hair's short enough," Sam yelled.

"Keep your voice down, son." Spracklin lowered his copy of the *Chronicle*. "Remember, you're turning eleven in December."

"You guys never listen to me when I speak normal." Sam hadn't touched his toast. "I'm not getting an effing haircut."

"You watch your lip, sonny," said Valerie. Her Texan accent was thick that morning, which was a sign to watch it. "Yer not too big to take outside for a tannin', you know."

"I'm big enough that I can say how long my hair should be."

"We'll discuss it later," said Spracklin. "Right now, just eat your toast and get ready for school." He could have added, "Like your brother" but thought better of it. Eight-year-old John-John—an aspiring hellion when he put his mind to it—always behaved best when his brother was catching it. He was angelic now.

"We can't discuss it later if I'm getting a haircut after school." The last sentence seemed to fade out, as if Sam was distracted by something.

Spracklin turned and saw his daughter at the doorway. Marie studied her family through strands of brown hair that fell over her green eyes. She wore men's pajama bottoms and a T-shirt with the midriff cut away. She muttered a good morning and took a seat. Her

5

dour presence silenced her family, who remembered how she used to be. Before she ran away to Haight-Ashbury the previous year, Marie had been a smiling, chattering girl, the life of the family. Since she had come home after a ten-month absence, she'd had a chilling effect on the house.

Looking at her, Spracklin recalled the stress of the night he'd finally caught up with her. It was the night that Robert Kennedy had been shot down in Los Angeles. Val and the boys didn't know the details of what happened, only what the papers said, and Spracklin had no intention of letting them or anyone else learn the truth. Let them continue to believe that he — Lt. James Spracklin — had been the one to apprehend and shoot two drug dealers, one of them fatally. No one — Val in particular — needed to know that Marie had killed Fox's sidekick. All Val needed to know was that her teenage daughter was home and safe.

"Good morning, sweetheart," Valerie said to Marie. "What can I get for you?"

"Coffee, I guess. Please."

"What about some food — you have to eat."

Marie fixed her mother with a stare that had become commonplace in the house. "I'm not hungry. Just some coffee, please."

"You know, Sam," said Spracklin. "When I was a teenager, we always used to look forward to haircuts. It was a chance to look our best."

"Yeah, but you wore greasy kid stuff in your hair and dorky straight-legged pants."

"Maybe when you're older," said Spracklin, trying to sound conciliatory. He folded the paper and studied the political news. Without Kennedy in the Democratic presidential race, it looked like Hubert Humphry was going to be the nominee. Lord Jesus, what a prospect.

"I mean, Jesus Christ, Marie's allowed to take off and live like a hippie. I can't even grow my hair a bit. It's not fair."

"I told you to button that lip." Valerie's voice had tightened with her growing impatience. Spracklin studied Marie as she sipped her coffee. Her T-shirt had a skull with a bolt of electricity going through the middle of it. It was cut so short the base of the skull was missing.

"Marie, tell her long hair is cool." Sam pointed at their mother.

"Don't you point at me. Just brush your teeth and get to school," Valerie said. "Marie, honey, do you think you should be drinking that coffee? It stains your teeth."

John-John placed his plate in the sink and ran upstairs to the washroom. Sam followed him. Spracklin noticed how big Sam was getting — not just tall, but broad as well. Marie ignored her mother and took another sip. Moments later, the boys were downstairs again. As they shouldered their bookbags, Valerie reminded them she'd be waiting after school to drive them to the barbershop. In a minute, they were out the door. John-John moved especially fast, knowing the dangers of lingering around his big brother at that moment.

Valerie shook her head. "What has got into Sam?" She was a slight, energetic woman. Her constant motion and freckles had always given her an air of youth, but her dark eyes and the strands of grey hair falling from her bun revealed the creep of age. Spracklin placed his newspaper on the table so Val could clip the coupons. She slumped on to a chair and smiled at her daughter.

"I'm not going to get you to stop drinking this stuff, am I?" Val asked, nodding at the coffee.

Marie glanced up and shook her head.

Val patted Marie's forearm. "I've done battling with your brother and, well, reached my quota of fights for one morning."

Marie smiled at her and looked away again.

"Nope," said Val. "I'm not going to badger you about coffee, or your clothes or — "

"My clothes are fine," said Marie. "They're pajamas."

Val placed her hand on Marie's arm again and squeezed. "Honey," she said. "It's all right to sleep in such things, but this is the breakfast table." Valerie looked to her husband for support, but he just finished his toast. Val should shut up but he couldn't say that and start another fight. Marie's T-shirt showed off more flesh than Spracklin would have tolerated a year ago. He couldn't explain to his wife that it now reassured him. Marie's arms were clearly visible and there were no needle tracks, no signs of bruising. He'd learned enough policing Haight-Ashbury to know that kids who showed a lot of flesh had no needle marks to hide.

"It's fine."

"All I'm saying, Marie — "

"Jesus Christ," Marie yelled. "I said it's fine." She stood and strode to the basement. Spracklin saw a tear silvering her cheek.

Valerie shook her head. "I just don't understand these kids…"

"We have two problems," said Spracklin as he stood and put his plate in the sink. "Sam's a kid. And Marie isn't."

"Marie isn't even seventeen years old."

"She's had a lifetime of experience. We have to remember that."

Valerie's glare told Spracklin she wasn't afraid to tangle with him. "I know how to deal with my own daughter," she said. "And I don't need you making me feel like I'm out of touch."

Jesus Christ, thought Spracklin. He could have pointed out the obvious — that if she knew how to handle *her own* daughter then *her own* daughter wouldn't be in the basement crying. He said nothing, hoping to avoid another reminder that Valerie, not Jimmy, was the girl's biological parent. Spracklin had only adopted her and served as her father, provider and guardian for the last thirteen years. He didn't have to say anything. They both knew he thought Valerie was at fault for picking another fight with Marie. He was relieved when his wife shuffled upstairs.

Spracklin descended to the little room in the basement that served as Marie's studio. One poster on the blue walls had fluorescent designs on a black background and another advertised a concert at the Fillmore with a band called Cream. The professional posters always paled in comparison to the other works on the wall, which Marie created herself: macramé wall hangings in multi-colored string, or studies for her more ambitious wall hangings.

Her biggest project was hanging on the fence in the back yard — a huge installation thirty feet across. The background was a swirl of blue and green, and across it ran a fiery orange message with one word "SOLSTICE." The "O" was a peace sign. She'd produced this orgy of color for some festival that was taking place in Golden Gate Park. The organizers had called Marie and asked her to come up with the backdrop. Spracklin was pleased for her, although the colors were too loud for his taste. He'd noticed over the past few weeks that Marie's mood seemed to brighten when she gathered her bundles of string and headed out back to work on the project.

Marie was seated at her work table and didn't try to hide the red moisture around her eyes. Spracklin bent down and wrapped his daughter in his arms. Marie's portable record player in the corner was playing "Sgt. Pepper's Lonely Hearts Club Band" loud enough that Valerie wouldn't be able to hear them talking.

"Why the tears, honey?"

He gently rocked her as she cried. She turned her head and whispered, "I killed him, Daddy. I murdered him."

"It wasn't murder." He patted her back and placed his lips to her ear. "You saved my life."

He had relived the moment several times each day in the previous few weeks. Early on the morning of June 6, just after he'd heard that Bobby Kennedy had been shot, Spracklin apprehended Andy Fox, the aging hippie who had controlled the heroin trade in Haight-Ashbury. There was one big reason Spracklin wanted to take Fox down: Marie and Fox had become lovers. Spracklin had learned Fox was importing heroin from Hong Kong and realized the courier was a Pan-Am stewardess. As he tried to intercept the stewardess at the airport, Marie showed up to drive her into the city. Spracklin followed them to a house off Haight Street, and Fox and his henchman overpowered Spracklin, beat him, and were about to kill him.

Then came the moment that had become a recurring nightmare: he was on the floor, preparing to die at the hands of Fox's thug. There was a report of a gun, and the henchman, a man later identified as Sam Lindgren, hit the floor. Spracklin looked up to see his daughter standing by the door, the smoking pistol in her hands. His initial reactions were pride and love. His daughter had saved him. But as he relived that moment over and over, his overwhelming emotion was guilt. His beautiful, intelligent daughter had to live with the knowledge she'd killed a man, and she'd done it to save him.

Spracklin squeezed Marie tight once again. She was calmer now than a few weeks earlier. She no longer got the shakes when she broke down. "Get hold of yourself," he said. "You have to be strong."

She nodded. "I will be."

"I'll protect you," he said. "I swear. I'll do everything in my power to protect you. But you have to be strong."

"I will be. For sure." She fished a tissue from her pocket and wiped her eyes and nose. "But can you do me a favor? Can you take me into the city today?"

They both knew he was leaving in a few minutes. "Are you going to the Haight?"

She shrugged. "Golden Gate Park. There's a dude organizing the concert for the solstice. I have to talk to him." She nodded to the studies for macramé she'd been working on for weeks. She looked up, into his eyes. "If I have to spend another day shopping with Mom in Sausalito, I'm going to go crazy."

Spracklin knew he couldn't keep his daughter imprisoned in the house. He nodded. He'd drop her off north of Haight-Ashbury, then continue on to the Hall of Justice.

CHAPTER 3

When Spracklin opened his office door, he found one of his closest friends flipping through the morning's *Examiner*. Raymond Handell was a solidly built man, beginning to grey at the temples. His pleasant face was marred by a scar that ran from his nose to his left ear—the result of a knife attack in the Presidio in the late 1950s. A cigarette dangled from his lips.

"Just what every cop wants—to find the Director of Internal Affairs in his office first thing on a Monday morning," said Spracklin as he hung up the jacket of his seersucker suit and opened the window. They'd known each other long enough that Spracklin could bust Handell's chops about heading the division that all cops hated.

"I'm not the worst of your problems, Jimbo," said Handell, his soft green eyes still studying the newspaper.

"No?"

"Uh-uh," said Handell. "It says so right here." He tapped the article. "It says here a community of hippies has retreated to Sugarloaf Mountain, somewhere in the Colorado Rockies, to escape the carnage that will ensue when the asteroid Icarus hits the Earth later this week."

"No shit."

"Oh yeah. About forty flower children have packed their *Whole Earth Catalogues* and sandals and gone back to the land while the rest of us are about to get squashed by a space rock."

"And what do scientists say about Asteroid Icarus?"

"They say Icarus will miss the Earth by 3.9 million miles." Handell looked up. "But you can't be too careful about these things." Spracklin started to chuckle and leaned back in his chair.

Handell flipped the pages and kept on going. "There's also some garbage on Page 3 about who's likely to become the next chief of the SFPD." He held it up so Spracklin could read the headline:

"Spracklin favored to Succeed Hawkings." Handell turned the page toward himself again. "It says right here that you're in poll position."

He squinted as he read. "Let's see, it says, Quote, dot, dot, dot: 'Lieutenant Spracklin is viewed by a majority of supervisors as an effective administrator with a progressive viewpoint needed to steer the department through the 1970s. Though not yet a Captain, Spracklin has won praise for his ability to crack cases, his clear and decisive communications, his volcanic flatulence, and for commanding the respect of the rank and file.'" Handell looked over at his friend. "End quote."

"That's a quote? Word for word?"

"I might have paraphrased a bit of it, but I captured the main points."

Spracklin knew what the article said. He'd heard about it on the car radio and bought the paper. It noted that Spracklin was a Protestant and a Democrat and those could work against him. His only rival within the force was Capt. Mark Patterson, the Catholic Head of Patrol. But the city fathers understood they needed a moderate to navigate the current racial climate. Handell didn't get into the meat of the story, only used it to josh his buddy.

Spracklin grinned at Handell. Ray had always been a guy who would sit at your desk and start telling jokes. He was the type of guy Spracklin needed. Bobby Kennedy, who Spracklin had once worked for in Washington, had been murdered two weeks earlier, Martin Luther King, Jr. six weeks before him. Spracklin's home life was in turmoil and he was under the political microscope as the heir apparent to Chief Bud Hawkings. The Chief had officially announced his retirement a week earlier, and since then the media, the other senior officers, even old friends had been a pain in the ass on the subject. Not Handell. Ray was kind enough to joke about it rather than ask prying questions. Spracklin knew Bud Hawkings had shown managerial genius in naming Handell as his head of the new Internal Affairs department two years earlier. The Chief had to create a department that would be hated by every cop on the force, so he named the SFPD's most popular officer to lead it.

It was a mistake to think Ray Handell a push-over. His pleasant demeanor masked keen instincts and a ruthless persistence that fools were known to underestimate. Handell and Spracklin had been SFPD rookies together as returning veterans in the late 1940s. They learned they'd both fought under General Patton in Europe, and they loved to swap war stories about Sicily and the Ardennes.

As Spracklin looked at his old friend, he thought how good it was that they'd stayed in touch after he was seconded to Kennedy's Justice Department in the early 1960s. They'd fallen back into a relaxed friendship when Spracklin returned to San Francisco once Johnson became President. Handell appreciated the way Jimmy and Val supported him through his messy divorce, and when he left the patrol division to head Internal Affairs. The rank and file, even many of the brass, didn't like the idea of a division that investigated police, but Spracklin spoke publicly and privately in favor of his friend. The cancer of an IA Division could never be as lethal as the cancer of dirty cops, he'd say. Spracklin was one of the few officers that Handell still saw on a social basis. Spracklin wondered if this was a social call.

"So, to what do I owe this visit?" Spracklin asked.

"I wanted to see how you're doing."

"Good, you?"

"I'm serious, Jimmy. I mean really, how have you been?"

Spracklin plucked a cigarette from his pack and offered one to Handell. The IA head took it and lit it off the butt of the one he was already smoking. Spracklin mulled the question. *How was he?* Really. He was still recovering. Andy Fox and his thug had beat the shit out of him, and it had taken a few weeks for the pain to subside. He still couldn't believe his hero Bobby Kennedy was dead. He had been trying to focus on the one bright spot—Marie was home. But he was worried about the girl, who seemed so depressed. And there was a lot of tension in his home.

"We're coping, Raymond. Thanks."

Handell smiled and nodded. "I know how much you revered Senator Kennedy. I'm sure it's been hard."

"Well, Ray, I've been mourning the Attorney General—I still think of him as the AG. And Val and I have been overjoyed to have Marie home again. And the last case, well, it was a hard one."

"True, but you have Marie home." Handell, tried to sound positive. "That must be great."

"Yeah, it is." Spracklin broke into a smile. "I mean, she's a teenager and all. Lot of attitude, you know? But it's wonderful to have her back with us."

"Great, great," said Handell. "And you're sliding back into work again?"

"Yeah," said Spracklin. He was beginning to wonder why Ray Handell was really visiting his office. The questions seemed prepared, the relaxed manner too relaxed. "No murders in the city since the Kennedy assassination. It's like even the crooks are numb at what happened."

They both laughed. "I've been getting my guys to go over old cases. The last few days, I started jotting down some notes on Landry and Jason." Spracklin looked up to see if Handell knew the cases he was referring to. "Jacques Landry and Emmett Jason, two Polgar lieutenants murdered last year. Two of the murders I still haven't cleared from last year."

Handell's easy smile grew into a broad grin. "Bogdan Polgar," he said, naming the gangster who controlled the Fillmore neighborhood. He remembered the cases. Over countless glasses of scotch, he'd heard Spracklin say he knew that Polgar ordered the murders but he couldn't prove it. Yet. "Bogdan Polgar," Handell repeated. "I always admired the hard-on you had for that guy."

They looked at each other, realizing Handell's poor choice of words.

"Well," said Spracklin. "There's no man I'd rather have admiring my hard-on than you."

"Can I rephrase that?" They chuckled.

"Too late, too late," said Spracklin.

As their laughter died down, Handell said, "Good to see you're still after him. I thought you'd be looking for Fox's donkey."

"Huh?"

"Sarah Byrne. The flight attendant who smuggled Fox's heroin into the country. I thought you'd be looking for her. To tie up loose ends."

Spracklin noticed that Handell was coming back again to the Fox case. His courier had been a flight attendant, later identified as Sarah Byrne. She'd escaped and was still at large. There was a want out across California for a slight strawberry blonde known to wear an emerald stud in her nose. "Sarah Byrne—she's an FBI matter," said Spracklin. "It would be imprudent for me to poke around that." It seemed obvious, thought Spracklin. Bringing contraband into the country was clearly a case for the feds. "The local guy working it is Merrill Flanagan," he added, mentioning the head of vice.

"So everything's wrapped up with Fox?"

"Pretty well. The bastard's being arraigned this morning." He glanced at his phone. "They're supposed to give me a call when he gets to the courtroom. I'll probably go. I was the arresting officer, after all." Spracklin felt mild worry, not full-blown paranoia yet. Handell was an old friend, but he was also the head of Internal Affairs. IA was always suspicious of a drug bust with no money seized. Spracklin had recovered no money the night he busted Fox.

"And Marie was there?" Spracklin thought Handell was trying to mention Marie too casually.

"That Sarah Byrne," said Spracklin. "It turns out her father is Harry Byrne." For the moment, Spracklin ignored Handell's question about his daughter, trying to keep the focus on the fugitive flight attendant.

"The donkey? Go away."

"I'm serious."

Handell laughed. "The industrialist?"

"The shipping magnate, mega-rich, Republican rainmaker — yeah, him. His daughter smuggles heroin." They shared a laugh.

"She stands to inherit hundreds of millions, and she's running drugs," said Spracklin. He shook his head. "Now she's a fugitive."

The smile faded from Handell's face, and he said, "Was she there when you were wrestling with the big guy, Lindgren?"

"Actually, she gave me the opening to deck him," said Spracklin. Handell raised an eyebrow, asking him to go on. "I came in and found Fox and Byrne unpacking the stuff. I had them, then Lindgren, he came up behind me with a gun, held it to my head, made me drop my weapon. That's when the girl panicked and ran out. It created a moment's diversion — just enough that I could sucker-punch the big guy and retrieve my weapon." He had to stick to the story he'd fabricated the night of the shooting and make sure no one linked Marie to the Lindgren shooting.

"And you started wrestling?"

"Yeah, till I shot him."

"You were on top of him? When you were wrestling?"

Spracklin thought for a moment. He was pretending to remember things precisely, but he was wondering what Ray Handell was playing at. "We were side by side, I think. Both struggling to get the advantage."

"And you reached around him, holding the gun perpendicular to the back of the head?"

"I think so. I mean, it happened fast and we were in motion." Spracklin tried to keep his tone light. They both wanted to maintain the appearance that this was just two old friends chatting. They both knew it was really an Internal Affairs officer investigating a cop.

"And Marie was there to witness it?"

"No, Marie was upstairs. I didn't even know it. By the time she came in, I'd shot Lindgren. She found me wrestling with Fox, just before I shot him. I wounded him in the shoulder."

"Now this is one thing I don't understand—what was Marie doing in that house?"

Now they were digging into the emotional depths of the investigation. Spracklin felt no guilt about Lindgren's death. He didn't regret shooting Andrew Fox—only that he hadn't killed the prick. The thing that punched Spracklin right in the gut was that his daughter had fallen in love with a piece of shit like Andrew Fox. The drugs, the sex, the rebellion—he had come to accept all that. What hurt was that Fox had meant something to her. He took a long drag on his Chesterfield.

"She was Fox's lover," said Spracklin.

The Internal Affairs head nodded as if it confirmed what he had already suspected. "I'm sorry, Jimmy." Spracklin did not respond. "She's a minor?" Handell asked. Spracklin nodded. "Are you pursuing statutory rape charges?" Spracklin shook his head.

Handell's tone was solemn. "You know we've got to talk to her."

Spracklin noted that Handell said "we" and wondered which of the IA turds would be sent to persecute his daughter. Raymond Handell was a gentleman, but his underlings were not. "And you know that's not going to happen," said Spracklin.

"I'm doing my job."

"And I've done mine. I interviewed her and took her statement. And I've claimed the Lindgren kill and I'm ready to live by whatever your department rules. But you're not interviewing Marie. She's been through a harrowing time and she's delicate."

For a moment, the two old friends stared at each other in silence.

"I have to make the request—"

"The answer is no. No one is interviewing my daughter. Fox is in custody, he's being arraigned today. Lindgren is dead. I'm responsible for bringing down both of them." He sent a jet of smoke toward the ceiling.

"Things don't add up with the Lindgren killing. We need to talk to witnesses."

"Talk to Fox."

"He's lawyered up."

"They'll get Byrne soon and you can talk to her. Otherwise, talk to me."

Raymond Handell knew there was no point in pushing the matter. Spracklin had always been the big brother in their fraternal friendship. Now the junior of the two was signaling that he wasn't going to let this drop. He stood without saying goodbye and left the office. Spracklin knew the matter wasn't over.

CHAPTER 4

As the elevator door opened, Spracklin checked his watch and wondered if he'd missed Fox's hearing. That was the problem with arraignments—you never knew when the guy's name came up, and once it did it was over in a flash. Spracklin had brought a few files to go through while he waited. He dashed down the hall, praying that Fox wouldn't make bail. There was no way— not even with the liberal judges in San Francisco—that they could grant bail to Andrew Fox. The prosecutor had solid evidence against him on twenty-four different counts, from first-degree murder to importing a banned substance to assaulting a police officer.

Spracklin recognized the hulking form and black curls of Sergeant Ed Burwell, slouched against the marble wainscoting outside the Superior Courtroom. Burwell liked to advertise his indifference with that slouch—he did it when he'd joined the Bureau of Inspectors a month earlier, and he was doing it now. The only thing that had changed over a month was the suit. On day one, Burwell's twenty-nine-dollar polyester suit was pressed to perfection. He'd worn it every day since, and it was now rumpled and misshapen. Spracklin wondered if any of the sheriffs had asked Burwell to move along, mistaking him for a street-corner hoodlum.

"Ed," said Spracklin, as he opened the heavy door.

"Jimmy," replied the sergeant, falling in behind him.

"They called him yet?"

Burwell shook his heavy head. "Just asked the clerk. It'll be another ten or fifteen minutes." They stepped inside and surveyed the packed courtroom. People of every race crammed the benches, coming to see friends or relatives arraigned before Judge Hugh Gleeson. Spracklin recognized about a dozen reporters, who were no doubt there to cover Fox. And of course, J.P. MacLean of the FBI sat in the second row. Fox was officially the feds' case, and MacLean didn't seem pleased to see Spracklin. They nodded to each other. Spracklin and Burwell squeezed by a couple of Latino women in the back row. Spracklin sat and placed the files on his lap.

"What's in the tubs?" asked Burwell, nodding at the manila folders.

"My files on Bogdan Polgar," said Spracklin. He pronounced the word "files" with emphasis. Typical Burwell, he thought. Spracklin knew goods files led to tight cases, ones that put criminals away. He hated the word "tubs", and had little time for cops who used the term. He wondered if he should tell Burwell to go find something useful to do.

"You're still going after Polgar," said Burwell.

"Jesus, keep your voice down," said Spracklin. He nodded to a thin black kid in the front row and whispered, "That black guy next to the kid in the blue hoodie. He works for Polgar. Monitors court for him." Spracklin studied Myron Adamson, and then the kid in the hoodie. Why would someone have his hood up in court. Was he also a member of the Polgar gang?

"You've got the Polgar network down, huh?" said Burwell.

Spracklin patted his files. "It's all in here."

Their conversation ended as two sheriffs led Andrew Fox into the courtroom and placed him in a front bench. Spracklin's ire rose at the mere sight of Fox. The dealer looked healthier than he had the night Spracklin shot him — hospital food obviously agreed with him. His reddish-brown hair was cut and combed, and there was a flush to his rugged complexion. It sickened Spracklin to think that Fox would get a trial. He wanted to take him out and shoot him now. Fox conferred with a young Hispanic defense attorney then scanned the courtroom. He stopped to study a few people, then his eyes locked on Spracklin. His thin lips curled into a smile.

Prosecuting Attorney Sherman Corbett introduced the case against Andrew Warren Fox of no fixed address, and read out the string of charges. He said Fox also faced murder charges in Fresno. He highlighted Fox's previous convictions and time served and demanded there be no bail granted. "Your Honor," said Corbett in the casual tone he always used in court. "The reason Mr. Fox has no fixed address is he lived in a van for the past number of years. He could not be a greater flight risk. I mean, his very home is on wheels."

A twitter of laughter rippled through the courtroom and the judge smiled.

"Jeffrey Fujimoto for the defense, Your Honor," said the young lawyer. Spracklin realized he had Japanese lineage. "And I'd like the court's forbearance in showing some leniency to my client. He is a victim of a recent police shooting, and has spent almost three weeks in a forensic unit of a hospital. He needs some access to the community to benefit from the support of loved ones and—"

"And where exactly in the community, Counselor?"

"I'm sorry, Your Honor?"

"Where in the community will your client reside while finding this support?"

"We could recommend any number of places. We'd be willing to agree to a house arrest."

The lawyer was going to continue but the judge's expression told him not to bother. The evidence against his client was too damning. Judge Gleeson's jowly face glared at the lawyer, almost daring him to continue.

"Bail denied," said the judge. "The accused will be remanded to County Jail, whereupon a psychiatric evaluation will be carried out. You'll report back to the court in three weeks to set a trial date."

Fujimoto said something inaudible and the judge asked him to repeat it. "Remanded to the general population of the county jail?" the lawyer asked.

"Yes," said the judge. "Of course."

The sheriffs took their positions beside Fox, who stood up. Fujimoto whispered something to Fox, who just stared at the kid in the hoodie. One sheriff pulled at Fox's arm, but the prisoner resisted. Myron Adamson was looking away. Both sheriffs tried to force Fox toward the exit, and the way Fox twisted his hips, Spracklin could see what was about to happen.

Fox's right arm broke free and swung around. His fist caught a sheriff square in the jaw. That man dropped and Fox jumped on the other sheriff hammering him in the face. The spectators drew back in horror as the bailiff and two policemen wrestled Fox to the floor. Judge Gleeson banged his gavel and people screamed and headed to the back of the room. As the crowd spread away from the melee, the person in the blue hoodie twisted so Spracklin could see the horrified face. It wasn't a guy at all.

It was Marie. Spracklin tried to get to his daughter—his instinct was to protect her from the fight. But he was wedged into the narrow bench. She joined a crush of people fleeing the courtroom. As Judge

Gleeson remanded the prisoner to solitary confinement, Spracklin edged his way out. He was about to follow Marie, when he caught sight of Cadet Tom Jackson striding toward him. Jackson had been with the Bureau a few months, and Spracklin hoped he would one day be an inspector.

Spracklin tried to avoid his gaze so he could follow Marie. "Lieutenant," he said, "they found her body. On Hippie Hill." Spracklin stopped. He'd talk to Marie later. He didn't know what Jackson was talking about.

"Whose body?"

"Sarah Byrne, Sir. Fox's donkey. At least, they think it's her. She's been beheaded."

CHAPTER 5

Jimmy Spracklin's evidence kit was the size of a large briefcase. It contained everything he needed at a crime scene—his camera and photographic equipment, magnifying glass, evidence bags, fingerprinting kit. It was heavy. As he left the shade of the trees near Park Station and went on to Sharon Meadow, he set it down on the asphalt path and surveyed the situation. Beside him, a young woman with curly red hair sat on a hand-woven blanket playing an acoustic guitar and singing. A dozen coins shone in her open guitar case.

Spracklin glanced at the girl, clean and cheerful with a flower in her hair. Just like in that song that his kids listened to. The hippies with the flowers had seemed like a pain in the ass two years earlier. They had flocked to Haight-Ashbury because it was the center of the LSD culture, reveling in the music and wild clothes. Now, the Summer of Love seemed like the good old days. Heroin had taken over, and those groovy flower children were becoming ravaged by addiction.

The girl smiled up at him, obviously unaware that a headless woman her age lay across the field. Sharon Meadow was a diamond-shaped field dotted with clusters of hippies. Beyond it was Hippie Hill. At about thirty feet tall, it wasn't much of a hill, especially by San Francisco standards. During the Summer of Love, it had become a Haight-Ashbury landmark.

Marie had told Spracklin some group was planning a concert on Hippie Hill in a few nights. The beginnings of a stage—the stage where Marie's wall hanging would serve as backdrop—could be seen at the crest. *Marie, goddamn Marie*, he thought. *What was she doing in the courtroom?* Beyond a frame of two-by-fours and stacks of plywood he could see a few patrolmen. They had removed the concert organizers to the bottom of Hippie Hill.

"You wanna carry the kit, Ed?" Spracklin said to Burwell. The sergeant lugged the evidence kit across the field, and Spracklin wondered if that would be the limit of his usefulness that day. They had hardly spoken on the drive across the peninsula. Spracklin was too annoyed by Marie and Ray Handell to engage in small talk. *Was Marie so infatuated with Fox that she showed up at his court hearing?* Spracklin could feel his blood pressure rising. He needed a drink.

Spracklin and Burwell climbed the hill and stepped around the pile of lumber and scattered hammers and saws. They joined four grim policemen beneath the towering eucalyptus trees on the rear slope. Deputy Medical Examiner Ernie Swanson and a Corporal were crouching on a patch of dirt by a stand of tall grass. All Spracklin could see sticking out of the vegetation was a pair of legs, toes pointing down. One foot wore a woman's sandal, and the other was bare. As Spracklin neared the body, he could see she was wearing a turquoise T-shirt, patterned with polka dots and stained with blood. Her left arm was under the body, the right outstretched. At first glance, it looked like her head was in the bushes, but he knew her head was missing.

"Lieutenant," said the uniform beside Swanson, his hand outstretched to Spracklin, "I'm Corporal Max O'Leary, Sir. We haven't moved the body. We've been waiting for you." O'Leary seemed a bit too eager to impress. Spracklin was really wishing the *Examiner* had never run that article about him.

"You found her?"

"No, Sir. Those hippies." He nodded toward the makeshift stage that they could barely see because of the rise of the hill. "The hippies on the other side of the hill are planning a concert, something like that. For sunrise on Thursday, they said. Anyway, one of them came to Park Station an hour ago, shaken, borderline hysterical, said they'd found a body."

Spracklin nodded. It was a small blessing the crime scene was so close to Park Station. Cops could walk over without radioing squad cars, which would have alerted the media. Spracklin could carry out the initial investigation without reporters hanging around.

"ID?" he asked the Corporal.

"None."

"The head?"

"We haven't located it yet, Sir," said O'Leary, nodding at two patrolmen moving slowly through the bushes along the east side of the hill. "We're searching for it."

Ernie Swanson looked up for the first time and nodded at the Lieutenant.

"Any tracks in the bushes?" asked Spracklin. He knew it was a longshot. It had been a dry summer and the ground was hard.

"None, Sir."

Spracklin was beginning to get a feel for the crime scene. By stepping only on the packed dirt, the perpetrator could easily have dumped her in the bushes without leaving any trace.

"Anything, Ernie?" said Spracklin.

Swanson shrugged. "I'd say she's been dead five or six hours. Rigor mortis has just set in. It seems the head was removed post-mortem, probably at that patch of blood there." He pointed to a circle of red on the ground. "The body's positioned in an inclined position with the head downhill from the body. There was little bleeding when the head was removed. There's wet staining on her jeans. I think she evacuated her bladder at the time of death."

"Cause of death?"

"Too soon to say. I would say strangulation—victims who are strangled often piss themselves." Swanson's father had been a beat cop in Oakland, and one thing Spracklin liked about the Deputy ME is he talked like a cop, not a doctor. Swanson pointed to the victim's right hand, which was curled into a loose fist. "There's slight discoloration of the fingernails, I think. That can be a sign of strangulation but it's not that strong in this case." He stood up and shook his head. "The laceration in the neck was not a clean cut. It looks like the perpetrator used a small hatchet or large knife to remove the head."

Until now, Spracklin had been caught up in his concern about Marie. Now he was taking on the gravity of the situation, becoming immersed in the evil of what had happened. He began to feel an overwhelming disgust, hatred, sorrow, in what he was witnessing and he knew that only he could avenge this poor girl. Sometimes, if he had a few days between cases, life seemed vapid because he was living a suburban existence without the weighty grimness of homicide. Now he was reverting to his normal life, to trying to right an appalling wrong.

"How long until we know the cause of death?" Spracklin asked Swanson as he studied the body.

"It will be in the rotation," said Swanson, not saying how many other autopsies would be ahead of this one. Spracklin didn't react. He simply continued to study the body, searching for any signs of a struggle. "Of course, I could do the autopsy myself," added Swanson. "Have the results to you this afternoon."

Spracklin placed a hand on the coroner's shoulder. "That would be a huge help, Ernie. I'd really appreciate it." Good old Swanson, he thought. In a world of brownnoses, none was browner than Swanson's. "Let me just get some photos of the scene, then we'll flip her over."

The Corporal looked puzzled at the mention of moving the body. "Sir, we've called the SID," he said. "They should be here soon."

"I'm the lead investigator," said Spracklin as he lugged the evidence kit to the edge of the bushes. "I'll give the SID any evidence I find."

"They might find things we can't," said Burwell. Spracklin turned and looked up at the sergeant. The useless boob was telling his boss how to investigate a murder. Spracklin believed the Scientific Investigation Division should stay in their labs. "There's one lead investigator," Spracklin said slowly. "He notices things, connects the dots, understands what has happened. I'll give the SID the evidence I want analyzed."

Spracklin crouched beside the evidence kit, and waved Corporal O'Leary over to his side. The Lieutenant took his Kodak Brownie Auto 27 camera from the case and stood. "Corporal, you see that sandal?" he asked, as be pointed the camera at the dead girl's feet and snapped a shot. O'Leary nodded. "We need the other one."

The Corporal looked puzzled. *There's a reason this guy's in patrol,* thought Spracklin.

"It's likely she lost that sandal during the struggle, if there was one, or while she was being carried over here. In either case, that missing sandal will tell us something about where she was before she ended up in these bushes — even if it just tells us the direction." He took a closeup shot of each foot. "We need to find it before someone picks it up, or before the garbage cans are emptied. I want your men to fan out in all directions and do a quick search, going through all trash cans. Then I want a tighter search, focusing on the turf between here and Haight Street."

"Yes, Sir," said the Corporal. Spracklin turned his attention to photographing the scene.

"Anything you think I should shoot, Ed?" he asked the sergeant.

Burwell was hovering uphill from him. He simply shook his head. Spracklin asked the sergeant to take notes on the photos.

Spracklin used a flash to make sure there was enough light to catch the details of the ragged neck wound. There was a ring on her right hand—did that rule out theft as a motive? It wasn't really an issue. The fact that the killer or killers decapitated her ruled out theft. If you kill someone for their wallet, you don't take the time to remove and hide the head.

Spracklin stepped back to photo the position of the body and the surrounding foliage. He bumped into Burwell, who was standing there watching him. "Well, Ed," said Spracklin. "Any thoughts on who would want to kill Sara Byrne?"

He heard no answer. He could almost see Burwell behind him shrugging his massive shoulders. Spracklin popped out the spent flash bulb and replaced it with another, then moved in for another closeup of the neck wound. He looked up at Burwell, and realized the sergeant had been pondering his question.

"She had imported heroin from Asia, so had she crossed into someone's turf?" asked Burwell. "The triads in Hong Kong have operatives in San Francisco. Do they decapitate their victims?" Now he shrugged his shoulders. "Was Fox involved? She could have testified against Fox, so he had a motive to put out a contract on her. But Fox is in jail."

Spracklin motioned to Swanson that he wanted to roll the body over. The medical examiner took the shoulders and Spracklin the feet, and together they lifted and rolled the cadaver.

"She was engaged," Burwell said flatly. He pointed to the left hand. A ring with a small diamond glistened on her ring finger. Somewhere out there, she had a fiancé. Spracklin stood and looked down at the headless body. A day earlier, she had been a fugitive who could have testified that Marie had picked her up at the airport. He believed she could have threatened his family. But Spracklin understood that she'd also been a young woman who was looking forward to marriage. She'd been an adventurous spirit who spent time in Asia. And like his own Marie, Spracklin knew she had fallen under the spell of Andy Fox.

"Do you know if she had an apartment?" asked Burwell. "Anywhere we should search?"

"From what I've heard, she lived at home. In her parents' mansion." Spracklin had quietly asked Marie about Sarah in the past few weeks. Marie knew from scuttlebutt around Haight Street that Sarah Byrne was from a wealthy family. People knew that she lived in the family mansion and was sometimes seen driving around San Francisco in a burgundy Mercedes convertible.

An ambulance pulled up beyond the bushes. Just up the rise of the hill, Spracklin saw the uniformed officers branch off in different directions to try to find the lost sandal. The wheels of the investigation were beginning to turn, which usually pleased Spracklin. But on this day, he just felt disgust. This girl had entered Fox's orbit and had been decapitated as a result. And his daughter, Marie, was in that same orbit. *Marie. Marie.* Spracklin wanted to focus on the case, but he couldn't rid his thoughts of the image of his daughter sitting near Fox in the courtroom.

CHAPTER 6

As he toweled the knife off, he noticed a reddish hair wedged into the crease between the blade and the guard. He gripped the knife, pinched the hair, jiggled, and pulled. After three tugs, the hair came out. He rolled it in his fingers and recalled again how her beautiful hair had filled his face with softness and a delicate strawberry scent as she struggled. He sniffed the single strand but could only smell the bleach he'd used to clean the knife. He flushed the hair down the toilet.

He checked the scabbard and found no blood on it. It had been tucked in his belt. He'd put it there so the leather wouldn't be stained with blood. It was a little detail that had paid off.

Details, he thought. As a boy, his father had stressed that he needed to pay attention to the minute details in everything he did. "Obsess about the small things, *Passerotto*," his father had said, using his pet name for his son. And with this operation, he had planned everything with microscopic precision. His father would be proud of him.

The girl had emerged on to the sidewalk at about 2 a.m., as expected. He'd been waiting about half an hour. He'd followed her west toward the park, as he had other nights. After being cooped up inside all day, he knew she liked to wander through the wooded park. He followed her across Stanyan Street. He was nervous. He'd been asking himself for a few days whether he could kill a woman. He knew he could stalk her, frighten her, beat her. But when it came time to actually kill her, did he have the balls to execute the plan? Others doubted him. They always had. Were they justified?

As she'd passed through the bushes near Hippie Hill, he grabbed her. He got his hand over her mouth so she couldn't scream and he was halfway up the hill with her before she began struggling. Within ten seconds, the wire was around her neck. She cried once—for half a second, he'd say—when he removed his right hand so he could pull the wire tight around her throat. Her warm body pressed hard against his, and he felt a surprising intimacy with her.

Then he recalled another thing his father had told him before he started this series of jobs: Ninety percent of a perfect mission lies in the planning you do beforehand. The other ten percent is in how you react to the things you can't plan for. And there's always something you can't plan for.

The previous night, the thing he hadn't planned for was the wire getting snagged in her neckbones. As she lay on the ground, he'd tugged and twisted it but it was wedged in tight. He'd made the garotte himself, and the handle could have been traced back to him. He'd tried cutting the wire with his knife, but it was too thick. He'd decided to get around the problem by hacking off the head and taking it with him. Cutting between the bones in her neck was hellish hard, but he was panicking and used all the strength he could to pry them apart.

Now, as he dried his knife and stashed it under his mattress, he told himself the next hit would be different. His handler had promised him a handgun for the next job. He didn't know much about guns, but he was certain it would be an easier kill than a strangling, although it might not be as thrilling, as intimate an experience.

CHAPTER 7

Standing at the crest of Hippie Hill, Spracklin tried to size up the circle of sullen hippies sitting across the asphalt path below. *Who was the leader? Would they cooperate? Did they know anything?* Most were sitting cross-legged on jackets or collapsed cartons to protect them from the damp grass. Carpentry tools and musical instruments were scattered near them. At least two girls were crying. One guy kept leaning over and whispering in the ear of a kid with curly hair. At the west end of the meadow, Spracklin noticed a tall black guy walking toward the group, adjusting his fly as if he'd just taken a piss in the bushes. He carried a clipboard.

"Hippies," said Burwell. "Just can't get away from 'em."

Spracklin and Burwell arrived at the circle of the hippies at the same time as the black guy with the clipboard. The Lieutenant introduced himself to the group, explaining they were investigating the death of the young woman found in the bushes. The slack-jawed hippies, in their ragged clothes, looked at him, and a few turned to the clipboard-holder. He wore a burgundy wool vest that reached to his hips and a canvas shoulder-bag hung by his side. He stuck out his hand and spat out his name, "J.D. Ehler."

"Jimmy Spracklin," said the Lieutenant, shaking his hand. He didn't bother introducing Burwell.

"Is it true, what they're saying? About the girl?" The kid had an earnest, direct quality about him and Spracklin wondered how much information he'd provide.

"You didn't see the body?"

"No, no. My friend, Martha, one of our performers." He nodded to an auburn-haired woman wrapped in a ragged quilt, probably in her thirties, older than the other kids. There were the beginnings of laugh lines at the corners of her eyes, which were now rimmed in red from crying. Yet there was a youthful air about her. "She found the body."

Spracklin nodded. "Well, Martha, I understand how upsetting this must be but—"

"When will we be able to get back to the stage?" blurted out Ehler. "Like, we gotta get it built today, dig?"

"What's that?"

"I'm sorry, man," said Ehler. Nothing in his manner suggested it was a sincere apology. "But like, man, we've been working for months to get a festival on this site and we have to finish the stage today."

Spracklin studied Ehler. The kid kept talking about the difficulties he'd had organizing the festival, about the stacks of speakers that would arrive the next day, but Spracklin wasn't listening. He was just studying this hippie. "And the cats at City Hall, man, nothing but aggravation from them. I've laid out almost a grand of my own money for the PA system and I have to stick to the schedule, you know. It's what we need to bring back the spirit of last year." He was pleading with the Lieutenant, genuinely worried that the cop didn't understand the importance of his festival.

Spracklin lit a cigarette as he eyed the man and said, "A young woman has been murdered."

He spoke as if it would be the end of the discussion. Martha, broke into a fresh round of tears and cupped her hands about her face. The others shifted uneasily. "I get it, man," said Ehler. "I get it. But we have to get the stage finished. We can't set up the speakers if there's no stage to put them on. Like we have three days till the Solstice."

"It's a crime scene."

"We don't need to go to the back of the hill." Ehler gestured toward the far side of the mound. "You can rope that off. We need to get to the stage."

"It's. A. Crime. Scene."

"No, it's not. Dude, she wasn't killed on the stage." Spracklin just stared at him. "I'm—we're going to help in any way possible, Sir. But can you let us know when we can get back to building our stage?"

"I need answers," Spracklin said, "about finding the body."

Ehler looked down at Martha. She nodded, letting him know that she'd be willing to talk. Spracklin squatted. He smiled. "There's nothing to worry about, Martha. I'm just going to ask a few questions and my partner, Sergeant Burwell, will take some notes." Behind him, he heard Burwell rustle in his jacket and remove a notebook. "Now, what's your name?"

She sat up, shed the tatty blanket, and said, "My name is Jordan Anne Baker." Spracklin now saw that she was wearing no bra beneath her white T-shirt. He tried to ignore the nipples poking against the thin cotton fabric.

"But you go by Martha?"

"I just go by..." She looked up at Burwell, back at Spracklin and said, "I don't like the name Jordan. I prefer Martha."

Her friends seemed surprised, as if they had never heard the name Jordan before.

"There's no reason to be nervous," said Spracklin. "Just tell me what happened this morning."

She looked up at Ehler, who nodded. "We arrived early, like eight." Ehler nodded. "We needed to get the stage—I'm J.D.'s assistant, right? And I'll be singing a few songs in the festival." She paused to catch her breath and calmly proceeded. "We weren't even looking at the—we'd called up seven guys to help put the stage together. The sound guys are coming tomorrow. We weren't even looking behind us. We were putting the frame of the stage together."

She glanced up at the hill. "Martin and Salinas Jim—he's trained as a carpenter—they were debating about where to put the steps up to the stage, or whether we needed steps. Martin wanted them, and he was like pleading with...." Her voice tapered off.

"Go on," said Spracklin. "You're doing well."

"I stood and looked around and I saw two feet sticking out of the long grass and I laughed like, you know, some cat had passed out in the bushes near our stage." She sobbed and took a deep breath. "Then I thought, shit, maybe he OD-ed. I thought it was a guy, right? One foot had a sandal on it and one was bare. And I looked, and saw it was a chick, and I thought her head was in the bushes." She tried to proceed but found it impossible. She collapsed into her friend's arms and began to cry again. "But she didn't have a head."

Spracklin's voice was soothing when he spoke. "Martha, I have one more question for you and then I'll leave you. Did you disturb the body, or the bushes around it?"

She shook her head without looking up at him. "I screamed and ran to the others."

Spracklin stood and looked up at the frame of the stage. He noted that the frame was just below the crest, on the side that sloped

31

toward Sharon Meadow. It was plausible that they had been working on the stage and didn't see the body in the bushes fifteen yards
away. The girl's feet were the only thing visible, and they were at
ground level. The curve of the hill could have hidden them.

"Well?" Spracklin heard a voice say.

He turned and saw J.D. Ehler gazing at him with an eager expression. "Well what?"

"Can we get back to our stage? We have to—"

"It's a crime scene. I told you that."

"But it's important that we get the stage set up. We have a tight
timeline. I'm paying people to be here."

"It's important to find out who killed this girl."

"Was it that Byrne chick, that millionaire drug runner?" asked a
hippie across the circle.

"We don't know. Did any of you know Sarah Byrne?" He looked
around the circle but all he got back was blank stares. "Do any of
you know anything about the dead girl up there?" Again no one said
anything. "Who was the first one here this morning?"

"I was," said Ehler. "I was here before eight because we need
this stage built. I'm going to lose money on this."

"People your age are always telling me money's not important,"
Spracklin said.

"People your age are always telling me it is."

"Was there anyone sleeping around here last night?" asked
Spracklin. "Last year there were always kids camping out here.
Anyone sleeping here last night?"

Ehler shook his head. "I didn't see anyone, but I was just worried
about the stage. We dropped the wood off yesterday and I was just,
like, dead set on building the stage, you know?"

"And where were you last night?"

"Me, Martha, Dale, Salinas Jim...." he nodded to hippies in the
circle as he named them. "We all had a planning meeting at the
Drugstore Café. Probably till three, four in the morning. Then we all
crashed at Jim's pad on Page. We had to be close to the site because
we're in the home stretch of this thing we've been planning for half
a year." He was off again talking about the importance of his work
and what it meant to everyone in the Haight. Spracklin wasn't listening. He was looking at one kid, a boy who looked no more than
sixteen with skinny, hairless limbs sticking out of cutoff jeans and
a T-shirt.

"Stand up, son," said Spracklin. He was oblivious to Ehler's ramblings now. The boy had been looking up at Ehler and now realized the policeman was talking to him. He seemed frightened to be singled out. Spracklin was looking at the collapsed cereal box he had been sitting on and a little piece of brown material sticking out from underneath it. He stepped into the circle and kicked the box to one side. Squashed under it was a flattened leather sandal. It could have matched the one he saw on the dead girl's right foot. "Did you place this here, son?"

"No, Sir," the kid said. He wasn't a hippie—just a local kid who had come along to hang out. No hippie would call him Sir. "I didn't know it was there."

Spracklin nodded and turned to Burwell. "We can tell that Corporal we found the other sandal."

CHAPTER 8

"Thing is," said Ed Burwell as hey strode down Post Street, "that asshole knew there was a dead girl lying just over the hill."

Spracklin nodded. He wasn't in the mood to chat. He'd had trouble finding a parking spot but hadn't minded. He dreaded the task ahead, and he was willing to park a few blocks away and walk back. Spracklin wished the pre-noon streets had been more crowded as it would have slowed them down.

"Think there's something about that stage?" asked Burwell, catching his breath. "That Ehler guy seemed too keen to get back there."

Spracklin had wondered the same thing. After they'd found the lone sandal, he had inspected the stage and everything around it. None of the scattered tools had any sign of blood or human tissue. He'd dug through tool boxes, bags of hardware, lumber, searching for…what? He didn't know—anything that Ehler might be hiding from him. There was nothing. Spracklin had decided the asshole—Burwell was right; Ehler was an asshole—cared only about his concert. He had Burwell take down the names and details of everyone—especially Ehler—who had been hanging around Hippie Hill.

"When we get back to the office, do a full check on Ehler."

Burwell was having trouble keeping up as they moved uphill. They crossed Mason Street and Spracklin stopped outside a Brooks Brothers outlet in a granite edifice. It was the second generation of buildings erected after the earthquake—those that showed San Francisco was, once again, prospering. Beside the store, bolted to the polished granite, a brass plaque read "The Poseidon Mercantile Group".

"We should have taken him in," said Burwell as he reached the Lieutenant. "He's a flight risk. All hippies are."

Spracklin ignored his sergeant and stepped into the building, whose directory showed the shipping company occupied the top five floors. They stepped into the elevator and asked the operator to take them to the twelfth floor. "What if he takes off?" said Burwell.

The brass elevator doors closed, and Spracklin said, "He's here at least till that festival's over. That's four days."

The old elevator rose slowly, but too fast for Spracklin. He had never met Harry Byrne, though he certainly knew the legend. Concluding a distinguished decade with the Navy in 1946, Byrne had bought decommissioned merchant marine ships to begin his own shipping company. As he built one of the leading shipping lines on the West Coast, Byrne became a Republican Party king-pin. He was confidant to presidential candidate Richard Nixon and Governor Ronald Reagan, not to mention several local politicians and supervisors. Spracklin's first contact with Byrne would be to tell him they'd found a headless body they believed was his daughter. The lone bright spot was that they were at Byrne's office, not his home. This job, the worst part of policing, only became worse when mothers were present.

The austere reception area was decorated with large black-and-white photos of Captain Harry taken during the Second World War. The boyish Byrne had been a lieutenant at Midway, then commanded his own destroyer off the coast of Africa and at Normandy. A fourth photo was hidden behind a poster on an easel advertising that Poseidon Mercantile was expanding and would move into the proposed Transamerica Pyramid.

A secretary led them to a corner office, pausing outside to knock gently. In the board room across the hall, two young men pored over notes at a long table with a bank of phones in the middle. A map of San Francisco was taped to one wall. Pins and notes stuck to important points, many of them clustered around Haight-Ashbury. A map of northern California was on the facing wall. Glossy prints of Sarah Byrne were taped to the wall and stacked on the table.

"Lieutenant," said the secretary. Spracklin realized she was waiting by the open door. He walked into the vast office that looked out on Union Square. The air was thick with the smoke of pipe tobacco, which added to the elegance of antique desk, credenza, and chairs.

Harry Byrne stood and stepped from behind his desk. He was a lean man in matching vest and trousers, his sandy grey hair was close cropped and his hazel eyes were friendly. He still had the youthful quality that he revealed in his war photographs. His left hand grasped a straight-stemmed pipe. He shook hands with Spracklin and Burwell and said, "Lieutenant Spracklin, I like to hear bad news quickly." His tone was polite, his manner somber. "They don't send out the head of homicide with good news."

"Captain Byrne, Sir, I'm afraid we've found the body of a young female in Golden Gate Park. We're investigating to see if it's your daughter."

"Investigating?" Byrne showed no emotion, only sucked rhythmically on his pipe. "You haven't confirmed the identification yet?"

"No, Sir. The medical examiner is looking into that. We'll know more in a few hours. I'm afraid her body...." He was going to say defiled, but that would imply post-mortem sexual assault. "She was beheaded, Captain Byrne. We haven't located the head yet, so we're fingerprinting the body."

Though Byrne maintained his martial bearing, the news rocked him to the marrow. He steadied himself and didn't seem to hear Spracklin's words of condolence. Spracklin knew Byrne had once lost a ship and two dozen sailors to German U-boats in the North Atlantic, and he knew how to prepare for the worst. But this was his own daughter. After a few seconds, Byrne set the pipe in an ashtray and pushed a button on his desk. "Mrs. Jenkins," he said. "Will you please have Martin come by with the car?" After a pause, he added, "And cancel my meetings for the day." He turned to Spracklin and said, "Lieutenant, thank you for coming in. My wife will want to know the news immediately."

"I understand, but we have a few questions."

"When my son was in Vietnam, my wife often told me I was to tell her any bad news the instant I heard it." It was as if he hadn't heard Spracklin. Byrne began to place papers into his briefcase. Spracklin assumed he did this every day he left the office and was operating on instinct now. Then the Captain grasped what Spracklin had said. "Questions?" Byrne said. "Yes. Go ahead." Once again, he was attentive, though he did not invite them to sit down.

"The victim we found wore an engagement ring."

"Yes, yes. Sarah got engaged about two months ago. An old flame had just returned from Vietnam. They surprised us all with the news—just before she left for Hong Kong the...the last time."

"His name?"

"Peter Menendez. Major Peter Menendez, 23rd Infantry." Spracklin jotted down the information.

"Tell me about him."

"We always adored Peter. He was a sterling lad, from New Mexico, studied at Berkeley, a member of its track team. I'm sure he'd have been a Rhodes Scholar if he hadn't volunteered for military service." His eyes grew misty. "He's been a great comfort to us the past few weeks. He and my son have grown very close. Even while Sarah was…was missing, Pete has been a regular at our house, for Sunday dinner and what have you." Byrne snapped shut his briefcase and grabbed his grey trilby hat.

"And he's in the Bay Area now?"

"Yes. He's working here at Poseidon."

"He's in the office?"

"No, no. He's part of a special detail we've assembled — to search for Sarah. You probably saw the command post in the board room. Pete's in the field now." Byrne came out from behind the desk. "Do you mind if we continue this as we head to my car?"

"I'm afraid I'm going to have to detain you for a few more minutes," said Spracklin. Byrne seemed taken aback by the firmness of his tone. "Captain Byrne, we're conducting a murder investigation. We still have more questions. Can you tell me about this task force?"

"Elias told me the SFPD might be like this, that you might resent the investigation and interfere." Byrne was frank without raising his voice.

"Who's Elias?"

Byrne looked surprised. "Elias Wong. You must know him — he used to head the Bureau of Inspectors." Spracklin was too dumbfounded to answer. Elias Wong, now a private investigator, was telling a client that the cops could *interfere* with his own investigation. "We contracted Captain Wong's services about two months ago to improve security at our container facility in Oakland. Two shipments of electronics had been stolen and we needed help. He's a good man — efficient with any task he's handed. When Sarah disappeared, he took over the role of — "

"Captain Byrne, we're the police force. We conduct the investigation."

The Captain wasn't used to being interrupted. He paused and continued calmly. "If that were true, your people would have found my daughter before, before...."

"Sir, how long ago did you bring in Wong?"

"Late March. As I said, he's done sterling work for us." Byrne could tell what Spracklin was thinking—that Wong's *sterling work* had not included actually finding the girl. He said, "Elias didn't have the resources available to the police department."

"Nor the competing responsibilities. I'll be handling the investigation of this young woman's death, whether it's your daughter or not. And it will be a thorough investigation of the highest priority. Now, tell me about your daughter."

"Why didn't you make it a high priority before today?" asked Byrne. Spracklin was learning how pointed the soft voice could be when the business titan was angry. "While she was alive?"

"Because I'm a homicide detective."

Spracklin knew what Byrne meant. Why were the cops showing an interest in his daughter now that she was dead? But he had to make the point and get information that only Byrne had. Byrne nodded and slumped into his chair. He gestured to two seats in front of the desk.

"Tell me about your task force," said Spracklin.

"We grew frustrated that the police were unable to locate Sarah after two weeks. So I transferred Captain Wong—you know him?"

"Oh yeah, we know each other." Spracklin wanted to ask what would happen to this task force now that Sarah Byrne was dead. But he knew the answer—Wong would now try to find his daughter's killer. Spracklin thought about trying to talk Byrne out of it, but he knew that could backfire. If the case went unsolved, Republicans would say Spracklin had thwarted the private investigation.

"Sir, can you think of anyone who would want to harm your daughter?"

Byrne picked up an unlit pipe. "Look-it, Lieutenant, you can appreciate that I realized a few weeks ago I didn't know my daughter as well as I thought I did." He tapped the last of the ash into an ashtray. "I couldn't believe my daughter was trafficking narcotics. But Elias looked into the evidence against Sarah, and he assured me it was rock solid. So, okay. My daughter, the little girl I bounced on my knee, smuggled drugs for some hood in Haight-Ashbury. There's no way she could do that and not make enemies."

"Did she have many enemies before?"

The Captain thought then he shrugged. It was hitting him that his daughter was dead. "She was a forceful character, Lieutenant. She...." His mind seemed to drift. "If Sarah wanted something, she would claw her way through a steel vault to get it. Some people, I guess, resented that."

"But you don't know any."

"No. Business contacts in the Far East, maybe."

"The Far East? Her job as a stewardess?"

"No, Sir. Her job as a stewardess was just preparation for the career she was planning." He smiled when he saw Spracklin's surprise. "Sarah only got that job because she wanted to start her own airline." He laughed. "Yes, a young woman with her own airline. She believed the future of transport was air freight. I told her nothing would ever replace sea shipping, but she argued that some products need to get to the market quickly. A live lobster costing seventy-eight cents in Maine is worth five dollars in Tokyo, she argued." His smile faded. "She became a stewardess to learn about airlines and the Asian market. During her two- to three-day layovers in Hong Kong, she'd meet with business people in the colony. She said she was building relationships. She was actually meeting businessmen in transport. I don't think it was just part of...." He looked up at the Lieutenant. "Her other activities we just learned about."

"Why do you think she was meeting bona fide businessmen?"

"I'd hear about it from my contacts in the Far East. Executives from Swire, from Hutchison Whampoa, the Jardines — these guys were always telling me how impressive my daughter was."

"So, she wanted to diversify your business into air freight."

"You don't understand, Lieutenant. She didn't want my help at all. Maritime shipping was the past to her. My son, William, my vice-president operations, he'd been a Lieutenant Commander in the Navy. She couldn't believe he was planning a career in an ancient industry like maritime transport. She called him Barnacle Bill. She wouldn't even talk about me backing her. She wanted to do it all herself."

Spracklin was about to move to another line of questioning, but he paused. "You're saying...your daughter preferred to finance her business by trafficking narcotics, rather than take help from her family."

After a few seconds of silence, the Captain said, "That occurred to me in the last few days." He ground his teeth on the empty pipe. "Elias told me her fingerprints were on the bags of heroin they took from that pusher, Andy Fox. It was an airtight case against her." He stood again and said, "Can we continue this, maybe tomorrow?" Spracklin nodded and the three men walked out toward the elevator. As they passed the command post, Spracklin asked if he could take a few of the photos of Sarah. Byrne agreed. Spracklin took four.

"We need to know more about your daughter," said Spracklin as they descended in the elevator. "As we proceed with the case. I understand she lived at home until she absconded—I'll need to search her bedroom, get her bank details and family phone records."

"Of course, Lieutenant. Right now, I need to see my wife."

Spracklin agreed. Byrne shook their hands and strode to a driver waiting beside a black Cadillac.

"Elias Wong?" asked Burwell.

"Problem," said Spracklin. "Big problem."

Burwell shrugged. "I heard he was a great cop. He got shafted— that's the word on the street."

Spracklin began walking toward his Monaco. He stopped and turned to Burwell. "Yes, Elias Wong was a great investigator— maybe the best I ever met."

"But...."

"But he wasn't shafted. He's an obsessive, a maniac." As they walked through the lunchtime crowd, Spracklin thought of his return from Washington in 1964. Bud Hawkings had placed him in the Bureau of Inspectors as Captain Wong's deputy, saying they needed a diplomat in the office. Wong was a Hollywood-style cop, a good-looking bachelor with a love of sports cars. Wong knew Spracklin was the Chief's boy and interpreted Spracklin's presence as a challenge. "If you can outwork me or out-police me, I'll be nervous," Wong had said. Spracklin had always been proud of his own work ethic, but he couldn't outwork Wong. Entering the office at 7 a.m., Spracklin often found Wong, wearing the same clothes as the day before, poring over files he'd been working on all night. On the scent of a criminal, he was relentless and merciless.

"I'm just going by what I heard," said Burwell. "He shot a pervert, in self-defense. But he had enemies in high places. They sacked him."

"That's the lore he's created," said Spracklin. He needed a drink. He checked his watch. It was almost lunchtime. "It's good for business. If you're a PI, you want that rep of being a renegade."

"So why is it bad news? Isn't it good to have that sort of investigator working beside us?"

"I'll tell you something about Elias Wong," said Spracklin, wheeling toward his Sergeant. "He sees himself as a private eye in a movie." Burwell looked puzzled. "Every movie about a private eye, they always outsmart the cops." Spracklin could hear the anger in his own voice. "The cops are always fatheads and the private dick sees clues they're too stupid to see. That's how Elias Wong sees himself. He's Bogey, Batman, the hero who sees things the cops miss. He lives to show up the force that fired him. So, he's going to do everything in his power to make us look bad. And he's got the ear of Harry Byrne, one of the most powerful men in the city."

CHAPTER 9

The troops were at lunch when Spracklin got back to the Bureau of Inspectors, so he quickly unlocked his desk drawer and took out a bottle of Johnnie Walker Black Label. He splashed two fingers into his coffee mug and got down to work. With his nerves settled, he turned his attention to the file and evidence carton from the Sarah Byrne case.

The evidence carton contained Byrne's overnight bag, which they had seized along with the heroin she'd brought into the country. It was full of women's clothes. He picked up a blouse then lowered it. There was something he had to do first. He unlocked his desk drawer again, pushed the scotch bottle to one side, and took out a file labeled Hugh Jennings MacTevish. He always kept this file locked in his desk.

Before Chief Bud Hawkings created the Internal Affairs department, he had formed a panel of three detectives to investigate a police shooting of Hugh MacTevish, who was suspected of raping and murdering minors. Wong had worked the case, in which two boys and a girl had been sodomized, and one of the boys murdered. All incidents occurred in the rain. The kids had been walking home from school near Lake Merced Park. The hoods of their raincoats were up, so they couldn't see who grabbed them. Wong made a point of patrolling the neighborhood during each rainstorm. One rainy day, he got a call. A housewife saw a child being grabbed. He responded fast enough to pursue the assailant into the park. The unarmed suspect ended up with three bullets in him, in the knee, chest, and a point-blank shot to the head.

There was no doubt Hugh MacTevish, the brother-in-law of a prominent banker, was the rapist. His fingerprints were on the girl's rain coat, and mementos from the previous victims were found at his Land's End house. But the civil rights community and MacTevish's sister forced an inquiry. The panel found "excessive force" and Wong was dismissed. Spracklin knew Elias got off easy—he should have faced a murder charge. But Wong thought he was sacrificed for political reasons. Wong's supporters on the force—there were many—were outraged. The Department rumor mill said Hawkings had his old friend Jimmy Spracklin—a guy who was on the investigating panel, for Chrissakes—take over the Bureau of Investigators. For the sake of appearances, Hawkings did not promote the Lieutenant to a full Captain. He'd told Spracklin it would take time, given sentiment within the force.

Spracklin anticipated trouble from Wong in the Byrne investigation, and he wanted to refresh his mind on the MacTevish case. He'd read a few pages when the phone rang.

"I tell you, Jimmy, that boy is pure Spracklin," said the woman's voice with a Texan drawl.

Despite himself, Spracklin smiled. If Sam were in big trouble, Val would have had a grimmer tone. "Is it worse than the haircut?"

"I dunno if anything's worse than the haircut—that boy looks like a caveman. But he's in trouble at school again."

"How bad?"

"Fighting in the schoolyard and engaging in subversive activities."

"Subversive activ—did he form a Communist cell?" Spracklin took a sip of whisky and chuckled.

"Sam was talking to school mates about organizing a protest against the war. Robby Markham—you know him?"

"Al Markham's boy. Baseball player, good pitcher."

"Yep. He starts calling Sam a hippie Communist and being unpatriotic and it ended up in fists. Robby's got a black eye and Sam's been warned. Next time he's suspended."

Spracklin started to laugh. He knew the Markham boy had a good twenty pounds on Sam. "So he's in trouble for pacifism and violence?"

"You said it."

"That takes some doing."

"And he's getting preachy about it. 'If people are in jail for opposing the war, I don't mind being suspended for it blah, blah, blah.' You've heard him before. Anyway, Loo-tenant. You gotta have a word with that boy."

"I'll add it to the list."

"Things busy at work?"

"You could say that." He sipped his scotch and told her about the girl's body and Wong's task force. He glanced at the evidence carton before him and knew he had to get back to work. "Whoa, Honey," he said. "I just got a signal from the receptionist. There's a call I have to take. I'll call you later." He told her he loved her then hung up and reached for his mug again.

After returning the MacTevish file to the drawer, Spracklin opened the evidence carton again and unpacked Sarah Byrne's business suit, underwear, blouses. He made sure they weren't wrapped around anything, that nothing was stashed in pockets. Inside the overnight bag itself, he could see the rips where Fox had cut away the fake bottom to get at the heroin. The heroin was now in an evidence locker awaiting the Fox trial.

Her toiletry bag contained soaps, shampoos, makeup, dental products. An unopened vial of YSL Rive Gauche perfume was still in its package, with a price tag with Chinese characters on it. At the bottom of the bag, he found a key ring with a Mercedes Benz fob, with six keys and a wallet. There was nothing else—no address book or notebook. He returned everything to the case and began to go through her wallet. He found receipts for drinks at the Dragon Boat Bar and dinner at the Mandarin Oriental hotel. There were business cards from Hong Kong shipping executives—two with Chinese names, one German, and one English. Spracklin set them aside to check with InterPol and see if the execs were legit. The wallet contained fifty-seven dollars in American currency, HK$237 in Hong Kong money, and her checkbook from a Bank of America branch on Haight Street. Sarah Byrne had not recorded her transactions—the ledger was blank.

Spracklin noticed the new receptionist—a widow in her forties—was at his door signaling to him. She held up four fingers and mouthed the word, "Chief." Bud Hawkings was on line four. Spracklin nodded and pushed the flashing button.

"Hey, Bud."

"Christ, Jimmy, I got incoming already," said the growling voice on the other end.

"Who's after you?"

"Casey and Mazursky." It figured. The two senior Republicans on the San Francisco Board of Supervisors were already on the phone to the Chief.

"They called you about the Byrne girl?"

"Indeed they did, Lieutenant. Indeed they did." Spracklin had expected this to happen in the next day or two, but the conservative politicians were at work already.

"What was their message?"

"What you'd expect: Harry Byrne is a great American and we have to do everything in our power to make sure the killer is brought to justice."

"We don't even know if it's Sarah Byrne yet," said Spracklin. "The ME's just doing the autopsy now."

"So where are you with the investigation?"

"I've got uniforms combing the area, looking for her head more than anything. There must have been some reason the killer decapitated her post-mortem, so we want that head. Assuming it's Sarah Byrne, I'll interview the family. One known associate is Andy Fox. I'll interview him. Then we'll proceed based on what we learn."

"Okay, Jimmy. You're taking this one yourself, right?"

"Yes, Sir."

"All right then. You focus on that and I'll keep the wolves at bay up here." Spracklin appreciated it. He didn't need political interference. "It's part of the job I will definitely not miss in six months' time, I'll tell you. I can't wait to be free of—"

"It's a bit more complicated than that, Bud," Spracklin said, cutting the Chief off. "The supervisors aren't our only problem. Harry Byrne hired Elias Wong to find the girl, and it seems like the Byrnes are keeping him on to investigate her murder."

"Oh shit," said the Chief. "How bad is it?"

"Byrne's turned the Mercantile Shipping board room into a command post. He's got Elias and Sarah Byrne's fiancé working it. They're well financed. And Elias…yeah, Elias is heading it."

"He's a good investigator."

"He wants my head on a platter."

"I think you're being a bit paranoid, Jimmy."

"But just a bit, right?" Chief Hawkings didn't respond.

"Just investigate the case—Elias is a side show right now." Spracklin knew the Chief was right. He thanked him and hung up. He realized his fingers were fiddling with the key ring. He liked the Mercedes Benz fob—who wouldn't like a key ring that showed that you drove a Benz? There were six different keys on it. Two were obviously for a Mercedes. But what of the others. Why would a twenty-three-year-old flight attendant need so many keys? Spracklin set the keys to one side, and replaced the lid on the carton.

CHAPTER 10

Something about a dismembered body on a gurney bothered Jimmy Spracklin. In the orderly lab, Ernie Swanson had already completed his dissection, disposed of organs and re-stitched incisions. The cadaver lay again under a crisp white sheet. The outline told any witness the ungodly truth—this woman's head was missing. There was something obscene about it. It was so clean, precise, brutal.

"I really appreciate you accelerating this one, Ernie," said Spracklin as the Deputy ME flipped through papers on a clipboard.

"Actually, it worked out well," said Swanson, finishing his notes and returning his pen to the plastic holder in the breast pocket of his lab coat. "The Chief called about an hour ago. I was able to tell him it's Sarah Byrne, and we'd almost completed the autopsy. Or at least the work we could do."

"You're sure it's Sarah?"

"The fingerprints match the prints they took off the pouches of heroin that were seized on June 5."

Spracklin nodded and focused immediately on the next big question. "She was decapitated post-mortem, as you expected?"

"Definitely."

"Then how did she die?"

"Good question. And I'm afraid I don't have an answer."

Spracklin sighed. "What does that mean?"

"It means we don't have a conclusive cause of death. To know what killed her, I'd need the head and we don't have her head. We have no evidence her throat was blocked, no evidence of dilated pupils or protruding tongue—the usual signs of strangling." He threw his hands into the air in exasperation. "Even the time of death, Lieutenant. We judge that by the temperature of the brain, but...." He looked knowingly at the Lieutenant.

"No brain."

"Exactly. Best I can estimate is between 10 p.m. and 3 a.m." He looked at his notes. "We know several things that didn't kill her. There were no poisons, drugs or alcohol in her system. I don't even think she drank. Her most recent meal was a salad. There was no damage to her heart. The only contusions are around the neck, which came post-mortem when the head was severed. There was no indication of gunshot residue, nor any blood patterns that would be consistent with a shot to the head. There were no signs of sexual assault, nor of the body being defiled in death."

"So there are no clues at all?" asked Spracklin.

"There are, but they're only clues."

Spracklin wished the doctor would cut to the chase.

"There were blood splatters on her shirt, and some of these contained mucus. During the commission of her murder, she bled from the nose. This could mean direct impact, a hit in the nose, or it could mean strangulation. There was no cranial matter mixed with the blood. That means that if she did die from head trauma, it was probably not severe enough to break through the skull. There was slight discoloration of her fingernails, but not enough to be conclusive."

"Strangulation is the most likely cause of death?"

"Certainly asphyxiation is a high probability, just because we can rule out so many other possible causes. My money would be on strangulation with some form of ligature, which caused bleeding from the nose."

Spracklin didn't jot this down as it would be in the autopsy. "What you're saying is we probably have a murderer who strangled her viciously enough to cause bleeding from the nose. But there is no other sign of trauma on the rest of the body."

"That's right. This appears to be a cold, calculated attack. There's no indication that the perpetrator wanted to inflict pain on the victim. I don't think it was a crime of passion."

"A clean kill, and then a beheading."

"Yes, the severing of the neck," said the doctor. Swanson peeled back the sheet, exposing the gaping wound at the base of the neck. Over the years, Spracklin had grown dispassionate about dead bodies, but he had seen this girl sitting in a car with Marie, with his own daughter. Now she was headless. He tried to overcome his craving for a sip of scotch, just one sip, and focus on what the doctor was saying. "The perpetrator used a knife to detach the head from the body," Swanson continued, using a pen as a pointer. "It's difficult to get a lot of information on the knife. It looks like the cadaver was on its back, and he was cutting from above. He used the edge of the blade first, slicing into the tissue, then cutting more aggressively between C5 and C6 — the fifth and sixth cervical vertebrae."

"The lower neck?"

"Yes."

"So if it had been strangulation, he removed all the evidence of it?"

"Yes. It seems he had difficulty once he was cutting into the vertebrae. The damage to the bone surface shows that he cut more and more aggressively. Then he used the point of the knife to try to pry the bones apart — you can see the sharp incisions on the bones. The incisions show clean cuts in the soft tissue, which suggests a blade long enough that he could pass it back and forth without the blade leaving the neck. I estimate a blade of at least seven inches."

Swanson replaced the sheet and then peeled it back at the side, so that he could reveal the woman's left hand. Spracklin noticed the engagement ring had been removed.

"One final thing," said the pathologist. "There was no discoloring in the extremities of her limbs. No blood has pooled in the fingertips and the toes."

"What does that mean?"

"She probably wasn't transported after she died. It appears she fell where she was killed."

Spracklin nodded. He turned to Burwell to see if he had any questions, but the Sergeant just shook his head. Spracklin thanked Swanson. Then he and Burwell took the elevator back to the Bureau of Inspectors. Spracklin was working through what they had already. And it wasn't much. He wondered what the hell Elias Wong knew.

"You get anything on J.D. Ehler?" Spracklin asked Burwell once they were in his office.

"I haven't had a minute," said the Sergeant. "I'll get on it this afternoon."

Spracklin accepted they'd been busy and told Burwell to take some notes. He'd already pinned a map of San Francisco on the wall, highlighting Golden Gate Park — the three-mile green rectangle in the middle of San Francisco — the West Coast equivalent of Central Park. Spracklin held a pen against the scale at the bottom of the map, measuring a mile, then held it over the width of the park. "So Golden

Gate Park, north to south, is about a half-mile wide, and Hippie Hill is about—let's estimate—about a quarter mile from the east end, and right in the middle. So that means...."

He turned and observed Burwell sitting on the edge of his desk, lighting a cigarette.

Spracklin finished his own sentence. "It means the killer could have been out of the park in less than five minutes after the murder." Spracklin lowered his hands from the map and flopped in his chair. Burwell didn't even swivel around so Spracklin was talking to his back.

"This isn't working out, Ed," he said. "I need inspectors who contribute to cases."

"I contribute."

"Downstairs, you didn't ask a single question. You didn't read the autopsy report."

"You were already taking care of that shit."

"That *shit* is what we do." He lit his own cigarette. "I need someone who digs out stuff I can't, who sees things I don't see."

"Tell you what, Jimmy," said Burwell. "Gimme a job to do. I'll get some poop on Ehler, but give me something more."

Spracklin wasn't convinced. He studied the map of Golden Gate Park as he smoked his cigarette. "Like what?"

"Like where does the investigation go from here? What are you doing this afternoon?"

Spracklin didn't even want to tell him. "I'm going to talk to Andy Fox." Burwell seemed surprised by the thought of Spracklin interviewing the drug dealer he'd shot a few weeks earlier. "He's the only guy that we know of who knew Sarah Byrne, other than her family."

Burwell nodded. "Let me come along and handle the interview. I'll show you what I can do. What do you want to get out of him?"

That was a good question, maybe the best Burwell had ever asked. Spracklin didn't know what he wanted to get out of the interview. "Just sound him out, really."

"Find out what he knows," said the sergeant. He was nodding now.

"Get him talking." Maybe there was hope for Burwell, thought Spracklin. "You know, Ed, like, don't go in there with a cop–suspect sort of thing. Sit down with him. Chat. Tell him a joke or two. Get him talking."

"I can do that."

"Sure you can. And then steer the conversation toward Sarah Byrne. You know, isn't it a shame? That sort of stuff."

"I can do that," said Burwell.

Spracklin glanced up at the map again. He noticed Park Station on the southeast corner. Spracklin remembered that Burwell had spent years in patrol at Park Station—he was probably drinking buddies with all the grounds crew in the park. "You know the maintenance department at the park grounds?"

"Sure. Edgar Hemmings and his gang."

"Great. Afterward, I want you to head back up to the park. Find out if anyone on the grounds staff noticed anything unusual this morning—anything weird in the area, trampled bushes, disturbed earth, anything."

"Leave it with me, Jimmy."

CHAPTER 11

He felt better being out on Haight Street. In the past twenty-four hours, his euphoria had alternated with waves of fear and apprehension. He'd got high and come down. He'd had almost no sleep. Now he felt calm as he walked with the kids down through the bustle of Haight-Ashbury. He was sick of hearing how much cooler the Haight had been a year earlier—the place seemed pretty freewheeling to him now. It had more of an edge, more adventure. The cats you met were more likely to be flashing knives than peace signs. If you were tripping, you were liable to get beat up by an addict who needed your money. It was a war zone, but a war zone with its own artistic flare. Killing time until he had to make his call, he leaned against a doorway and watched two pretty chicks dancing on the sidewalk to a tune playing from an open window.

> *People push and shove me*
> *But I got the lord above me*
> *I'm heading back to Oakland*
> *Where I'll find some folks who love me*

He'd heard the song the past few days. Jasmine. It was Jasmine's new single, recorded around the corner at a studio on Clayton Street, the place with the egg cartons plastered to the walls. He checked his watch and tapped his toe as he watched the young girls jive to the sound.

> *I know the outlook's stormy*
> *But your dire views just bore me*
> *I'm heading back to Oakland*
> *Where my baby's waiting for me*

It was time. The assassin stepped around the dancers into the street, just as a biker on a chopper revved the engine and zoomed off toward Lower Haight. The assassin moved inside the phone booth on the corner of Cole. He was glad the girls' radio was playing so loud. No one would be able to hear his call. He plugged in a dime, and his client picked up on the second ring.

"It's done," he said.

"I heard," said the client. The old guy's voice was calm. He wondered whether the client would compliment him on a job well done.

"It went off without a hitch. Just like I said."

There was silence at the other end of the line, and the assassin knew the client could hear the pop song in the background. Suddenly, Haight Street felt childish and inconsequential. "I kept up my end. I'm ready for the next step."

Through the music, he thought he heard the client chuckling. "A girl. A flight attendant."

He'd known that would be the old guy's attitude. He'd known people would sneer at his hit. "I...did what had to be done."

There was another pause, and the client said, "What's with the head?"

He was sure this was a test. He knew he shouldn't say anything over the phone. He couldn't say the wire had been caught in the vertebrae of her neck. His knife wouldn't cut the metal wire, so he'd had to take the head off. The wire would have been evidence, so he'd taken the whole head. "I'll explain it when we meet," was all he said.

"Smart boy," said the voice. Then he added. "Across the street, you see Eddie's Convenience?" The assassin turned and looked at the store across the busy road. "There's a noticeboard just inside the door. There's an address on a green card. Go get it. Be at the address at eight tonight."

There was a click and a dial tone, and he heard the dime drop into the change box. The client had been waiting for his call and placed the card in the store beforehand. No one tapping his line would know where they were meeting. He left the phone booth and headed across the street. The client hadn't praised him, but they were meeting again — that was a start.

CHAPTER 12

Spracklin didn't like the holding area below the courthouse. It stank and it was filled with low-lifes who didn't interest him. Drunks, robbers, druggies, pimps, brawlers. Most were known to the cops, but not to Spracklin. He knew the murderers, few of whom were repeat offenders. As he and Burwell entered the brightly lit detention area, he tried not to look at the manacled crooks waiting to be shipped back to the County Jail on 7th Street.

He badged the Sergeant behind the operations desk and said: "There was a guy in Courtroom 4 this morning, Andy Fox. Decked a sheriff. He been shipped yet?"

"In solitary," answered the sergeant.

"What cell?"

"I said he's in solitary. He's there till the last shipment."

"We need to see him and his file," said Spracklin. He pushed forward his lieutenant's badge. The Sergeant looked at it. He pulled a file from a carton, handing it to Spracklin. It showed the recent details of Andy Fox's life. After being shot, he had been isolated in the forensic ward at the General Hospital. He had been discharged to the County Jail the previous day and brought to lockup. He'd been allowed two guests in the forensic unit—his lawyer Jeff Fujimoto, and someone called David Terceira. Spracklin pointed the names out to Burwell and jotted the details of the visits down in his notebook.

"Cell 6," said the sergeant. "Mikey, show the Lieutenant and Sergeant to Cell 6." A sheriff at the back of the operations area grabbed a key ring and told Spracklin and Burwell to follow him. They passed under the glaring fluorescent lights, following a painted yellow line on the floor past the grid of cells. Decades of white paint had built up on the iron bars. The cells were almost empty as the previous night's hoods were being processed in court, released or transported, and a fresh lot had yet to be arrested. One lunatic was howling in a back corner, and a guy in a Black Panthers T-shirt stood at the sight of the sheriff and demanded his phone call. They walked to the end of the corridor, where the sheriff unlocked an iron-plated door and swung it open.

Andy Fox was on a cot, his back against the cinderblock wall. The cell included a bunk, chair, sink, and toilet. No soap. No toilet paper. Fox's left eye was swollen shut and discolored. Blood was smeared around his nostrils and on his denim prison shirt, though he'd washed most of it off his face. Spracklin half laughed. Good enough for the bastard.

"Lieutenant," Fox said. Then he gave a slight smile that seemed to say he was so bored that he was happy even to see the cop who had shot him. Then he spied Burwell's hulking form behind Spracklin and he grew serious. "Who's he?"

Spracklin knew Fox wouldn't say anything if he thought they were going to beat him up. Much as he enjoyed Fox's panic, Spracklin knew he had to calm the guy's nerves. "Good day, Fox," he said. "This is Sergeant Burwell." The Sergeant stepped past Spracklin into the cell and sat on the wooden chair by the basin. Spracklin looked back at the sheriff who had taken up a position at the door. "Thank you, Sheriff," said Spracklin. "We'll be fine."

"I'm under instructions to remain, Sir."

"And I said we'll be fine." Spracklin kept his gaze on the man until he left. Spracklin noticed for the first time that Burwell had a clipboard. Burwell looked at his boss and at Fox.

"What is this?" asked Fox.

"We're just here to talk," said Burwell.

"About what?"

"Well, about—" Burwell pulled a pack of cigarettes from his pocket. "We're investigating a case and we need your help."

"Your buddies got their pound of flesh an hour ago."

"Calm down, Andy," said Burwell. He had a slight smile. He offered a cigarette to Fox, who declined. "We're just wondering if you can tell us some things about Sarah Byrne."

"Sarah," he said. "Why are there two of you here?"

"I'm helping out Jimmy. He's the lead investigator, I'm here to ask a few questions."

"Lead investigator."

"Yeah," said Burwell, lighting his cigarette. "So, he'll get to go to your execution and actually hear you sizzling in the chair." Burwell chuckled and looked up to see if Spracklin would join in the joke.

"What the fuck?" yelled Fox.

"But I can only hear about it on the evening news," said Burwell, still laughing. "So, I have some questions—"

"Get the fuck out of here," screamed Fox.

Spracklin rolled his eyes and sighed. "Calm down, Fox," he said. "We just want to talk."

"Get this asshole out of here. I got enough problems without him."

Spracklin knew it had been a mistake to bring Burwell. "Sergeant, let me speak with the prisoner." Burwell looked over at him, as if to say it was only a joke. "You're excused." Spracklin and Fox both waited while Ed Burwell rose and walked down the corridor between the prison cells. They heard his feet receding. Spracklin took Burwell's place in the chair and decided he needed a cigarette as well.

Fox looked away. "So, are you here so we can team up?"

Spracklin was just lighting his cigarette but he stopped with the flame inches from the tip. *Team up with Fox?* "What are you talking about?"

Fox sat up on the bunk, grunting from the pain in his sides. "Marie," he said. He ignored the pain to get close to Spracklin. "We need to work together to protect Marie."

"The day I work with you will be—"

"Some cops came in last night, asking about her."

Spracklin finished lighting his cigarette and pocketed his lighter. "Who?"

"Dunno. Two of them. One was Irish."

"That narrows it down."

"Listen up, man. This Irish guy did the talking. He was asking questions about how Sarah got from the airport. You know, the night you shot me."

Spracklin took a long draw on the cigarette and studied Fox. He still wished he'd killed the guy, but the dealer seemed to be sincere now. "What did he say, this Irish cop?"

"He was playing heavy, you know. Threatening me. And he kept asking who drove Sarah. He said there was a witness who saw the driver."

"What witness?"

"He didn't say. But you have to get to Sarah before these guys do."

Fox obviously thought Spracklin would help Sarah Byrne, a drug smuggler, if it would benefit Marie. It was a moot point now. "Sarah's dead," he said.

Fox nodded and settled back into his cot. He thought for a moment and asked, "Murdered?"

"How'd you know?"

"It just makes sense, doesn't it?"

"Not to me, it doesn't. Why would it make sense?"

"For three weeks, she'd been a fugitive on drug-smuggling charges. Now she shows up dead. Someone would want her out of the way, or to get back at her. You got a cigarette, Jimmy?" Spracklin took the pack of Chesterfields and shook one out. "I can light it myself," said Fox. Spracklin lit it off the end of his and handed it to Fox. The dealer was talking and Spracklin had to keep him talking.

"Who are these people who might want her dead?"

"Me." Fox blew a stream of smoke toward the ceiling. "And your daughter."

"You wanted her dead?"

Fox took another drag on the cigarette. "You asked who *might* want her dead. I suppose I *might*." He placed a comic emphasis on the word. "Well, if I were you, I'd suspect me. If she's dead, then there's one major witness who won't be testifying against me. Maybe I snuck out last night and iced her." He tapped the ash of his cigarette on to the floor. "And then there's Marie because Sarah is the one person who could testify against her. Do you have an alibi for your little girl?"

The guy was now becoming the smartass Spracklin had been expecting. Spracklin knew he was trying to goad him and he had to keep calm and keep him talking. "You could have had David Terceira do it."

Fox smiled. He was enjoying the verbal jousting. "Never know, do you? You'd have to find him and ask him."

"You don't feel an ounce of guilt about what you did to the Byrne girl, do you? No remorse now that she's dead."

"I couldn't have done it, Jimmy. I was in the pen."

"Not her murder. Getting her involved in running drugs for you."

Fox took another long drag on the cigarette. "You didn't know Sarah, did you, Lieutenant?"

"I know you used her international flights to supply your drug ring."

"I didn't get her involved in anything. She...." He could have continued, but he gave Spracklin a look that said he was too smart to say anything else.

"You're saying she got into it herself?" asked Spracklin.

"I don't know what you mean by 'into it' but I will tell you this about Sarah: no one told her what to do." He took a final drag on the cigarette and flicked it into the toilet beside his bunk. "She was a bit like Marie that way."

Spracklin studied Fox. In the past few weeks, he'd been dealing with kids, brats really, who pretended to be rebellious because they took drugs. Few had the grit to be outlaws, or to survive the violence of the drug trade. Andrew Fox was different. He was in his thirties—a beatnik, not a hippie. Spracklin knew his strength and agility, and his skill with fists, knives or live ammunition. He was unencumbered by conscience or compassion. He liked operating among the hippies, but he wasn't one of them and shared none of their beliefs in love, peace, and social justice. Spracklin hated his guts, but he felt closer to Fox, at least in terms of age, than the hippies.

"What's the story with you and Marie?"

Fox laughed, then clutched his side. "We're in love. Didn't she tell you?" He paused and added, "Can't wait to call you Dad."

Spracklin held his gaze. "I want to know what's going on." Now he wanted to kill the bastard again.

"Ask her."

"I'm asking you." Spracklin tried to keep his voice low. He didn't want the sheriffs to hear.

"I've told you the truth of the situation, Lieutenant. And think of this: If I didn't love Marie, I'd tell the truth about what happened the night you busted me." Fox let that sink in. The two men knew what was on the line. They both loved Marie and couldn't let the truth about her role in Sam Lindgren's death get out.

Spracklin said, "Why was she in court this morning?"

"Ask her."

Spracklin knew Fox would say nothing about Marie. The Lieutenant had one last question: "Who's David Terceira?"

"A friend. How is Marie doing?"

"You saw her yourself, this morning."

"But tell me how she's doing."

"Stay away from her. Even if she tries to see you."

"How was Sarah killed?"

"Stay away from Marie."

Fox leaned forward and whispered, "We both know I did Marie the greatest favor in the world. I went along with that bullshit story that you killed my best friend. You better keep me onside."

"You're irrelevant now. No one would believe you if you did change your story."

"I could make trouble."

"The only one you'd hurt is Marie. And yourself."

"Tell me what happened to Sarah—toss me a bone."

Spracklin dropped his butt on the floor and ground it under his shoe. "They found her this morning on Hippie Hill. She'd been decapitated."

Fox took in the information. "It's too bad. She was a good shit, lot of fun."

"No idea who did it?"

"Could be anyone. I'd wonder about her contacts in Asia."

"Sheriff," yelled Spracklin. He wasn't going to get anything more out of Fox. He stood and took one last look at the prisoner. He was beaten and bloody, but Andy Fox was not defeated.

Spracklin thanked the sheriffs and walked to the elevators. He hadn't learned much. He still didn't know who David Terceira was.

"You seem lost in thought," said a voice. Spracklin looked up and saw Ray Handell leaning against the far wall. For a second, he forgot their argument and was glad to see his old friend.

"Where the hell did you come from?"

"I was coming to see you—they told me at your office you were down here. You just walked right by me."

"Something on my mind."

"My bet is it's a case."

"They found the body of this Byrne girl. The brass is up in arms about it and—well, it's getting complicated."

Handell put his arm around Spracklin's shoulder. "Jimmy, Jimmy, Jimmy," he said. "You've got too much on your mind. Listen, I just wanted to clear up our misunderstanding of this morning."

"Aw, don't worry about that," said Spracklin, trying not to sound suspicious. He wondered if Handell could be the "Irish" cop Fox had mentioned. He doubted it, but his guard was up.

"Listen, Jimmy. I've talked to the guys. We don't think we need to go to Marie. We understand she's been traumatized, but there are a few things we have to clean up. Can you come up to the office sometime tomorrow?"

"Just a few questions, eh?"

"Sure. First thing in the morning."

"I've got to focus on this case, but I can give you guys some time."

He sincerely liked Handell, but agreeing was pure self-interest. It helped to be on the good side of the head of Internal Affairs.

CHAPTER 13

It took Spracklin a half-hour to track down Burwell once he arrived at Park Station. A Sergeant directed him to walk about half a mile to the Structural Maintenance Division. From there, a groundsman rolling his own cigarette pointed him toward a small shed at the end of a row of equipment garages.

Spracklin walked into the dark shed and waited for his eyes to adjust. Forms began to emerge—stacks of dusty machinery, wheelbarrows, gardening tools. The junk covered about three-quarters of the floor and was stacked at least shoulder high. In the free space, Spracklin could make out three men: Burwell in his rumpled suit, and two black men in coveralls. They all held Dixie cups.

"Jimmy," said Burwell. His jacket hung from a nail on the wall, his top button was undone.

"Ed." Spracklin waited for Burwell to ask what he was doing there, but the Sergeant said nothing. Spracklin said, "Just came by to see if you had anything to report."

"Just talking to Edgar and Jack about it," Burwell said. He took a sip.

Spracklin nodded at the men, introduced himself and shook their hands. Their names were Edgar Hemmings and Jack Cashman.

"So, what do you have, Ed?" asked Spracklin.

The big Sergeant shrugged. "James Donald Ehler is a twenty-two-year-old from Sacramento. Dropped out from UC San Diego. He was studying engineering. No record." He took a sip from his paper cup. "Around the park, no one found anything suspicious last night, least of all a girl's head." The other two laughed. "Last night, everything was normal. Kids were sleeping in the park. But there usually are."

"Usually?"

Burwell stood, and reached for a bottle of Bacardi on a window ledge. "Edgar was saying kids sleep rough in the park every night. You don't notice them on patrol, but they're under bushes, in the woods." He tipped some rum into his cup. Spracklin wondered when the Sergeant would offer his boss a drink.

"Everywhere," agreed Hemmings, who accepted a topping up from Burwell. He'd sat down at a cluttered desk. Three centerfolds were tacked on the wall behind him — Miss December, Miss April and Miss June.

"And one place they like to sleep is the maintenance buildings," said Burwell. Cashman declined another drink, and the Sergeant returned the bottle to the window ledge. "But none of the sheds was broken into last night."

"So, what do we make of that?" asked Spracklin.

Burwell sipped, shrugged. "Dunno. We're just going over it."

After an awkward silence, Spracklin nodded. He said to Edgar Hemmings, "If you notice anything, just let us know." He shook their hands again and headed back toward his car. He didn't need Burwell's shitty rum. He had Black Label under the front seat. Spracklin mouthed a cigarette from his pack, paused to light it and muttered, "Prick."

As he approached Kezar Stadium, Spracklin heard guitars and voices from Hippie Hill. A woman was singing. He was aching for a drink, but he wanted to see what was going on near the crime scene.

Crossing Sharon Meadow, Spracklin could see the kids had been busy. They'd completed the platform, and placed a console to the left of the stage. A young woman was standing on the stage strumming a guitar, he could catch only snippets of her music as there was no sound system yet. Behind her, three long-haired carpenters were erecting the frame for a backdrop, which would hold Marie's tapestry.

Marie, thought Spracklin. *Jesus Christ, Marie.* He looked for her, but she wasn't among the two dozen people milling about. Ehler had all his workers putting the stage together beneath the great eucalyptus trees. Spracklin surveyed the hill, wondering if he should be looking for anything in the crowd. But again, he didn't know what.

Spracklin noticed a young man with shoulder-length red hair waving to him from the pathway to the west. The kid was lean with a prominent chest and shoulders. When he saw Spracklin coming toward him, he walked slowly away, down the path. Spracklin caught up with him just around the bend and the young man shook Spracklin's hand, introducing himself as Dave Bloom.

"You're investigating that girl's death?" he said.

"That's right. Lieutenant James Spracklin, head of the Bureau of Inspectors."

Bloom glanced behind Spracklin, then looked him in the eye. "I've been around here all day and kept an eye open. I've been working on the stage the past few days. People are, you know, shocked, but you'd expect that. I've only seen one person who hasn't been here earlier in the week, just one guy I'd call suspicious."

Spracklin tried to size up this hippie-jock who wanted to help a cop. His tone was almost conspiratorial, as if they were in on something together. "Go on," said the Lieutenant.

"There's a big guy in a green army jacket," Bloom said. He dropped his voice. "He's pissed out of his mind and he's hanging around Hippie Hill."

"He's not working on the concert."

"No, man—Sir. It's like he keeps looking at the place where the girl died. He's fixated on it." He tried to find the words to describe it, and blurted out, "Sitting by a tree, drinking wine. I think I saw him crying earlier." Bloom looked at Spracklin as if waiting for approval or reassurance.

"Is he there now?" asked Spracklin.

"He was a while ago."

"Thank you."

Spracklin turned to follow up on the lead and the boy grabbed his wrist. "Lieutenant," he said. "If I can help you, I'd like to. I'm, ah, I'm interested in applying to the Police Academy." Spracklin understood now. He pulled a card from his wallet and handed it to the young man. Placing a hand on his shoulder he said, "Sure, sure. Call me any time. And keep your eyes open. If you see anything else call that number. Leave a message if I'm not there."

He turned back toward Hippie Hill, wondering if the big drunk in the green jacket was still there. As he climbed the hill, he realized he knew the singer. It was Martha, the woman with auburn hair who had found the body. She wore blue jeans and a red checked shirt tied at the waist. She still hadn't managed to find a bra. She was smiling, geeing, and hawing with the technicians.

"Sing a song," yelled a young man.

"Not with all the hammering going on."

"Once you start singing, they'll stop."

Spracklin strode down to the trampled ground where the body had been found. There was nothing nagging him about the crime scene but he wanted to find the guy in the green coat.

"Lieutenant," he heard someone calling behind him. He turned and saw J.D. Ehler striding toward him with a piece of paper in his hand. He looked even more annoyed than usual. "Did you do this?"

"It depends on what 'this' is," said Spracklin. Ehler handed him the paper. It was an order from the Parks and Recreation Department canceling the supply of electricity for the concert. It said there had been an act of violence on the site, which violated the terms of Ehler's agreement with the department. The festival license had been revoked.

"For Chrissakes," yelled Ehler. "I told you we had nothing to do with the girl."

He continued yelling while Spracklin read the order. He knew the Parks and Recreation director and three deputies, but the person who'd signed the order was someone he'd never heard of. Spracklin held up a hand to silence Ehler. "You seen a guy hanging around here, a big guy in a green jacket?"

Ehler was taken aback. "A guy in army surplus stuff. Drinking wine. Yeah. What about him?"

"I want to talk to him."

"Well, he's gone and this is important. This is the same grief we got from the city when we wanted to hold a festival commemorating Bobby Kennedy a few weeks ago. I need at least electricity and I can't get a hookup without Parks and Rec approval."

Spracklin held up a hand again. He knew the concert had to proceed for the sake of his daughter if nothing else.

"I need watts, man," said Ehler, raising his voice. "We're going to have fifty-thousand people here Thursday night and we need the power to reach 'em."

Spracklin glared at the boy until he shut up. "Tell you what, J.D.," he said. "I know the Parks Department General Manager — Jackie Andrietti. Old friend of mine. I'll call him about this and get it straightened out."

Spracklin patted him on his shoulder and nodded at the surprised Ehler. He was speechless, and behind him the long-haired kid was still trying to get Martha to sing. Ehler looked at Spracklin.

"You'd do that?" Spracklin realized the kid had probably never had anyone from the city, certainly not the SFPD, helping him in any way.

"Think I want this thing canceled when my daughter's doing the backdrop?"

Spracklin didn't know what to make of Ehler. He'd been lingering around the crime scene enough to make Spracklin suspicious. But Spracklin had never met a murder suspect who badgered an investigating officer as much as Ehler had. If he was the killer, he was either a genius or an idiot.

"All I want to do, Detective, all we're trying to do here, is put on a good concert," he said, stammering on the words. "Did you hear about the Grateful Dead show on Haight Street in March?" Spracklin laughed, wondering if the kid was serious. "Honest, Sir, it closed down the whole street. People are still talking about it." He pointed at the stage as they began to move back uphill. "This will be as big. I swear. This show is something thousands of people will remember all their lives."

Spracklin couldn't have cared less, but he made a mental note to call Jack Andrietti. Ehler kept telling him how great his concert was going to be, dropping the names of bands he'd never heard of. On the stage now, Martha was tuning her guitar and flirting with the guys at the console.

Others cheered for the song and the singer began to strum her guitar, her hips swaying with the rhythm of the song. "Okay then," she crooned. "Here's the Environment Song." Spracklin tried and failed not to fixate on the swaying of her body, the swing of her breasts, as she sang.

> Toxic gases blind me. I can barely breathe
> All the family's gasping. We've fallen to our knees.
> This cloud of noxious gas will soon have us entombed.
> History will end! All life on earth is doomed
> It's like an evil spell from a dark Satanic text
> Daddy did a double-flusher, and now we're most perplexed.

Spracklin smirked, then chuckled. The technicians whooped. The singer winked at them. Spracklin looked again at the crime scene. There was no sign of the drunk in the green jacket—maybe the red-haired kid was leading him on.

CHAPTER 14

A blue MG—a sporty little number with the top down—sat in the driveway when Spracklin got home. Spracklin got out of his Monaco and inspected the sports car. It was spotless, recently waxed, the ashtray unused. The only sign of disorder was the leather driving gloves on the passenger seat. Spracklin wondered what affluent young Romeo was calling on his daughter. A rock star? A millionaire's son? Whoever he was, he had to be a step up from Andy Fox. *Shit*, he thought. He had to speak to the girl about Fox.

As he grabbed his briefcase and seersucker jacket, the front door flew open, and Marie came out, smiling. "Daddy," she said, pulling him toward the house. "There's someone I want you to meet." Spracklin hadn't seen Marie this happy in…maybe a year. "I was hoping you'd be home before he left."

Spracklin tried to figure out who could afford that sort of car— maybe John Brodie or one of the other 49ers. He stopped in the doorway. Val was shaking hands with a dumpy guy, maybe fifty, with a bad comb-over. He had a Mediterranean complexion and wore a mauve silk shirt with puffy sleeves.

"Daddy," said Marie, "I'd like you to meet Luigi Prodi."

Spracklin stepped up and shook hands with the Italian. It was a firm shake, a creditable shake.

"Lieutenant Spracklin," said the guest with a refined English accent. "I was just telling your wife what a pleasure it is to meet your charming daughter." He placed a hand gently on Marie's back. "And now this pleasure is only amplified by meeting her charming family."

"You're English, Mister…."

"Prodi," the man said. "Luigi Prodi, owner of the Prodi Gallery on Haight Street." He said it like Spracklin should know of it. "Born in

65

Italy, but my family moved to Portsmouth in 1932, fleeing Mussolini. Now, I'm in exile from a more nefarious foe—Inland Revenue."

They laughed politely, and Marie said, "Mr. Prodi came to see my work."

"Yes, a friend told me of your daughter's textiles and insisted I come to meet her. Marie described the work to me, and I offered to drive her home so I could witness them first-hand." He laughed gently and added. "I couldn't wait to see the Solstice wall hanging at the festival Thursday. And my impatience was rewarded."

"Will you stay for dinner, Mr. Prodi?" said Val, obviously taken with him. "We have more than enough."

"I'm afraid I can't, Mrs. Spracklin," he said as he placed a red beret on his head and turned to leave. "I'm afraid I must return to the city. I have a meeting this evening. But I hope I will be invited again and witness more of your daughter's work. She is a precocious talent."

He shook Val's hand, and she held his so he couldn't get away.

"Well, at least tell my husband what you said. You know, about the archetypes."

Prodi smiled and obliged. "Lieutenant, I'm struck by Marie's dexterity in applying the archetypes of Haight-Ashbury's graphic designers to a new medium. The Haight artists in two years have created motifs that are now famous throughout the world, and your daughter, with her appreciation of hues and texture, is now applying them to new medium. It's exciting work." He was patting his pockets as he spoke. "My gloves?"

"In your car," said Spracklin.

"Ah yes," said the gallery owner. Spracklin watched him waddle to his car, don his gloves and drive off.

"Funny little fella, huh?" he said.

"He is not a 'funny little fella'," said Marie, trying not to laugh.

"Then why are you laughing?" asked Spracklin, bending to kiss his wife.

"I'm not. I'm just happy—happy to meet such a brilliant artistic mind and have him see my work."

Spracklin walked to the kitchen and pulled a bottle of scotch from the liquor cabinet. "Naw, you were laughing," he said, grabbing two glasses. "Because the term 'funny little fella' summed him up perfectly."

Spracklin handed Val a scotch and took his into the den. He flicked on the knob on the cabinet television and waited a few seconds for the color picture to appear on the screen. He needed to see how the local news was covering the Byrne killing. Checking his watch, he saw he had a few minutes before the news came on. So, he went to his office and called Parks General Manager, Jack Andrietti. He recommended the concert proceed and said the crime scene was near but not at the stage. They chatted until Val came in, and Spracklin excused himself and hung up.

"Dinner's ready so maybe you could speak with him after," she said.

"Who? I just hung up."

"Sam. You were going to talk to him about fighting in the schoolyard."

"Right, right," said Spracklin. "Just let me catch the headlines."

The lead news story was the decapitated body found on Hippie Hill. The reporter mentioned that police had been searching for the daughter of industrialist Harry Byrne but didn't have enough to tie Sarah Byrne to the body. It would be a bigger story tomorrow when they confirmed the identity.

Spracklin turned off the TV and joined his family in the dining room.

"So, Sarah's dead, huh?" asked Marie as she picked at her vegetables. The boys lifted their heads, and Spracklin knew he'd made a mistake mentioning the Byrnes. Valerie shot him a look before she turned to Marie. Spracklin realized they could all hear the news report.

"You know, honey," she said, "that we don't discuss your father's work at the dinner table. There are more pleasant subjects."

"I was only asking about someone I met once." The excitement of entertaining Luigi Prodi had worn off. Marie put her fork down. "Is it true what they hinted at on the radio? That they found her near the stage on Hippie Hill?"

"Well, honey," said Spracklin. His wife's piercing blue eyes were telling him to change the subject. "There was a body found today near the concert site. But I can't really say much."

"Is she the headless hippie in the park?" asked the youngest boy.

"John-John Spracklin, you mind your manners," said Valerie. "A young woman has lost her life."

"John, m' boy," said Spracklin. "It's just not the sort of thing you discuss at the dinner table."

"That's right," said Valerie, with a forced smile. "Now, Marie, tell us about your day."

"Not much to say really. I went to the city and came home."

"Tell your father about your macramé."

"They're picking up my backdrop for the Solstice Festival tomorrow. They've got a truck coming for it."

Spracklin was about to congratulate her, and Val jumped in. "Your father can drop it off tomorrow. On his way in."

"It's too big," said the girl. "We've arranged for them to pick it up. And I'll go in with them — to make sure they hang it properly."

"Oh, honey, you don't want to trek all the way into the city if you don't have to."

"I've got to meet with the organizers before the festival Thursday night and help position it." Marie gave an awkward laugh. "I'd, like, die if I was standing there all night and my work wasn't displayed properly."

There was an awkward silence, broken only be the sound of Sam's knife grating against the china. "You sound like you're planning on going to that festival," said Val.

"I'm not going to miss it. My work is going to be on display."

"We'll discuss it —"

"I am not missing it."

"I said, we'll discuss it. After dinner."

"This isn't a prison and you and Sergeant Schultz" — she nodded her head at Spracklin — "can't hold me here against my will." She pushed her chair out and stomped off to the basement.

"Why that girl," said Val when she was gone. "When will she learn?"

Spracklin chewed his pork chops and hoped to avoid a fight. He thought his best course of action was just to eat his dinner. His wife glared at him. He hadn't backed her up the way she had expected.

"Sergeant Schultz?" he said, with a smile. "I thought I'd at least be Colonel Klink." The boys giggled then finished their meal in silence. The silence continued as Val cleared the table. Spracklin downed the rest of his scotch and wandered down to the basement. Marie was sitting on the overstuffed couch in the corner. Dusk had fallen and he couldn't make out the music posters and art work she'd taped to the wall.

"Are you here to bust me, Detective?" she asked.

"My jurisdiction ends at the Golden Gate Bridge," he said, taking a seat across from her. "Your mom's just trying to protect you. It's what parents do."

"Can't she understand this is a big break. I mean, Jasmine is going to be on stage, and there are rumors the Grateful Dead are going to show up and play a set. The Grateful Frigging Dead."

"Given what's happened, we don't like you hanging around that stage. Please try to understand. I mean, how did you even meet these guys?"

"A dude called J.D. Ey-ler or Ee-ler or something like that—he put an ad in *The Oracle*, the underground paper on Haight Street. Just a little thing saying he was looking for The Seamstress to do some work."

Spracklin winced to hear her use the term—Marie had used "The Seamstress" as her alias when she'd run away to Haight-Ashbury.

"You met with him?"

"It was just after I came back home. There was a phone number on the ad so I called it. This weirdo called J.D. answered. He's like, 'We want to help you out, we really do. We can't pay you nuthin' but it will be great exposure.'"

Her imitation of Ehler was deadly accurate, and Spracklin couldn't help laughing. "I met the guy today, down at the festival site. You've got him down pat."

"We're going to help you out. I promise you that," she said, again imitating Ehler. They both erupted into laughter. "I haven't met him yet. I imagine this little guy looking up at everyone telling them what he'll do for them."

"No, he's tall and gangly, a black guy, and you're right, a bit of a weirdo. So, what were you doing in court today when Andy Fox was arraigned?" He'd hoped to meander into the subject but he'd blurted it out. The smile vanished from her face.

"I could ask you why the hell were you following me today?" Marie lowered her voice so her mother wouldn't hear, but her tone was harsh.

Spracklin chuckled. "You know I'm a policeman, right?"

"I don't need sarcasm."

"I was the arresting officer. I apprehended Fox. I had to be in court today. Now you tell me: Why were you in court?"

Marie looked at her feet and whispered, "I just wanted to see him. Okay? It's nothing big. I've just been wondering about him and wanted to know his wounds had healed."

Since she'd returned home, Spracklin had been trying to understand his sixteen-year-old daughter's wants and desires. He'd wanted to cut her some slack, worried she would run away again. Val thought she needed discipline, but Spracklin just wanted to feel happy at home.

"You're in love with Andy Fox?" he asked, the words heavy in his mouth.

"No, it's not that. I've seen what he's done. I know he's guilty. It's just...." She clutched a pillow to her stomach. "I'm confined here and I just miss my freedom. I heard you on the phone last night, saying he'd be arraigned. I wanted to go see. I'm human, you know."

Spracklin nodded. He shifted over to the couch and put an arm around her shoulder and pulled her into him. She hugged him back.

"And you want to go to this solstice thing in Golden Gate Park."

"I could go with Rachael," she said, naming a childhood friend. "You could drive us and pick us up at 1 a.m." He held her gaze and she burst out laughing. "Okay, midnight."

"Let me think about it and talk to your mother."

"And you don't mind me going down there with the wall hanging tomorrow? In broad daylight?"

"Let me work on it. But I need to know something. It's important."

"What's that?"

"Are there any members of the Fox gang still at large?"

"The Fox gang. You make it sound like something out of a bad western."

"You know what I mean. Were there people who worked for Fox who are still hanging around Haight Street?"

"Is this about Sarah?" He nodded. She thought for a moment and said, "I don't know. Honestly, I don't. We didn't talk much about his business. I only knew him for a few days."

"What did you know about Sarah Byrne?"

"I just met her that one time. I know her more from the legend she's become."

"Legend?"

"All the hip people knew where she was holed up, who was hiding her. It's like knowing that Paul McCartney's dead. But I just picked her up once, after she'd made a transpacific flight. Neither of us said much."

"Okay." Spracklin stood and kissed her on the cheek. He climbed the narrow stairs and wondered if a brandy would help him relax while he took care of some paperwork. Val was in the kitchen.

"What were you two laughing about?" she asked without turning from the sink.

"Oh nothing. She was just imitating some goof on Haight Street."

"Tell me, who?"

Spracklin poured some brandy into a snifter. "It's just a guy who's organizing this concert."

Val continued to do the dishes. Spracklin wondered if now was the time to mention Marie wanting to go to the concert. "Are you going to have that word with Sam?" she asked him.

"Yup," he said. Lecturing his son seemed preferable to the awkward silences or shouting matches with his wife. He took his brandy upstairs to the sound of the transistor radio. Sam always claimed he couldn't do his homework unless he was listening to his favorite AM station. Spracklin wasn't going to pretend to be mad with the boy. A bigger kid had picked a fight and Sam had whipped him—nothing wrong with that. He would mention that rules are rules and when they're broken there are consequences.

CHAPTER 15

Haight-Ashbury had to be the easiest place in the world for a stakeout. He just had to sit on the sidewalk and look strung out. He'd been sitting under a big oak tree in the Panhandle for two hours and no one had looked twice at him. The narrow park two blocks from Haight Street was busy. Clusters of kids dotted the paved public space. Their numbers always increased when a big concert took place, and the Solstice Festival was a draw. Some hippies a half-block away were playing guitars and singing songs about the joys of vagrancy.

From his position, he could see up Clayton Street. His back was stiff but he wouldn't move. He was pissed off at the way the old guy had condescended to him, first on the phone, and then in their meeting. He would see this assignment through.

Finally, he saw his quarry. Beneath a street light near Page Street, there was the husky guy in his rumpled green jacket. The assassin had marked him that afternoon on Hippie Hill, but he'd lost the guy when that detective showed up.

The drunk moved in jerky movements, heading toward the building where he lived. The assassin checked his watch. Ten-thirty-two. There was no set pattern to the mark's movements. The assassin rose and walked toward the three-story apartment building. He wondered if he should do it now.

The assassin had tailed the man for days. He'd learned the guy's habits, his motions, his weakness. The target was physically strong and had a military background, but he'd been drinking all day long. The assassin was going to exploit that weakness. The client had come through and now the assassin was armed. It was an old Ballester-Molina pistol, the type he'd seen in war movies. It was old but he'd cleaned it. He had three clips of ammunition. His knife and gloves were in the backpack slung casually over his shoulder. He was ready to take care of business.

He neared the apartment building where the mark was fumbling with his keys. It would be now, thought the assassin. He would follow him in and complete another part of the contract.

He was standing behind the mark, as if he were also going into the apartment building. The drunk had just found the key when the door flew open and three hippies came striding out. The last one, a pretty blonde in hipster jeans and a thick headband, held the door open for them. The assassin let his backpack slip off his shoulder and dipped to grab it, so the others wouldn't see his face. He and the drunk stepped into the building.

Had the cats exiting the building seen him? He couldn't tell. He bypassed the drunk who was still messing with his keys. The assassin began up the stairs. Now he had to confirm the mark's apartment. He stood at the top landing, listening for the man as he shuffled upward. The mark moved no further than the second floor. The assassin crept down and peered down the hall. The guy was outside a door at the end of the corridor. He found the right key and opened the door.

The assassin felt a sudden doubt. The kids leaving the building could maybe identify him. The client would mock him, but it could wait a day. When he nailed the guy, he had to make sure it was at a time when no one had seen him enter the building.

CHAPTER 16

Spracklin taped a photo of Sarah Byrne next to the map on his office wall, and wrote her name in black marker in the margin. Beside it was her official airline identification, which let her sail to the front of Customs lines with minimal suspicion.

"What do we have?" he asked.

"We have motives," said Burwell from a chair by Spracklin's desk. He was going through the motions of being a detective. "She was in the drug trade. That in itself could get her killed."

Spracklin taped a sheet of paper to the wall and began to list the motives.

"She was an heiress," Burwell said. "With her dead, her brother inherits everything. Fox could have had her knocked off so she couldn't testify against him."

Spracklin waited for the Sergeant to continue, the marker hovering above the paper. "Anything else?"

"It's just...." The Sergeant was puzzled by something.

"Yes."

"Why did he behead her? I mean, the autopsy said she was strangled, right?"

"Ernie Swanson said we should assume she was strangled."

"So why remove the head?"

"A mark of anger, perversion?"

"If the guy was a perv, he would have raped her. She'd been in Hong Kong, right? Meeting with drug dealers, so organized crime."

"You're thinking triads?"

"I don't know. We grabbed her stash so someone was out money. She knew too much about their operations. She refused to blow a king-pin. I dunno. It's too early in the investigation to rule anything out."

Spracklin nodded. He had never heard of the Oriental crime families beheading their victims, but it was a possibility. Triads were active in Chinatown and the waterfront. He jotted down the word, "Triads." He waited to see if Burwell would add anything. When he didn't, Spracklin listed more, speaking out loud as he wrote: "Was her fiancé jealous of anyone? Was another lover jealous of her fiancé? She'd embarrassed her family by running drugs. Were they embarrassed enough, angry enough, to kill her? Did she have partners in this airline business she was planning?"

The fact that Burwell had left so many obvious possibilities off the list convinced him again that he had to transfer the guy out of the Bureau of Inspectors. Burwell studied the motives. "It seems to me the big one, the first one to follow, is that she was a member of the Fox gang."

Before Spracklin could point out how obvious that was, the phone rang and he picked up.

"Jimmy? Bud," said the voice on the other end. "You've seen the *Chronicle?*" It was never a good sign when Chief Bud Hawkings started a conversation in a tone that carried equal measures of question and accusation.

"I was just getting to it, Sir." He wrote CHRONICLE on a piece of paper and held it up to Burwell. He mouthed the word, "Now." Burwell went off to fetch the paper.

"Well, the entire Board of Fucking Supervisors has read it and they're howling."

"How many have you heard from?"

"Rounded off to the nearest ten...."

"Okay, okay, I get the idea."

Burwell came bursting through the door with the paper, and they spread it on the desk as the Chief described the ass-chewing he'd received that morning. The main story was about the Supreme Court outlawing racial discrimination in housing. The story on the Byrne murder took up the bottom half of the front page:

The Dead Dealer of Haight Street
By Abbey Garson, Chronicle Reporter

A headless body found in Golden Gate Park on Monday has been identified as Sarah Byrne, the heiress and flight attendant who has been missing since smuggling ten ounces of heroin into the U.S. three weeks ago....

Below the headline was a black-and-white photo of Sarah Byrne, wearing a tank top and bellbottom jeans, and walking down Haight Street. Spracklin could just make out the glint of her nose stud, but only because he was looking for it. What stood out was the broad smile that spoke of a carefree attitude and boundless determination. Some hippie with a camera must have made a few bucks selling the shot to the *Chronicle*. As the Chief complained about the bellyaching supervisors, Spracklin skimmed through the article. The first few paragraphs detailed the drug bust three weeks earlier and Sarah Byrne's involvement in smuggling narcotics. On an inside page, Spracklin found the material Hawkings had been referring to.

Miss Byrne was a partner of Andrew Fox, who was arrested in a drug seizure in Haight-Ashbury on June 5. The arrest of Fox and the shooting death of his second-in-command had led police to believe they had broken up the organization.

But sources within law enforcement circles say Fox's arrest has left a vacuum in Haight-Ashbury, one of the country's most active heroin markets. These sources say several organizations — both from within the Bay Area and outside it — are now moving to fill the void. These new parties include organized crime syndicates from the East Coast, and groups from Los Angeles. Sources also say the Fox gang is trying to reclaim its stranglehold on this valuable turf.

One group that has begun to move into the Haight is Satan's Host, a small but vicious bike gang in Los Angeles known to decapitate its enemies. Sgt. Laurie Lopez, a source in the Los Angeles Police Department confirmed two gang members are suspects in a recent murder case involving decapitation....

"Jimmy," said the Chief. "Is any of this shit in the paper true?"

"We're looking into it, Sir."

Spracklin kept reading, hoping the Chief would continue talking, but there was nothing but silence for a few moments. Then the Chief said, "I never like it when you call me 'Sir,' Jimmy. It means there's something wrong."

"Well, Bud, what's wrong is that there's a dead girl, we don't know who killed her and we're wasting time following up unsubstantiated claims in the press."

"You should be able to substantiate them real fast, Jimmy. I'm getting my face ripped off up here."

The Chief hung up and Spracklin put the phone down slowly. The Lieutenant took the time to read the article. The journalist had stuff he didn't.

"Elias Wong been leaking them stuff?" asked Burwell. Spracklin ignored his stupid question. Of course, it was Wong. He flipped back to the front page and checked the byline. The story had been written by the *Chronicle*'s police reporter, Abbey Garson, who he knew to be dependable. Spracklin noted that she referred to "law enforcement circles" sources, not police sources. It had to be Wong.

He folded the paper. "There are three things here that are interesting. One, this bike gang that decapitates its enemies. Call LAPD and find out what you can about them. Two, the Fox gang trying to come back. Fox was visited in the forensic ward by that David Terceira guy—T-E-R-C-E-I-R-A. Look into that one." Spracklin looked down at the paper again and reread the key passage.

"What's number three?"

"It's just—it might just be the reporter using the wrong word. But the article says Sarah Byrne was a 'partner' of Andy Fox's. Not a donkey or an underling, but a partner. Fox yesterday told me that no one told her what to do—she did things for herself. It seems that Wong thinks that she was on an equal footing to Fox."

Spracklin watched Burwell slouch off to call Los Angeles. *No sense of urgency*, thought Spracklin. The Lieutenant opened a window. A gentle rain was falling, enough that he could hear the tires against the wet pavement below. Spracklin looked at what they'd taped to the wall. The fucking newspaper had more than they did.

He needed better information. No, he told himself. That wasn't right. They needed some information. They had none.

Spracklin lit a cigarette and thought about the Johnnie Walker in the personnel drawer. There were too many people around. He had a long drag on the cigarette, picked up the phone receiver, and dialed Captain Mark Patterson, the head of patrol.

Spracklin's rivalry with Patterson was well known, and it had only intensified now that the Chief had announced his retirement date. Spracklin liked to think he was a better cop and administrator than Patterson. Patterson's easy manner and popularity gave him an effortless air of leadership. What Spracklin considered smug sarcasm others considered a great sense of humor.

"How are you today, Lieutenant Spracklin?" asked Patterson, sounding cheerful. Patterson often addressed him that way, reminding them both that the head of patrol outranked the head of the vaunted Bureau of Inspectors.

"I've had better days."

"And it's only 9:15. What can I do for you, Jimmy?"

"I need an undercover guy, Mark," Spracklin said. "I've got a dog of a case, this Sarah Byrne thing, and I need better intel than what I've got now. You got anyone I can rein in quick? Someone at Park Station?" He was laying himself bare before his greatest rival. He had little choice.

"Park Station?" blurted out Patterson with a laugh. "What about the pool?"

Spracklin had expected Patterson to be difficult. "What pool?"

"There's a pool to see who can get the next repeat sting."

"What?"

"I got this guy at Park, Breck McKinley. Good guy. Last month he nailed this junkie, a piece of shit from South Dakota, by selling him a packet of heroin. He arrests the kid, who comes up with bail. This week, the same kid bought LSD from McKinley. The same kid bought drugs from the same undercover cop *twice*. Can you believe it?"

"Not really."

"So anyway, McKinley and two other undercover guys on Haight Street, they have a pool going to see who can be the next double sting. I've got ten bucks on McKinley. I figure if he can do it once, he can do it again. You want in on it, Sprack? The pot's $240."

Spracklin said he didn't. And he didn't believe Patterson had money on McKinley. It would be like him to convince people to back someone other than the guy he was backing. Whoever Patterson was backing was getting a lot of overtime approved—Spracklin was sure of that.

"Mark," said Spracklin as he lit a cigarette off the butt of the last one. "I need an undercover guy." He hated sounding desperate to Patterson. He might have been helping Wong for all Spracklin knew.

"If I reassign any of the undercover guys I got at Park I'll have a revolt on my hands," Patterson said. "They're all busting ass to win the pool." Spracklin could have begged, but he could only let himself sink so low. He knew Patterson wasn't going to help him out.

"Jesus Christ, Jimmy," said Patterson. "It's Haight-Ashbury."

Spracklin wondered what he meant. The Patrol Captain continued, "A bunch of drug-crazed losers who drift in and out of town each day. If it were up to me, we wouldn't waste time patrolling it—just pull out and deploy the manpower in places it's needed." Spracklin had heard it all before from other cops. "But here's what I'll do for you, Jimmy. I'll put word out that we need intel on this Byrne girl. We'll read it out at roll call. Now, I gotta go—"

"One more thing, Mark."

"Yeah."

"You need a sergeant?"

"A sergeant. You just poached a sergeant away from me."

"Poached him? You called me and told me how great he was."

"He wanted a promotion and I was backing him. It's what a good manager does."

"Cut the shit, Mark. You want him back?"

"Give him time, Jimmy. He's a good cop—a bad underling but a good cop." He heard Patterson try to suppress a laugh. "Just wait a few months—when you're chief, you can send him wherever you like."

They hung up. Spracklin tapped the ash of his cigarette into the ashtray. He grabbed his jacket and stopped by Burwell's desk. The Sergeant was about to make a call and his finger hovered over the rotary dial. "I gotta meet with Ray Handell and his team, and then interview the Byrne family," Spracklin said.

"Handell? IA?" asked Burwell. Spracklin nodded. "Why are you meeting with them?"

"They have questions"—Spracklin emphasized the word—"about the guy I shot the night we caught Fox."

Burwell put the receiver back in its cradle. "IA's going after you?" he asked in disbelief. "You're about to be chief and they're going after you?"

Spracklin shrugged. "They told me they had questions."

Burwell stood and slapped his boss on the shoulder. "Well, don't take any shit off those assholes," he said. Spracklin said he wouldn't and walked away. He'd finally found a way to get through to Burwell—just let him know he was on the wrong side of the biggest assholes in the SFPD.

CHAPTER 17

Spracklin had always tried to give the Internal Affairs office the benefit of the doubt. He got it—there were bad cops and they had to be rooted out. It was good for the whole department, the whole industry, that Ray Handell and his crew were willing to do the job. But he hated their office. The place had the feel of a government department, not a division of the SFPD. It was tidy. The furniture was new. There was a plant—a plant for Chrissakes—on the receptionist's desk. There was a flag in the corner, a photo of the mayor on the wall, along with a photo of the Golden Gate Bridge at sunset.

The receptionist asked him to have a seat in the waiting area. There was no ashtray on the coffee table, only magazines. They were even current issues, that IA actually subscribed to. He examined that week's issue of *Time*. The cover illustration was a painting of a smoking handgun pointing at the reader. It was by that New York artist who did paintings that looked like stuff from comic books. The headline read The Gun in America. In the wake of the King and Kennedy assassinations, the whole country was up in arms about gun murders. And the head of homicide at the SFPD was wasting his time answering stupid questions from Internal Affairs. Spracklin wondered if the IA brain trust thought they'd make him sweat if they took their time calling him in.

Five minutes later, just as Spracklin was preparing to leave, he heard his name called. He looked up and saw Ray Handell standing at the doors that read IA STAFF ONLY. Handell was smiling. Spracklin stood and walked by him saying, "I have to be at Mount Sutro at eleven."

"Sorry, Jimbo," said Handell, as he followed Spracklin in to the interview room. "I was on a call." Spracklin stopped when he saw the shirt-sleeved man at the far end of the conference table. "We'll try to get you out of here as fast as we can."

"Mickie," said Spracklin as he took a seat near the door, at far as possible from Mickie O'Neill. O'Neill was built like a British rugby player — lean, broad shoulders, big arms. His hair was thinner than when Spracklin had worked with him, and his most noticeable feature was the broken nose that had never set properly. He had been in the Bureau of Inspectors when Spracklin first joined, but had left for IA after Elias Wong was forced out. Hawkings liked the idea of the new IA team including one of Wong's guys. It showed, the Chief believed, that the faction outraged by Wong's ouster had bought into the new department. O'Neill was a Wong disciple, hard-working and thorough. He lacked Wong's intelligence, but he compensated with a mean streak as wide as a freeway. A joke went around the force when he joined IA: With Mickey O'Neill investigating bad cops, who would investigate Mickie O'Neill's unnecessary use of force?

"Well," said Handell, "why don't we all sit together and we can have a chat?"

"Sounds good," said Spracklin as he shook a cigarette out of his pack. He wasn't moving. "I've got half an hour." He lit the cigarette. Handell pushed a tape recorder down toward Spracklin, and O'Neill wandered down to Spracklin's end. Handell turned on the tape recorder, gave the details of time, date and who was present and said, "Tell us what happened the morning of June 5, Lieutenant."

Spracklin gave them a bland narrative about receiving a tip about a drug shipment, said he'd been at the airport as part of the team intercepting it. He recognized a stewardess — later identified as Sarah Byrne — as someone he'd seen on Haight Street and followed her to a house. He entered and found Byrne and Andy Fox unpacking a shipment of white powder. Byrne escaped, and Spracklin described his arrest of Fox.

"My focus was on Andrew Fox," Spracklin said. "He's a murderer and he had a knife. My handgun was pointed directly at him, and I instructed him to push his knife out of his reach on the coffee table in front of him." It felt painful to think back to that night. At the time, Spracklin knew Senator Kennedy was dead or dying and he'd tried to push that knowledge out of his mind and focus on the task at hand.

"Hold it a second, Lieutenant — why did you tail her alone?" asked O'Neill. "Why didn't you just have someone else pick up the tail?"

"I was acting on instinct—I had seen Sarah Byrne once in Fox's presence. I doubted anyone else would act on the hunch I was acting on." Spracklin tried to speak in a relaxed manner, but O'Neill was focusing in on his weak point. He had followed the girl himself because he'd seen that his own daughter was Byrne's driver. He couldn't call in backup while Marie was in the picture.

"Tell us something, Jimmy," said Handell. "How did Lindgren get involved?"

Spracklin was about to answer, but O'Neill cut him off. "There's something I want to get straight first. Describe your pursuit of the girl. Where were you when you saw her?"

"In the arrivals lounge."

"And you followed her?" Spracklin nodded. "And she was picked up?"

"I followed her to the parking garage, and she got in the car and drove off."

"She was driving herself?"

"Someone was driving. I couldn't see who. I thought it could have been Fox. In a blue Pontiac."

O'Neill sat back in his chair, holding Spracklin's gaze. Handell asked again how Lindgren came into the picture.

"I had my weapon trained on Fox and I heard something behind me." Spracklin closed his eyes as if remembering. "I recognized the sound of a gun being cocked. I knew in a second my brains would be on the walls. I wheeled around—real quick—and struck the assailant behind me in the side of the head with the butt of my weapon."

"That was Lindgren?" asked Handell.

"I didn't know who it was at the time—a big goddamn hippie. I didn't know his name. He was identified post-mortem as Sam Lindgren. Anyway, I tried to neutralize him with the pistol butt, but he was too strong. He hit me back." Spracklin made it look like he was struggling to remember. "I think we traded blows. I was determined to hang on to my sidearm, so I think I jabbed him with a left. He clobbered me and I went to the ground. Then he was on me."

"Where was Fox during all this?"

Spracklin thought and shook his head. "I don't know. But I know moments later he'd retrieved his knife."

"And you ended up winning that struggle?" said O'Neill. "With a guy like Lindgren?"

"He didn't have his gun any more. I think he dropped it when I hit him. I don't remember."

"How can't you remember?" said O'Neill, raising his voice. "You remember every detail when your life's on the line."

"We were struggling, asshole."

"Were you drunk?"

"We were fighting. It was a struggle. Unlike you, I don't handcuff my opponents before I fight them."

"Gentlemen," said Handell. "Enough. Enough. We have work to do and we're going to be professional." He glared at his underling. Spracklin felt good—he'd got the last word in. "Look, Jimmy, here's the question: you and this ape were wrestling. How did you end up in a position to shoot him through the back of the skull with the barrel perpendicular to the back of his head?"

Spracklin let out a loud sigh. So, this was it: they had forensic evidence that raised suspicions. The angle of the shot was wrong for two men wrestling on the ground. "Ray, God's truth. I've asked myself the same thing again and again."

"Like hell you have," said O'Neill.

Spracklin let it pass. "We were wrestling, but I still had my gun. He was trying his damnedest to punch me silly. He got in a couple of good shots. But when he drew back his hand, I sort of squirmed out from under him. As I recall it—and it all happened fast—I squirmed out, twisted, and fired. I don't remember aiming for his head, but I might have. When I saw he was down, I turned to face Fox."

"And then somehow, your daughter showed up? That's what your report said."

"Haight-Ashbury is a small place," said Spracklin. He tried not to react. He'd rehearsed the lines and he hoped they were convincing. "My daughter made Fox's acquaintance when she was a runaway on Haight Street. I didn't know it at the time but Marie was upstairs while I was struggling with Lindgren."

"That's a big coincidence."

"I believe Fox learned that I was looking for her. So, he tracked her down and got close to her. She came in after I'd shot Lindgren. Her arrival distracted me. Fox lunged at me with his knife and I shot him. Him I caught in the shoulder."

O'Neill smiled. "'Made Fox's acquaintance.' Is that some new term for banging him?"

Handell held up a hand, signaling to his underling to tone it down.

"They had a relationship," said Spracklin. He wondered if Handell—the man his kids called Uncle Ray—was going to let O'Neill continue to talk like this about Marie. "Marie is a victim in all this. She was preyed upon by a criminal and now we're doing our best to put her life back together."

"She can corroborate what happened that night?" said O'Neill. "She might know how you made that impossible shot?"

"Impossible shots happen. Lee Harvey Oswald made one."

O'Neill leaned across the table toward Spracklin. One of his heavy forearms was on the table, in a pose that Spracklin felt was supposed to be threatening. "What was your daughter's role in the drug ring?"

Spracklin leaned in toward O'Neill. He wasn't going to be intimidated. "Nothing. There was no deal. The guy seduced her and that's it."

"It's statutory rape. You haven't pressed charges."

"He's going to get the chair for murder. I wouldn't put my daughter through a rape trial for a guy who's going to fry anyway."

"We've got to ask her."

"You're not going fucking near her."

"We want her wallet, address book, bank records. Does she have a safe deposit box?"

"Safe deposit box. The kid's sixteen years old, you tool."

"Now, Jimmy," said Handell.

"You guys go after cops," Spracklin addressed Handell. "That's fine. People hate you for it but that's part of the game. You start going after cops' kids—with no evidence, nothing to hang a case on—and you're asking for trouble. Big trouble. Now I have a murder to investigate. Real police work. Just stay away from my daughter. She's been traumatized enough without a gorilla like O'Neill going after her."

Spracklin took two seconds to look each of the men in the eye. He needed them to know he was serious. They all knew he had enough power to make life difficult for them. He stood and left the Internal Affairs office.

CHAPTER 18

Driving through a light rain, Spracklin wound his way up Mount Sutro. The higher he climbed, the more it seemed like he was far from a city and in an Alpine nature reserve. He remembered his grandfather describing it as a place no one wanted to live because no one wanted to climb hills to get home. Now millionaires like Harry Byrne were chauffeured up the hill into its wooded beauty.

As he pulled on to Johnstone Drive, Spracklin had to brake because of the number of cars parked on the narrow street and a crowd of people. Spracklin reversed, parked, and got out. About a dozen reporters were gathered near the side street, huddled under umbrellas. As he got closer, Spracklin saw three security men keeping the press at bay. One reporter recognized Spracklin, then the others clued in and rushed toward him, shouting questions. He shook his head and brushed past them, badged the security men and walked toward the square house with large windows huddled amid the trees. In front of it was parked a crowd of luxury cars. In a cordoned off area near the house, there were two Cadillacs — a Fleetwood Brougham and a Coupe Deville — a Mercedes convertible and a European roadster. The Byrne fleet, Spracklin assumed.

A staff member opened an oak door. Given the Old World aura of Byrne's office downtown, Spracklin had expected a Victorian, or at least Edwardian, edifice. He saw that the home was full of antiques of polished dark wood, but the house itself was mid-century modern — large square spaces, white walls and light hardwood floors. Even on an overcast day, Spracklin couldn't help but notice the huge windows. Appointed in white and silver, the corner living room presented views on two sides of a well-tended garden bordered by trees. The modernism of the structure was tempered by the antiques, pipe smoke, and a group of elderly mourners. The only modern item in the room was a poster-sized painting by that New York artist—the same one who did the recent cover of *Time*. It shared the largest wall with an ornate crucifix. The mourners had gathered in small groups and were speaking in hushed tones. The steady ticking of a grandfather clock in the hall cut through their murmurs.

Flowers occupied every table, and more were on the floor. Spracklin knew the cards bore the names of friends and sycophants who'd tried in vain to find words of consolation. About two dozen of them were now in the room. Against the east wall, Marjory Byrne was being comforted by two nuns and a young woman. Spracklin picked out three city supervisors and several Republican grandees. On another day, he'd have made a point of chatting with them, getting them onside for the decision on the next chief. Today was not such a day.

Harry Byrne was talking to three men in black robes and recognized one as the Archbishop. Byrne excused himself and came to greet Spracklin. "Good morning, Lieutenant," said Byrne, shaking his hand. He wore a white shirt, dark tie, and no jacket. Surrounded by the city's elite, his light movements seemed even more youthful than the day before. But his eyes were heavy, his complexion sallow.

"Mr. Byrne, I apologize for coming at such a time but—"

"It's fine, Lieutenant. We all want the killer caught, and we will catch him."

Spracklin wondered who the Captain was referring to when he used the word "we." Byrne waved to a young man among the mourners—a younger, more muscular version of himself. With a rigid bearing, William Byrne bowed to the two women with whom he was talking and joined his father and Spracklin. The young man shook hands with an iron grip and said, "How do you do, Sir?" The elder Byrne led them to his study, the younger Byrne insisting that Spracklin precede him.

"Will your daughter's fiancé be joining us?" asked Spracklin once the study door was shut.

The Captain said, "I'm afraid Pete isn't with us this morning."

The study was more conventional than the rest of the house. A ceiling-high bookcase with a library of naval history on one wall, paintings of old ships on another. The tables were full of silver-framed photos of Marjory Byrne christening ships, the Byrnes smiling with President Eisenhower, Governor Reagan, Richard Nixon, President Kennedy, and the Pope. After Spracklin repeated his condolences and a Hispanic maid brought in coffee, Captain Byrne filled in his son.

"Lieutenant Spracklin leads the Bureau of Inspectors, the homicide department," Byrne said as he filled his pipe from a tin of Troost tobacco. "He's heading the official investigation." He placed a hand on his son's shoulder and said, "William is our operations wizard, deals with our counterparties around the world. He came home from Vietnam in 1965, and headed our New York office for two years. Now he's in head office, though he's spending a lot of time in the Far East, opening new routes for us."

Taking his cue from his father, William Byrne said, "We'll help in any way we can, Sir."

Spracklin didn't like the term "official" investigation, as if Elias Wong was doing the work that mattered. But for now, he wanted to get Byrne's tight-assed son to relax and talk. "You're a naval man as well?" he asked.

"I was an officer aboard the USS Maddox, Sir."

"You followed your father's footsteps, serving aboard a capital ship?"

"I wanted to serve where I was most needed, Sir. I considered joining the Brown Water Navy in my second tour to serve inland, closer to the action. But I felt I could make my greatest contribution at sea." He paused a second, and added: "Sir." After another beat, he added: "We were at the Gulf of Tonkin in '64."

Sipping his coffee, Spracklin wondered how he was going to get through to this kid. It was like interviewing a tape recording. "Tell me about your sister, William."

"Sarah was two years older than me and attended—"

"Ah, William, I have the biography. What was she like?"

"Well, Sir, well, she was strong-willed and adventurous." Spracklin paused mid-sip, gazing at the young man over the rim of the coffee cup. "Sarah was the most determined person I ever met, Sir." He unwound a bit, choked up, then continued. "What I mean is, she worked in our shipping office one summer and would work harder than anyone. But she didn't want to work for anyone, not even our dad. Being a stewardess was the first step in her having her own transport company." He gave a weak smile. "We used to have this debate around the dinner table: what's the future of cargo transport? I agree with my father's view: it's containers. Intermodal transport is rising twenty-four percent annually and it's not slowing down. But Sarah saw it differently. She thought air transport was the future." Captain Byrne lit his pipe and the thick, sweet-smelling smoke filled the room.

"And when did you last see her? I mean of course both of you."

"I last saw her May 30, at 2 p.m. in the afternoon at the Poseidon offices," said William. "We spoke for about five minutes. She had dinner with Mother and Father here that night at 7 p.m. She left at 9:15, going to the airport for her flight to Hong Kong."

Spracklin studied the young man in astonishment. He was robotic in reciting the times, dates and locations. He sat in his chair with military rigidity. "That's awfully precise," he said. William Byrne was beginning to make him long for the ragged hippies in Golden Gate Park.

"I helped Captain Wong prepare a timeline of Sarah's movements before her disappearance. I remember the times we came up with."

"It's recorded? Written down?"

William glanced at his father, who gave an easy smile. "Yes, Sir," said the younger man.

"I'll need to see that."

"We'll take that under advisement."

"There's no advisement about it, William. I'm investigating your sister's murder and I will need to see the material you have on her. I have the greatest sympathy and respect for you and your family, but I intend to catch her killer."

"So do we, Lieutenant," said the younger Byrne. "And with all due respect we're the ones who've been doing the legwork so far."

"Does that mean you're refusing to let me see those papers?"

William was about to respond but his father silenced him with a gentle wave of his pipe. "Now, Lieutenant," he said with a smile. "Have you noticed we're referring to each other by our ranks? Captain and Lieutenant and so on? You must have fought in the Second War."

"MP. General Patton's Third Army."

"Yes. We're all military men, and it's obvious we're allies here." Spracklin was impressed with his style of leadership, akin to President Kennedy's — gently steering everyone in his desired direction. "Lieutenant Spracklin, we want to help you. But Elias Wong is conducting our inquiry and the documents are all his. You'll have to ask him for them."

"But you know their contents?"

"Some."

"What do you know about Sarah's whereabouts since June 5?"

"Again, you'll have to ask Elias."

"I'm asking you." They knew Wong would refuse to grant anything without a warrant and getting a warrant would slow everything down. Spracklin wanted to get an idea of what Elias had and whether it was worth the bother.

"Elias will give you more definitive answers."

"No, he won't. Captain Byrne, you've got to understand there is only one murder investigation. I'm the only investigator working with the prosecutor's office, the only one who can present evidence in court. We're not allies. I am investigating everyone, and I will need to know where both of you were two nights ago. I need to search her bedroom now. I'll get search warrants to access any location, any documents I need to find her killer. Am I making myself clear?"

Captain Byrne took another sip of coffee. He was no longer smiling. "I was at my house with my wife all evening Sunday. She and the staff can vouch for me."

The younger Byrne took a moment to answer. "I was at the office, working, till nine." He smiled and added: "I like working nights and weekends so I can work with the radio on." He glanced at his father, as if he may have been breaking a company rule. "It was the weekend so I signed in and out with the doorman in the lobby. Then I went home, to my apartment in Pacific Heights, arriving at about 9:30. I was alone, watching TV — Ed Sullivan reruns, and part of the Giants game."

The elder Byrne set down his coffee cup and replaced the pipe in his mouth. "Our team has found out —"

"Who's the team?"

"It's mainly Elias Wong at the head, and Pete Menendes assisting him. Then we have two researchers back at the Poseidon office."

"Menendes? Sarah's fiancé?"

"That's right."

"He has investigative experience?"

"He was airborne in the military. We've learned he has talents in gathering intelligence."

"What does that mean?" Spracklin wondered if they were examining phone or bank records, or interrogating Sarah's friends.

"Pete has an easy personality. He can move through Haight-Ashbury and learn whether people had seen Sarah. He was desperate to find her — the man was deeply in love." He lowered his voice and added, "Yesterday was a devastating day for him. As it was for all of us."

"What did he learn?"

The Byrnes looked at one another. "He learned a lot of misinformation," said the Captain. "People talked about Sarah sightings like she was Adolf Eichmann or Jimmy Hoffa. Everybody knew where she was hiding, and Jack and Elias spent days, weeks, tracking down wild rumors. In Haight-Ashbury, Castro, different places in Oakland, up and down the coast. And then yesterday, we learned that someone else had found her. Someone evil. And now she's gone."

Spracklin finished his coffee and lit a cigarette. "I realize how difficult this is, gentlemen." He checked his watch. "I'm going to need to talk to Menendes and —"

"You don't need to talk to him." It was William Byrne this time. "I'll say who I need to talk to and her fiancé is high on the list."

"I can tell you everything Peter knows." William Byrne seemed assertive on the point.

"Not everything. William, I need to talk to that young man."

"It's just that...." said the elder Byrne. "It's just that Pete is taking the news very hard. But I will make sure that he's at the Poseidon office this afternoon. Let's say 4 p.m., and if there's any change I will tell your office. Now, you said you would like to see Sarah's bedroom. William will assist you."

Spracklin shook the Captain's hand and followed the younger Byrne up a broad staircase. The Lieutenant had been expecting something akin to what he had seen in Haight-Ashbury — unmade bed, Beatles posters taped to the walls. But there was a grand air about Sarah Byrne's bedroom. The large bed was draped with a quilt. The hardwood headboard complemented a mahogany dresser, fold-out desk and oil paintings on the wall.

"She liked antiques," said Spracklin.

"The furnishings were my grandmother's, Sir," said William Byrne. His voice was beginning to quiver. "Sarah and she were close, and Sarah asked for them when Nan died six years ago."

"You know I have to search the room?" William nodded, and Spracklin began to go through the drawers in the bedside table.

"Is that really necessary, Sir?" William blurted out. He was standing at the door, almost at attention. "My sister died yesterday."

"I understand it's distressing, William." He used the first name to try to sound sympathetic. "But I am going to find and prosecute her killer. The clues leading me to him may be in this room."

The young man gave a reluctant nod. Spracklin continued his search as the dead woman's brother studied him through tear-soaked eyes. Spracklin knew Wong had already gone through the room, but there was a chance his former boss had missed something.

A copy of *The Quiet American* sat on the table. Spracklin flipped through it and found no papers or notes. There was nothing in the bedside table drawers, under the mattress, behind the headboard, nor behind the paintings. In the dresser and closet, Spracklin found separate wardrobes—blouses and business suits for her trips to Hong Kong, and blue jeans and tie-dyed T-shirts for her nights in Haight-Ashbury.

Spracklin at last came to her desk, which also served as her dressing table. The drawers were filled with stationery—fountain pens, stamps, typewriter ribbons still in their packages.

"Did Elias find an address book in here?" he asked William Byrne.

Byrne didn't bother denying Wong had searched the room. "If he did, he didn't mention it."

Spracklin opened the lid of a small jewelry box. It held a few rings, with a few empty slots. Spracklin remembered the rings on both her hands. He also saw a few small emerald studs that she liked to wear in her nose. The first thing he'd noticed about her was her green nose stud. She'd had a selection of them. One was very likely still embedded in her nose, wherever it may be.

With the young soldier by the door still watching and trembling, Spracklin flipped through a notebook on the desk. It was completely blank, but an envelope fell out. Spracklin picked it up. The Bank of America logo was on the top left-hand corner. It appeared to be a bank statement. Spracklin checked the date on the franking mark—June 7, 1968. The bank had sent it out more than a week after Sarah went missing.

"I can't let you open that, Lieutenant," said Byrne. "If Sarah's personal...." His voice faded off as he realized Spracklin wasn't listening. The Lieutenant was deep in thought, pondering the notice from the bank.

"Mail kept coming after Sarah disappeared," Byrne said. "Captain Wong has asked us just to keep it here. I know he went through some of it three weeks ago, but that must be a recent addition." Spracklin was fixated by the envelope. The paper on the back showed evidence of water damage—more specifically steam damage. The paper had yellowed and was wavy near the opening, and the flap was now only half-sealed.

"Who's had access to this room lately?" he asked Byrne. "In the last week?"

"I beg your pardon, Sir?"

"I want to know who's had access to this room. I need to know details."

Byrne seemed taken back. "Well, my family, the staff, the task force...." He looked out the door, toward the living room where the mourners were gathered. It was clear to them both that anyone in the main room could have slipped into Sarah's chamber. Spracklin looked again at the corrupted envelope, and began to open it. "You can't do that," protested Byrne. Spracklin gave him a dirty look. "It's my sister's private mail."

"Someone has tampered with this." Spracklin held out the envelope, still unopened so Byrne could see it. "There's discoloring. It hasn't been resealed properly. Someone has tampered with this envelope. I need to know what that person wanted me to see, so I can look for what they didn't want me to see."

Spracklin switched on a desk lamp and eased open the envelope. William Byrne watched. The seal broke easily having been weakened by the steam. Spracklin removed the contents and set the envelope to one side.

He found a single bank statement, three withdrawal slips, and two deposit slips. Spracklin studied the statement. He held the paper at an angle so they could both read it. He wanted Byrne to know he had not fudged the evidence.

"Your sister was thrifty," said Spracklin.

Spracklin handed the slip of paper to the young man and studied the reaction. William Byrne's eyes went right to the bottom of the ledger, and widened as he stared at the figure.

"Two things stand out, right?" said Spracklin.

"Two?" asked Byrne. "I only noticed the amount she was sitting on." Byrne ran a hand through his hair as he tried to comprehend what he had seen.

"That's the first thing. A hundred and thirty-two thousand dollars is a lot of money."

Byrne held his gaze and said quietly, "I had no idea. She used to ask Dad for spending money—you know, telling him she couldn't do much on a stewardess' salary." His anger rose slowly but it was pronounced. "She had Dad convinced she was hard up. I mean, bad enough she was crying poor and driving a Mercedes, but... Jesus Christ."

William dropped all his reserve and shook his head in disgust. Spracklin wanted him to keep talking. "She was saving for her business, maybe?" Spracklin said.

William Byrne sighed and shook his head. "You have no idea what she put my parents, my father, through." He choked up. "He did everything for her, and she turned around and humiliated him." He seemed to remember who he was talking to. He looked at Spracklin and regained his military bearing. "I'm sorry," he said. "I mustn't speak ill of the dead." He returned his gaze to the envelope and said, "You said two things stand out. What was the other?"

"The date." Spracklin held the sheet up again so the boy could read it. "This bank statement was dated April 12. But the date on the envelope is June 14. Since when do banks send out statements that are two months out of date?"

CHAPTER 19

The Duty Sergeant was eating his lunch as Spracklin entered Park Station. The guy had a mouthful of hamburger from some greasy spoon when he realized the next chief was in front of him. He sat up, almost knocking over his Thermos of coffee. "Lieutenant," he mumbled.

Spracklin smiled. "Relax," he said, showing his badge, just to follow procedure. "I need a phone."

The Sergeant swallowed, stood and led Spracklin down a corridor. "Who's your money on in the pool?" asked Spracklin to make conversation.

"Young Luke Steinman," said the Sergeant with a smile. Spracklin didn't even have to explain what pool. Patterson was right—it was the talk of the station. The Sergeant led Spracklin to a vacant office, bare except for a desk, chair, phone, and photo of President Johnson. Burwell picked up on the fourth ring.

"It's Spracklin," he said.

"You survived the grilling by IA?"

"Yeah. They brought in Mickie O'Neill. It was, uh, not pleasant."

"O'Neill," sniffed Burwell. "Gorilla with a glass jaw." Spracklin hadn't heard the description before. Before he could ask, Burwell went on. "That O'Neill likes to act tough 'cause he's big and got his nose broken way back. You ask me, the tough guy was the one who broke his nose, not the guy who got his nose broke."

Spracklin laughed and told Burwell what he'd learned at the Byrne mansion. "You got anything for me, Ed?"

"I've got a few bits and pieces for you, boss," said Burwell. "I checked with a Lieutenant Emilio Rodriguez at Parker Center in Los Angeles. He laughed when I read him the newspaper story about Satan's Host."

"Laughed?"

"Yeah. Not a knee-slapper. But he chuckled. He said it's a stretch to say the gang has been known to behead their enemies. They're not a big gang, sort of a bunch of garage mechanics with some attitude. They peddle dope down at Santa Monica Pier. So, on March 3, some greaseball called Ernest...." He paused while he read the name. "Ernest Julian Brezinski washes up under the pier minus his head. He'd been a small-time hustler and word on the street is he'd ripped off one of the guys from Satan's Host. No evidence. No arrest. All they got is some penny-ante scrote who got beheaded where the gang hangs out."

Spracklin digested the information. "And what did you get on David Terceira?"

"Absolutely nothing. A union organizer by that name was charged with racketeering in Detroit in the forties, but other than that, nada. No driver's license or birth records in California." After a pause, Burwell asked, "You want me to keep looking?"

"No, no," said Spracklin. "We have to find out why someone tampered with that bank envelope."

"You want me to ask the bank?"

"The bank wouldn't do anything without a warrant. I need you to type up an affidavit for a warrant. Do it carefully and—"

"I know how to apply for a search warrant."

"You've been sloppy in writing them before. We need access to the girl's account and anything she did at the bank. Make it broad. Double-check everything and get someone to proofread it—"

"I know, and I'll find a sympathetic judge. I've done it before, Jimmy."

Spracklin read him the bank's Haight Street address and the details of the account. They arranged to meet back at Park Station at 3 p.m. Spracklin hung up wondering if Burwell would screw it up.

With a few hours to kill, Spracklin thanked the Duty Sergeant and strode outside. He considered going to Zam Zam for a lunchtime martini. As he lit a cigarette, he heard the music from Sharon Meadow—amplified music. J.D. Ehler had got his electrical hookup and was testing his sound system. Spracklin remembered they were putting up Marie's banner that day. He decided to take a look.

The grass was wet, so Spracklin stuck to the asphalt paths as he moved into the open field. Straggles of kids were coming from all directions and gathering at the foot of Hippie Hill. Two banks of black speakers stood like bookends on the stage, and technicians milled about, checking the equipment and working on the set. A good-looking guy in aviator sunglasses strummed his guitar at one of three microphones. His gravelly voice projected across the field.

> *I long for racial harmony*
> *I'll fight for human rights*
> *I'll march to finally ensure*
> *All men get voting rights*

Good God, thought Spracklin. If self-righteousness were a crime, this brat would be doing hard time. The kids around the stage seemed to like it. They swayed to the beat of the music. Two girls shouted the singer's name "Ralph" then sang along, and an old guy with fuzzy grey locks held up a peace sign. Spracklin estimated there were probably a hundred people, the acoustic guitar lending itself well to the intimate gathering.

The music created an aura of joy, but it was interrupted by the rumble of motorcycle engines. Spracklin and others looked around to see where the racket was coming from. In seconds they saw two solid men astride Harley Davidsons driving down the path from Haight Street. They motored on to the grass, braking at the rear of the growing crowd. They both revved their engines before killing them. Spracklin noticed a patrolman near the arts center at the back of Sharon Meadow. He seemed unbothered by the bikers on the grass, or the puffs of smoke that drifted from the crowd. Spracklin got it. Go lightly until someone crossed a line.

With the choppers silent, the bikers seemed content to straddle their bikes and enjoy the music. The singer—Ralph, if Spracklin remembered correctly—smiled and nodded at them and continued to sing. Spracklin approached the swaying crowd, which had begun to seem uneasy with the bikers there. The Lieutenant focused on the backdrop that was stretched across the back of the stage. It should probably have been larger, but to him it was magnificent. Thick cords were tied together to resemble vines that provided the framework of the fabric. Leaves made from green and purple string sprouted from them. Between the branches, Marie had stitched a single word—Solstice. Each letter was a different fluorescent color—and the peace sign within the "o" delivered a simple message of hope. He soon found Marie standing amid the roadies, lost in her own dance as she moved to the beat of the song. He could see her mouth moving as she sang along. Spracklin forgot about the investigation for a moment and smiled as he looked at his little girl. He knew she was bursting with pride, but for now she just wanted to enjoy the music.

Spracklin was wondering if he could get the bikers to rev their engines again, just to drown out this bleeding heart. Then a sudden movement at the corner of the hill caught his eye. A guy was moving along the edge of the crowd. A husky guy in a green coat was moving like a soldier on patrol, not a hippie at a concert. Green coat—the guy was wearing an army surplus jacket, just like the one that red-haired kid had told Spracklin about the day before. The kid kept low to the ground, his arms swinging low for balance, his eyes up. He had a target, and it looked like the bikers. It was then that Spracklin realized the bikers—one stocky; the other larger and muscle-bound—were wearing the colors of a bike gang. Their torn denim vests had crests on the back with the words SATAN'S HOST.

Spracklin left the asphalt and strode across the damp field toward them. He could see fire in the young soldier's eyes. The kid wasn't drunk now. He moved smoothly, athletically, like a member of a commando group. Maybe, thought Spracklin, the combat coat was legit.

The soldier took out the bigger biker first. He blindsided the giant, tackling him from the rear with a shoulder to the ribs, knocking him off his bike. Girls screamed and revelers scrambled away as the two men rolled into them. The soldier hammered at the big guy with his left fist. The biker struggled to get up, but the soldier had pinned him with a half nelson.

The smaller biker sprang to action, fumbling in a saddle bag for something. Spracklin was about twenty yards away when the little guy drew out a chain. He swung it around twice to build momentum as he stepped toward the fighting men. People screamed and scuttled away. The music stopped. The chain whistled as it swung through the air and came down on the soldier's back with a sickening thud. The crowd backed away farther.

"Cut it out, man," the singer yelled into the mic.

Spracklin had been aiming to tackle the soldier, but he now knew he had to stop the runt with the chain. "Stop," he yelled. "Police." He couldn't get any closer because of the swirling chain. The little guy ignored Spracklin and yelled, "Get off my fucking partner, dude."

Gaining his strength, the big guy broke the half nelson, he was fighting back. The soldier, reeling from the strike by the chain, still had him in a choke hold and flailed at his face with his fist.

"Let him fuckin' go," yelled the little guy, who was using the arc of the chain to keep Spracklin away. Spracklin and the kid at the microphone were both yelling at them to stop. The chain circled and glanced off the soldier's shoulder and head. The guy didn't scream or grimace.

The blow gave Spracklin the opening he needed. He launched himself at the smaller man, planting a shoulder in the guy's gut. The biker groaned as the air left his chest and he hit the ground. The chain fell on to the grass beside him. Spracklin rolled the guy over, and tried to get a handcuff on him. The biker was strong and began flailing his arms and kicking. Spracklin reverted to a choke hold, just hoping to hold him until the cop he'd seen near the arts center arrived. It was like something out of a rodeo, as Spracklin and the soldier both tried to keep their hold on the bikers who were fighting to throw them off.

Spracklin grunted as he tightened his hold on the little guy. He sensed something happening to his right. From the corner of his eye, he saw a lean man grab the soldier and lift him off the big biker. The newcomer had his back to Spracklin. All the Lieutenant knew was that the guy wore well pressed slacks, silk shirt and had salt-and-pepper hair. He wondered if it was a cop. Then he saw the pistol on the guy's belt—a sidearm Spracklin knew was a Smith & Weston Model 39. The lean man pushed the soldier away and stood between him and the big biker, who was getting up off the ground. As the lean man turned, Spracklin recognized him. It was Elias Wong.

"Get the fuck outa here, Pete," Wong said over his shoulder and he grappled with the big biker. The biker was trying to get at the soldier, but Wong was stronger than he looked and held the guy back.

"I said get out of here," he yelled. "The cops are coming."

Pete, likely Pete Menendes, had begun to back away, but now he stopped and pointed at the biker. "This isn't over."

"You got that right, asshole," yelled the biker, fighting to get by Wong.

Spracklin noticed someone on his left—the patrolman he'd seen earlier. He grabbed and handcuffed the little biker's left wrist and tried to bend his arm behind his back. But he failed. Spracklin grabbed the biker's right arm with both hands but was unable to subdue him.

Two other cops came rushing over, handcuffed the big biker and wrestled him away from Wong. They recognized Wong as the former head of homicide and left him alone, choosing instead to help subdue the smaller biker.

"You really think four of you guys can take Lou on?" said the big biker as he rolled on the grass. His right eye was swelling shut, but he laughed at the sight of the four cops trying to wrestle his little friend. One patrolman used his nightstick for leverage and they were able to bend the arms enough to handcuff both wrists. It didn't stop Lou from struggling—he fought against the manacles and kicked at the officers.

"You fellas better bring some leg restraints," called the big biker. "Lou ain't done yet."

The policemen ignored him. They looked at each other, shook their heads and laughed. "Crazy little shit," said one red-haired officer as he bent over to pick up his blue hat.

Spracklin laughed along with the cops—a nervous laugh. He patted his sidearm to make sure it was still in its holster. The little guy, still struggling against the handcuffs, had a rugged complexion and a look of fiery hatred in his eyes. The veins in his neck bulged as he tugged on his cuffs—the guy actually believed he could break the chains. Spracklin realized he was lucky the other cops had been close by. Little guys in outlaw gangs survive by being smart or crazy, and this guy was definitely crazy. Spracklin looked after Wong and saw him wandering over to sit on a windbreaker on the grassy slope of the hill. The big guy he'd called Pete had already disappeared down one of the winding paths leading from the meadow.

"Take them in," Spracklin said to one cop, handing him the keys to handcuffs on the big guy. "Lockup."

"Downtown?"

Spracklin thought. "Park Station for now." The big biker howled with protest, saying he was the one who had been assaulted. "Book them with assault, assaulting an officer, and resisting arrest," Spracklin said.

"That's bullshit, man," groaned the big biker as a police cruiser pulled up. Spracklin stood aside as the three patrolmen dragged the bikers to the black-and-white. He dusted the dirt off his knees and elbows, and realized the grass stains on his knees would need dry-cleaning. He walked to the side of a hill and sat down beside Elias Wong.

Around them, the audience returned to the bottom of the hill, and an engineer did a fresh sound check of the mic. Spracklin noticed that the handsome singer had left the stage, and was now comforting Marie near the sound console. She looked worried, but Spracklin waved to her, signaling that he was all right.

"We're getting too old for this shit, Sprack," said Wong.

He was a tall man with prominent cheeks and a salt-and-pepper buzzcut. Wong had always been a dashing bachelor known for his love of sports cars. He wore neither a jacket nor tie, and the S&M semi-automatic clipped to his belt was visible to anyone. He'd always liked everyone to know he was armed and would use the gun if necessary. He'd never made any bones of the fact that he'd killed that MacTevish kid — he'd just insisted it was self-defense.

"Not really," said Spracklin. "I find it exhilarating." He wondered where Wong had come from and why he was hanging around. *What in hell did he know?*

"You're full of shit," said Wong with a laugh. He offered Spracklin a cigarette and lit both of their smokes. "You know, I was wondering when you'd get here, Sprack," said Wong. "You always were a day late in any investigation."

Spracklin didn't need to justify his actions to the likes of Elias Wong. But he knew the patrolmen nearby could hear this exchange. He needed a comeback. "It only became a homicide case a day ago."

They watched the patrolmen struggle with the smaller biker, whose powerful hands were grabbing the cruiser door. "Don't pout, Jimmy," said Wong. He gave a little chuckle. "You have the lead suspects. You may even pull ahead of me once you interview them."

Spracklin watched one cop whack the biker's hand with his baton and the others push the little guy into the squad car. He wondered if Wong actually believed the bikers were the lead suspects. "It's going to take more than an interview to get anything out of those guys," said Spracklin. "LAPD, Seattle, KC, none of them could make anything stick. I've got my work cut out for me." Spracklin wondered if Wong would buy the line about Seattle and Kansas City. He liked the thought of his old boss spending a day on the line chasing phantom leads involving Satan's Host. He took a long drag on his cigarette and said: "I need to talk to Pete Menendes."

"You don't need to talk to Pete. He's got an alibi."

"Jesus Christ, Elias, I need to bloody talk to him. And don't tell me my job."

Wong tapped the ash off his cigarette and smiled. "It used to be my job to tell you your job." He chuckled. "Then it was your job to end my job. I'm sure there's irony in there somewhere."

"Where can I find Menendes?"

"I told you, Jimmy: He's got an alibi. Me. He and I were down in San Mateo the night the girl was killed." He caught Spracklin's dubious stare. "He got a tip Sunday that the girl was hanging out at a commune down in San Mateo. We were checking it, staking it out."

"San Mateo."

"Yeah, he and I went and hung out till about two in the morning—looking for intel on the girl. We got nothing and left the commune at two. I dropped him off at about 4 a.m."

"Dropped him off where?"

"Haight and Ashbury. He likes the neighborhood. Jimmy you can check with the kids at this commune in San Mateo. I mean, they saw us. I stood out there." He laughed. "They'd remember Pete and me."

"Where does Menendes live?"

"I don't know."

"Cut the shit, Elias."

"There's no shit. You just apprehended my two leading suspects, those two bikers. They're the ones I was tailing."

"Menendes knew they were your focus?"

"Yeah, sure." He said it as if it were information he wasn't protecting and could share with the Lieutenant. "Look, Jimmy, you've made a career out of following my leads." He was speaking loud enough that the two patrolmen lingering nearby could hear him. "My lead was those bikers and now you have them. Follow it."

Wong stood and grabbed his windbreaker from the grass. He flicked his butt into the woods. Spracklin let the statement hang in the air. Wong always liked to get the last word in. The cops lingering nearby had heard him taunt Spracklin about being late on the investigation. Spracklin wondered if he should follow him, hoping he would lead to Menendes. Wong would make him in a second. Spracklin would get to Menendes through the Byrne family. Wong paused and glanced at the stage. The good-looking singer was back at the mic now. He was taking it on himself to make the spectators forget about the fracas. Spracklin glanced at him and was struck by the gleaming smile and the way the others took to him. He told the crowd that he wanted to sing a new song. Two girls responded yes, again calling him Ralph. He had a rugged voice, but the tune was pleasant, the refrain catchy. It was better than his dreadful song about racial harmony.

> *'Cause I'm made, made in the shade*
> *The world is unfoldin'*
> *So, it's streamlined and golden*
> *And what today shows is*
> *It's all coming up roses*
> *'Cause I'm made, made, made – in the shade.*

As Ralph jumped into an instrumental, Wong turned to walk away. "Hey, Elias," shouted Spracklin. The private eye was about twenty yards away. "Answer me one question." Spracklin had to shout above the music to make sure Wong and the cops all heard him.

"If you found the girl when she was alive, would you have turned her in to the Department?"

Spracklin was sure the patrolmen heard that question. They knew the girl had smuggled narcotics into the country, and the Byrne family would probably have shielded her if they'd found her first. Wong turned, faced Spracklin and spoke evenly. "Everything I've ever done in my career, Lieutenant, I've done to solve crime and apprehend criminals."

"So, you took money from a multi-millionaire to find his drug-smuggling daughter, with the goal of handing her over to the police if you caught her."

"Yes," said Wong. He stepped toward Spracklin. "When I took the job, I looked into it. I knew she was dirty. I told Captain Byrne I'd find his daughter, but we had to turn her in." He looked at the patrolmen who were staring at him. Then he returned his attention to Spracklin. "I let him down on my promise. Now I'm going to find her killer."

He held his gaze on Spracklin, to make sure the Lieutenant understood. Then Wong walked away. Spracklin let him go. The guy was an asshole, and you never emerge unscathed from an argument with an asshole. Now Spracklin stood and walked toward Haight Street. He had a few minutes to have lunch and get a drink. He could have asked Marie to join him, but she was busy with her friends and he wanted to go to a bar. Ralph was still on stage, still screaming out that he was made, made, made in the shade.

CHAPTER 20

According to his driver's license, the biker who had wrestled with Pete Menedez was called John Arthur Rimshaw, and he was a big fellow all right. Standing about six-foot-five, he looked to weigh about two-hundred-and-eighty pounds—big-bellied, broad-shouldered, round-armed. He had a manner of casual brutality. He didn't strain against his shackles as he sat in a detention cell. But when a patrolman showed him into the interview room, he flung the door open and threw himself into a chair, not caring whether it broke. The chair held, and the constable handcuffed Rimshaw's right hand to it. He sat calmly with his broad left arm on the table. His partner, Louis Duble, had to be wrestled through the booking procedure then flung into a cell, where he paced back and forth, waiting.

Spracklin was in no rush to interview either of them. He'd gone to a lunch counter for a sandwich, and back to his car for a nip of scotch. Chewing Wrigley's and smoking a Chesterfield, he'd taken care of a few admin tasks and put out a warrant on Peter Menendes. He'd checked with Burwell, who'd got the search warrant so they could get the girl's bank records. And he'd briefed the prosecuting attorney on what they had so far. Now he had to find out what was going on with these bikers. He planned to interview the big guy for an hour then leave him for an hour or so while he and Burwell went to the bank. If he was getting anywhere, he would probably go back and forth between the bikers, persuading each that the other was caving.

Rimshaw looked up when Spracklin walked in. "Only one of you?" the biker said with a chuckle, taking in Spracklin's grass-stained jacket and his Colt revolver hanging in its shoulder holster. "So, who's missing—Good Cop or Bad Cop?"

Spracklin sat opposite the biker.

"I'd shake your hand and introduce myself, but you might have noticed it's chained to a chair," the biker continued with a voice as big as his body. Spracklin liked witnesses and suspects who talked, and he decided to play along.

"We'll start with introductions and maybe we'll shake hands in a while. I'm Lieutenant Spracklin and I want to ask you a few questions."

"Jack Rimshaw," he said. "My brothers call me Jack-Attack. Ask away."

"What are you doing in San Francisco?"

"Here for the concert."

"To see which act?"

"Jasmine."

Spracklin was surprised. Rimshaw had quickly named one act Spracklin knew was playing at the festival, almost as if it were the truth. Spracklin knew Jasmine—he had met her during an earlier investigation. She was a whimsical blonde, beautiful, flighty, her young brain already addled with LSD. "You came all the way from LA to see Jasmine?"

"Sure. We're going to get married."

"She's agreed to marry you?"

"Well," said Rimshaw with a chuckle. "No, she's never met me. But we're getting married. I figured the first step was coming up here and meeting her." Spracklin wanted to keep the guy talking, so he laughed. "You're blowing your role as Bad Cop," the biker said. Spracklin shrugged and offered the big guy a cigarette.

"Whatever," said Spracklin, as he lit both their smokes. "When did you get into town, Jack?"

"Last night." He spoke the words with great emphasis. "Which by my count is twenty-four hours after the heiress got beheaded."

"How do you know about that?"

"When your club is named in the newspaper, you tend to find out about it. Especially when they're writing bullshit about you beheading people." Rimshaw blew a stream of smoke toward the ceiling and lowered his voice. Spracklin loved it when suspects lowered their voices, like they were letting the interrogating officer in on a secret. Sure sign of bullshit, he thought. "Look, Sir, we're just a few guys who like to enjoy ourselves. We don't hurt anyone. We come up here for a concert and there's all this shit in the newspaper and *The Oracle* and—"

"The what?"

"*The Oracle*. Underground newspaper. You saw it, right?"

"Tell me about it."

"*The Oracle*. Cats all around Haight are rapping about it. It just came out with an interview with the dead heiress — they interviewed her a few days before she was killed."

Spracklin wrote down the name of the magazine. "So where were you Sunday night?"

"Pismo. Jenny Mac's Bar and Grill. Check with their cops — they came to break up a rumble. Took down our names. 'Bout three in the morning. Me and my brothers drove up here yesterday afternoon along the coast."

"Anyone see you at Jenny Mac's?"

Jack Rimshaw gave a hearty laugh that rattled the chains on his right wrist. "Lieutenant, everyone at Jenny Mac's saw us." Spracklin laughed with him and was about to ask him another question, but Rimshaw cut him off. "Look, Lieutenant, we don't behead people. We don't kill people. We only fight if provoked. Check on me — I have no criminal record. I have two years of college at ULVN in animal husbandry. What you saw at the park today was me getting attacked. We're loud and brash, and we draw attention. But we're not killers. And what you read in the paper is complete bullshit. Did ya notice there was no source for it?"

Spracklin studied Rimshaw. "How many of you were at Jenny Mac's?" he asked.

"There were three of us. With a few chicks we met on the beach. We had a party. Some guy was hasslin' one of the girls and there was a brawl. I mean, shit man, if anyone was in the bar, they saw us."

Spracklin stood and said, "Jack, you sit tight." He moved toward the door.

"What the fuck else am I going to do?" asked the big man.

Spracklin closed the door behind him and lit a cigarette. He walked out to the holding area and studied the clock on the wall. There was a mid-afternoon sleepiness in Park Station. Two cops were typing up reports and the Duty Sergeant was doing a crossword puzzle. Three kids — two white, one black — were lounging on the bench, obviously waiting to be charged and shipped downtown. Spracklin assumed they'd been nailed on narcotics charges. He wondered if an undercover officer had busted any of them for the second time. The Duty Sergeant noticed Spracklin and straightened up. He knew it was too late to cover up his crossword puzzle.

"Can I help you, Lieutenant?" he asked.

"Can you place a call for me? To Pismo? Get me the local police squad." The Sergeant nodded and scribbled out a note. "Ask for Captain Jones, Mark Jones. They call him Sparky down there."

The Sergeant nodded again and Spracklin wandered into the pantry to get a paper cup of coffee. Back in the squad room, he looked at the arrests so far that day. Across the room, a young woman with a German accent was weeping and telling an officer she'd been robbed. She'd lost her money, passport, and plane ticket back to Europe. Her dirty bare feet stuck out from frayed bellbottom jeans.

The phone rang. "Captain Jones in Pismo for you, Lieutenant," said the Sergeant. Spracklin asked him to hang on, noted the line the call was on and found an empty interview room.

"Spracklin," he said.

"Lieutenant Spracklin, Eric Hanlon down in Pismo," said a chipper voice. "Great to talk to you again."

Again, thought Spracklin. Who the hell was this guy? "Yes, Eric," he said slowly trying to recall when and where he had spoken to Hanlon before. Spracklin was hoping to talk to his old friend Sparky Jones. "How have you been?"

Hanlon was talking, but Spracklin kept trying to remember him. He could not place him, until he mentioned something about the information the Pismo Beach Police Department had provided before.

"I hope it was helpful," Hanlon said.

"In more ways than we'll ever know," said Spracklin, trying to recall a case that required information from Pismo.

"Delighted to hear it," said Hanlon. "I always tell my boys to cooperate with other forces. You never know, the guy you help today could end up being the San Francisco Police Chief tomorrow." Spracklin rolled his eyes as he listened to the chuckle on the other end of the line. Was there anyone who hadn't heard about the race to be chief.

"So how can I help you today?" asked Hanlon.

Spracklin told him about the murder, the newspaper reports and the bikers he had in custody. And he asked if there had been any disturbance in Pismo on Sunday evening. Hanlon told him to hang on while he got a report.

"I can say, Lieutenant, that at 01:50 on Monday, June 17, a patrol was dispatched to Jenny Mac's Bar and Grill after a report of a disturbance, a brawl." *Jesus*, thought Spracklin. He wished the guy would just tell him the dirt. "Patrolmen Enricho and Haverstock were met by the owner Rory MacCallum—do you need the spelling."

"It's all right."

"—Who had called the complaint in. The patrolmen entered and found the establishment almost empty, except for a table with three males, all wearing Satan's Host colors, and three women. The patrolmen got the impression there had been a brawl because of the women. In fact, Haverstock told me it appeared the bikers had come into the club, talked with the women, whose boyfriends were in the club. That started a brawl, which Satan's Host won. The boyfriends left and the women stayed, along with the bikers." He paused to laugh.

"Did you get the names of the bikers?"

"Yes, Sir, we did. Our men asked to see ID and took down the names of the Satan's Host guys—John Rimshaw, Louis Dupre and one Adrian Van Flanders. Yes, somewhere in the world, there's a biker called Adrian Van Flanders."

He laughed again, but Spracklin didn't. "So, they were in Pismo Beach at 2 a.m. on Monday?"

"Absolutely," said the Captain. He seemed less jocular, probably noticing Spracklin's somber tone. Spracklin thanked him and hung up. The main suspects in his case had iron-clad alibis. They'd been getting into trouble in a bohemian haunt just north of LA. He lit a cigarette and thought about it. How did Satan's Host become suspects in the first place? They had been in the newspaper, and the dead girl's fiancé attacked them. Other than that, he had nothing on them.

He checked the clock again. He had to meet Burwell at the bank. He strolled out to the reception area and thanked the Sergeant. He requested that the two bikers be detained and taken to lockup downtown. He'd get to them later.

CHAPTER 21

The assassin stepped into the phone booth on Haight near the corner of Cole. As he waited for the client to pick up, he gazed at the convenience store and wondered if instructions were pinned to the noticeboard again. Maybe the old fucker had people tailing him. He glanced up and down Haight Street, but no one seemed suspicious. The only thing out of the ordinary was the television crew—a clean cut reporter, grumpy producer, overweight cameraman with a heavy camera on his shoulder—interviewing flower children. He had drawn close enough to hear the discussion about the dead flight attendant. As the phone rang, he studied the nervous gestures of a pudgy girl as she spoke of the killing.

"Yeah," said the voice. The client could unnerve him with just one word. There was no anger or threat in his voice. It was just the knowledge of what he could do.

"Just checking in."

"And."

"I'm watching. Making sure everything's right."

There was silence. He hated it when the client went silent. "Nervous?"

"Not in the least." He probably would be when the time came, but now he just wanted to get on with the job. He wanted the exhilaration of two nights earlier. The client could be as silent as he wanted. The assassin knew in his heart of hearts he would keep his nerve.

"Seen the papers?" It was the client breaking the silence.

"Yeah."

"You noticed what they focused on?"

He thought about it for a second. "The head."

"Yeah—keep doing it."

The assassin turned around in the booth and leaned against the door. The client wanted the next one beheaded as well. It seemed like a needless complication to the mission, but it wasn't his job to question the boss—he just had to do it.

"Okay."

"I want it done."

"He's in the neighborhood. I'm on him. I'll catch up with him. I think...."

The assassin realized his client had hung up. He knew his contact was right—the guy had to be eliminated. The longer he left it, the greater the risk the guy would flee the Haight or retaliate. Neither could happen.

CHAPTER 22

As he rushed to meet Burwell at the bank, Spracklin noticed something across the street. He paused for a VW Bug to chug by him, then paced across the road to a storefront whose temporary sign read Prodi Gallery. He hadn't noticed it before. Stepping around a group of flower children sitting by the door, he peered in the window. It had sounded grand when the owner with the flouncy British accent described it, but the reality was it was just another store on Haight Street—scuffed floorboards, a counter at the back, bare lights dangling from the ceiling. Modern paintings hung on the walls, but no customers were looking at them, let alone buying.

A few posters were taped to the window. One read "SOLSTICE" in bold aqua-marine letters that curved across the top of the page. It advertised the concert Thursday night and listed the entertainers. The biggest billing was given to Jasmine, after whom there were a bunch of bands and singers Spracklin had never heard of. He was sure his kids would know them. He read to the end to see if Marie was given any credit for her backdrop, but there was no mention of her. All it said at the bottom was: "And we may have a few surprise guests."

Running late, Spracklin chugged across the street and into the Bank of America branch. He found Ed Burwell leaning against the counter filled with deposit slips and chained pens. He was fanning himself with the warrant in the afternoon heat. Beside him was a fidgety guy who introduced himself as Bud Margeson, a trim man in his forties who was clutching a file that Spracklin assumed was Sarah Byrne's bank records. His checked sports coat and Brylcreamed hair attempted a youthful image. He fit in well with the orange and yellow posters on the wall showing mini-skirted girls and frat boys in white sweaters, all smiling at their bank books. The banker led them to his office.

"Sergeant Burwell has told you what we want?" asked Spracklin as they sat down.

"I read the warrant," Margeson said. "I've pulled Miss Byrne's records and checked with our legal department. I'm advised I should give you access to any material named in the warrant and withhold anything not covered by the warrant."

"We were really careful writing this, Mr. Margeson," said Spracklin, nodding at the warrant. "The judge made no amendments. We should have full access to the records of all Sarah Byrnes' dealings with Bank of America. There were no stipulations or restrictions placed on our powers to view this material."

"Yes, yes," he said. "It was a shame about poor Sarah. The accusations against her were shocking and the end — well, simply horrifying."

"You knew her?"

"We handled her business. She always wanted to know the best interest rates, always wondering about new products that could improve her returns. Completely averse to risk — wouldn't consider stocks." He put the papers down and smiled. "She'd wander in with her frayed blue jeans and her sandals, and the tellers would figure she was just another hippie. Then she'd start giving orders, asking about interest rates and FDIC limits. It was something to behold. Now, what exactly do you want to look at?"

"First, I'm wondering if you could help me with something." Spracklin pulled from his breast pocket the envelope that he had seized from Sarah Byrne's bedroom. "I want you to have the look at this — the envelope and its contents." The banker studied the envelope then removed the statement and accompanying documents. "Here's the thing," Spracklin said. "The statement date on the envelope is last Friday, June 7, and the bank statement inside is April's."

"That can't be."

"Why not?"

"Bank of America has the most efficient processing system in the world. We're a generation ahead of our competitors. We'd never be a month and a half late with a statement."

"We got the envelope this morning. Can you confirm that this is an authentic B of A statement?" He gestured to the statement, which Margeson was studying.

"Yes, absolutely. But we sent out the May statements two Fridays ago, not April's."

"We need to see your records of Sarah Byrne's accounts for May and June," said Spracklin. The manager flipped through his file and withdrew two slips of paper. "And the deposit slips and checks as well."

"We mail checks back to the account holder. All the information we have is in the statements."

The bank statement for April was more detailed than the one they had found in Sarah Byrne's bedroom. Spracklin checked the numbers, making sure they were all the same. Burwell asked him something but he waved the Sergeant off. Then he examined who had made the deposits. Other than her paychecks, Spracklin had expected that Byrne herself would have made all the deposits. But most of the deposits were from an offshore corporation, something called Minglewood Cayman Islands Ltd. Twice a week, since early May, this corporation had deposited between eight-hundred and fifteen-hundred dollars in her accounts.

"What do you know about this Minglewood Cayman Islands?" Spracklin asked the bank manager.

Margeson looked at the statement. "Nothing. I was unaware of it until now."

"They've been putting seven thousand a month into your bank and you don't know anything about them."

"What I do know is they paid by check in the overnight deposit slots. That's how Sarah Byrne's account grew." He held up his hands, gesturing that he knew nothing more. "We have a lot of clients. We can't know everything about all of them."

"It didn't seem odd to you?"

"Lieutenant Spracklin, the Byrne family is very wealthy. They do business all over the world. It wouldn't seem odd that a family member was being paid by an offshore entity."

Spracklin wrote down the name of the company and looked at the record for May. There were more deposits from the Cayman Islands company—big ones, two of them worth more than $2000. The total in Sarah Byrne's account reached almost $145,000 by the end of May. And there were two more paychecks from Pan-Am. The only thing that seemed out of place was a single withdrawal of two-hundred dollars on May 30. Then Spracklin noticed it. Under the withdrawal line, all it said was "Cash."

"It seems like she made a single withdrawal in the last few months," said Spracklin.

"It seems that way," said Margeson.

"And we don't have the withdrawal slip?"

"That would have been mailed out to the account holder."

Spracklin nodded and began to think about this. Whoever swapped the bank statements did not want investigators to know about the deposits from the Cayman Islands company, or the withdrawal late in May. He wondered what could be significant about Sarah Byrne withdrawing a couple hundred bucks from her six-figure account.

"I need to see the records for June," he said.

He said it with enough force that Margeson was taken aback. "Of course," he said. "We don't have a statement prepared yet but we have deposit and withdrawal slips." He slid them across the desk. Spracklin fanned through them and figured there were about ten slips of paper. Removing the elastic band, he moved first to the withdrawal slips. There were four of them. "Holy Jesus," he said. He looked at the bank manager and then at Burwell, who was flicking through the deposit slips. "She wasn't withdrawing money at all."

"Huh," said Burwell.

"These are all signed by Peter Menendes." He pointed at the slips and they could all see the signature, signed with a basic cursive scrawl.

Margeson fingered through the file and pulled out one form. "Sarah Byrne had granted signing authority to her fiancé. I handled it myself, about two months ago."

"Jesus Christ, you could have mentioned it."

"I'm supposed to give you the information you ask for," said the manager.

"Did anyone else have signing authority?"

"No."

Spracklin spread the withdrawal slips out on the desk in front of him and studied them. Four times that month, Menendes had come to the bank and withdrawn two-hundred dollars on each visit. The money was removed on June 4, 8, 16, and 18. "The guy made a withdrawal after she'd been murdered," said Spracklin. He turned to Burwell. "He was taking money out of the account all the time she was on the run, and even after she'd died. He's probably the one who steamed open the envelope with the bank statement. He'd been in the Byrne house in the last month."

"What about Byrne herself?" asked Burwell.

"No sign of her taking money out. She was probably scared to be seen here after she went underground."

"Well someone was visiting the bank for her," said Burwell. He spread out five deposit slips on the desk beside the withdrawal forms. "Minglewood Cayman Islands kept on making deposits right up till the end of last week. They deposited almost five grand. No Pan-Am paycheck though."

"The airline suspended her when she went missing," Spracklin said. "But we have no indication that she made those deposits herself. There haven't been any since she died?"

"Not yet."

Spracklin thanked Margeson and told him he may have to get in touch again. Outside, he gave Burwell a cigarette and took one for himself. "We need to find Menendes," he said to Burwell. "We have to find out what we can about Minglewood Cayman Islands, but above all else we need to get to Menendes. Right now."

CHAPTER 23

Spracklin sent Burwell back to the Hall of Justice to do a background check on Menendes and look into Sarah Byrnes' employment records with and payments from Pan-Am. Now the Lieutenant felt drawn to Hippie Hill, as if it were a pagan talisman calling to him. It was the only place he had seen Pete Menendes and he had to wonder if the drunken soldier would return. Spracklin slowed down as he passed through the tall pines on the east side of the pasture, then came to a stop. He studied what was happening on the stage.

The sound check had become a celebration, and there were more than a hundred kids cloistered at the foot of Hippie Hill dancing, chatting, moving with the rhythm of the two performers on the stage. Ehler's people had finished the stage. The platform looked secure, able to bear the weight of the massive black speakers. Ehler and a technician were fiddling with knobs on a sound console to the left of the stage. The stage held four microphones, a drum kit, and a tangle of wires running to a bank of amplifiers. Two women with acoustic guitars were on the stage singing, and it almost seemed that the organizers were recreating the better parts of the Summer of Love. Behind it all, shimmering in the late afternoon sun, was Marie's multi-colored wall hanging. The performers seemed dwarfed by the one blazing word: SOLSTICE.

There was no sign of a husky kid in military fatigues. Spracklin scanned the scene again for another target—Elias Wong. He eyed the audience, the people flanking the stage, the stragglers clinging to the edges. He caught sight of his daughter, but neither Wong nor Menendes. There was music and sunshine and an easy feeling in the park. The women sang:

Rachael dons the saffron gown she bought from George
  the Third
It cost her three months' wages. She calls the price absurd
She pours me thistle tea and though centuries have passed
Her wrinkles run with tears about the day she was harassed
Into buying mustard dresses when she wanted Day-Glo rings
Pretty shabby treatment from the crazy English king

As Spracklin drew closer to the stage, he realized one of the sing-ers was Jasmine. In a floppy felt hat and hipster jeans, she strummed her guitar and harmonized with the other singer, who Spracklin didn't know. Given her growing fame, it was no doubt a coup for Ehler to have her at the warm-ups, not to mention the concert. Her blonde hair spilled on to her shoulders, and she sang a stream of surreal lyrics that Spracklin had come to expect from her.

She beams a checkered smile when I bring her gifts of garbage
Her hair is rinsed but never combed, a blue electric barbage
A tattoo fading calmly on her soggy wrinkled wrist
Initials of a lover lost, Rembrandt, maybe Liszt
We sit and sip her teas brewed from thistle down and rye
She bakes licorice and garlic into halitosis pie

Spracklin found no sign of Menendes in the rear of the field, so he began to make his way toward the stage. He had to remind him-self that he was on patrol, because his eyes were repeatedly drawn to the stage. It wasn't the singers. It was the single word behind them:

SOLSTICE

Spracklin looked at it and smiled then caught sight of a familiar face—the kid with the red hair, walking down the same path as the previous day and looking back at Spracklin. Spracklin followed him around the corner and caught up with him out of sight of the kids around Hippie Hill.

They shook hands. "How are you today?" Spracklin asked, for-getting the kid's name.

"Dave Bloom," said the boy.

"Sure, I remember, Dave," said Spracklin. "How are you?"

117

"Good," said the boy. He seemed hurt that the detective had forgotten his name. "I have some stuff for you. On the guy in the green jacket."

"Pete Menendes?" Spracklin offered the boy a cigarette, but he shook his head.

Again, he looked hurt, this time that Spracklin already knew the name Pete Menendes. "Yeah, Menendes. You must know where he lives then, huh?"

Spracklin held his lighter in front of his cigarette and looked up at the boy. "Actually, Dave, that is one detail we're missing." He lit the cigarette, pocketed the lighter and took out his notebook. Bloom gave him an address on Clayton Street. "It's an apartment building, three stories," he said. "Near Oak Street, down by the Panhandle." He looked apologetic and said, "I don't know what apartment he's in. But I saw him at the hill last night and I followed him back. I could only see what building he went into. I didn't see any lights coming on, so I can't say what floor or anything."

Spracklin was about to put the notebook back in his jacket pocket, and said, "Anything else?"

"He was dating that girl who died, engaged to her in fact. People would see the two of them around the Haight after dark. They were a bit of a folk legend — the wealthy heiress who ran heroin and became a fugitive. She'd sometimes go for walks at night. Also, this magazine interviewed her."

He handed Spracklin a rolled-up copy of a newsprint publication. The Lieutenant unrolled it to see the bannerline reading *The Oracle*. The cover showed a photo of a hippie with a guitar, and the headline said "Solstice Redux" about the festival taking place that week.

"*The Oracle*. The underground newspaper. It came out yesterday with its latest issue and they have an interview with Sarah Byrne."

"I've heard about this interview," said Spracklin.

"Page 27."

Spracklin nodded and rolled the magazine up again. He kind of liked that the boy was nervous around him. "So, you want to be a cop, do you?"

"Yes, Sir," said Bloom. "I enlisted for the marines but got rejected because I'm deaf in my left ear. I think I'd be a good officer. A good detective."

"I'm sure you would." He glanced back toward Hippie Hill. He knew he had to get Marie and head home. "Listen, Dave, I want you to apply to the Police Academy and use me as a reference. Also, write me a letter, give me your background. And...." He thought for a moment and remembered that he had no undercover presence in Haight-Ashbury. Here was a conduit to the street. "And keep your ear to the ground for me, Dave. You've been a big help already but I can always use more."

"What are you looking for?"

"Any information on who was following Sarah Byrne. Anything at all would help."

They shook hands again, and Spracklin returned to Hippie Hill. He found Marie left of the stage with the singer called Ralph and Luigi Prodi. The young guy was gesturing at the backdrop, and Marie was barely concealing her pride. Ralph leaned into her space as he spoke, pointing to the wall hanging with his left hand while also touching her elbow. Spracklin didn't like it. He figured the guy was in his early twenties—certainly too old for his sixteen-year-old daughter.

As he made his way toward them, Marie saw him and waved.

"Daddy, you remember Luigi, and this is Ralph," she said, introducing him to the singer. Her right hand rose and clasped Ralph on the shoulder. Spracklin made a mental note to warn her not to touch young men she'd just met. Ralph reached out and grasped Spracklin's right hand in both of his.

"Lieutenant Spracklin," said the young man. His green eyes looked deep into Spracklin's. "Ralph May, Sir. It's a pleasure to meet Marie's father. I've been a fan of her work for a while and told my friend Luigi about it. I'm delighted he agrees that I wasn't exaggerating."

He gestured to the older man, who had a mauve kerchief tied around his neck. Marie beamed at the compliment. "Ralph was singing earlier," she said. "He's, like, so talented." Spracklin nodded weakly. "He's trying to get Jasmine to play his new song, *Made in the Shade*."

Prodi glanced at her to make sure he could speak without interrupting. "We were just discussing your daughter's palette, Lieutenant. The technical aspects of her craft, I have to say, are very sound."

Marie was about to say something, but Ralph cut her off. "Like I was telling Luigi," he said. "This chick's the real deal, the future of visual arts in Haight-Ashbury. Talent like hers has to be exhibited." He put both hands on Prodi's shoulders, shaking him lightly. "I told Luigi here he had to come see this girl's work and it blew him away, man."

A drummer and bass player had taken the stage with Jasmine and the other girl, and they'd picked up the tempo of the song. The kids were moving to the beat of the music, and Prodi was gesturing at the wall hanging and trumpeting its virtues in his flowery English accent. "The strands of maroon cord form three crossing veins that amplify the harmony of the composition," he yelled above the music. The women on stage, now with a rhythm section, jacked up the tempo for one final chorus.

> Now let me walk beside you. I don't care if people stare
> If the world wants to deride you, the world's the loser there
> But Rachael shakes her head and says that it's the world
> to blame
> "Me outrageous? Goodness gracious! I'm the one
> who's sane."

Jimmy Spracklin forgot for a moment about Wong and Menendes, and even that they'd found a headless girl not twenty yards from where he was standing. The only thing that mattered was the beaming smile on his daughter's face. She looked from him to Ralph May to the tapestry and basked in the rock music and the praise of an art critic.

Marie wanted Prodi to join her in talking to Ehler's crew about how the tapestry should be hung. And Ralph May scurried on the stage to tell Jasmine about his song. So Spracklin sat on a crate and flipped through *The Oracle* as he waited for her. On Page 27, he saw a black-and-white photo of Sarah Byrne. He recalled seeing her the night Senator Kennedy was shot. In the picture, she was sitting on a bed, in some apartment on Haight Street, he assumed. He still had to find it. She was in a nondescript apartment. There was no window behind her, nothing Spracklin could nail down as a landmark. The room seemed neat. The bed was made. There were three cartons behind her with the word Marantz printed on them. From the angle of the camera, Spracklin couldn't tell if she still wore her nose stud. She was dressed neatly in white blouse and black pants, but her eyes looked nervous and there were bags under her eyes showing her exhaustion.

The headline read, Persecution of a Renegade Heiress. Beneath it, a sub-head told the gist of the article: "Sarah Byrne wanted to build great things rather than raise rich children. The establishment wouldn't stand for it." The article, obviously written before news of her murder had broken, developed its theme quickly. Sarah Byrne was a product of the moneyed San Francisco establishment, but she refused to play by its rules. She worked and was planning to launch her own business. Because of this rebellious streak, the establishment had turned against her and fabricated reports that she had smuggled narcotics into the country. She was now hiding in the Haight, working to clear her name so she could continue her pursuit of her air freight and electronics businesses.

No one could have accused the writer Sheryl d'Angelo of excessive objectivity, or of over-researching her work. She had tracked down a fugitive, Spracklin had to give her that. But her full-page feature in the underground newspaper read like one of those sappy novels that Val bought at the drug store each week.

> Sara isn't a high-society bitch, or even the type of over-sexed fly-girl you read about in Coffee, Tea or Me? She's not even a flower child. She's a modern business woman with bold ambitions in the shipping and electronics industries. "I work hard," the no-nonsense fugitive told The Oracle in a location we can't reveal. "I want to—I will— build up my own business. Some people don't like the thought of women building businesses, so they're fabricating lies against me. Once I clear my name, I can go back to planning my business career."

The writer started out with the conviction that Byrne was innocent—after all, Sara (d'Angelo's spelling) said so—and then built her story from there. The writer had obviously bought into this women's lib stuff that was so popular in the papers. The combination of a female entrepreneur and persecution by the establishment made a compelling tale that would be gobbled up by her unquestioning readers, Spracklin knew.

CHAPTER 24

Spracklin let Marie control the radio as they drove across the Golden Gate Bridge. She was hellbent on listening to the AM chart-topping crap that usually made his head swim, but he was so relieved to see her happy that he didn't want anything to spoil her mood. Marie produced a jumble of static as she jumped channels, finally settling on a song Spracklin recognized—"The Sound of Silence" by Simon and Garfunkel.

Marie settled back into the green bench seat, crossed her leg and tapped her toe along with the tune. She looked over at her father and saw he was smiling. "What?" she asked.

"I was going to ask you to leave it on this song," he said. "I thought you'd flip to another station if I admitted to liking it."

"No. I like these guys. Even their old stuff."

"This is their old stuff?"

"They're more experimental, bolder on their new album."

Spracklin nodded and was happy when Marie sang along with the song—she sounded young, happy. They left the bridge and headed up the 101 toward their house. He was looking forward to a whisky. He hoped Burwell had turned up something on Menendes. At least they had an address now. Jesus Christ. He should be able to find something on the guy. Menendes couldn't be the choirboy that the Byrnes were telling him about.

As the song wound down, a goofy disc jockey shouted out some blather that drowned out the final chorus. Marie's hand fiddled with the knob in pursuit of a decent song.

"When I rule the world, I will outlaw all DJs," she said.

"Can I be in charge of your anti-DJ division?"

"What was your clear rate last year?" she asked with a mischievous grin.

"Sixty-three percent," he said, knowing she had heard it before.

"Sorry, Daddy," she said. "Nothing less than one hundred will do."

"Total eradication of all DJs," he said. "Harsh."

Marie found something she liked, an instrumental dominated by a strumming guitar, backed by an organ, bass, and drums. It had a galloping pace, more up-tempo than the Simon and Garfunkel number.

"Oh wow," said Marie. She looked over at her father, as if he should recognize the song. Spracklin shrugged his shoulders. "You just heard her at Hippie Hill," said Marie.

Spracklin was confused until her heard the loon-like voice.

> *Eleven springtimes blossomed on an August afternoon*
> *As we paddled past the ghost-town, an antique*
> *Quebec ruin*

"Jasmine," said Spracklin.

"Her new song. It's getting a lot of airtime."

"She's on her way up, huh?"

"Yeah. I heard a DJ saying this morning that it's getting airtime across the country, not just in the Bay Area. He was expecting her to make the Billboard charts this week."

Spracklin nodded and smiled. "You can learn a lot from DJs."

She laughed at herself. He patted her shoulder and they drove along listening to the songwriter they had been twenty yards away from an hour earlier.

> *A toast to you Old Dougie Boy, a toast to Tim as well*
> *You're living large in Heaven after leaving us in Hell*
> *We weep and mourn and miss you with a howling,*
> *loving strife*
> *Two generous mad buddies with a lethal dose of life.*

"I can't wait to see her set tomorrow night—I hear she's going to be the headline act."

"What about the Grateful Dead?" He wanted to show his daughter how hip he could be.

"That's the rumor." She shifted in her seat so she was facing him. "Here's what Ralph told me. The Dead are in New York right now and scheduled to play a few East Coast dates through the rest of the month. J.D. probably started those rumors and is doing nothing—NOTHING—to deny them."

Spracklin laughed. "J.D. is a hustler."

"Yeah, so without the Dead he still has Jasmine as the headliner."

"So, if it's an all-night concert, what time does the headliner come on?"

"Probably just before dawn," she said, then realized she spoke too quickly. "I'm not missing it, Dad. I mean, my tapestry is the backdrop. I am not—NOT—missing this festival."

Spracklin turned down the volume on the radio and paused while he turned off the freeway. "Did I say you had to miss the festival?"

As they began to drive through Sausalito, Marie launched into her defense. "I have been at home for three weeks and felt like I was in prison...." Her voice tapered off as Spracklin held up his hand to silence her.

"I've been investigating a violent crime near the festival site," Spracklin said. "But I know it would be an overreaction to say you're not going to the festival because of that. The concert's going ahead, and I think you should attend. You're one of the stars. But—"

"Oh, Daddy, thank you," she squealed before he could raise the hand again.

"But. That crime did take place and it would be irresponsible of me to let you stay out alone all night. I know you've traveled on your own, Marie, but that murder was brutal. We don't have the murderer yet. So here is the compromise."

She waited for what was coming.

"You and I will go to the festival, until about one in the morning." He paused to let it sink in. "Yes, you'll be with your dad, and no you won't see the whole concert. But I have to work the next day and I simply cannot let you go on your own. Not with that lunatic still on the loose."

They pulled into the driveway and Spracklin put the car in park. They both sat for a moment while she pondered his proposal. "Can we negotiate?"

"Take it or leave it."

"Your best offer?"

"My best offer."

She thought a moment longer and nodded. "All right." She said it slowly, like she was doing him a favor.

He smiled. "I'm looking forward to it," he said. "It does my soul good to see you so happy." He put his arm around her shoulder and gave her a squeeze. She threw her arms around his neck and kissed him on the cheek. "One more thing, while I think of it," Spracklin said. "If we get separated, we meet at the stage, by the sound console."

She nodded and they walked into the house. Spracklin had planned to make a beeline for the liquor cabinet, but his wife came rushing to her daughter.

"Thank the Lord you're home," she said, clasping both Marie's hands in hers.

Both Spracklin and Marie asked her in unison what was wrong. "Are the boys all right?" Spracklin asked.

"They're fine. Sam's about to be banned as a Communist, but I can tell you about that later. But my goodness, they said on the news this morning that that poor girl was murdered right beside the stage where that festival's being held. I'm just happy you're home safely."

"Mom," Marie said with a laugh. "You didn't have to worry."

Val extended her arms and held her daughter by both shoulders. "Marie," she said. "Darling," she added for emphasis. "A girl little older than you was murdered and beheaded there not two nights ago." She gave a laugh. "I've been a detective's wife long enough to know where there's danger."

"But it was light out today. And there's lots of people around. And on Thursday night we're going to—"

"Thursday night?"

"Yes. Thursday night. That's when the concert is. Dad and I—"

"Marie, you are not going back there Thursday night." Val crossed her arms and adopted the stance that told the world she would not budge. Spracklin moved into the kitchen, where he could get his scotch. "That place is full of creeps and criminals and you're not going there at nighttime."

"But my tapestry is on display. It's the centerpiece of the whole stage."

"There's a homicidal madman on the loose. I said no."

Spracklin thought Marie was going to start yelling, but she was calm. She walked into the kitchen after her father and simply put her little backpack on the kitchen table, which was already set for dinner. "Don't worry, Mom," she said in a tone Spracklin knew was far too condescending to be effective. "I'm going to have personal police protection." She emptied her backpack and threw the empty sack down the basement steps. "The head of homicide himself is going to escort me." She kissed her mother on the cheek. "And he'll be armed."

Spracklin had filled his glass with ice and was floating it in Johnnie Walker as he felt his wife's glare. Val was ignoring his daughter's olive branch and staring at her husband. Spracklin took a sip of scotch and faced his wife. "Marie and I discussed this in the car," he said and took another sip. "What we agreed is that I would accompany her and stay with her the whole time. And we'll leave at one o'clock — she won't be able to see the part of the show that goes till dawn."

"And you reached this agreement without even checking with me?" He saw Val biting on her lower lip, as she did when her volcanic Texan fury was building up.

"We discussed it in the car and reached a compromise."

"For her to go all night to a place where a young woman was just beheaded?"

"Till one o'clock. I'll be with her. There's no danger."

With lips pursed, Val began to move Marie's junk to the side counter. The spaghetti was draining and the Bolognese sauce was simmering on the stove. They would soon have to gather around the table and act like a family. As she finished the chore, Val studied a long strip of leather rolled into a coil. "What's this, Honey?" she asked Marie as the family took their seats.

"A belt," Marie said. She took it from her mother and unfurled it and they could see it was a wide leather belt. The fringes were imprinted with swirling designs, which were heaviest at the rounded tip.

"Did you buy it? Down on Haight Street?"

"No," she said. "It was a gift from Luigi. You met him last night. He told me I'd appreciate the workmanship given my gift for texture."

"Oh him. Right. He makes belts?"

"He's got a network of craftsmen. One of them made this. I'm really flattered that he thought of me."

Spracklin gazed across the table to try to catch his wife's eye. He didn't want Val to get into it tonight.

"I just don't know if it's proper for a man of his age to be giving a young lady presents."

"Well, he originally offered me a brimmed hat that he had in stock — they are so cool, suede and out to here." She held her hands up over her shoulders. "But it was too nice. I mean, if I accepted it, I really would have had to sleep with him."

"Marie Annette Spracklin," screamed her mother. *Jesus Christ*, thought Spracklin. He walked to the counter to give himself another splash of scotch. "Don't you dare use that kind of language in our house," shouted Valerie.

Marie laughed despite herself. "It was a joke, Mom."

"A joke that was strikingly void of humor," said Val. She stared at her husband, pleading with him to back her up. But he could only chuckle at the girl's pluck. The boys tried to stifle their laughter, but they soon were laughing as well. Only the mother of the family was stern-faced.

"Honey," said Spracklin as he sat again, "we're just having a bit of fun."

"Oh sure, it's a joke to you," said Val, her Texas accent thickening. The boys were now shoveling spaghetti into their mouths, hoping to get out of the kitchen before the yelling started. Spracklin tried to think of something to change the subject.

The phone on the wall rang and Spracklin wondered if he should answer it or let it ring out. He glanced at his wife, at the tears welling in her eyes. He stood and took the receiver off the wall. "Hello."

"Jimmy, it's Burwell."

"Where are you?"

"Clayton, just off Haight Street. You told me to look into Menendes."

Shit, Spracklin thought, he'd meant to call Burwell about Menendes. "What did you learn about him?"

"Where he lives for one thing."

"You found him?"

"Most of him." Spracklin didn't understand. He was tired and didn't have time for games. Burwell continued. "I'm in a fleabag just off Haight Street and there's a dead body in a second-floor room that might be Menendes. But I can't tell for sure because his head is missing."

Spracklin shifted his attention from the fight with his wife to the latest homicide in Haight-Ashbury. It took a few seconds for him to understand what had happened.

"We've got multiple homicides with what appears to be post-mortem beheadings, Jimmy," said Burwell. "You better get down here."

CHAPTER 25

Night and a light drizzle had fallen on Haight-Ashbury by the time Spracklin's Monaco pulled to a halt on Oak Street. Up Clayton Street, two patrol cars were parked diagonally against the sidewalk outside a walkup apartment building with a convenience store on the ground floor. The cruisers' spinning red lights reflected off the wet pavement. A crowd of freaks, bathed in the crimson glare, were pressed against the police barricade to get a look at the crime scene. Two patrolmen with beads of rain on their uniforms held the onlookers back. "Evening, Lieutenant," said one when he recognized Spracklin. Dragging his evidence kit, Spracklin stepped inside, where he could hear the fuzzy chatter of a walkie-talkie upstairs.

At the first landing, he found Ed Burwell talking to a woman in her mid-fifties, who was sipping from a large steaming mug. The ripples in her coffee highlighted how much her hands were shaking. "What you got, Ed?" Spracklin asked, lowering the briefcase to the weathered linoleum.

"Mrs. Ainslie, here, who owns the building, called Park Station at 7:15 this evening. A tenant had called her to say she could see blood seeping out from under the door of Flat D over there." He gestured down the dark hall to an open door. Even in the dim light, he could see the red blotch worming its way into the hallway.

Spracklin introduced himself and said, "Who called you, Ma'am?"

"Her name," she said with a trembling voice. She caught her breath and tried again. "Her name, the name on the rent checks, is Marnie Blackstone. The kids all call her Keepsake."

Ed Burwell said, "Mrs. Ainslie lives over Laurel Heights and drove over as soon as she got the call. She says she unlocked the door and called us as soon as she saw the body in the room."

"It was horrible," she said.

"I'm sure it was, Ma'am," said Spracklin. "Who leased the room from you?"

"It was a nice young woman, Margot her name was, Margot Kempt."

"That's how she signed her checks?"

"She—actually, she always paid in cash. Fifty-five dollars a month."

"But you had identification from her, so you knew who she was."

"Of course," the woman said, though the response came slowly.

"Can you describe her?"

"She was different than the other kids, Lieutenant. More poised, more professional. She met me in a suit. She shook hands. She spoke well."

"Hair color?"

"Light blonde. Touch of red. And once I ran into her in the street, not long ago, and she had jewelry in her nose."

"A nose stud? Emerald?"

The woman thought for a moment and nodded. "Yes, yes, it was green."

Spracklin thanked the landlady, and asked her to remain in the building. He lugged his evidence kit toward the open door. A lamp inside was casting light into the dim hallway. The headless body was lying rigid not far from the door, with a piece of wood pried from the doorjamb tossed on top of it. Male. Caucasian. Probably six feet tall. Blue jeans and khaki military jacket. Running shoes. The body was facing downward, all four limbs stretching out. The left arm was flung out so the sleeve was pushed up, revealing a tattoo of his regimental crest. At first glance, it looked like the neck had once again been hacked off with a knife. It was not a clean cut. There was a lot of blood this time, a small lake that spewed out from the neck wound.

"I haven't touched the body," said Burwell. "I called the medical examiner—someone's on the way."

"Anything else?"

"I have some uniforms on the neighbors, residents of the building. Rooms are all empty on this floor—not a single answer at any door. The guys are checking the other floors."

Spracklin took in the room, which smelled of BO and cordite. The bed was a tangle of dirty sheets, the floor littered with grubby clothes, and food wrappers. Spracklin counted seven empty wine bottles at a glance, and an ashtray holding a mound of butts and roaches. A shiny component stereo sat on a beat-up dresser. The amplifier, which was still on, bore the brand name Marantz, the same as the three cartons in the corner, beside a crate of records. Two posters of Impressionist paintings were taped to the wall. Spracklin opened two doors—one a toilet, the other a walk-in closet.

Stepping around the dead man, Spracklin studied the area around the door. A plume of blood coated the wall and the back of the door itself. There was a gap in the blood plume where some-one—the killer he assumed—had pried off one plank of the door-jamb. It was now on the dead man, with the unpainted side facing up. Spracklin could see a bullet hole in the plank.

"You want a check on her?" said Burwell.

It took Spracklin a second to realize the Sergeant was talking about the landlady. He nodded.

"Also run the alias that the tenant gave. I'm assuming it was Sarah Byrne but we need to check it."

Burwell nodded and added: "I already asked the lady for a list of the tenants."

As he pulled on rubber gloves, Spracklin looked at the plaster and doorframe where the doorjamb plank had been removed. There were marks on the plaster, and a big gouge in a stud with nicks all around it. The perp must have used a knife to pry the board off. "All right, Ed," he said. "What do you make of it all?"

"Here's the way I see it," said Burwell. "He lined the guy up here, probably against the wall. My bet is we'll find the vic's prints on the door and the wall where he leaned up against it." He looked at Spracklin to make sure the Lieutenant was following him. "The perp popped him once—there's only one hole in the plank, see? Point blank—one shot was probably enough. But the bullet passed through the head and lodged in the wall. The guy took his knife—right?—and he pried off that piece of wood. But the bullet had passed though the plank, so he had to use the knife to dig it out of the plaster there."

He looked at Spracklin, as if to ask for approval. The Lieutenant took another look at the space where the doorjamb had been removed. He closed the door and looked at the back of it.

"Not bad, Ed," he said. "But he fired two shots."

"But there's just the one hole."

"I know, but look at the blood plumes. One stretched out across the back of the door, and the other goes off to the left, away from the door. He must have had the guy forced up against the wall, and got off two quick shots. Fast enough to get two in his head before he dropped to the floor." He looked again at the headless body. "My bet is that when we find the head, we'll find a slug in it."

"Any doubt that it's Menendes?"

Spracklin shook his head. "We'll have to ID it, but I'd put money on it. Same build, same clothes. Tattoos from the 23rd Infantry." Spracklin stepped over the body, stooped and lifted the tail of the combat jacket. They could both see the outline of a wallet in the back pocket. Spracklin withdrew the wallet, set it down on the dresser, and flipped it open. They could see a plastic window with a driver's license behind it. They looked at each other, then Burwell read it out loud.

"David Terceira." The sergeant looked up at Spracklin.

Spracklin wasn't listening. This had to be Menendes. He emptied the wallet on the dresser beside the stereo. He counted four twenties, and three photos—four military personnel smiling in front of a helicopter, a family of five in front of a Christmas tree, and a head and shoulders shot of Sarah Byrne. He pulled out the driver's license. It felt thick to him, then he realized there were two laminated cards. He separated them and saw two driver's licenses—one for David Terceira and one for Peter Louis Menendes. They both had the same photo of the guy he had seen in the park the day before.

"What is it?" asked Burwell.

Spracklin handed over the license identifying Pete Menendes. "This is his real ID," he said. "And he had a fake ID for some guy called David Terceira."

"So, is this guy's real name Menendes or Terceira?" the Sergeant asked.

Spracklin shrugged. The case was changing quickly and he needed to sort it out fast. He kept casting his eyes around the room— the stiff, the door, the blood on the floor, the sparse furnishings. The room was more disorderly, than dirty. It was the same apartment as the photo in *The Oracle*, and it had looked neat in that picture. His eyes were again drawn to the Marantz amplifier. It was a nicer stereo than most people could afford. *Hippies*, he thought. They'd live in a dump like this but spend a king's ransom on a stereo. He spun the turntable to read the label on the record. "Axis: Bold as Love," he read aloud. He focused in on the door. "Was the door locked when the landlady came in?" he asked Burwell.

"She didn't say."

"Make sure you ask her. There's no sign the lock was jimmied. Maybe the door was open when the perp came in here, or maybe the vic let him in. What we've got here is a repeat murderer with a semi-automatic weapon and a knife with" — He checked the marks left from prying off the door frame — "a minimum eight-inch blade. He's walking around Haight Street without anyone noticing and he's been able to find two fugitives that the SFPD came up clueless on. He's changing his MO — why did he use a gun this time but not with Sarah Byrne?"

Spracklin began to search the room, starting with the closet. Women's clothes were hanging in it. He walked to the dresser and opened drawers to find men's and women's underwear. He glanced at the wastepaper basket and rooted through the food wrappers and papers. He began to look at receipts from local restaurants and shops.

"We need to fingerprint this place soon. My bet is that we're going to find prints from Sarah Byrne."

"Sarah Byrne?" asked Burwell. Spracklin looked over at him and saw him standing over the body with a puzzled expression. "She vanished three weeks ago. Her prints wouldn't still be here."

Spracklin didn't turn around to show the look of disgust on his face. "You don't get it, Ed. There are women's clothes in Pete Menendes' apartment. There's receipts from last Friday for Tampax and skin cream. They were ordering takeout two dishes at a time. She was hiding at his place all the time." The Lieutenant looked at the body and took a deep breath again. "The SFPD, Elias Wong, the shipping magnate's task force — we were all looking for the girl for weeks. All the while she was holed up in her boyfriend's apartment. Menendes was hiding her. But he couldn't protect her. Not in the end. Then whoever got her came after him tonight."

Spracklin thought again about Sarah Byrne and the bedroom he had seen that morning at the Byrne mansion. She had gone from the splendor of her family home on Mount Sutro to this. She'd spent her last couple of weeks holed up in a room little bigger than a jail cell.

"Jimmy," Spracklin heard Burwell say. Looking up, he saw the Sergeant pointing at the door. A patrolman, an older guy who he recognized but couldn't name, was standing by the body. The guy had been knocking but Spracklin had been too lost in thought to hear.

"Lieutenant," said the cop. "Captain Wong wants to come up. I'm assuming it's all ri—"

"Where is he?" Spracklin asked.

"Ah, down on the sidewalk," said the patrolman. "In the rain."

Spracklin knew Wong still had a lot of friends in the force. He couldn't just blow him off. "I'll come see him," he said, tossing his gloves on the bed. Turning to Burwell, Spracklin added, "Don't touch anything."

Spracklin stopped and looked again at the door. He told the patrolman he'd meet him downstairs. He retrieved Sarah Byrne's key ring from the evidence kit. He chose one of the keys he hadn't identified yet, and inserted it in the door. The Yale lock clicked open.

The drizzle had turned to rain, which had helped clear away most of the spectators. Two dripping cops were huddled in the doorway, Elias Wong with them. He kept glancing into the hallway, and stepped into the building when he saw Spracklin.

"Is it true?" he asked. There was a look of desperation in his eyes. Spracklin patted his coat pockets, found his cigarettes, and shook one into his mouth. "Is it Pete?" asked Wong.

Spracklin nodded as he lit the cigarette and watched Wong slump with the shock of what he heard. The PI looked up at Spracklin and asked, "Definitely murder?"

"We're investigating," said Spracklin.

"Can I see him? I can—"

"No."

Wong was shocked. It was as if Wong had forgotten that he'd been trying for days to humiliate Spracklin and the department.

"I can help you, Jimmy. Another set of eyeballs could only help you."

"You should have thought about that before you started leaking dirt on us to the papers."

Wong didn't bother denying it. "I was trying to flush out the killer. We'd considered every angle and needed to push the case forward."

Spracklin took a long drag on his cigarette. He actually wanted the men to hear the argument now. "The girl had been dead less than a day when you went to the press. There was no way you could have looked at every angle."

"Pete and I had been searching for her for weeks."

"Well here's an angle you didn't look at, Elias. Menendes was hiding the girl the whole time." Wong was about to call bullshit but Spracklin cut him off. "The girl's clothes are all up there. Receipts from last week for women's things, takeout for two. She was hiding at Menendes' apartment the whole time, writing checks for him on her bank account. All the time you were working with him, he was leading you away from her."

"I don't believe it."

"Watch this, Elias," said Spracklin. He held up Sarah Byrne's key ring and told the private eye what they were. "We found them in her overnight case the night we busted Fox a month ago." He chose a house key on the ring and inserted it in the front door. Again, the bolt opened with ease.

"I know you don't believe it," he said to Wong. "But she had a key to this place and she was here all the while she was a fugitive. And you not believing it, that's one reason we're not letting you into the crime scene. Because you don't want to admit you got hosed by Pete Menendes."

CHAPTER 26

The rain was beating on the windows, drowning out the sound of the patrolmen's radios in the lobby. Standing again at the door of Menendes' room, Spracklin stared at the bloody mess before him. Ed Burwell was waiting for him to begin photographing the scene. Then the ME would inspect and move the body. Then they would have to search and fingerprint the room. Spracklin found the body nauseating. It wasn't the gore. He'd grown used to that years ago, in Normandy and the Ardennes. This body made him think of the vibrant young woman with the green nose stud who Menendes had been engaged to. What would they have become if they hadn't got entangled in the drug trade? She was a dynamic entrepreneur. He was an all-rounder, an athlete, scholar, and war hero, adored by all who encountered him. Spracklin thought of Elias Wong's pleading face. Wong wasn't a guy who got sentimental about homicide victims, but he was shaken to the core about Menendes. Sarah and Peter Menendes could have become more successful than her father.

Spracklin was thinking about another cigarette before getting down to work, when he caught a flash of movement from the corner of his eye. A door across the hall closed. He could just hear the click above the sound of the driving rain. Burwell had said the rooms were empty, but someone was obviously across the hall. The odd thing was he was certain it was a child.

Spracklin knocked lightly on the door. There was no answer so he knocked again, louder.

"Hello," he called. He was polite. Whoever was in there had information he needed so he would be charming. He had his hand on his sidearm, just to be sure. "Hello. Can you open up?" All he could hear was the rain and the men's voices downstairs. "Hello. My name is Spracklin. I'm a homicide detective." Still nothing. "We're going to be camped out in the room across the hall for the next few days—you're going to have to come out sometime."

After another pause, a faint voice said, "Can I see your badge, please?"

Please, thought Spracklin. These kids had grown up on television and knew cops had to show their badges, though not all of them said, "Please."

"Of course, you can," said Spracklin producing it from his pocket. "But you'll have to open the door for me to show it to you."

He heard a lock grinding, and the door opened a crack. Spracklin realized he was holding his badge too high for the person behind the door, so he lowered it. A single eye studied the badge. The kid had no other stalling tactic.

"I'm a detective," he said. "Honest." The eye kept on staring at the badge. "If you let me in, I can explain what I want. I'm not here to hurt you."

After a pause, the door opened and Spracklin stepped into a room whose floor was covered with mattresses overflowing with tangled sheets and dirty clothes. The walls were plastered with Beatles posters, the only furnishing taller than a foot was a table with an eight-inch TV and aerials. Facing him, a thin girl stood pigeon-toed against the wall. Her hazel eyes studied his face. She didn't tremble or cower, but her stillness revealed her terror. Spracklin guessed she was fifteen.

"Hello there," he said. He tried to forget the carnage across the hall and bring some warmth and reassurance to the girl. "I'm Jimmy Spracklin and I'd like to just ask you a few questions." She continued to stare at him. Spracklin looked around the room, which had three bedrolls, a few backpacks and a chair in the corner. Spracklin knelt so he would be on her level.

"So, what's your name?" he asked. "You know, I bet—"

"Nancy," she said. "Nancy Jones."

A false name was better than no name. "Nice to meet you, Nancy. Where you from."

After a pause she said, "New York City?"

"Oh yeah. Which borough?"

Another pause. Then she said, "New York borough. I'm eighteen."

Too young to know how to lie well, thought Spracklin. She was scared, probably terrified. He had to find out quickly what she knew.

"Nancy," he said, "I need your help." She continued to look into his eyes. "Have you been here all day?"

After a beat, she nodded.

"Did you see anything unusual?" No response. Just the stare. "Anything in the room across the hall?"

He was wondering if he should change tack when she blurted out, "There was loud music. Then a man left carrying a backpack."

Good, he thought. "Tell me the whole story, Nancy. When was this?"

"It was about five-forty. I know that because I was watching The Banana Splits on the box here." She gestured to the little television by his elbow. Spracklin knew The Banana Splits. His son John-John, age eight, liked the show while Sam sneered at it as kid's stuff. But this young waif, alone in Haight-Ashbury, liked to watch it. Spracklin checked his Timex. Four hours had passed since the incident she described. "It starts at five-thirty, and it's a show I really dig, and I was getting into it, and then the room was just shaking with Jimi Hendrix and I couldn't hear the show."

"Jimmy who?"

"Jimi Hendrix. Someone was playing his *Axis: Bold as Love* album super loud. 'She's So Fine.' The song was 'She's So Fine'. Then you could hear banging and thudding and a minute or two later who-ever it was turned the music down. But I could still hear him bang-ing around."

"How do you know it was a 'him' and not a 'her'?"

"I saw him. It was a man." She paused then realized she should go on. "After a minute or two, there was a commercial, and I was going to ask whoever it was to turn it down. I opened the door and realized the music was off now. It was quiet, and I was closing the door, and I noticed a guy leaving the apartment."

"You saw his face?"

She thought for a moment and slowly shook her head. "He was wearing a raincoat, a black raincoat with the hood up, and all I saw was him leave the room and he pulled the door behind him and left. I thought it might be Big Pete, the guy who lives there with some girl, but this guy was smaller than Pete."

"You're sure it was a man?"

"He moved like a man and he was wearing men's shoes and the backpack he was carrying looked heavy but he carried it easily."

"Describe the backpack."

"It was blue or black, and it was canvas and big, and it looked like it was wet. It sort of glistened. And he held it in his right hand and it was weighted down so there was something heavy in it. And he was wearing gloves, which was strange because it's not cold. He carried it to the stairs and then went upstairs with it."

"Upstairs? How do you know he went upstairs?"

"I heard the footsteps, and I heard a door close. He went upstairs. Just above me."

Spracklin was on his feet in an instant, striding to the door. "Burwell," he called. "Ed," he repeated as he reached the door. Ed Burwell appeared at the door across the hall. "Seal off all the entrances."

"We have."

"Double it. Get the landlady and a patrolman up here. And fast."

Burwell took off down the hall, and Spracklin turned back to the girl. His tone had changed and she was shaking now. "Am I in trouble?" she asked.

"No Nancy, or…What's your real name?"

A beat. "Janet."

"Janet, I'm going to get a police officer to look after you, and, and…." He could hear men coming up the hallway. "Janet, this place, Haight-Ashbury, it's not safe anymore. It probably never was, but you're a good girl. You should go home."

He had no time to give her a fatherly talk. He assigned a patrolman to guard the crime scene and the girl, and to call the social services department to get a social worker for her. He led Burwell to the stairwell. As he climbed the stairs, he began to wonder how good a lead this was. The girl could be mistaken, but she seemed intelligent and was specific about the time of the incident.

"Jimmy," he heard. Looking back, he saw Ed Burwell pointing down at the step. In the dim light, he could see something on the stairs. Burwell flicked on his lighter and held it over the mark—a single red dot, about an eighth of an inch in diameter.

"Blood?" asked Burwell.

"That would be my guess." Spracklin straightened up. He charged up the stairs. A constable was leading the landlady—he forgot her name—down the hall. "Ma'am," he said. "We need your help." He didn't have the time to fuck around with warrants. If she was going to be difficult, he'd kick doors in. He stepped into the wing above the girl's room and said: "Can you open these doors for us?"

"All of them?" There were four doors before them.

"Yes, please."

She opened the first on the right and it was the standard Haight-Ashbury bedroom, with two single beds and a double mattress on the floor. It was the landlady opening the doors, not the police, he thought. Anything they found might stand up in court.

The next room was empty. It wasn't just that there was no one in it—there was nothing in it but a bed, dresser, and chair. What hit him instantly was the smell. He was used to rooms in Haight-Ashbury reeking of sweat, dope or incense. But now he smelt anti-septic cleaners. It was weird enough that Spracklin drew his weapon and stepped into the room. He opened the closet door, found nothing but cleaning products and garbage bags. The bathroom was empty. Spracklin holstered his gun and began putting on rubber gloves.

"Who rented this room?" he asked the landlady—Ainslie. Her name was Mrs. Ainslie.

"I'd have to check."

"Open the other doors with Sergeant Burwell and then get me the name of the tenant here. And whether they paid by check."

Spracklin felt he was on to something. The guy had wiped the room down and left. After donning rubber gloves, the Lieutenant began opening drawers and cupboards. They were empty. He looked under the bed. Nothing. He stood and pulled the bed back from the wall. He could see the floor had been wiped clean, but there were red smears across the floor boards. There had been blood on the floor, under the guy's bed, and he had done a bad job of wiping it away. If the guy had done this bad a job of cleaning up blood, Spracklin wondered if he would have left fingerprints in the room.

The only things the suspect had left were some half-used cleaning products and an overflowing wastepaper basket in the bathroom. The trash was all that the guy had left behind, so he began picking through it piece by piece—apple cores, banana peels, discarded packaging, grocery bags, candy wrappers, old receipts, all coated in coffee grinds. There were torn up fliers for concerts and art exhibitions around the Haight. Spracklin wondered if these could be a clue about the perp's future movements. He began to piece together the shreds of paper. The papers—blotched and wet from coffee grinds—were different colors and ripped into sixteenths, so they came together quickly. Two were for concerts in early July and one was for a surrealist exhibition at a coffee shop. There was one sheet of paper he didn't understand. It was half a mimeographed sheet that read:

Jack
Jake and Mabel
Mabel
Still Lifes
Poetry

The paper had been torn below the word "Poetry." Spracklin wondered if the whole paper contained something incriminating and he had torn it off so the police would never find it. Then again, it might just be sundry trash.

Spracklin looked up and saw Mrs. Ainslie come in. She paused at the door, gazing at the mess he had made with the garbage on the floor. "Lieutenant," she said. "I just spoke to my husband on the phone, and he checked the records. The tenant in this room is a Rebecca Napo...." She looked at notes she had scribbled down. "Rebecca Napolitano. She paid by cash. We haven't seen her for a couple of months, but for the past two months we received cash payment by mail. We still have her damage deposit. Thirty-two dollars."

Spracklin thought about it. "Do kids often leave before their lease is up?"

"It's more common than not." Mrs. Ainslie was catching her breath now. She had held up through a trying evening and now she was beginning to weaken. Her voice broke. "Kids leave and they sublet their rooms to other kids. There's not a lot we can do to stop it."

Spracklin knew the horror of what she had seen downstairs was beginning to set in, and it was compounded by the knowledge that the killer had been living in her building. Spracklin thanked her and went downstairs to get his evidence kit. He needed to search the killer's room for fingerprints.

CHAPTER 27

The best operatives did not work quickly. They worked efficiently. He told himself to work efficiently. He held the branches of the shrub to one side and drove the spade into the ground. He was careful to place the earth in a neat pile beside the hole. Disregarding the rain, he kept digging. He ignored the handgun digging into his waist when he bent to lift another scoop of dirt. He even tried to ignore the surges of euphoria that kept welling up inside him. The only thing that mattered now was digging.

Lubricated by the rain, the branch slipped and he reached a gloved hand down to yank it back. He now had a hole deep enough for one of the garbage bags, but he needed it twice the size. He had to get rid of both of the heads.

He shifted position so he was digging under a different bough. He drove the shovel into the earth and hit a rock. He adjusted the shovel, dug lower and kept going. He felt the cold rainwater drip down his neck and under his shirt. The T-shirt—the clean shirt he'd changed into after burning the one covered in blood—was soaked and clung to his back. The cuffs of his jeans were getting muddy. He had to keep digging.

The hole looked big enough. He reached into his backpack and withdrew one plastic bag and tossed it in. It took up more space than he'd thought, so he took a few more scoops from the wall of the hole. He tossed in the other bag and pressed them down with his foot. He quickly—efficiently—pushed the earth back over the hole. He'd swallowed a few uppers with a single Budweiser and now he felt himself working with clear-headed competence. He'd rented another room, a basement flat up on Waller Street, and moved everything he owned there that morning. He'd wiped down the apartment on Clayton Street. There would be no fingerprints. Then he'd carried out the hit—not a scared woman this time but a decorated Vietnam vet. He had become a man to be feared. A hitman. A button man. A wise guy.

He picked up his rucksack and threw it on his back. Now he had to be careful. No careless mistakes. He patted down the earth atop the hole and pushed the excess under the bush where it wouldn't be seen. He took care to mess up the patch of dirt where he'd been standing, making sure to leave no footprints. As one last precaution, he cut up the hill and tossed the spade — which he'd pinched the day before — over the fence into the maintenance grounds so it wouldn't be missed. Moments later, he was out of the park. Then he let his emotions take hold of him. He felt his chest and shoulders lift. He was triumphant. He'd carried out two perfect missions in three nights. He'd done it solo. He hadn't flinched. And the latest hit was against a soldier.

He was moving up. The next hit, the third and final hit under this contract, would be more difficult. No one would scoff after the next one. Yes, it was another woman. He had to admit that. But walking erect in the driving rain, he took pride in the fact that it was a complicated mission, one that would test his mettle. The target was under the protection of her father, an SFPD Lieutenant. It would be tough.

CHAPTER 28

The rain had cleared by the time Spracklin steered the Monaco up the steep slope of Clarendon Avenue. Spracklin was not feeling sunny. He had got just two hours sleep and had barely had a drink the previous night. He had stopped by the office that morning to find his in-basket full of pink message slips he didn't want to return—the public relations department (the least of his worries), reporters, two Republican supervisors, and the thugs at Internal Affairs. He'd called Chief Hawkings and asked him to run interference with the Republican grandees. He'd grabbed Burwell and fled the office.

"So, I checked with the personnel office at Pan-Am," said Burwell as the car struggled to make it up the hill.

"And...."

"Sarah Byrne made weekly flights to Asia in April—four in all—spending forty-eight hours in Hong Kong on each trip." He held up some papers and pointed to the dates of her departures and returns on a makeshift calendar he'd made. "The airline paid her $314.98 every two weeks, and you can see the entries here." He pointed to two entries on the bank statement. "She had three checks from her old man for about seven-hundred dollars total. But then there were eight payments that are unaccounted for—there were no checks in the bundle showing where that money came from. Those checks were large, ranging between $832 and $1,320."

"So, it's about ten-thousand coming from somewhere," said Spracklin.

"Yup—$9,301.14," said Burwell. "One thing I noticed: there's no relationship between the timing of these mystery payments and her trips to Asia. Some of them were paid in while she was supposedly in Hong Kong. The paychecks from the airline, those were both deposited while she was in San Francisco."

They arrived at the Byrne mansion and, as there were neither mourners nor media there, Spracklin parked close to the house. Spracklin and Burwell showed their badges to the security detail and walked along the white gravel driveway to the residence that looked like an assembly of stark white cubes. There were only three cars in the driveway, one Cadillac, the roadster, and the burgundy Mercedes 230 SL convertible.

A Latina maid told them the Captain was at the Holy Virgin Mary Cathedral making arrangements for his daughter's funeral. Mrs. Byrne was resting and not to be disturbed. But William Byrne was in the study. They found the younger Byrne at his father's desk, poring over shipping manifolds. The jacket of his three-piece suit was hanging on the back of his chair, and the radio on the bookshelf blared some music with screaming guitars. The maid had to knock twice to get his attention. When he saw the officers, he turned off the radio and asked them to sit.

"What can I do for you?" he asked, as he picked up a pipe from the ashtray.

"We're sorry about the death of yet another member of your extended family, but I'm afraid we have to ask more questions," said Spracklin. "We are trying to retrace Peter Menendes' steps in the final days of his life, and are wondering if you could give us some information."

Spracklin realized Byrne wasn't listening. He was leaning on his left elbow and gazing at a point on the wall. His fingers stuffed tobacco from a Troost tin into a pipe. Perhaps he was in shock following this latest death.

"I'm sorry, Detective, what was the question?"

"When did you last see Peter Menendes?"

As Byrne thought about the question, he patted his vest pocket, obviously searching for matches. Spracklin fished a book of matches from his own pocket and handed it to the young man.

"Pete, yes," said Byrne. "He wasn't around the office when we found out about...about Sarah on Monday. And he didn't come to any of the visitations here at the house."

"Was there a problem between Menendes and your family? Any hostility?"

Byrne held the match over the bowl as he sucked on the pipe. "None. I think it's just that...." He fumbled for the right words. "Everyone grieves in their own way. We'd been trying to contact him about the funeral, but he hadn't installed a phone at his apartment." He continued to stare into space, then returned to the question. "I think Pete was in the office on Friday. He and Elias Wong were in the command post in the afternoon and I stopped by to say hello, find out how the search for Sarah was going."

"And what did they say?"

William Byrne puffed on his pipe. It looked incongruous to Spracklin. A pipe just didn't look right in the hands of someone so young. "Elias told me they felt they had exhausted their leads in San Francisco and were working on intelligence Pete had brought in that she may have left the city."

Spracklin shifted in his seat and wondered how far he should push this. "And you took him at his word?"

"I don't micromanage, Lieutenant. My father always says: 'Hire the best people and leave them to do their job.'"

Spracklin took back his matches, lit a cigarette and handed the pack to Burwell beside him. "Look-it," said Spracklin. "William," he said, assuming he could call the young fella by his first name. The guy tried so hard to emulate his father that Spracklin wondered whether he should address Byrne by his rank and surname. "The thing is that Pete Menendes was living with Sarah all the time she was a fugitive. They had a room together in Haight-Ashbury—the room we found his body in. He was just pretending—"

"You have proof of that?"

"Definite proof. Her stuff was at his apartment. He was cashing checks on her account as recently as last week."

"Let me see the checks." Byrne then seemed to realize he wasn't in a position to demand evidence from the police. He stood and began to pace the study. "I knew Pete—he wouldn't do that. Pete is...Pete was a great friend, a family member. He wouldn't do that to us."

"The guy I saw was a drunk barely able to stand," said Spracklin. He was growing tired of the niceties with the Byrnes.

"Pete was fond of drink," said Byrne. He strode past his desk and back pensively. "I think it was his crutch when Sarah disappeared. But we all have our crutches. My dad says the bottle is a marvelous servant and a terrible master. It became Pete's master."

Spracklin started to say something but Byrne burst in. "You wouldn't believe what a nice guy he could be. He'd look for—he'd search for—things to do that were just plain nice. In my office at Poseidon, I have photos of my crew on *The Maddox*. Like those." He gestured to three eight-by-tens on the wall in gilded frames, showing the elder Captain Byrne on the bridge of a ship. "Pete saw the photographs lying on my desk and he just took them and got them framed. It was the sort of thing he did—he was this big, gregarious jock who sort of brought you into his world and made you part of it. I mean, he invited me along to a reunion dinner with members of his platoon. I saw they respected Pete. You'll see them at his funeral. He was king to everyone who knew him."

William Byrne wasn't pacing any more. He was stationed in front of the detectives, trying to convince them he was right. Spracklin stubbed out his cigarette in the nearest ashtray and looked up at the young man. He was worn out and not in any mood to humor Will Byrne.

"The evidence shows that—"

"Yes, yes, yes. I know what the evidence shows," said Byrne. He sat again on the hard-backed chair and leaned toward them. "What I'm trying to tell you is just how difficult it is to accept the evidence. It's not the guy I knew. He was the guy anyone would want his sister to marry." His gaze again seemed to fall on a distant point only he could see. "He was perfect for her, perfect."

"Because he...."

"Because he brought out the best in her. He softened her and made her human."

"You found her inhuman sometimes?"

At first, Byrne said nothing. "Sarah was my little sister, and I loved her. But she was so stubborn. She had to have her own company. I know now she'd rather smuggle heroin than work for Dad. When my Granma died, she wouldn't even let Dad hold on to the stock certificates she inherited. She had to hold them herself. But Pete, Pete made her...warmer."

"Stock certificates," Ed Burwell said. "What stock certificates?"

"My grandmother had holdings in a few companies—General Motors, GE, Citibank. Blue chips. They were divided among her grandchildren. We each got about $11,000 in stock."

"What happened to Sarah's shares?"

Byrne shrugged. "They must be with her stuff somewhere."

Spracklin said: "I have to ask you, William: where were you last night at about 5:30?"

He expected the question. "I was on my way home from the office. Walking over to my place in Pacific Heights. Then I spent the evening at home watching the Giants game on TV. Unwinding. Working on a few accounts"

"Alone?"

"Alone."

Spracklin didn't think he could gain anything more from William Byrne and asked for a time when he could speak to the elder Byrne. He again offered his condolences, stood to leave. As they shook hands, Burwell held Byrne's hand, he had a puzzled look on his face. "You and Elias, did you guys find those stock certificates in your sister's bedroom, here, in the house?"

"I told you. I don't know where they are."

"But you searched?"

"Elias searched the room. He made no mention of them."

The inspectors were silent as they left the house. Burwell began to say something but Spracklin stopped him. He pulled out Sarah Byrnes' keyring with the Mercedes fob. He'd had it in his pocket since the previous night. There were six keys on the ring, and he knew two of them opened the front door and apartment door at the building where Sarah Byrne and Pete Menendes had hidden. He looked at the Mercedes 230 SL, its exterior still coated in the previous night's rain. Spracklin remembered Marie saying Sarah was known to drive it through Haight-Ashbury, and he could imagine the brash young heiress zipping by the flower children with the top down.

What's on your mind, Ed?" Spracklin asked as he paced toward the Mercedes, holding up Sarah Byrne's key ring. He opened the car door with one key, got in, and turned the car on with another. He now knew what four of the six keys were for.

"Eleven thousand dollars of stocks," said the Sergeant. "We haven't accounted for them."

Spracklin had noticed the same thing. He nodded and walked back to the front door. He opened it with another of the keys. Spracklin nodded and smiled. "You're wondering where the stock certificates are," said Spracklin. He now knew what five of the six keys were for and he studied the sixth—a flat, dull grey key.

"I'm thinking if we find those certificates, we find the killer," said Burwell. "I mean, $11,000 is a pretty good reason to kill someone."

"So, the perp killed the girl, and then the boyfriend ended up with the share certificates. So, he had to kill Menendes too?"

"Dunno. I'm just thinking it through. Maybe Menendes killed her to get the certificates —"

"But she had more than that in her bank account...." Spracklin's voice trailed off and he looked at the mystery key again.

"Then maybe someone else killed him to get the papers. He was in rough shape after the girl died and...What?"

Spracklin was studying the final dull grey key that he hadn't identified yet.

"The bank," said Spracklin.

"What about it?"

"I think I know what this key is." Before he realized what he was doing, he slapped Burwell on the shoulder and added: "And I think it may lead us to your stock certificates."

CHAPTER 29

Ed Burwell was growing short of breath as they strode along Haight Street. They only had to go from Park Station to Clayton, but the Sergeant just couldn't move quickly. Spracklin paused at a corner and noticed the posters for the Solstice Festival stapled to a lamppost. The bold red and blue lettering reminded him again that he was on Haight Street, the epicenter of the acid movement. Looking around, he saw hippies were returning to the street now that the rain had stopped. Three were sitting against a sandwich shop storefront to his right, begging for money. A female junkie across the road was smiling at him, hoping to turn a trick to get her fix. Panhandlers and hookers—that's what the flower children were becoming. Spracklin studied the poster for the festival. Once again, the last line about surprise guests stood out to him. He wondered who J.D. Ehler had lined up for the concert.

"So, it's a hunch?" said Burwell as he drew abreast of Spracklin.

"It's a hunch now," said Spracklin. He was holding Sarah Byrne's key ring in his right hand, as if it were a talisman left him by the dead drug smuggler. "It's the art of being an inspector, Ed. You follow your hunches without falling in love with 'em. If the facts prove 'em wrong, you abandon them."

"I just think it's a longshot."

Spracklin held up the one key they had not yet identified. "Tell me what else this could be. I should have seen it sooner."

They crossed the street and entered the Bank of America. Spracklin peered around—a few customers were filling out slips at a counter. Bud Margeson was sitting in his office with an elderly woman. Spracklin knocked gently, then spoke firmly.

"Mr. Margeson," he said, "I'm going to have to interrupt." He stepped back from the door, inviting the bank manager to join him.

"Lieutenant," said Margeson, looking up front his desk. He was wearing a blue pinstripe suit and a bowtie. "I'm with a customer now."

"And I'm exercising a warrant," said Spracklin. He held up the warrant they'd received a day earlier.

"As soon as I'm finished, I'll be with you."

"If you'd been up front with me yesterday, I wouldn't be here today. I'm investigating a double homicide."

The old woman recoiled at the mention of a double homicide, and Margeson got the message. He excused himself and joined Spracklin at the door. "That was thoroughly unprofessional," said Margeson as they stepped into the main hall of the bank.

Spracklin shrugged. "Did Sarah Byrne or any of her associates have a safety deposit box here?"

"I can't tell you about any of her associates. I wouldn't know who they are."

"Cut the shit. Did she have a safety deposit box?"

"If you'd asked yesterday, I would have told you. Yes, yes, she had a safety deposit box with us."

"I need to get into it. This search warrant allows me access to it."

"Well, we only have the bank's key. Given that the owner of the box is deceased, we'll need to fill out the forms arranging for a locksmith to come...."

Spracklin silenced him by holding up Sarah Byrne's key. "This might help," he said.

Margeson nodded and led Spracklin and Burwell down a pebbled stairway to the basement and asked a bank employee to help the officers. Together they searched a ledger and found the right box. Margeson didn't say goodbye to the investigators—he just moved back up the stairs. The employee, a guy in his forties whose white shirt had grown tight on him, wrote down their names, took a ring of keys and led them into a room full of safe boxes. He took them to box number 1049.

"Do you have a record of who's had access to this box?" asked Spracklin.

"It's in the log," he said. With his head, he motioned back to the log book at his desk.

"Good," said Spracklin. "I want to know the last time anyone accessed this security box."

Box 1049 was a wide door with two key holes. The bank employee inserted his key into one, and Spracklin did the same in the other. They turned the keys in unison, and the door swung open.

"Would you like a private room?" he asked as he withdrew the metal compartment from the safe.

"Yes please," said Spracklin.

They were led to a dark room with wooden tables and chair and a framed photo of Big Sur on the wall. The banker placed the metal box on a table and left the two policemen on their own.

"One moment," Spracklin said to the guy before he could leave. "What's your name?"

"Frank Jones."

"Okay, Frank, here's what I need you to do. You're going to stand at the door and watch us. You can go through your log book, but I want you to make sure that we don't take anything from this box, or put anything in."

Spracklin jotted down Jones' name in his notebook and positioned the box so Jones could see it. The clerk stood just outside the door flipping through the log book.

The metal box was crammed with papers. On top they found share certificates. Not only did Sarah Byrne have more than a hundred-thousand in cash in her bank account, she had shares of blue-chip companies like City Bank of New York, Pan-American Airline and International Business Machines. He set them to one side.

"March 4," Jones called out, closing the book. "The last time anyone accessed this security box was March 4. It was Miss Byrne herself."

"No one else has been in since then?"

"No one. They would have had to sign in."

Spracklin thanked him and went back to his work. Underneath the share certificates, he found the documents incorporating Mercantile Airlines, based in San Francisco. Sarah Byrne herself held one hundred percent of the share capital, and it had three directors—Sarah Byrne, Peter Menendes and David Rosenburg, the general counsel of Poseidon Mercantile. The company had incorporated in February, and Spracklin supposed it had no assets yet. He wondered whether this seeming shell company had anything to do with the murder. He set the legal documents on top of the stack of share certificates.

The next documents were all in a single manila envelope whose return address read "Lane & Slaughter, Solicitors" based in the

Cayman Islands. Spracklin pulled several sheets of paper from the envelope and found a letter from a lawyer called Nigel Lane to "Miss Byrne" saying that they had incorporated Minglewood Cayman Islands. The letter was signed in January, a month before the San Francisco company had been incorporated. The share capital of Minglewood Cayman Islands was divided evenly between Byrne and someone called Edward Schultz. Schultz had signed the document, saying it had been signed in San Francisco on January 23.

Burwell had been looking over Spracklin's shoulder at the papers, and he asked, "Can you figure it out, Jimmy?"

"Not yet," murmured Spracklin. "It looks like this Cayman Islands company has paid her tens of thousands, maybe hundreds of thousands of dollars. But...." He paused as he thought about it.

"We'll have to bring in Schultz and ask him," Burwell said.

"We might want to get some more information first," said Spracklin. He picked up the final envelope in the metal container. There was no lettering on it and the contents felt more rigid than the others. Spracklin pulled out a stack of black-and-white photos. Several strips of negatives fell on to the table.

There were nine eight-by-ten black-and-whites and they looked like they had been developed by an amateur, with a few overexposed blotches on some of the photos. They had been taken on different days and various locations. Most showed young men outside notorious gay bars. Even Spracklin, who knew nothing about that scene, had heard of the Tool Box on Fourth Street and Compton's Cafeteria on Taylor.

Spracklin then picked up the cut negatives and looked at the shots. They appeared to match the printed shots, but there were sixteen negatives — seven more than the prints. He handed the prints to Burwell. "Recognize anyone?" he asked. As Burwell flipped through the photos, Spracklin looked at the negatives and tried to figure out what they revealed.

"Nope," said Burwell.

Spracklin ran a hand across the inside of the safe deposit box and placed the stock receipts back inside. He showed the other material to Frank Jones, saying they needed it as evidence. He put the documents into the briefcase and handed Burwell the negatives.

"I have two jobs for you, Ed," he said as they ascended the stairs. "Get those negatives to the lab and get prints on them. Put a rush on it. And look into Edward Schultz. I need to know about him. We'll meet at Park Station at 2 p.m."

"What are you doing?"

Spracklin didn't bother answering. He had other things on his mind.

CHAPTER 30

*T*he *Oracle* office at 1371 Haight Street was a mauve store front with big windows. The newspaper office took up the ground floor of a three-story structure with two columns of ornate bay windows at the front. From the door of *The Oracle*'s office, Spracklin could see the corner of Haight and Clayton. It was entirely possible *The Oracle* staff could have seen the "chick with the nose stud" from their office as she went on her nighttime strolls.

The Lieutenant had expected a typical newspaper office — type-writers, phones ringing, an editor barking orders. Only this one would have had hippies at the worn wooden desks. But what he stepped into was more like an art gallery. Brightly colored prints, each precise in its detail, were taped on to the walls. They were wild prints of flowing lines, swirling letters and vibrant colors, the style that Haight-Ashbury was known for. No one was typing. There were two men and a woman at easels working on some sort of art, and three others were placing things in boxes.

One guy with a neat haircut was talking to the three artists, pointing out details of their work. At the sight of Spracklin, he lowered his hands to his sides and stopped talking.

"Get out," he said, pointing toward the door. Spracklin stopped, confused, but held his ground. "I'd call my lawyer, man, but there's no point," he said, his tone not angry so much as disgusted. "And after what you fuckers have done, I got no more bread to pay him."

Spracklin held up his hands in a surrender gesture. "I'm just here to talk about—"

The young man threw down the magazines he was holding and yelled, "Look, I've fucking had it with you CIA types or FBI or what-ever you are grinding our rights into the dirt." He wore a golf shirt and a pair of faded jeans. He looked sane but Spracklin wondered if he was clinically paranoid or on something.

"Your campaign of oppression has driven us out of business. Dig the packing boxes, man. We're shutting *The Oracle* down." Spracklin looked at the wall. He knew he wouldn't like *The Oracle* if he chose to read it, but it was a shame there would no longer be an outlet for these tremendous illustrations. "So, all you CIA types can head over to J. Edgar's house and have a big bash to celebrate another nail in the coffin of the First Amendment."

Spracklin smiled. "Did you say CIA?"

"Don't fuck with me, man," said the editor—Spracklin assumed he was the editor. "I don't know what agency you're from, but who-ever you're with the answer's the same. I need to see a warrant if you're coming in."

Spracklin reached in his pocket and pulled out his badge. If the guy wanted to check his credentials, he could come close enough to read them. "My name is Jimmy Spracklin. I'm a Lieutenant with the Bureau of Inspectors of the San Francisco Police Department."

"Are you telling me you're not a federal agent or ever have been?" The guy kept talking about his rights, and Spracklin let him talk himself out. Once he was silent, the Lieutenant said, "I'm inves-tigating a murder." The guy started talking again so Spracklin held up the page of *The Oracle*. "Sarah Byrne," he said. "You interviewed her. I want to talk to the reporter who met with her."

"Look, man," said the editor. "I don't know who you are but we've had it with federal agents coming in here and fucking up our work. We're shutting down because of the harassment." He slumped into an old easy chair in front of a desk piled high with papers. "You want to rap with Sheryl d'Angelo? You're gonna have to fly to New York City. She might be there now. She was stopping by her folks' place in Oklahoma City before taking up her new job there."

"With who?"

"*Village Voice*. I'm sure you subscribe and Sheryl's illustrations will be in the next issue when it arrives in the mail." One of the hip-pies laughed along with him.

"Illustrations? I thought she was a reporter."

"Dude, everyone here has been a reporter for the last few months. I can't pay anyone and the writers are sick of the harass-ment. We heard about the chick with the nose stud down the street so I sent Sheryl out to interview her. Sheryl got some notes and took a picture. She and I wrote the story together. Now, unless you have a warrant, run along and oppress someone else."

"Sarah Byrne, did she say if anyone was after her or if she was scared of anyone?"

"Your whole fucking police force was after her—she was scared shitless."

"But did she say anything that wasn't in the article?"

"Yeah, she gave Sheryl four bucks to place a classified ad in the paper for her."

"Did you run it?"

"Sure, we did. Now scram."

"Look, just show me the ad and I'll leave."

The editor—Spracklin still didn't know the guy's name—grabbed a copy of the magazine and flipped through to the last few pages. "Here," he said, pointing to the bottom of the classified sector. "It was the last one we got in before going to press."

Spracklin followed his finger and read the small rectangle of newsprint.

MINGMAN 6.18.68 0200 @ Red House. MERCGIRL

Spracklin took out a pen, jotted down the ad in his notebook and wondered if he should try to get more out of the guy. There didn't seem much point. The woman he wanted to talk to had left the state. Maybe he could try calling her in New York. "You said the magazine is called *Village Voice*?"

"The door's that way," said the editor, pointing beyond Spracklin to the street. The Lieutenant decided to leave and stepped out to the street. He lit a cigarette and surveyed the road. He had time for lunch, and thought the best martini in the city would satisfy his appetite.

A kid with a beaded headband was sitting cross-legged on a blanket outside Zam Zam. He was selling beaded products with Navajo designs—earrings, wrist bands, chokers. To get in the bar, Spracklin had to maneuver his way around two tourists haggling with the kid. He stepped through the arched doorway set in purple stucco beneath a sign that read Aub Zam Zam. There was jazz playing on the sound system, that recording of the Duke at Newport that he'd always liked. Maybe he could find a refuge of jazz on Haight Street.

He walked past a table of hippies laughing hysterically at something, to the far end of the bar, next to a guy in his thirties who was trying hard to be a hippie—muttonchop sideburns, salt-and-pepper hair down to his shoulders, flared pants. He didn't quite cut it. Spracklin ordered a martini. The swarthy bartender said nothing but set about pouring the gin and vermouth.

Spracklin didn't want to chat with the pretend hippie, so he took his notebook out of his pocket and set to work. The case was moving, but he didn't know where it was going. He had no answers yet, but at least he had questions. As he sipped the dry martini, he began to jot them down:

> Was SB killed for her money?
> Are the photos linked to the murders?
> Why did the killer murder PM as well as SB?
> Why were they beheaded?
> Who's Ed Schultz?
> Why did Menendes have fake ID?

Spracklin circled the name Ed Schultz and wondered about the transactions. The martini was ice cold and he thought about having another. He felt a firm hand on his shoulder and heard a warm voice say, "Why, Lieutenant Spracklin. What a pleasant surprise."

Spracklin closed the notebook, turned and saw Bogdan Polgar beside him. One of Polgar's henchmen Lester Fredericks (born Leonid Fedorov in Leningrad in 1938) was at his elbow, and suggested to the aging hippie that he find another seat. The hippie complied and Polgar slipped into his chair. Fredericks joined another of Polgar's thugs at the door. He was a white guy, well dressed, silent, built and moved like a welterweight. Spracklin had seen him a couple of times with Polgar but still hadn't learned his name.

"Do you mind if I join you, Lieutenant?" asked Polgar once he was seated. Dressed in a worn jacket with patches on the elbows and an open collar, Polgar looked like a gentleman. He had deep laugh lines and greying sideburns. No one would know he was the head of a crime syndicate in Fillmore, the black district just east of Haight-Ashbury. He was a patrician figure, a guy who arranged apartments for his thugs, and made sure their children had the proper schooling. And he could put a contract out on those same henchmen without batting an eye if he thought they'd crossed him. His people, an army of Eastern European emigres and blacks from Fillmore, loved and feared him. Spracklin had been trying for fifteen months to link two murders in the Western Addition to Polgar, and had not succeeded. To the bartender, Polgar said, "I'll have what my friend is having, Bruno, and top up his glass."

"You know the bartender's name?" asked Spracklin. He capped his pen, returned it to his pocket and shook a cigarette out of the package.

"I've told you before, my friend. I keep my finger on the pulse of Haight-Ashbury. This place is a goldmine. People come here from all over the world and spend money. I saw you come in and I thought I'd stop by and say hello."

Spracklin knew it was bullshit but he wanted to know what the Russian wanted. Spracklin lit their cigarettes and pocketed his lighter.

"I guess you're spending all your time around here again," said Polgar after he'd taken a sip of his martini and nodded his approval to Bruno.

"And why is that?"

"The Byrne girl, of course. My goodness, that is a grisly one."

"What's your interest in it, Bogdan?"

"Me? No interest at all. But Lieutenant Spracklin, as a citizen and businessman, I don't like this sort of thing." He took another sip. "No, Sir, I don't. And I'm just glad we have the two best law enforcement minds in the state working on it."

"The two best?"

"Yes, Sir, you and Captain Wong."

"You're aware that Elias is working the case."

"Indeed I am. He came to see me about a week ago, asking about young Miss Byrne."

"Why'd he do that?"

"That's what I asked him." Polgar let out a chuckle. "Great minds do think alike, don't they? I said to him, 'Why ask me?' He thought I might have some insights given my interests in the area."

"What did you tell him, Bogdan?"

"Nothing much. I said the kids in the neighborhood had all these stories about seeing her in the Haight. My employees kept hearing them. We didn't know which ones were true, but there were too many for them all to be wrong. I was pretty sure she was in Haight-Ashbury somewhere."

"What did Elias say to that?"

Polgar shrugged. "He didn't say much of anything. He got excited about Satan's Host moving into the area, but he didn't say much about the girl. But enough of that. How are you, Lieutenant?"

"Hold on, Polgar. You told him about the bikers? What do you mean he got excited?"

Polgar took another sip of his drink and smiled again at the bartender. "Best martinis in the city," he said. "I should ask him to make mine a vodka martini, being Russian and all." He smiled and looked again at Bruno. "But the guy terrifies me."

"Just answer my question."

"Oh, you know. I mentioned that all the hippies were saying they saw Sarah Byrne here or there. But the big news for Captain Wong was that Satan's Host was on the Haight."

"No one had heard of Satan's Host before they were in the *Chronicle*."

"Never heard of them? Everyone had read those stories, newspaper stories, out of LA about what those animals did to their victims."

Spracklin started to say something but Polgar kept talking.

"I tell you, Captain Wong's eyes lit up when I told him five members of Satan's Host were holed up on Haight Street. You know how Elias Wong gets that look in his eye when he hears something that intrigues him? Wong always had the sharpest mind of anyone on the SFPD. It was great to see him get excited about a lead again."

Spracklin took a long drag on his cigarette and tapped the ash into the ashtray. He was trying to figure out Bogdan Polgar's game. Polgar wanted him to think the bikers killed Byrne and Menendes. Why? Was he involved?

"Three."

"Huh?"

"Three. There are three members of Satan's Host in town. We checked them out. They have alibis for the girl's murder. They're clear."

Polgar chuckled. There was something so charming about his grandfatherly laugh that it could almost make Spracklin forget he had spent over a year investigating a double homicide the guy had ordered. "Oh, Lieutenant Spracklin.... Can I call you Jimmy?"

"No, you can't. Call me Lieutenant Spracklin. Or Sir."

"Lieutenant. I've told you before: I keep my ear to the ground. I talk to people." He downed his martini. "People in this neighborhood are worried, Lieutenant. I mean, Hell's Angels have that house up on Ashbury, then a week ago those bikers started trickling in." He held up a hand with all the fingers outstretched. "Five of them."

"There's freedom of movement in this country, Bogdan," said Spracklin, just to keep him talking. He would check around at Park Station to see if they had any gen on the Satan's Host bikers arriving before the Byrne girl was killed. "The days of the sheriffs running outlaws out of town are past."

"I'm just glad you have the boss, the leader of the gang, locked up. That's what my neighbors want. The Angels don't like them hanging around. People are getting nervous."

"And you've followed me into this club to relay the concerns of the good citizens of Haight-Ashbury," said Spracklin.

"You know I'm always eager to help the law enforcement personnel."

"What I know, Bogdan, is that you're full of shit. And I know that one day I'm going to nail your ass to the wall, and it will be the best day of my career." He finished the last few drops of his martini and pocketed his cigarettes and lighter.

Spracklin stood and walked out, brushing past the bodyguards. The sun was still shining on Haight Street, and it took a few seconds for his eyes to adjust. Tomorrow was June 21, the longest day of the year, he reminded himself. As he walked by the hippie landmarks that had been so vibrant a year earlier—the signs at Haight and Ashbury, the Stanyan Park Hotel—he thought about the timing of Polgar's visit. He had been talking to Elias Wong. Polgar had said as much. Could the two of them have been working together? No. Elias wouldn't sink that low.

CHAPTER 31

Spracklin paused by the pines towering over Park Station and studied his Monaco. There was white paper stuck under the brown sedan's left windshield wiper. It couldn't be a ticket—it was a police vehicle in a police parking lot. It looked like a white envelope. He crossed between the tree trunks and into the car park. Three kids were sitting just outside the entrance singing anti-war songs—as if the cops were responsible for the war in Vietnam. He tried to ignore them and pulled the envelope out from under the wiper and saw the word "Spracklin" printed on the outside. Inside was a handwritten note on foolscap.

Lieutenant

Here is a list of people who entered and left Menendes apartment building on Clayton y'day p.m.:

16:10: Arrived. Two chicks with shopping, one blonde in poncho, one overweight brunette.

16:35: Left. A black guy with a backpack. Afro. Jean jacket. Short.

16:42: Left. Four people, two old, one child, one teenager. Old man had camera.

16:53: Arrived. Fat guy with briefcase wearing a suit. Maybe Mexican....

Spracklin cast an eye over the list, which had another two dozen entries, then studied the signature at the bottom: Dave Bloom. Spracklin looked around and for the first time studied the kids seated just outside the gates. Dave Bloom was sitting beside the guitar player, looking back at him as he sang along to "Where Have All the Flowers Gone." Spracklin held his gaze for a few seconds, tucked the envelope into his breast pocket and strode out of the car park. He walked past the singers and headed down to the arch under the Alvord Lake Bridge. He had a cigarette as he studied the list again. He didn't think "Fat guy with briefcase" would help much with this case. In fact, there was no one on the list that seemed to match what they knew of the killer.

"Lieutenant," said a polite voice.

Spracklin turned and saw Dave Bloom. He made sure the boy hadn't been followed and said, "How did you know which car was mine?"

"I've been watching the building on Clayton where Sarah and Menendes lived. I saw you going to the bank. I knew you would have parked at Park Station."

"But how did you know which car was mine?"

"Yesterday, when you lit a cigarette, you removed the keys from your pocket when you fished out your lighter. You had a Ford key on the ring. There were three Fords at Park Station. The Monaco was the only one with a full ashtray."

Spracklin thought about it and nodded. The kid could use his head. "So, explain this list."

"Like I said, I was observing the apartment yesterday—at least until the rain started. I looked like I was just hanging out. I got a list of who came and went."

"Starting at 4 p.m."

"Yeah. I just thought it might help."

Spracklin pocketed the list and looked around again. "This is good work, Dave."

"Will you be able to use it?"

"I don't know. But keep your ears open. Just one thing: if you suspect someone, don't go near him. Just let me know."

"I'll be okay."

"I said, don't go near him." He patted the boy's shoulder and thanked him. "I have to get back to work."

At Park Station, Spracklin asked the Duty Sergeant for an interview room where his team could work. Minutes later, he was seated beneath a faded photo of President Eisenhower in a windowless ten-by-ten room with the yellow legal pad spread before him. His jacket was on the back of his chair. And he was making the list he should have made a day or two before:

Sarah Byrne and Peter Menendes – Suspects

He paused to ask himself whether they had the same killer. Both had been decapitated. Both were working on her venture. But she was likely strangled and he was likely shot. He needed to work off a theory so he assumed for now it was one killer. He began to write.

Harry Byrne	*Has money to order a contract*
	Outraged daughter was a drug smuggler
William Byrne	*Competing for father's affection*
	Stood to gain inheritance if his sister was dead
Andrew Fox	*Sarah Byrne could have testified against him*
	Menendes used fake ID to meet him
	Could put out a contract from jail
Satan's Host	*Some, but maybe not all, have alibis*
	Turf war with Fox???
Ed Schulz	*?????*

Spracklin thought for a moment about something that had been bothering him for half an hour. Then he wrote:

Bogdan Polgar	*No apparent motive but for some reason he's tailing me and following this case.*

He was wondering whether any of these guys might be found on Bloom's list when the door flew open and Ed Burwell burst in.

"Hey, Jimmy," he said as he strode into the room and took the other chair. "Good thing you're not back at the office." He took a pack of cigarettes from his jacket. "The Chief's looking for you. I hear some supervisor is calling for your head 'cause you're hassling the Byrnes again and the PR department wants you. And your buddy from IA, Handell, he was asking for you as well."

Spracklin thought about each item as Burwell reeled them off and dismissed each in turn. "Don't worry about any of that. What about the case?"

Burwell draped his jacket on the back of the facing chair and sat down. "Okay, I dropped off the negatives, put a rush on it, and I found your Edward Schultz." He paused to light his cigarette, then pulled a sheet of paper from his jacket pocket. "Edward James Schultz, born July 17, 1939 in Portland, Oregon. Attended Oregon State, did not graduate. Enlisted Navy, May 1961, dishonorable discharge after a year. In June 1964, he was busted for bootlegging in Salt Lake City."

Spracklin laughed. "Bootlegging to Mormons?"

"Niche market," said Burwell. He was wearing a broad smile, telegraphing that the best part of the story was coming. "March '66, he—heh, heh—he was sentenced to eight months—heh, heh—for accessory to armed robbery. Twenty-four thousand from a bank in Salinas."

"What's so funny?"

"He drove the getaway car." He laughed again. "They made a clean getaway."

Spracklin was laughing with him now. "And...."

"Schultz is color blind. He got pulled over for going through a red light. He thought it was green. He can't distinguish red from green." Spracklin slapped his knee. Burwell fought to speak through his laughter. "Pulled over for going through a red light. Leaving a bank heist. The cop saw duffle bags in the back seat with cash pouring out of them. He did eight months in Folsom."

They both bent double. "What's he doing now?" gasped Spracklin.

"It looks like he's gone straight. He owns a stereo store now, down on Irving near UCSF." He glanced at his notes again, and his tone grew more serious. "It's called Minglewood Stereo."

"He owns the store?"

"Yeah. I spoke to his parole officer. Says Schultz has straightened himself out. Went into business. Employs twelve people. Pillar of the community."

"Where did he get the money to open a stereo store?" Spracklin spoke slowly as he turned things over in his head. He shook out a new cigarette and signaled to Burwell he needed a light.

"He didn't say," said Burwell, handing his cigarette to Spracklin.

The Lieutenant lit his cigarette and leaned back in his chair. He blew a stream of smoke at the grey ceiling and thought aloud. "So, this ex-con, this guy who needed money so badly he robbed a bank, this complete fathead, has opened his own business. Not only that, he has formed a business in the Cayman Islands with a millionaire heiress who's running drugs from Asia." He took a long drag on the cigarette. Burwell said something but Spracklin didn't hear him.

"An heiress, an ex-con, and a vet form a business. It generates enough cash that it pays the heiress up to fifteen-hundred a month. All on the QT." He stood and began pacing the small room. "It's a retail business, a stereo shop. It's...." He stopped and looked at Burwell. "Why stereos?"

"It's a good business," said Burwell. "I mean, every fucking rathole we've been in in Haight-Ashbury, the kids have these million-dollar sound systems." He kept blabbering but Spracklin stopped listening. He took his notebook from his briefcase. Burwell didn't seem to notice the Lieutenant was on to something. "No sheets, no bed. Just a mattress on the floor. No soap. No arsewipe. But they have these record players that would...." He noticed Spracklin was flipping through the notebook and reaching for the phone. "What's going on?" asked Burwell.

"Byrne," said Spracklin as he dialed the number. "He said they brought in Elias Wong because of an electronics heist at their terminal." Spracklin thought Burwell would get it, but the sergeant looked puzzled. Spracklin held up a finger to tell him to wait. "Hello," he said. "Captain Byrne, please. Harry Byrne.... Yes, thank you."

"What is it?" asked Burwell impatiently.

"It's.... Hello, Captain Byrne? Jimmy Spracklin."

"Yes, Detective," said the mogul in a dull voice. Spracklin couldn't tell if it was the voice of a man in mourning or one who was sick of hearing from the cops.

"I hate to bother you, Sir. I just have one question. You mentioned the other day that you had some robberies at your terminal in Oakland."

"Yes. In March. Two separate incidents."

"Can you please give me details?"

"We reported it to the Oakland Police Department. March 16 and 18, either side of St. Paddy's Day. On each day a container of electronics was stolen from our terminal."

"What sort of equipment?"

"Stereo equipment from Japan. Brand name Marantz. Two containers full. It had a retail value of about one hundred and sixty thousand dollars." He sighed and said, "You can get the details from your colleagues in Oakland."

"Yes, Sir. Sorry to bother you. Thank you."

Spracklin placed the receiver back in the cradle and told Burwell what the shipping magnate had said. The Sergeant smiled and nodded and said, "Great." He repeated, "Great." Then he added: "What does it mean?"

"What it *might* mean is that Minglewood is a fence for the stolen stereos," Spracklin said. "What I'd bet is that Sarah Byrne was involved with the stereo heist at her family's shipping terminal. She fenced them through Minglewood. Then they channeled her cut of the money through an offshore company, which paid money back to her." He jotted some notes down in his notebook. "What we need to do is get the details of the police report. We need details of the stolen shipment."

"We need a warrant," said Burwell.

"We wouldn't get a warrant on what we have now. We need details of what was stolen, serial numbers, and model numbers. We'll get them from the Commercial Crimes division in Oakland. Then we'll go into the store, like any other stereo buyers, and see if there is product matching what was stolen. Once we've got reason to believe the stuff is hot, we'll get the warrant."

Spracklin was about to place a call to the Oakland police, when the door opened and Mickie O'Neill stepped into the room. The Internal Affairs officer placed his finger on the phone cradle and nodded his head toward the door. "C'mon, Jimmy," he said. "We're going downtown."

CHAPTER 32

O'Neill stood with one thick finger suppressing the button on the phone, emphasizing that Spracklin wasn't going to make the phone call. His stance, his glare, the way the crooked nose was thrust forward, all dared Spracklin to defy him. Burwell was poised, ready to take action to help Spracklin. Soon two more IA officers were in the room, positioning themselves to neutralize the Sergeant. Spracklin knew Burwell didn't like him, but the Sergeant liked O'Neill and his type a hell of a lot less.

"One way or another, you're coming with me, Sprack," said O'Neill.

"We have work to do, O'Neill. Police work." Burwell tried edging one of the IA goons to one side, but the guy pushed back.

"Let's go, Lieutenant," repeated O'Neill. He didn't have to say Spracklin could cooperate or they would drag him out.

"What is this shit, O'Neill?" asked Spracklin. He lowered the receiver and grabbed his notebook. He didn't know what was going on, but a sixth sense told him to make sure he kept his notes. He put on his jacket, with Bloom's note in the pocket, and tucked his notebook in beside it.

"We're going downtown," said O'Neill, speaking over the sound of Burwell struggling with the IA officers. They had grabbed him by the upper arms and he was fighting to get free. He was tying them up, meaning that Spracklin and O'Neill could square off against each other.

"Not now. We just caught our first break in the Byrne case."

"Yeah. I've been hearing that crap from you for a week now."

"We're closing in on a suspect."

"So am I." O'Neill raised a thick arm and pointed out the door. "The car's waiting outside."

Spracklin knew he was cornered as long as he remained in the little interview room, so he walked out to the hall. He thought of telling Burwell to ease up but decided against it. Spracklin began to lengthen his stride and walk down the hall in front of O'Neill. "I told you guys I would cooperate fully."

"You've missed every meeting we set."

"Do you follow the fucking news, O'Neill?" They were passing the main desk now. "We're on the biggest case in the city."

"Just keep walking, Sprack."

"I'm closing in on a killer in a double homicide, asshole," Spracklin yelled. He wanted to humiliate O'Neill in front of the NCOs and patrolmen. He stepped into the shady parking lot. "We've had our first break and I have to follow it."

O'Neill stepped through the door. Spracklin could feel the big man looming over him. He remembered what Burwell had said about O'Neill: if he was as tough as he liked to pretend, the other guy from that fight long ago would have been the one with the broken nose. "You're not going anywhere but our office," O'Neill said. "Handell is getting your daughter and we're—"

"You guys told me you'd leave my daughter out of this."

"That was before we learned she was the one who met Sarah Byrne at the airport."

"Bullshit."

"We've got a witness from the airport, Sprack. Marie was Sarah Byrne's driver that night. You've been lying to us. Your daughter's a suspect in a drug ring."

Handell was after Marie. Spracklin knew he had to act fast to warn her. He turned and began walking off. "You're full of shit, O'Neill. You've had a grudge against me because you couldn't cut it as an inspector." He had to warn Marie. He couldn't go back into Park Station. He kept walking. "I have a murder to investigate."

"I'll arrest you if I have to."

"Fuck you."

Spracklin could feel the muscular man stepping up behind him. O'Neill grabbed his left shoulder. Spracklin wheeled around. He swung his right fist tight, keeping it close to his body to preserve the power. He caught O'Neill under the jaw. It wasn't enough to knock him out, but the IA sergeant took two steps backward and then landed on his ass. He was dazed, just enough that Spracklin could flee into the bushes.

"You're finished, Spracklin," he heard behind him. "We'll get your girl," O'Neill yelled. "And you won't be there to lie for her."

Spracklin knew he had to keep to the bushes in case the IA guys were following him. And he had to get to a phone. He walked swiftly, cutting west through the shaded paths along Kezar Drive, trying to get as far as he could from Park Station. He wondered why O'Neill's henchmen weren't pursuing him. Then he remembered Burwell. If the Sergeant had any use at all — a big if in Spracklin's books — it was as muscle. He was probably still wrestling with them. He saw a phone booth outside the bowling greens and tried to keep calm as he crossed the street. He didn't dare look around, and he wondered if there were officers coming up behind him. He lifted the receiver, plugged in a dime, dialed his home and stared at the hand-written notices of rooms for rent and peace rallies. He thought about what had just happened.

He had punched an Internal Affairs officer.

"Hellooo," said Valerie. Her chipper voice seemed surreal to him. He had just thrown away his career, their daughter faced criminal charges, and Val was sounding like a housewife in a laundry commercial. Spracklin knew he had to sound calm.

"Hi honey," he said. "How's everything?"

"Just fine. I was just about to start dinner. Roast chicken. It's going to get hot later in the week and we'll have cold chicken to pick at. You just missed Raymond Handell."

Shit, Spracklin thought. "Missed him?"

"Yes. He's in great form. Like the old days. Said he was north of Golden Gate so he stopped by to see if you were around."

That prick, thought Spracklin. *That bastard.* "Weird that he'd stop by looking for me in the middle of a work day."

"He said he knew what weird hours you kept. He set in to joshing Marie like he used to, singing that song from Westside Story to her." It was an old joke — Ray on one knee singing "Maria" — that had been funny when Marie was eight.

"But he left?"

"Yeah, he said he had to get back downtown. He and Marie left a few minutes ago."

"Marie?"

"He was asking her about that thing at the park, the concert her tapestry is hanging at. He offered to give her a ride into town to check on it."

Spracklin damned Ray Handell under his breath. He couldn't believe the bastard would go after his family.

"I thought Marie wasn't going in to the city today—not till tomorrow night, when I'm with her."

There was a pause at the other end. "It's odd, Jimmy. It was like when she saw Ray, she made an excuse that she had to go out, to the park, and Ray instantly offered to drive her. Said he was going that way anyway."

Spracklin wondered if he could get to the IA office before Handell got her inside. The more he thought about it, the more ridiculous he knew it was. Handell had Marie and he couldn't get her away from him. She would have to hold up under questioning. She would simply have to stick with his story. He realized Val was saying something.

"What's that, honey?" he asked.

"I said," she demanded slowly, "What's going on?"

"Nothing's going on."

"Jimmy, Marie acted strange as soon as she saw Raymond. Then he started acting strange—insisting he take her to the city. Now you're asking about it. What is this thing that everyone knows about except me?"

"Nothing. Ray, I guess, just wanted to give her a lift."

"Jimmy, tell me—"

"Listen, Val, I have to go. Something's come up. I'll call later."

He hung up on his wife and strode away from the payphone. He'd been in the open too long and had to get in the bushes. He wondered if he should just jump in a cab and head to the IA office. He could run interference for Marie. No, he thought. He'd just decked one of their officers and Marie would only get upset seeing her father arrested. He could only hope that she would hold up. He still could not believe what he'd done.

He had to take cover. He knew that the word among the patrolmen would spread—the head homicide detective had decked an IA tool and was on the lamb. Everyone on the force would be on the lookout for him—just so they could tell their buddies about being the one to bring him in. He had to hide.

He quickened his pace, but hoped it still looked casual. Once he hit the tree line on the road, he began to sprint to the thickest clump of trees he could find. As if by instinct, he headed toward Hippie Hill. If Marie did get free, he knew that she would meet him there. That's what they'd agreed—meet by the sound console near the stage. He clung to the trees as he climbed the gentle slope and found the hubbub of activity around the stage. Spracklin huddled by the eucalyptus trees and lit a cigarette. He needed to calm down. Someone on the stage was tuning a guitar, but Spracklin was focused only on the field, scanning it for cops. He searched for his daughter. She wasn't there. A woman on the stage began strumming her guitar and the kids near him began dancing. As he released a lungful of smoke, he realized he knew the singer. It was Martha, voluptuous Martha, swaying with the beat of her own strumming.

Spracklin saw J.D. Ehler standing at the far end of the stage, nodding his head with the beat. His folded arms clasped his clipboard to his chest and his hips moved to the music. He was smiling—possibly the first time Spracklin had ever seen it. Spracklin didn't need to talk to him to know what he was thinking: the festival was falling into place. The crowd was growing and the kids were even enjoying the acts they'd never heard of.

CHAPTER 33

Ray Handell continued to sing "Maria" as they crested the Golden Gate Bridge and began their smooth descent into San Francisco. He'd lowered the windows of his Lincoln Continental with an electric switch on the arm rest, and he belted out the West Side Story standard in a goofball baritone over the sound of the rushing wind. He was doing all he could to be Good Ol' Uncle Ray to the girl he'd always adored. And she smiled when he glanced over at her.

"You used to always get a kick out of this song," he yelled. "It's not funny anymore?"

"Sure it is," she said, and summoned up a laugh.

The problem was that she was no longer innocent little Marie who used to delight at bouncing on his knee and giggling at his funny faces. She was old enough to know he had overspent on this car in the middle of his divorce proceedings, figuring his greedy wife couldn't scoff it because he needed it for work. Her father had also told her Uncle Ray could barely afford payments on the car, and Spracklin always had to pay for the drinks when they got together at the bar. And now Uncle Ray was taking her in. He had betrayed her father and was ferrying her into San Francisco under the pretense of doing her a favor.

"I hope I'm not taking you out of your way, Uncle Ray," she said.

"Why would it be out of my way?"

"Well, you're heading downtown and I need to go to the Park."

She awaited his response but none came. She was right—he was up to something. He had been too insistent that he drive her into the city. She tried to act relaxed but her mind was racing. She had to figure out how to escape. She wondered what her father would do. Her father would keep him talking.

"Actually, Marie, honey, we have to make one stop before we go to the park."

"Where?"

"Downtown. It will take you out of the way a bit."

"Just let me out in the Presidio. I can take a bus."

"No, no, come see where I work."

"Internal Affairs?"

He seemed a bit taken aback. "Yes," he said. "Internal Affairs." She tried to think of something to say. He seemed to interpret her silence as disapproval. "I don't know what your dad told you about IA, but it's not like what people say. I want you to come and see it. I have a corner office, you know."

Corner office. It was a weird thing to say. She actually felt sorry for him. Her parents called him "Poor childless, divorced Ray." Maybe he wanted—yearned—for her to be impressed by his corner office. He was taking her in for questioning, but part of him still wanted to be the kindly uncle.

"Daddy hasn't really said much about IA," she said.

"Not much?"

"Well. Not when he's sober."

They stopped at a red light in the Presidio with the pine trees stretching high above them. A half-dozen anti-war protestors were crossing the road, carrying placards to the protest at the gates of the military base. Handell frowned at the hippies. He shook a cigarette out of its box and mouthed it. "What does he say when he's tanked?"

After a pause, Marie said, "Nothing."

"You can tell me, Marie. I won't tell him."

"You promise you won't tell him?"

Handell lit his cigarette. "Sure."

"He thinks the problem is you're not showing enough leader-ship." Marie swiveled in her seat and faced him. "You can't tell him, all right. He'd kill me, but I love you so much and I want you to do the right thing."

"Jesus, what did he say?" He took a long drag.

"Daddy, really respects you. You know that."

"Just tell me what he said."

"He said there are young Turks—that's what he called them, young Turks—who are calling the shots in IA and you should take control more. And he thinks there will be problems down the road."

"What sort of problems?"

She shifted back to face the front again. They were now rolling along the drive. "Daddy said if he becomes chief one thing he'll do is rein in Internal Affairs."

"He said that?"

"He wants you to stay in your post. He just wants you to lead the guys beneath you."

"I do lead them."

"Really, Uncle Ray? Are you the one who wants to bring me in now? Or is it the guys who work for you?"

He held his cigarette out the window and tapped off the ash. "It's me."

"So, you are bringing me in for questioning?"

Handell pulled up to another red light. "Marie, there are just a few things we want to get cleared up. Once we get some answers, I'll drive you to the park."

"Is it about the night Daddy arrested Fox and shot that man?"

"We need some answers."

She waited, actually forced herself to count three. Then she blurted out: "I have an alibi—but you can't tell Daddy. And especially not Mother."

He was surprised. "Everything will be confidential."

"I can tell you everything. Just you can't tell my parents."

CHAPTER 34

As Martha finished a song, Spracklin sat on a crate, drawing the final inches from a butt and trying to figure out what was happening. Handell had Marie—the one thing Ray had promised would not happen. He and his daughter were both wanted by the police force he'd devoted his life to. And it had happened just as he was making headway in finding the Byrne and Menendes killer.

With dusk falling and the temperature dropping, Ehler was halfway across Sharon Meadow, working with his lighting crew at two standards they'd set up in the middle of the field. The platforms were rickety, and the ancient spotlights looked like they'd been sitting in some high school auditorium since the Depression. Ehler and a couple of minions experimented with broadening and narrowing one spotlight as Martha sang one of Jasmine's standards.

> January in Oregon, a sunny, salty day
> Noon up on a sandstone cliff, admiring foamy spray
> My second tin of Schlitz Bull, chased with airy brine
> How can I take this with me, this perfect place in time?

Spracklin finished his cigarette and shuddered. He needed a drink. Nicotine just wasn't doing the trick. But he couldn't wander too far from Hippie Hill. The only thing he could do was wait and work the case. Maybe he could do right by Sarah Byrne and Pete Menendes.

He emptied his pockets to see what he'd grabbed before escaping O'Neill. He had his notebook—that was essential. Folded into it was the article torn from *The Oracle*, and also the photo of Sarah Byrne sitting in the room where her fiancé would be shot. And he had Bloom's note and the scrap of paper he found in the murderer's bedroom. He was going to take a look at his list of suspects, but something caught his eye.

As Martha came out of a guitar solo, a red glow reflected on to his notes. Looking up, he saw Ehler had moved to the other lighting booth. That projector had a disc of colored screens in front of the lens, so it could cast light in different colors. A long-haired kid was turning the disc, changing the beam of light from red to green. He had no shirt but wore an oven mitt to protect his hand from the light. As the light washing over her changed color, Martha kept singing.

> *Eight-thousand miles' meandering have led me to*
> *   this place*
> *A year since I first thought I'd brave*
> *   suburbanite disgrace*
> *It's led me to a state of mind, for I'm just realizin'*
> *The endless possibilities stretched 'cross the blue horizon*

The hundred-odd people at the foot of the hill erupted in cheers as she finished the song. Martha bowed, and pointed to the far side of the stage. The spotlight shone a narrow beam on to Jasmine, who was hanging out with a few musicians, listening to Martha sing her song. The crowd howled their approval. Spracklin heard a male voice yell, "Marry me, Jasmine!" It was Rimshaw, swaying and grinning like a drunken lout.

Spracklin had not noticed the bikers before. There were five guys in Satan's Hosts colors at the foot of the hill, blending into the crowd in the fading light. Rimshaw was the biggest and stood out. Spracklin saw Duble and three others he hadn't seen before, they obviously had a good lawyer. Polgar was right about there being five of them.

Spracklin looked at the sky and wondered if it was dark enough to steal out of the park to a bar. It was risky. He stood, stretched, and looked across the field to the lights around Park Station shining through the trees. He had an idea. It was audacious but it could work. He began to walk down the hill. As he reached the bottom, he glanced around and noticed the bikers camped out with the other revelers. Rimshaw had noticed him, and pointed him out to Duble. Spracklin would worry about that later. Crossing the field, Spracklin glanced at Ehler. He was arguing with the lighting crew member, who insisted the spotlight was burning his hand, even with the oven mitt. Spracklin turned at the Sharon Art Center and headed up toward Park Station. It was a quiet time of day. Patrols were out but it would be hours before they brought in burglars or brawlers for booking. Spracklin paused once then walked at a normal pace into the parking lot. No one was there, but he still looked nonchalant. He took out his keys as he strode to the Monaco. Still no one. He unlocked the door, retrieved the flask of scotch from under the seat and stashed it in his pocket. He pushed down the door lock, slammed the door, and walked out of the parking lot, heading west back toward the payphone he had used earlier.

In the shadows of the trees, he took a belt of scotch. The whisky fortified him, and he felt bold enough to check in with the office again. He walked casually to the payphone, and plugged in a dime and dialed. He finished off the scotch as the phone rang and he tossed the empty into the bushes.

"Inspectors, Burwell," said a gruff voice after the third ring.

"Spracklin," said the Lieutenant, turning away from the road. "What's happening?"

"What's happening?" repeated Burwell. "Let's see. What's happening is that we've recovered a few hundred grand in stereo gear from Minglewood Music, and Commercial Crimes is taking credit for it. We're closing in on a double murderer and all that the brass cares about is where you are. And the head of the homicide division is a fugitive. Other than that, nothing much."

"What do you mean, closing in on a double murderer?" asked Spracklin.

Burwell quickly told him about the raid at Minglewood Music. He'd gone to the store in the afternoon, posing as a shopper, and saw a large sale on Marantz amplifiers and receivers. He jotted down model and serial numbers and ran it by the Oakland police by phone. The numbers matched, so they brought in the SFPD Commercial Crimes division. They raided the place at about 5:30 p.m. and began questioning Edward Schultz, the owner and manager of the store. Burwell said that Schultz wasn't the dummy he'd expected: no prison tats or denim, just pressed flares and an expensive mod haircut. And he held up well in the first half-hour of questioning. "So, in the middle of it, Gillis is needling him about—"

"Who?"

"The head of Commercial Crimes."

"Arty Gillis."

"Yeah him. He's needling him about the heist from the container terminal, and I jump in and start asking about the company in Cayman Islands. Gillis looks at me like I got three heads. So, Gillis is trying to hush me up and Schultz is denying any knowledge and—"

"Ed, I can't talk long."

Burwell thought about it for a second, and said, "Yeah. Right. We brought Schultz back downtown but it was just as much of a shitshow. I wanted to get to the bottom of his relationship with Sarah Byrne, and Gillis wants a medal for busting him on a 496 PC." Spracklin had to think back to his days before homicide to remember—possession of stolen property.

"Ed."

"Right. Here's what I got. Schultz lawyered up and won't discuss the Cayman Islands company. He admitted to knowing Sarah Byrne, but not well. And he has alibis for Sunday night and last night. Home with his family all Sunday night—a bit weak, I guess. But last night he and his staff kept the shop open till 9 p.m. That one's iron-clad."

"No evidence linking him to the killings?"

"No. I asked him if he had two heads hidden in his shop and he said no."

"Look, Ed, I got—"

"That was a joke, Jimmy."

"Yeah, I get it. Now listen up. The Satan's Host bikers, we have alibis for three of 'em, right?"

"Meant to tell you—they got a lawyer and they walked."

"But there are five of them here tonight. I ran into Bogdan Polgar today and he told me there have been five in San Francisco all along. There's two members of the gang we don't have alibis for on Sunday night."

"Should I put out an APB?"

Spracklin could have told Burwell where they were. But he didn't need cops from Park Station flooding Hippie Hill right now. He had to stay there in case Marie showed up.

"Sure," said Spracklin. There was silence on the line and Spracklin said, "What did the IA guys say?"

"That you're a criminal and need to be brought in."

"Are you buying it?"

"Would I be talking to you now if I bought it?" Spracklin wanted to thank him but couldn't find the words. "IA and your wife don't buy it, but I do."

"My wife?"

"She's been calling. Repeatedly."

"Calling you?" Spracklin's heart sank as he thought about what the recent events would be doing to Val.

"Calling everybody. Where's my husband? Where's my daughter? What's going on? And she's telling anyone who'll listen that you can return her daughter to her then go check yourself into the YMCA."

Spracklin keyed in on the word "daughter." Val didn't know where Marie was. "Marie," he said. "What's going on with Marie?"

"Everyone wants to know that. Even the IA guys were asking me if I knew anything about your daughter. That girl's in a world of trouble, Jimmy." He chuckled. "By the way, your photos came in—the prints of the negatives in the safe deposit box. You were right—there were incriminating shots in there. William Byrne going into The Stud and getting into a sports car outside Compton's Cafeteria."

"Gay bars?"

"Yep. Looks like there's still an heiress to the Byrne fortune." Burwell paused for Spracklin to laugh, but the joke fell flat.

"Lock those photos away," said Spracklin. "And don't spend too much time on Schultz. I doubt he killed her and he'll be locked up on the possession charges if we need him."

Spracklin hung up and thought about what he'd learned. William Byrne was a homosexual. The perfect son from an upstanding Catholic family, a man who worshiped his straight-as-an-arrow father, was gay. Spracklin understood what the young man would do to keep that secret. Val was hysterical and IA was asking about Marie. Spracklin should have asked Burwell how long ago they'd been asking. For all he knew, they could have released Marie by now. He had to get back to Hippie Hill.

CHAPTER 35

He didn't like using a phone booth so close to Park Station, but he was in a rush. He needed to talk to the boss, the arrogant old prick, and he needed to do it fast. He looked up and down Stanyon but couldn't see anyone suspicious. The boss's phone had rung eight or nine times now, but he wasn't going to hang up. *Pick up, asshole*, he thought. He checked the street again.

He'd been in a bad mood all day. It had begun with the let-down of the job the night before. He knew he should have been pleased with the hit going so smoothly. Get in the room, put the guy against the wall, turn up the music, two shots to the head, cut the head off, and leave. It was — he'd pondered the right word all morning — clinical. It was a clinical strike with none of the euphoria of killing Sarah Byrne. It was a job.

Dusk was falling and the late afternoon crowd was moving into Haight-Ashbury — the young San Franciscans who worked in other parts of the city and came to the Haight after dark to find a party. Their numbers were dwindling but some still came. Two college kids — you could tell college kids a mile away — were walking hand in hand toward the park. Three gays were across the street photographing each other with Haight Street in the background. It was becoming familiar, but it was still intoxicating.

"What is it?" asked the husky voice.

"It's me."

"Were you successful?"

"Are you shadowing me?"

"Huh." He heard a rustling of papers. The boss was doing something else and didn't want to be disturbed.

"I asked you a simple question and...."

"Hang on." The boss muzzled the receiver. There were voices, some discussion, and then the boss was back again. "Have you been successful?"

"What do you think?"

"Don't give me that shit, Sonny. I gave you a job to do. Have you done it?"

"No. I was at the place we agreed on but the person in question never emerged." He was careful not to mention Spracklin, his daughter or the house in Sausalito. "Then a cop came. At least he looked like a cop."

"Her father?"

"No. Someone else. And he left with her. Driving a Lincoln Continental. But someone else is following me around Haight-Ashbury. I can tell he's following me. I need to know if it's you."

"Why would I tail you? Unless it's to see if you're doing your job, which you obviously aren't."

"Well someone is tailing me."

There was no response. There wasn't even the sound of papers being shuffled. Finally, the boss spoke: "Do you need to be recalled?"

"No."

"You've done the easy part. We knew it was going to get harder. Now just go do it. You should head north."

He looked up and down Stanyon again. He couldn't help himself. "She'll be coming across the bridge. As long as that concert's on, she'll be coming. It's just." He looked again. "I'm noticing the presence of people I don't like. I need to know whether it's you."

"No. Now should I give this job to someone else?"

"No. I'm good. I'll get it done." He replaced the receiver and checked the change slot to see if his dime had been returned. It hadn't. He looked up and down the street again and headed back to work. He tried not to think of it as work. The next mark was female. It would be as intimate as the first one.

CHAPTER 36

Marie wondered why she hadn't tried crying before. Men were suckers for tears, and none more so than Uncle Ray. She buried her face in her hands and tried to fake crying. It was a good enough act that he pulled the car over.

"Marie, honey."

"I'm sorry, Uncle Ray. It's just that...." She lowered her hands and shuddered. "That night is like a nightmare to me. I came in and that man was lying in a pool of blood and the gun smoke and...." She stopped. She didn't know if she should risk her fake crying again so she just stared into space. She tried to get her bearings without looking around. They were on Lombard, near Divisadero. She wanted to just throw open the door and run, but she was about a mile north of the shelter of Haight-Ashbury. It was a hilly mile as well. Ray had a car. She wouldn't make it to the Haight on foot. She needed a plan to get away from him.

"I'm sure it was hard, Marie. Now look...." He was choosing his words carefully, trying to calm her. He took out a cigarette and pushed in the lighter on the dashboard. "I've known you forever. I don't want you to get into trouble. If there's information you need to share with me, but don't want your parents to know, let me know. I won't tell them." He broke into a smile that bordered on a chuckle. "Nothing would make me happier, sweetheart, than to just cross Marie off my list."

She said nothing. She hadn't realized she was on his fucking list. She pretended to just be staring ahead in shock, but she was trying to think of a plan. Her father always said a slow liar was bad liar. She had to make something up fast.

"That's all that would happen, Marie," said Handell, lighting his cigarette. "If you just tell me what happened that night, then we can just stop worrying about you."

"I only got to Andy's pad when it happened. I mean, I was coming in the door when I heard a shot. I had no idea Daddy was inside, or what was happening. I went in. Andy's friend was...." She buried her face in her hands. "There was smoke in the air. Daddy was there and he shot Andy."

"I thought you were upstairs?"

She looked at her feet and said, "That's what I told Daddy. I was, well, I was out."

"Can you prove it?"

"Someone can back up my story, Uncle Ray," she said slowly.

"Who?"

"You can't tell my parents. You just can't."

"I won't."

"It was a woman. Annie Driscoll. She teaches transcendental meditation, has a studio on Page Street."

"Okay. You were with her that night?"

"Yes. Yes. I was." She was silent, motionless.

"Where?"

Marie waited a beat and said, "In her bed."

Handell took a long drag on his cigarette. He nodded, clearly understanding why Marie couldn't tell her parents. "What time were you with her?"

"Well, this is the thing, Uncle Ray. I know exactly when I left. We were in bed, just rapping. At her place in the back of her studio. And suddenly we hear noise outside. People screaming. Television was blasting from upstairs. So, Annie switches on her clock radio and we hear that Senator Kennedy has been shot. And I'm like, I know that man. I remember sitting on his knee in Washington. And Annie—she's a real peacenik—she's going, 'It's the military industrial complex that killed him.' I'm in mourning and she's launching a sermon about the war industry—"

"Do you know when you left her studio?"

"That's the thing: I'd had enough of her and I wanted to be with Andy, my boyfriend." She looked at him with a bashful glance. "I know. It was complicated. But I do remember that clock radio said zero-zero-four-three when I left. It was one of those new ones that have two zeros for midnight. So, I probably got to that house where Andy was staying at about 1 a.m."

"And Annie can back up your story?"

"Sure. You want to meet her? You just can't tell my parents about her."

"That would be great. Where's her studio?"

"Over in Haight-Ashbury."

Handell started the car again, and turned right on to Divisadero. As he moved up and down the hills leading to Haight-Ashbury, Marie sat in silence, working on the next part of her plan.

"What time is it?" she asked.

Handell checked his watch. "Ten to five."

"Oh."

"Problem?"

"Well, at five each day Annie does outdoor meditation session with her followers. That's what she calls them. They'll be outside now."

"You know where?"

"Yeah. Just park on Haight, near Baker."

Handell turned on to Haight Street and found a parking spot uphill on Buena Vista Avenue East, beneath the turret of a beige Victorian house. The vast hill of Buena Vista rose above them. They got out of the car, and Marie looked up at the wooded hill. "Annie likes to get away from the smog and noise of the city in her sessions. She thinks Buena Vista has the best ambience for her group."

She crossed the street to the wall at the foot of the great, tree-lined mound. Ray Handell fell in behind her and they began to climb. The afternoon was growing cooler and they avoided the discomfort of climbing the hill in the heat.

"You're sure she's here?" puffed Handell, beginning to fall behind Marie. "And she can corroborate your story?"

Marie looked back and kept walking. "Oh yes. I mean, it was the last time we had a…meaningful encounter. She remembers it."

"Marie, can you slow down?" He laughed. "I'm not young anymore."

"Come on, Uncle Ray," she said, quickening her pace. "You'll like Annie. Don't be prejudiced about my relationship with her." She glanced back again. Handell was leaning against a tree, panting. "She's just a wonderful person."

"Marie, hold up."

"I can't wait to see her."

Marie was panting as well now, but she kept climbing. It was always a bugger of a hill. She had probably been up there twice in all the time she'd been around Haight-Ashbury. She hated climbing it. But she didn't smoke and Ray Handell was a pack-a-day man. The winding paths were shrouded in trees. Soon she could no longer hear Ray Handell shouting after her. She just kept climbing. At the top, she would go down the west side and make her way to Golden Gate Park.

CHAPTER 37

Spracklin stood in the dark at the base of Hippie Hill and estimated about a hundred kids were huddled into little groups
in front of the empty stage. Someone in the field was playing
Top 40 hits on a transistor radio. Some hippies were passing a joint
around as they sat on the hood of a Mercury Comet parked at the
far end of the crowd. The Satan's Host bikers — five of them — were
sitting cross-legged on blankets, their bikes standing in a row behind
them. As well as the two thugs they had arrested the previous day,
there were three new guys, two of them younger bucks with slicked
back hair. They seemed quiet for now, and Spracklin was happy just
to leave them where they were, in his sight.

Then one of the younger bikers stirred. Spracklin wondered
if the guy was going to come after him. But no, he was going the
other way, toward Haight Street. Spracklin then noticed two people coming toward Hippie Hill from Haight-Ashbury. A black man
and a white woman, walking hand in hand. The guy was carrying
a bedroll. They stopped and looked at the biker advancing toward
them. Spracklin couldn't hear what was being said, but he saw the
mixed-race couple turn and head back the way they'd come. The
biker watched them go then returned to his comrades and their
bikes. Spracklin realized that Jack Rimshaw had spotted him and
was studying him. The biker chieftain said something to Duble, who
turned to watch the Lieutenant.

Spracklin strode up the hill, keen to get away from the bik-
ers, and looking without success for Marie. He wondered whether
Handell was keeping her for the night. *That bastard.* Handell was the
IA turd he should have belted.

Ehler and his team were sitting in a circle beneath some electric
lights attached to the soundboard. They were drinking Budweiser
and smoking cigarettes. They would be here all night, making sure

no one vandalized the stage or equipment. There were about twenty of them, including some of the singers who would perform the next day — Martha, Ralph May, some fat guy with a headband that Spracklin had seen before.

May was strumming a guitar and singing a folk song. It was that "Blowing in the Wind" song that Peter, Paul and Mary had recorded a few years back. Spracklin sat on the edge of the stage and assessed May's talent — mediocre guitarist, all right singer, extremely good looking. There was another quality he had — he sang with conviction, as if he believed the message of someone else's song. Martha stood and fetched two Budweisers from a tub of ice behind the stage. She sat beside Spracklin, levered the caps off with a church key and handed him one.

"That's a buck for two beer, you know," said Ehler, who'd been eyeing the beer vat.

"Dock it from my pay," said Martha. She winked at him and clinked bottles with Spracklin.

Ehler had no response. Spracklin couldn't see the clipboard. For once Ehler was relaxing, leaning on an elbow, drinking a beer, and listening to the music. He seemed less intense now. May finished "Blowing in the Wind" and launched immediately into a song about marines landing at Santo Domingo.

"Catchy tune," said Spracklin to Martha. "Did he write that?"

She shook her head and took a swig of beer. "A guy called Phil Ochs wrote it. A Greenwich Village activist and songwriter. Ralph's hero." She was speaking loud enough that May could hear her.

"He seems to like the topical songs — must be committed to the cause." Spracklin took a sip of his watery beer and wished he still had his flask of whisky.

Martha laughed.

"What's so funny?"

"He's committed to his own libido." May flinched, clearly hearing what she said. "Look at the girls around him. Cheryl there and the redhead with the tattoos." Spracklin looked at the two young women she gestured at. They were entranced by May, hanging on every note he sang. "We're in the sixties, Lieutenant. There's no more effective aphrodisiac than moral outrage in four-four time. Post-modern panty-remover."

May looked over at her with a sour expression. Without interrupting his strumming, he said, "I heard that." Then he added, "Unfair."

She laughed again. "He knows it's the truth." Spracklin noticed the girls had also heard her and didn't seem put off. She nodded at a quiet boy who wore a blue bandana as a headband. "Alvin here is into the music." Spracklin thought he had heard Alvin playing keyboards earlier. "But Ralph, he sings instead of spiking their drinks."

A blush spread across Ralph's clear complexion, and the olive eyes gleamed with a smile. Just looking at him, Spracklin knew the kid didn't need music to break hearts. He was good looking and had an easy charm. "We can agree on one thing," he told Martha. "Alvin was born to play jazz. He's the next Monk."

Spracklin tossed the empty beer can into the bushes and circled the crowd to get another. He noticed Ehler's eyes following him. *Cheap bastard*, thought Spracklin. "That didn't last long?" said Ehler.

"Beer never does it for me," said Spracklin. "Like drinking water."

Ehler nodded, stood, and gestured for Spracklin to follow him. They wandered behind Marie's backdrop to a place where Ehler's crew had piled crates of gear, coils of wire, and leftover scaffolding. He lifted a guitar case off a crate, unlocked the box and lifted the wooden lid. He didn't open it wide, just enough for Spracklin to see dozens of pint bottles. Ehler reached in and pulled out a mickey of Bacardi.

"Five bucks," he said to Spracklin.

"Five? For that piss?"

"I'll get six bucks for it tomorrow night, maybe seven," said Ehler. "And don't tell me you helped me out today. I already gave you a beer for that."

"So, you're a bootlegger."

"I'm a businessman. I gotta cover my losses on this concert."

"You're not much of a businessman if it loses money."

"Gotta start somewhere. Once I do this one, I'll make a name for myself and do others. Five bucks."

Spracklin looked at the rum. "You got any scotch?" Ehler shook his head. "Four bucks," said Spracklin. Ehler moved to return the bottle to the crate and Spracklin stopped him. "Okay, okay." He removed a five-dollar bill from his wallet and paid the young man. He knew bootleggers needed a markup. Ehler pocketed the money, locked the crate, and patted Spracklin on the shoulder.

As Ehler sauntered back to the side of the stage, Spracklin tore the seal on the rum, took a sip, then another. He took another before slipping the bottle into his back pocket. He decided to wander into the bushes for a piss and a few more nips. Up by the stage, he could hear Martha now teasing a teenage girl about her mushy poems for someone called Bob Weir. Spracklin tried to act nonchalant as he wandered into the bushes.

He walked past the spot where they'd found the headless girl and into the stand of eucalyptus trees. He looked around to make sure no one could see him. He found a secluded spot and began to relieve himself against a tree. Spracklin drank a bit more rum, a big gulp this time. It filled his mouth and burned its way down his throat, filling him with slight nausea and overwhelming relief.

He slipped the flask into his back pocket, and did up his zipper. He was about to head up the hill when he realized how much rum he'd drunk. That last gulp was a big one. He steadied himself against a tree, and realized he wasn't alone. Standing off across a dirt path, maybe thirty yards away, was Louis Dupre. The stocky biker was frozen in the ambient light of the park at nighttime. He seemed to be smiling at Spracklin. Then everything went dark.

Someone had thrown a coat over Spracklin's head and yanked him backward. He was blinded and the collar cut into his throat. He couldn't breathe. He flailed at the attacker behind him. His fist hit a head, but at an angle that wouldn't hurt anyone. He could feel greasy hair on his forearm. Then came the blow to his ribs. As one guy held him from behind, someone was in front hammering him in the gut. He doubted Dupre could have got to him that quickly.

Satan's Host was after him. He was getting too close, and Dupre had taken a beating from the cops earlier that day. Now they were retaliating. The rumors about the bike gang now flooded Spracklin's thoughts—revenge killings, territorial reprisals, beheadings. With the pain shooting up and down his left side, he tried kicking in front of him, but his legs caught in the thick ferns and he couldn't land a blow.

Spracklin reached inside his coat and brought out his revolver as another fist hit his gut. He struggled to breathe and secure the handgun. The guy in front of him whacked the gun out of his hands. All Spracklin could do now was to go on the defensive. He crossed his forearms in front of his face and tried to crouch over to deny his attacker another shot at his gut.

The guy behind kicked out Spracklin's left foot and he crashed to the bushy ground. One of them tried kicking him, but now the ferns were helping Spracklin. The smelly coat was still on his head but he could just see his attacker's boot ensnared in the ferns. Spracklin rolled on to his belly and lay as flat as he could. The two bikers — they had to be bikers — were standing on either side of him and kicking. With each kick, they tore ferns from the ground and delivered painful blows to his side.

Spracklin grabbed one of the legs and pulled at it. He felt the biker hit the ground beside him. Driven by panic, Spracklin moved like a man half his age. Springing on to the prostrate biker, he flailed at the young man's head with his fists. He was straddling one of the guys with the slick-backed hair, hammering him with both hands. He felt a kick in the ribs but he just kept thumping his victim. If he could knock one out, at least it would be a fair fight.

There was a crash on the side of Spracklin's head and he toppled to the ground again. Dazed he looked up to see a biker moving in on him. It was the other kid with slicked hair. The guy was muscular — not as big as Rimshaw but strong. He'd picked up a stick, about a yard of thick hardwood, and he was angry that Spracklin had fought back. Spracklin looked around for a weapon of his own, but could find nothing.

"Freeze," said a woman's voice.

Spracklin and the biker both looked in the same direction. Marie was crouching by a tree with Spracklin's handgun trained on the biker. Her arm was braced on a low branch. It would be a dead certain kill if she pulled the trigger.

"Drop the stick."

The biker, his slicked hair now disheveled, looked at the girl. Spracklin could tell he was wondering if he should take his chances with this tender young thing. But there was something in Marie's voice — its even tone, its certainty. He lowered the stick and tossed it into the far bushes. Spracklin and the second biker both rose and looked at the girl with the gun. The two young bikers glanced at each other and began to move away. There was no sign of Dupre, who had obviously left the beating to the two juniors. Spracklin walked over to his daughter. His priority now was taking the revolver from her. The worst thing that could happen would be for her to pull the trigger. As the two bikers retreated into the darkness, Spracklin placed his hand on his daughter's wrist. He could feel it trembling. He knew she was having flashbacks to the last time she had held a handgun.

Spracklin holstered the gun and hugged his daughter. She wrapped her arms around him and breathed heavily. His aches and bruises were nothing to him now. He felt as if a massive weight had been lifted from his shoulders. Marie was safe.

"Handell let you go?" he said.

"I got away. What was this about?"

Spracklin looked into the darkness where the bikers had retreated. "We, ah, had a melee with one of Satan's Host this morning. It looks like they put these two rookies up to paying me back— an initiation ritual." He turned to her. "You ran from Ray?"

She broke away from her father and shook her head. They began to walk up toward the stage and Marie explained what had happened. "So," she said when they were seated on the grass near the stage. She was trying to put a brave face on what had happened, "the good news is I got away. The bad news is you have a gay daughter."

She gave a weak laugh, and Spracklin just nodded. "They came to get me at Park Station today," he said. "One of Handell's flunkies. I, ah, I got away from them. I tried warning you at home but Ray had already picked you up."

"What do you mean they came to get you?"

"O'Neill, this guy who works under Ray. He said they have a witness who saw a dark-haired girl at the airport, picking up Sarah Byrne. If it's you, then it contradicts my story." He let her digest the implications of what he was saying. "We've delayed them today, but eventually they're going to catch us. We may have to admit you picked up Sarah. I still have to claim the shooting."

They sat in silence and listened to the banter of the hippies, dominated by Martha. "Come on, Ralph," she was laughing. "Sing with some feeling. Sororities across America want to feel your outrage."

"If I just wanted to attract women, wouldn't I sing love songs?" he asked. "I sing protest songs—listen carefully—as an act of protest."

"Protesting against a few hours of celibacy, maybe but...." She continued talking, but Spracklin couldn't hear above the laughter of the others. Even the pretty girls were laughing with her now. Spracklin was trying to understand the dynamic. Ralph seemed to be enjoying the ribbing, the notoriety of being a ladies' man. But the other guys in the circle were laughing too loud, as if they enjoyed seeing the lover-boy taken down a peg or two. As he thought about it, Marie got up and walked to the tub of ice and beer. Ehler was eyeing her but said nothing.

"Say what you will. I've written songs that have meaning for me. I sing them from the heart."

Marie opened two beer and walked back to her father, handing one to him. He felt he should forbid her from having beer, but it just didn't seem right.

"So, what are you going to do?" she asked. The circle of hippies was singing along with Ralph May as he strummed "We Shall Overcome." The two Spracklins could now talk between themselves. "Hide out here for the rest of your career?"

He shrugged and took another sip of beer. Inferior goddamn drink, he thought. You feel bloated before you feel drunk. He didn't want to take out his rum bottle with Marie around. "Dunno," he said. "I just...." His voice faded. He couldn't tell his daughter that his career was through and that her mother wanted to throw him out. He couldn't bear the thought of Marie knowing that he was becoming a colossal failure. "I'm reverting to my natural state, honey." He reached into his pocket and pulled out his notebook and other papers that he'd saved before he fled Park Station. "I'm doing the only thing I know how to do. I'm working on solving the case and figuring out who killed Sarah Byrne and her boyfriend."

He flipped open his notebook to the list of suspects. Marie squinted in the dim light, quickly reading over the list of suspects and Spracklin's notes by name. She nodded slowly, knowing just enough about what had been in the newspaper to understand most of it.

"Her brother was being blackmailed?"

Spracklin glanced at the hippies nearby to make sure no one was listening. He whispered, "Sarah had photos of him outside a gay bar. They were in her safe deposit box."

Marie nodded and then pointed to the other paper in his left hand. "And why do you have a set list?"

"This was a piece of trash we found in the murderer's apartment. I didn't know what it was. What did you call it? A set list?"

"Sure. J.D. handed it out to everyone two days ago. To performers and staff."

Marie went silent and her eyes widened as she studied the names on the crumpled paper. She slowly turned her head and her eyes met her father's. She glanced toward the others, and he knew not to say anything. She kept an eye on J.D. Ehler as she reached for the clipboard on the far side of her father. She flicked one sheet then another till she found the page she was looking for. The heading at the top of the mimeographed sheet read:

SET LIST - TOP SECRET

And below there was a list of people. Ehler had penciled in notes around them—the times they would play at the concert and the songs they would sing. The middle of the mimeographed sheet was exactly the same as the paper Spracklin had found in the murderer's wastepaper basket. It listed performers called Jack, Mabel, the Still Lifes, and a poetry reading, all to take place between 1:30 and 3:40 Friday morning. The list then moved on to acts that even Spracklin had heard of, ending with Jasmine at 4:35 followed by the entire cast singing "Morning Has Broken."

Marie pointed to the two words at the heading—TOP SECRET. She slid the clipboard back to its previous position and leaned over.

"I was here the other day when J.D. handed out the set lists. He told everyone to keep it secret." She looked at the circle of hippies, including J.D. Ehler. They were still gabbing and ignoring Spracklin and his daughter. "He wants everyone to believe the rumors that the Grateful Dead is going to show up. He only gave the set list to a few people."

"A few people? So, the killer has something to do with this concert," mumbled Spracklin, afraid even to move his lips.

Marie nodded her head and they surveyed the circle of hippies, singing songs and telling jokes.

CHAPTER 38

The sound of birds woke Spracklin, then he became aware of other sounds: men talking, distorted music from a transistor radio, far-off traffic. He opened his eyes and saw great eucalyptus trees against blue sky. The sun was high—he had slept until mid-morning. To his right, he saw a tangle of black hair beside him. Marie. Marie had come to Hippie Hill the night before. In the fog of semi-sleep, he smiled at the joy he felt when he saw his little girl—now a brave young woman. He tried lifting his head and felt electrifying pain—in his side from his bruises, and his head from a hangover.

Beer, he knew, was a dreadful drink, and no matter how much rum he drank to wash away its evils, he still felt like crap the day after drinking it. It never got him drunk or happy but he always felt like hell the morning after. He lit a cigarette, hoping it would get the shitty beer taste out of his mouth. He knew he looked like a wino—his pants and jacket were wrinkled and he hadn't shaved in days. He was about to stretch, but pain shot through his ribs. He remembered the bikers put a beating on him. As his head cleared, he began to remember the tasks ahead. He removed the cigarette, coughed up a wad of phlegm, which he hawked into the bushes. He shook Marie gently. They had to move. Handell and his gang would be looking for them, they had to keep their eyes peeled.

Marie sat up, looking as bad as he felt. He and Martha had allowed Marie to have a few beers, he guessed. The headache told him he had drunk more than he thought, and obviously his daughter had as well. He couldn't see Martha anywhere.

"Morning," said Spracklin. "Any idea what happened to Martha?"

When Marie spoke, her voice was groggy. "Probably went off to discover underwear."

Spracklin walked into the bushes to take a leak, and began to think about the case. He had to get to William Byrne immediately. But he couldn't drive downtown as his car was at Park Station. He would have to get a cab, and that meant he would have to wait until a bank opened. He needed cash. What a fucking mess. He surveyed his surroundings. Ehler was on the stage, getting organized for his big day, and volunteers were poking around the stage. In all, there were about twenty kids sleeping at the foot of Hippie Hill, making sure they would have prime spots that night. The bikers were still in their bedrolls near their bikes. *Bastards*, thought Spracklin.

Marie hobbled out of the bushes, wiping her mouth. She staggered up to him and he put his arm around her, feeling guilty. He could smell the vomit on her breath. He should never have let her drink beer. He thought she'd only had a couple, but maybe she had snuck a few while he wasn't watching. Or while he was in the bushes polishing off his rum. He squeezed her tight and asked if she was all right. She nodded. He looked up to see Martha coming over the crest of the hill, carrying coffees and a paper bag. She stopped by the stage, where Ehler was going over some notes. She handed him a coffee and a newspaper, and wandered over to Spracklin and Marie.

"I thought my campers might need some breakfast," she said with a smile, flopping down on the slope facing them. She had changed her shirt to a looser afghan. When she moved, Spracklin could tell she still wasn't wearing a bra, but it was a bit more discreet than her white T-shirt. Martha handed over the coffees and set the bag in front of them. It was full of donuts.

Marie accepted the coffee but decided against a donut.

"You must be starving," said Martha. "Go ahead. Today will be busy with the festival. Who knows when you'll be eating again?"

Marie thanked her. She took a coffee and sipped it. Spracklin took a loud slurp of his coffee and pulled a donut from the paper bag. "This is just what the doctor ordered," said Spracklin. "Marie, have a donut."

Marie looked away. "I'm not big on breakfast," she said.

"All the more for you, Jimmy," said Martha with a wink. "And I can always get extra if you need them. Maybe some sandwiches."

"I may need some cigarettes later."

"Just let me know," said Martha. Gesturing uphill toward J.D. Ehler, she added, "And give me a bit of warning. I'm on call."

Ehler was poring over the newspaper, and he looked up at Spracklin. Something in his expression told the Lieutenant there was a problem.

"I think you got bigger problems than a hangover," J.D. Ehler called over to him.

"What d'ya mean?" asked Spracklin, his voice hoarse.

Ehler gestured with his head, telling the Lieutenant to come over. Spracklin and Marie wandered over, and their eyes were immediately drawn to the photo at the bottom of Page 1. It showed the Department's file photo of Spracklin in his lieutenant's uniform

SFPD Searches for Spracklin After Assault
By Jack Pittman

The San Francisco Police Department is searching for one of its most senior officers, Lieut. James Spracklin, after the head of the Bureau of Inspectors allegedly assaulted another officer yesterday.

The SFPD is making no public statements, however people close to the matter say Spracklin is wanted for questioning regarding a fatal shooting during a drug seizure in Haight-Ashbury earlier this month. When Internal Affairs officers questioned Spracklin at Park Station on Wednesday, the lieutenant assaulted one of the IA officers and fled.

It is a bizarre turn of events for an officer who has recently been touted as a possible replacement for Chief Edgar "Bud" Hawkings....

Spracklin seethed as he skimmed the article. He glanced over his shoulder in the direction of Park Station, as if he should see hordes of cops—his colleagues—charging across the field to get him. He wanted to kill Ray Handell. He'd crossed the line twice now. He'd gone after Spracklin's daughter and he'd leaked stuff against an officer to the press. It wasn't the way to handle things.

"I got a copy of the paper to check the ad I put in about the concert," said Ehler, as if he should apologize for having the paper. "When I looked at it, like, all I saw was your photo. Kind of freaked me out."

Spracklin was too angry for words. He felt as if all the world was scrutinizing him. But he looked around and the hippies were still in their morning fog. None seemed aware of the brewing scandal that engulfed someone in their midst. Only Marie seemed stunned. Her bleary eyes stared at him in disbelief.

"You assaulted an officer?" she asked.

Spracklin shrugged his shoulders. "I got in a scrap."

He wanted to leave it at that but she pressed him. "When?"

"In the afternoon."

"So, you decked a cop in the afternoon and got in a fight with bikers at night?"

Before Spracklin could answer, Ehler cut in. "You were fighting with bikers?" He glanced down the hill and pointed at the sleeping Satan's Host members. "Them?"

Spracklin shrugged again. "They jumped me in the woods."

Ehler stared at him in disbelief. "You're a cop, for Godsakes. Bust 'em."

"And take them where?" Spracklin realized how bizarre this was. He was explaining to a hippie why he couldn't arrest outlaws on Haight Street. "What's it to you, anyway?"

"I'd love to get rid of those fascists," said Ehler. "They were in that fight yesterday. They scare people. They're beating up on any African-American who comes near this stage. They threatened to run me off till I told them there's no show without me."

Spracklin looked over at the sleeping bikers. "When did this happen?"

"Two days ago. They were pushing me around, asking me what part of Fillmore I was from and who I work for. Weird shit like that." Ehler folded the newspaper and shoved it in an accordion file into the crate. "I don't want them here. Shit, if you can get rid of them, it's fine with me."

"Fillmore, huh?" said Spracklin. He looked again at the five bikers in their sleeping bags, bottles littered around them. He knew that now was his time to act. Spracklin didn't like taking his daughter into the circle of bikers, but he couldn't leave her alone. He grabbed her hand and led her down the hill. There was a gap of about two yards around the five members of Satan's Host and the other kids, as if the hippies themselves didn't like to get too close to them. Jack

Rimshaw stirred as Spracklin stepped into their space and straddled one of the kids who'd attacked him last night. Marie crouched at the edge of the circle.

"You here to arrest me again?" asked Rimshaw. He stared up at Spracklin and broke into a slow, stoned smile.

Spracklin already had his handcuffs out and secured the wrist of one of the young kids. The boy seemed to be still drunk or stoned — he barely moved. Moving swiftly, Spracklin passed the handcuffs through the spokes and prongs of the nearest chopper.

"What the fuck are you doing?" asked Rimshaw, struggling to get out of his sleeping bag. He was too slow. Spracklin already had the wrist of Louis Duble. Spracklin heard the cuffs click, and he stepped back from the bikers.

"You fucking bastard," cried Rimshaw. He was out of his sleeping bag and struggling to his feet. Barefoot in jeans and a T-shirt, he moved on Spracklin and the cop came at him. "Back off, Rimshaw," he shouted. The flower children around them were coming to now, and creeping away from another brawl. Marie held her ground.

One of the bikers, the other young kid, was awake now and getting to his feet. Spracklin moved his jacket just enough so they could see the grip of his revolver.

"Just some questions," said Spracklin. "I need to know why you're here?"

"What?"

"Since you've been in the Bay Area. Have you been involved in the concert, the festival?"

Rimshaw looked at the Lieutenant in a strange way, wondering what trick he was trying to pull.

"I told you before. The guys and me came here to see the show. I wanna see Jasmine live."

"You don't strike me as a Jasmine fan," Spracklin said.

"You don't strike me as a brilliant detective, but someone gave you the job." The other biker laughed. Duble was waking up. He tugged at his left arm and realized he was shackled. Spracklin knew he didn't have much time.

"And which of you boarded at the apartment on Clayton?"

Rimshaw was starting to get annoyed now. "Look fella," he said. "I don't know what you're trying to pin on us now, but we're here to listen to some fucking tunes."

"Just camp out here." The biker was nodding. "Commune with nature. Pick a few fights with some darkies and—"

"Hold on there," yelled the biker. "We haven't picked fights with anyone."

"You guys have been picking fights with any black that comes near here."

Spracklin was about to say something more but Jack Rimshaw held up his hand. "Look, we've been playing defense since we got here. Those 'darkies'—your word, not mine—belong to a gang down in Fillmore. They've jumped us three times now. Show him, Marco."

The biker sitting across from Rimshaw pulled up his jean jacket. There was a wide purple and brown bruise that ran from his hairy chest down to his belt.

"They did that with a baseball bat. A guy came at me with a knife our first night here. And they're following us everywhere. I mean it, man. They got cats posted all over the Haight, all over the park. We go after anyone we think is a spy."

"The spies are all black?" asked Spracklin.

"As far as we know. All we know is we get black cats trailing us and then an hour later their brothers jump us."

"Pigs," said one of the bikers. Spracklin looked over and realized the punk he'd handcuffed was now awake. He and Duble were both tugging at the chains. Spracklin laughed, nodded to Marie and began to walk up the hill again.

"Aw shit, man," said Rimshaw. "Let 'em go."

Spracklin turned back to the biker. "You'll be fine." He tugged at Marie's sleeve and led her away from Hippie Hill. With the bikers screaming behind him and trying to break free of the handcuffs, he moved quickly to the west, back toward the phone booth.

CHAPTER 39

The benzedrine had helped, but he couldn't tell whether he was running on bennies or adrenaline. All he knew was that he was operating in overdrive. He didn't want to call the boss, but he had to. The old bastard was expecting results and he had to check in. He could complete the contract. He was close. He just had to keep his cool.

As the phone rang, he looked up and down Haight Street. He was expecting the cops to come get him. It was an emotional response. He knew the cops weren't on to him but the cops were lingering. He saw them all over the place. Their presence was wearing him down. He had to be cool, but it was getting more difficult. He could feel himself becoming paranoid. Three killings in one week was a lot. And it turned out that killing was easier than living with it, with the fear of discovery. He tried to suppress his emotions, to be rational. If he was rational, things would go smoothly.

"Hello," said the boss. He was always even-keeled, always the same tone.

"It's me," said the assassin. "Just checking in."

"And…."

"I'm working on it."

"You're taking your time."

"Look. She's, she's with him the whole time. You know who I'm referring to. He won't let her out of his sight. And I told you about the tail yesterday." The boss was silent at the other end. The assassin wished he would react with yelling or sarcasm. The silence was pure torture. He looked down at his boot and saw blood splattered on the brown leather. It wasn't that noticeable, but it could be dicey if he were brought in for questioning. He should have spotted it before.

"You got a lot of excuses."

"I couldn't do it yesterday—that other cop picked her up. I told you."

"She escaped him."

"I know. And she's with her old man now. As long as he's guarding her...."

The silence persisted. Finally, the boss said, "So, take care of both of them."

Now it was the assassin who was silent. The boss wanted him to knock off a San Francisco cop? And not just any cop. The head of the homicide division. "Do you understand what you're saying."

"Completely. Read the paper. You'll see there's never been a better time."

He wondered what was in the paper. And which paper? "There's never a good time for something like that."

The boss sighed. The assassin could picture him sitting in his office, behind his desk, surrounded by his muscle. The young man wondered if the boss understood the shitstorm that would be unleashed if he iced both a police lieutenant and his daughter.

"That guy, he's poking his nose where it doesn't belong. He has powerful enemies. Take care of both of them. You can leave their heads on."

There was a click and the line went dead. The assassin hung up the phone and turned back toward the traffic on Haight Street. The sun was rising in the sky. He was dumbstruck and edgy from the bennies. He had to move. He stepped into the street and heard the screech of brakes. A girl in a Ford sedan shouted something, but her car radio was too loud for him to hear. All he heard was Buffalo Springfield. He stepped back on to the sidewalk and shouldered his backpack. It contained his knife and the handgun the boss had given him. He began to walk toward Golden Gate Park.

CHAPTER 40

Searching constantly for patrolmen, Spracklin led Marie along an asphalt path toward the bowling greens. Now that his story had been in the *Chronicle*, he knew all patrol cops would be on the lookout for him. He had to keep out of sight. Together, they moved quickly down the path as Marie peppered him with questions about the cop he assaulted.

"Mickie O'Neill," he said. "Allegedly," he added. "The guy outweighs me by thirty pounds. He should have cleaned my clock. But he'd rather fight battles by leaking dirt on me to the papers."

Marie struggled to keep up with her father as they moved through the cover of the woods. They could see kids huddled in blankets beneath the trees, pairs of legs sticking out from the bushes. The community of modern hobos was stirring. One topless woman was unabashedly washing herself with a cloth and a bottle of water. Two guys about twenty—both fit for work—shouted to Spracklin, asking for money. Spracklin ignored them all and kept walking until he got to the phone booth. After checking the coin slot, he fished in his pockets for another dime but only found a quarter. His last one. He plugged it into the slot and was put through to Ed Burwell at the Bureau of Inspectors.

"Burwell," growled the familiar voice.

"It's Spracklin."

"Jesus, man, you gotta rein in that wife of yours."

Spracklin wasn't surprised by the news that Val was calling. She'd be frantic by now about Marie. "When she calls back, tell her Marie is safe and with me. I don't have long. Now listen. Those bikers, Satan's Host."

"You know they've pulled you from the case. I mean, have you seen the newspapers?"

"No one's told me," said Spracklin. Burwell would get the message: without an official order, Spracklin was still on the case. "We pulled in two Satan's Host yesterday but there are five hanging around Haight Street right now, right? Two of them, kids really, don't have an alibi. One of them is handcuffed to his bike at Hippie Hill."

"What?"

"Trust me. Get there fast, and you'll get him. Maybe him and his partner. I want them questioned about the Byrne and Menendes cases. Keep 'em for as long as you can." Spracklin hoped Burwell wouldn't start asking questions, and for once he wasn't disappointed by the sergeant's lack of curiosity. "Anything at your end?"

Burwell sighed. Spracklin could hear the thud of his feet being placed on his desk. "Where to start? I just talked with our friend Andy Fox."

Spracklin wanted to get off the line, but he had to ask: "What did he say?"

"Not much. He said nothing about Peter Terceira. Just said he was a friend. I pressed him on Menendes but he said he didn't know him. All he wanted to talk about was your daughter."

"What about her?"

"When he heard she was on the lamb—"

"How did he hear that?"

"You always said you have to get suspects talking. So, I told him IA was after her but lost her. Twats. And he all of a sudden sat up on his bunk and said we had to help Marie. Like I was in cahoots with Fox and his gang. I tried getting intel on Menendes but he just kept asking about IA and Marie. So, I asked him the obvious question: If Marie was so important to him, why did he punch a sheriff when he saw her Monday morning. You know what he said?"

"Tell me."

"That courtroom rat that Bogdan Polgar had in the courtroom."

"Myron Adamson."

"Yeah. Him. Fox saw Marie in the courtroom but he also saw Adamson. He knows the kid is Polgar's guy, so he knew Polgar was monitoring what was going on with Fox. Fox knows Polgar has people in prison, so he figured the only way he could survive was to get stuck in solitary."

"So, he decked a sheriff."

"What a dickhead, huh? Oh yeah, and he has a message."

"What's that?"

"He said, and this is a quote, 'Tell Marie, I'm going to get out and we'll be together again.'"

Spracklin chose not to reply. Marie was a few paces away. He was certain she couldn't hear what Burwell had said. He said, "What's going on with Schultz?"

"Shultz has lawyered up and isn't saying anything, but Commercial Crimes has Larry Nesbitt, their forensic accountant, going through Schultz's books and Sarah Byrne's papers. This is what I could get off him. Schultz had forged papers showing that he paid for the stereo gear. Nesbitt showed it to me—even I could tell it was a forgery. So, he sold these stereo components at a discount in his shop. They sold like hot cakes. He deposited the cash at his Wells Fargo branch, and once a week he'd wire some of the proceeds to the account in the Cayman Islands. They would send money back to his account and Sarah Byrne's account at Bank of America. They were dividing the proceeds evenly. So if he got Sarah Byrne and her boyfriend out of the way...."

"He could keep all the profits," said Spracklin. "But there's one thing."

"What's that?"

"If he got rid of Sarah, he could never gain access again to the Poseidon terminals. He wouldn't be able to blackmail William Byrne again. Unless he has copies of those photos."

Burwell was silent for a second, then said, "Maybe."

Spracklin checked the road again and as a throwaway comment asked, "Anything else happening?"

"Yeah, Joe Dixon caught a case in Richmond," Burwell said, referring to one of the homicide veterans. "He's at the scene now. Some poor schmuck got knifed but there's almost relief around here that there's something to do."

"Shit. What's the details?"

"Kid found dead last night outside his flat at Geary and 27th. Stabbed a few times in the gut, and defensive wounds on his left hand. No apparent motive—his wallet was still in his back pocket."

Spracklin tensed up and asked, "What was his name?"

"Bloom, I think."

"David Bloom?" Spracklin yelled. Marie looked over at him, studying the look of horror on his face.

"Yeah, that's it," said Burwell. He kept talking but Spracklin didn't hear. The pounding in his head drowned out anything coming out of the phone. Young David Bloom was murdered. He'd got too close to the killer, and the guy had knifed him. The sweet young man who wanted to help Spracklin, to join the force. Killed. Spracklin wondered if he himself had got the boy killed. His head began throbbing with a message that kept repeating itself: he had got David Bloom killed. He saw Marie mouth some words. Marie. Seeing Marie brought him back to the moment. He had to protect his daughter.

"Are you all right?" she said.

He nodded as he heard the voice on the phone say, "Is that what you want, Jimmy?"

"What's that?"

"Do you want me to keep working the Schultz lead or—"

"Ed, I knew David Bloom. I met him on Hippie Hill. I want you to tell Dixon to look into the angle that Bloom may have been killed by the same guy who got Byrne and Menendes."

"How do you figure that?"

"The kid wanted to be a cop. He kept coming to me on Hippie Hill with intel on the case, and...." Spracklin looked up and down the street again and knew he had to get away from the open space. He also needed a drink. A real drink. Something to help him think straight and get out of this mess. "I think he got too close to our perp."

"Yeah but how—"

"Ed, I gotta go." He hung up and faced his daughter. The look on her face told him she wanted some answers. "Another murder," he said. He looked over toward Haight Street and he knew to get to Zam Zam he would have to go by Hippie Hill and closer to Park Station. If Burwell acted, cops would be swarming around Hippie Hill for the next few hours. It was enemy territory. He had to seek cover and find a drink and he had to move quickly.

He checked for change in the coin return, found none, and took his daughter's hand. Thunderstruck and silent, he led her across the street and into the bushes, where he collapsed on the ground.

CHAPTER 41

The killer had got David Bloom. That was all that Spracklin could comprehend. There were defensive wounds, so the kid had been terrorized and suffered unimaginable pain before he died. Spracklin sat up and fumbled for a cigarette. His hand shook as he lit it. He snapped the lighter shut and began to make a plan. He would tell Marie that the park was no longer safe, that they had to get over to Haight Street. They could go around Kezar Stadium and give Park Station a wide berth. There was something he had to investigate on Masonic. That's what he'd tell her. He could sneak to a corner store and get a bottle. Then he could sort out whether he should just hand himself in. Maybe he could cut a deal—he would come in if they left Marie alone.

"Honey," he said. "Honey, I think we should head over to Haight Street."

She looked down at him, her face filled with concern. "Why?"

"There's something I need to look into."

"What?"

"Something about the case."

"You told me every detail of the case after a few beers last night. What's happened now?" Before he could stammer out an answer, she said, "Who's been murdered?"

Spracklin took a long haul on his cigarette and told her about David Bloom. He tried to control the shaking in his hand.

"And what do you need to look into on Haight Street?" she asked. He tried to think of something, but all he knew was that David Bloom was dead and that he, Spracklin, had got the kid killed. "I know that look, Daddy. You don't need a drink." He wanted to argue with her, but he didn't have the strength. He looked away.

"Let's get out of this park," said Spracklin. He sucked on the cigarette. "I'll buy you lunch."

"We're going to crack this case." She knelt down and faced him.

"Lunch would be good."

"Dad, we're going to crack this case," she yelled. Spracklin looked through the bushes to see if anyone had heard. Marie held out her hand. "Give me that list of suspects again," she said.

Spracklin reached inside his jacket and pulled out the note-book with papers tucked inside it. Marie studied his list of suspects, then flicked through the notebook. She turned back to the suspects, naming them as her finger moved down the page. "Harry Byrne, William Byrne, Andy, Satan's Host, Ed Schultz, Bogdan Polgar...." She flipped the yellow paper over to see if there was anything else printed on the back.

"I don't know if it's a complete list," said Spracklin.

She studied the list again and said, "There are two things...." Her voice faded as she concentrated.

"Huh?"

"I was just thinking there were two things we know about the killer or killers. He—let's assume it was a man—he knew where Sarah lived, and he had the means and incentive to behead her. I don't see anyone on this list who meets both those criteria."

"Only one I know is Andy Fox," said Spracklin. "He's a vicious man with a knife."

Marie didn't blink at the name of her former lover. "How do you know Andy knew where Sarah lived?"

"I don't, but Pete Menendes went and saw Andy in jail. Used an alias to get in. We found the fake ID in his wallet."

"You think Andy ordered the hit—or hits?"

"I don't think anything. I'm just looking at the evidence and try-ing to figure out where it leads me."

"Three things," she corrected herself. "We also know the killer had access to a list of performers that J.D. gave to a handful of peo-ple." She flicked through the notes again and looked up at her father. "I don't like your list," she said. "No one on your list would have had access to the set list. The only ones who have any connection to the concert are Satan's Host."

"They're not part of the organization," he said.

"But they're here and they could have got the set list." She contin-ued to go over his notes. "What about all this stuff about Sarah Byrne and that stereo heist?" She flicked through more papers. "And the money laundering? And the photos of her brother?" She looked up at him. "Have you asked William Byrne what he knew about them?"

"I was going to, but...." He didn't have to say the rest.

"So, let's call him," she said. She got to her feet. "No one had a bigger motive than him to kill Sarah. He'd get her half of the inheritance and punish her for embarrassing his father."

"But he hasn't been at the concert."

"Call him." Spracklin studied Marie. She was holding out her hand to help him to his feet. He couldn't take her hand now. She'd be able feel him trembling. He had to hide it from her. He had to live up to her image of him. He stood and flicked his cigarette butt into the bushes. He thought of something—he knew of a place where he could get a drink if he could distract Marie.

They began to cross the street, and he began to feel better. He was on the hunt for a killer. He was doing what he was born to do. And he knew where he could get a drink. Yes, he thought, a drink.

"So where did you learn to be a junior investigator?" he asked his daughter as they crossed the street again.

"I've spent a lifetime listening to you take calls in the kitchen while we were at the dinner table." She gave a weak smile. "I'd be pretty stupid if I didn't pick up a bit of it." She smiled. "It helps when you learn from the best."

Spracklin folded the papers and put them back in his pocket. He patted his sidearm and strode past the phone booth.

"I thought you were going to call Byrne?" said Marie.

"I have another plan."

CHAPTER 42

It was early afternoon when Spracklin and Marie reached the maintenance yard. It was lunchtime and groundskeeper Edgar Hemmings would understand that Spracklin needed to wet his whistle on a hot day. He would pay for the bottle, even a glass, but he had to get Marie out of the way first. Spracklin knocked and they stepped into the cluttered shed whose low ceiling radiated the heat of the afternoon sun. It took a moment for his eyes to adjust to the dark. After a couple of seconds, he noticed some movement at the far end of the room. He made out the slim outline of Edgar Hemmings leaning back in a chair by an old battered desk stacked high with papers and gardening magazines. His open lunchbox was in front of him and he held half a sandwich in his hand. As Spracklin moved inside, he saw a husky young man sitting against the far wall, eating his own sandwich.

"Well, well, Lieutenant Spracklin," said Hemmings.

"Mr. Hemmings," said Spracklin. "I was in the neighborhood. Thought I'd stop by." He nodded hello to the younger man. "This is my daughter, Marie." They said hello. The young man did not introduce himself.

"Anything I can do for you?" asked Hemmings.

"Yes, is there a bathroom?" asked Marie. Spracklin tried to hide his joy. Marie would be gone for a few minutes. Hemmings directed her to an outbuilding just past the utility shed, and she strode out the door and disappeared.

Spracklin took a chair by Hemmings's desk. He could tell the groundskeeper was studying his wrinkled suit and bashed up face. "I'm wondering...." Spracklin tried to be calm, to not think about David Bloom, or the story in the newspaper, or the abrasions on his face. "Would you have another Dixie cup? Those Dixie cups we had the other day. I'm happy to pay." He glanced at the door. Marie had just left. He had to calm down. "Just, it should be fast."

"Think nothing of it, my friend," said Hemmings, opening a desk drawer and withdrawing a bottle of Captain Morgan and a few cups. He splashed a shot in a cup, then poured a bit into his own Thermos. He waved the bottle at the other young man, who just shook his head. "You've been working hard."

"Yeah," said Spracklin. "Up all night, working this case." He downed his rum. "These kids." He shook his head. "I just found out another has died." The drink began to wash through his system and he felt his strength returning. "Listen, Edgar...." He felt he could call him by his first name. "Could I ask another favor? Could I use your phone?"

Hemmings gestured to it and Spracklin picked up the receiver. He wondered if he could get some privacy, but Edgar and his helper stayed where they were, chomping on their lunch. Spracklin dialed the number he'd committed to memory.

"Poseidon Mercantile," said the nasal voice of the Byrnes' receptionist.

"William Byrne, please," he said. He looked at Hemmings, who appeared to be taking no notice of him. Then he added, "My name is Spracklin, SFPD."

After a few moments, the younger Byrne picked up with the words, "Yes, Lieutenant."

"Good afternoon, William. Listen, a few things have come up in the investigation—"

"Lieutenant Spracklin," said Byrne, raising his voice. In the background, Spracklin could hear music, that kid with the Jewish nose who couldn't sing. Dylan. Marie used to play his stuff. "Stop right there."

Spracklin was taken aback. The young man had always been unfailingly polite.

"I'll take the lead here, William," Spracklin said.

"No, you won't."

The fucking Byrnes were still acting like Wong was leading the investigation. William Byrne wasn't even turning down his stereo while talking to him. "I'm the lead investigator." Spracklin wanted to raise his voice but he was conscious of the two Parks employees listening to every word.

"You've been suspended. I do read the newspapers, Lieutenant."

Shit. Spracklin had to keep the edge over Byrne. "You can't believe everything you read in the papers."

"You're a fugitive, for Godsakes. You've been reduced to the same status as my sister. You'd have come here in person if there weren't a search for you all over the city."

"I've got the photos, William."

Byrne paused before answering. "Look, I don't know what you're talking about. But the papers say you're wanted for questioning in the shooting death of a guy, the night my sister disappeared. As soon as I get off the phone, I'm calling the police."

Spracklin could hear the edge in the young man's voice. But he turned off the music and Spracklin spoke into the silence. Spracklin tried to think of what he could say that wouldn't tell the groundsmen what they were talking about. But then Marie came in. She saw her father on the phone and launched into a conversation with Hemmings. While his daughter engaged in small talk, Spracklin went after William Byrne. "There's one of you leaving The Stud. There's another of you getting into a sports car outside the Compton Café." He could tell from Byrne's silence that he was making inroads. "You're wearing glasses in the shots, but it's you. I'd have no problem establishing that it's you in those photos. You've seen them. You know it."

William Byrne wasn't threatening to call the police now. "Are you blackmailing me?"

"I need information. Who sent you the photos?"

After a pause, Byrne said, "I don't know." His voice was strained and he spoke as if his teeth were clenched. "How did you get the photos?"

"Don't worry about that. Tell me what happened."

"You're not on the case anymore."

"No, but I have the photos. And I'm going to find out who killed your sister."

Spracklin placed a finger to his free ear so he couldn't hear Marie and Hemmings. Marie was asking Hemmings and his lunch companion about the gardens. "What does this have to do with Sarah?" asked Byrne.

"Just tell me who's blackmailing you. I've got enough copies of the photos to send them to whoever takes over the case, to Elias Wong, to your father, to—"

"Don't. Don't send them to my father. I told you I don't know who's blackmailing me. I simply don't know."

"Tell me what happened."

"It was April 5, a Friday, the day after Doctor King was shot. An envelope arrived at the office addressed to me. The address was typed. Mailed from the Rincon Annex Post Office the day before. The photos were inside it. There was no note or anything."

Spracklin got the sense that it was easier for him to talk about the package, the photos, the post office, than to mention what they showed. This young executive and soldier would probably never be able to discuss his secret life as a homosexual. "Do you still have the package?" asked the Lieutenant.

"I burned the whole thing. But the following Monday another package arrived with more photos. I kept these ones—at my apartment, not at the office." He went silent for a moment, and Spracklin began to wonder if they'd lost their connection. "You saw what they were. Someone is out to ruin my life."

After another pause, Byrne added, "The next day, April 9, I got a call. I was going into a planning meeting for a new route we're planning to Manila. It was a male voice. I didn't recognize it. He said, 'William Byrne, gotta pen?' I knew what it was about—I'd thought of nothing else for four days. Then he said: 'Bring three signed requisition forms, completely blank but your signature, to the Balboa Theatre for the 3 p.m. show tomorrow. Sit in the second row from the back. Don't turn around. I'll have the negatives.'"

Spracklin lit a cigarette. He should have been taking notes, but given his status with the force he wondered whether it mattered. "What are the requisitions?"

"They're the forms truckers need to gain access to the terminal and the containers. They had my signature on them, but the rest of it was blank. I wasn't too concerned because whoever got it would have had to fill in the rest of it. Not many people would know how to fill it in, not to mention the container numbers."

"You did what the guy wanted?"

"Yes. I canceled meetings for the afternoon and told my father I'd caught a bug of some sort. Instead of going home, I went to the matinee of Doctor Doolittle. I sat alone in the second row from the back. After about fifteen minutes, someone whispered in my ear to hand over the requisitions. I asked for the negatives. As he took the requisition forms, he handed me an envelope—I could feel negatives in it."

"Overexposed film?"

"Yes. It wasn't the negatives of the shots of me. They were all blank. The negatives, the genuine negatives, are still in the hands of whoever took the photos."

Spracklin didn't tell him the people who'd blackmailed him were probably dead. "You didn't follow him?"

"He told me I was being watched and to stay where I was. By the time I turned around, the guy was gone."

"So, what happened?"

"Seven days later, at 2:14 a.m., a man, estimated to be in his thirties, drove a tractor trailer into Terminal 2, presented requisitions and was admitted. He had to be directed to the proper spot but he left with two containers full of Marantz electronics. No one has seen them since." Byrne was focused on the theft now, and his voice was steely. Spracklin noticed how precise he was with the details. "But here's the thing. That form was filled out perfectly. It was filled out by someone with knowledge of our operations. It was an inside job."

"Who had knowledge of the shipments?"

"My father and me. Our senior team. And then the shipping crew right down to the stevedores. We were excited with the inroads we'd made into Japan, so we celebrated every time we got a new Japanese client. Marantz is a growing business, and stereos are a booming market. My dad was thrilled when we got that contract. Lots of people know about the Marantz contract. But only a few people knew when product was moving through the port."

"But the requisitions had your signature?"

"When my father asked about that, I said it was forged. It didn't actually look like my signature."

"So, you brought in Elias Wong to help find out who could have been on the inside?"

"Exactly. We had a universe of about a hundred people within the company who had these details. Elias was beginning his investigation when Sarah disappeared. We had a management meeting, and agreed unanimously to make our priority finding Sarah. Until Monday."

His voice trailed off. Spracklin dropped his cigarette and ground it out with his shoe. "I can't tell you where I found the photos, William. At least not yet."

"Are you going to make them public?"

"I don't know."

Spracklin paused for a moment then hung up. He didn't need to make William Byrne feel at ease about anything. He polished off his rum, hoping Marie would think he was just drinking water. As the conversation in the room faded out, he thought about what he'd learned from the phone call.

"More hippies giving you grief, Detective?" Hemmings asked as he swiveled in his chair.

Spracklin blew out his cheeks, remembered where he was and laughed. "If it wasn't them, it would be someone else."

Hemmings let out a guttural laugh, reached out and slapped the Lieutenant's shoulder. "Wish I could say that."

"They hassle you, the hippies?" asked Spracklin.

"Hassle. Steal. Mooch. Beg. And bother." He bit into the second half of his sandwich and said, "Mercy me, they make a mess of our work. I say to James all the time," —he nodded to the younger man— "if these hippies make life this bad for us, just think of what it's like for the police."

"How exactly do hippies make life bad for you?" asked Marie. She seemed more curious than insulted.

"No offence, but they've changed everything. Kids are passed out in the bushes, the flower beds. Trampling the gardens, plucking mushrooms from the lawns. We trim the bushes, we never know if kids are lying down in them."

"Going to amputate something one day," said James, speaking for the first time.

Hemmings finished his sandwich and offered his guests each a homemade chocolate square. Marie took one. Spracklin declined.

James was starting in on another sandwich. "They shit in the bushes. Like, all the time."

"Why, Marie," said Hemmings. "Most mornings I open this shed and find some hippie has broken in, or else he's lying here, still asleep."

"Like we're running a hotel," said James.

"And the equipment they've stolen," said Hemmings.

"Two, three nights ago someone broke in here and ripped off a shovel," said James, leaning forward and eyeing Spracklin intently. Spracklin figured this guy was thirty, he was clearly sick of the hippies. "I mean, a shovel. What would these kids need a shovel for?"

"That got returned," said Hemmings. James turned and looked at him with incredulity. "Yeah, someone chucked it over the fence in the back of the compound. Someone had been digging in the de Laveaga Dell with it."

"It's back?" asked James.

He was cut off by Marie. "I'm sorry, but when did you say the shovel disappeared?"

They all looked at Marie, and Spracklin started to understand why she'd asked this key question. He'd been pondering a way to get more rum or some other liquor. Now he was focusing on his daughter.

"Let's see," said Edgar Hemmings. "Today's Thursday. So, it was…I opened the shop here Monday morning and a window was broken and the only thing that was missing was the shovel. And then Ernie Pearson handed it into me yesterday morning. Yeah, yesterday we got it back."

Marie turned slowly and stared at her father. Spracklin had tied it all together, just as she had. Someone had stolen a shovel the night that Sarah Byrne was murdered, and returned it after Pete Menendes had been killed. Someone had needed to dig a hole or two in Golden Gate Park.

"What's de Laveaga Dell?" Spracklin asked Hemmings.

"It's a gulch just beyond the far end of the compound."

"And how can you tell someone was digging in it?"

"The dell is the deepest depression in the park. It's like a dried-up swamp. Darkest soil in the whole park. There was soil from the dell on the shovel. Someone had been digging in the dell, and hadn't bothered to wipe down the shovel."

Spracklin nodded slowly. He was no longer missing liquor. He was a cop again.

"Edgar," he said slowly. "I need to ask a favor. I'm wondering if I could borrow that shovel, and maybe a spare pair of coveralls?"

CHAPTER 43

They met at the southwest corner of Sharon Meadow, by the arts pavilion. Their view of the stage was partly obstructed by one of the banners that dotted the field. If the assassin moved slightly, he could see a folk-singing duo harmonizing, just like Simon and Garfunkel, without the talent. He'd seen them warming up and wished they would stop looking at each other and giggling during the guitar riffs. They played no original material, just a little Donovan, and a dab of Dylan. He liked to be charitable, but these two needed to improve.

A stream of young people was now feeding the crowd, which stretched halfway across the field. It would fill the field in a few hours. A strengthening afternoon wind flicked two peace sign flags and carried wafts of smoke across the crowd. Most people were still sitting so he could make out the Satan's Host choppers, though the bikers themselves still hadn't returned.

"Are you looking for her in the crowd?" asked the old man. "She ain't there. I told you."

"Just looking at the crowd," he replied.

"Well pay attention to me."

"I'm listening. Just looking at the show."

"If you paid more attention to your job, we'd be done by now."

The assassin didn't like his boss's tone. He'd been kowtowing to the old fart for a couple of weeks now and he was getting sick of it. He cared less and less about the relationship between their families. He was now a killer and deserved more respect. "I told you, I couldn't do anything about her last night. I had to take care of the guy who was tailing me. Then there were too many people around her."

"I wanted to talk to you about the guy tailing you."

"He was following me everywhere, drawing attention to me. He was so goddamn clumsy about it. People were staring at me, wondering why this guy was watching me."

"You didn't have to kill him."

"Um yes, I did."

"It was too much."

"He was dangerous. He was talking to Spracklin."

"We could have removed him quietly, scared him away. You didn't have to kill him. The cops are talking about a mass murderer."

"It was one more. And it was a good hit—a good hit against a fit young man."

"The job was to get the girl and her father."

"They were surrounded by people all night long." He said it louder than he meant to and hoped none of the passing concert-goers could hear him. He glanced at them and looked back at his boss, who was glaring at him. Bogdan Polgar, he had learned, could be charming when he chose to be. But he had an ability to turn off his charm instantly and for extended periods. Today he was all business and he'd wasted no time in telling his hired gun how disgusted he was with the delays. The assassin had been surprised when Polgar suggested they meet at the Sharon Arts Center, he'd wondered whether the kingpin would actually show up. But he'd been there on time, with two of his bodyguards, one black, and one Eastern European. "It wasn't my fault that cop picked her up yesterday," said the assassin.

"She was hanging around here all last night. They both were. But results? Zilch."

"Jesus, man, I got the first two. I got the tail. And I'll get her and her old man. Last night there were just too many people around. Her father was armed. I will get her tonight when she's not around him."

"You don't get it, do you?" asked the Russian. His face was sharp with anger, but his voice maintained its even tone. "I told you. At the beginning of the job—you have to get rid of Andy Fox's people and their protectors. You have to get her AND her father."

The assassin nodded. "I got Fox's people. You're the one who said you'd get to Fox in prison. But I believe he's still alive." The old man had admitted before that he made an error by sending one of his people to the bail hearing. Fox saw the kid in court and got himself put in solitary. Polgar's gang couldn't get to him.

"Fair enough," said Polgar. "We'll get Fox. We'll take care of that. But you have to take care of Marie and Spracklin."

The assassin looked into the Russian's cold blue eyes and understood what he was saying. If he wanted the credit he needed, he had to kill the cop. Killing a couple of girls, a snitch, even a Vietnam vet—those wouldn't bring him the cache he wanted. He had to kill someone dangerous. He had to kill Jimmy Spracklin.

"I have to ice the cop?"

"You need to get both of them." Polgar's voice softened now. "You have to kill Marie—she's the last link to Fox in Haight-Ashbury. And if she's dead, none of us are safe as long as Spracklin's alive, even in his weakened state." Polgar put his hand on the killer's shoulder. "You have to get rid of him when you kill her."

"I could kill her without him knowing it was me."

"He'll find out. Don't underestimate that man. He's a tiger that never stops prowling until he has his quarry. He's been on me two years, slowly getting closer. You have to finish him off."

"The deal was three of them."

"Yes, and if you want to stay alive, once you kill the third, you have to kill a fourth. It's a simple matter of survival. I will make sure it's worth your while."

The assassin took a deep breath. He now had to kill an armed detective. He wondered if it would be harder than killing a seasoned Vietnam vet. "They've been hanging around the stage, hiding among the crowd. I'll have to get them away from everyone else."

Polgar shook his head. "He's at a maintenance shed over there, beyond the trees." Polgar pointed to the west. "The entrance is to the left of the bowling green. We've had an eye on him. He and the girl went in there half an hour ago. So now you can do your job."

"You know for sure where he is?"

"For sure. Go pick up their trail. Lester will go with you." Polgar nodded to the Eastern European bodyguard. "He can help you."

The assassin looked at Lester Fredericks, who was scanning the field to make sure no one was approaching who shouldn't. "No way," said the assassin. "I work alone."

"Lester can help you."

"The deal was—"

"You've proven unable to meet your end of the deal. Lester will be there to help you and make sure the job gets done. He's a resourceful man."

The assassin looked at the lean bodyguard with the sunken eyes. He wondered if Lester's mission was to kill the assassin once the job was done. He wondered if he could lose Polgar's man and then do the job himself. That would be dangerous. The best course of action would be to kill the Spracklins and then get out of the way as quickly as possible.

CHAPTER 44

Hemmings had found not only a pair of coveralls but also a Giants baseball cap, even a pair of work boots for the Lieutenant. Spracklin still thought of the Giants' move to the Bay Area as recent, but the baseball cap said otherwise. It was tattered and dusty and reminded Spracklin that a decade had passed since the team moved from New York. He and Marie strolled out of the compound and around the winding road toward de Laveaga Dell. He was on the hunt. A couple belts of rum had helped, and he liked his disguise. Gone was the rumpled suit, replaced by the duds of a groundskeeper, marching along with a spade in his hand. His revolver was in its shoulder holster under the coveralls, his notes and wallet were tucked in one back pocket. The visor of his baseball cap shaded his face. He was ready to investigate a triple killing.

"What did you learn from Byrne?" asked Marie as she paced along beside him.

"Someone was blackmailing him and he helped them steal electronics from the container terminal."

"Doesn't that make him the main suspect?"

"I don't think he knew the blackmailer was his sister." He dipped his head to hide his face from the groups of young people strolling toward Sharon Meadow. They were hauling blankets, bags of food, bottles. Beyond the trees, they could hear folksongs. There was a carnival atmosphere in Golden Gate Park, Spracklin realized. He and Marie were oblivious to it. They were heading into a ravine in search of two severed heads.

"Think this will lead to anything?" asked Marie.

"Those heads are somewhere. This is the best lead we've got."

"The more I think about it, the lamer it seems."

Spracklin stopped and stared at his daughter. Taken aback, she looked into his stern eyes. "Listen to me, Marie," he said and, from the way she flinched, he knew she could smell the liquor on his breath. "I've scraped together cases on way lamer leads than this. The Maquire case in '64, the guy's wife was missing and all we had was their Dachshund kept scratching at the new paneling in the basement. I ripped out the paneling and found her." He lit a cigarette and turned to his daughter again. "When you got nothing, you grab whatever you can." He took a drag and removed the cigarette from his mouth. "We've got nothing, and the stakes couldn't be higher."

"I thought the stakes were always high with a murder case."

He gazed at his daughter in disbelief. "This case is everything," he said, his voice softening. "Ray Handell and his thugs, they have too much on us. The only way I can get ahead of them, the only thing that can save us, is cracking this case." He began walking again and continued speaking. He spoke out loud for Marie to hear it, but it felt as if he were speaking to himself. "Harry Byrne is a powerful man. If I can find his daughter's killer, it might be enough to gain powerful friends, to save my job, and protect you."

They turned on to a path that descended into de Laveaga Dell in the shadows of the overhanging trees. There was a cool dampness in the winding path. When they came to a clearing, Spracklin took his first scan of the area. The center of the dell was grassy, about the size of a football field. It had three picnic tables at the center, and the area was fringed with gardens of shrubs, all of which had lost their springtime blossoms. The banks of the grove surrounding them were blanketed with dense woods.

"We don't have to worry about the grassy spots," said Marie.

Spracklin glanced at his daughter and realized she was surveying the area along with him. "Why's that?" he asked. He agreed with her, but he wanted to hear her reasoning.

"He wouldn't bury under the grass. The dig marks would show. He'd dig among those shrubs, in the dirt."

Spracklin nodded. There were probably two-hundred or three-hundred yards of shrubbed garden around the perimeter. He decided to start at one end and walk around the edge until they found a patch that looked like it had been disturbed.

"Over there," said Marie, pointing to a patch that receded behind high bushes. "It gives the best cover. He could hide in there while he was digging."

Spracklin thought about it. "It was dark and raining. He might have just wanted to get in and out as quick as possible."

They began on the south side and walked slowly along the edge. Spracklin didn't have high hopes and they completed one circuit without finding anything obvious. It had been a while since the grounds crew had disturbed the soil, so Spracklin had hoped recent digging would be noticeable, even if it had been raining when the digging supposedly took place. "Let's go over it once more," said Spracklin. Maybe it would be a waste of time. They could return the shovel to Edgar Hemmings and go back to Hippie Hill. They covered the perimeter again, this time going in the opposite direction. They had almost completed another loop when Marie grabbed Spracklin's upper arm and said, "There." She was pointing to a place where the dirt had been trampled but there were no signs of digging.

"They're just footprints in the soil," said Spracklin.

"But they're all pointing into that bush. Like he was working under the bush."

Spracklin snuck close to the garden, while remaining on the grass. There were marks. It looked like the soil had been disturbed near a rhododendron bush and someone had tried to cover it up. The bush's lower branches skirted the ground with broad leaves. Spracklin raised a hand to make sure Marie did not step on the soil and planned his approach. He wanted to look under the rhododendron branches without disturbing the marks. He skirted around the bush and tried to approach from the uphill slope.

The ground was hardpacked now and he was able to pull back the thick foliage. Beneath the broad leaves, he could clearly see someone had been digging. The killer had been clever, digging under the branches. But the leaves had also preserved the signs of the disturbed soil, and it was obvious now where the digging had taken place. Spracklin pulled back the nearest rhododendron branch but it snapped. To hell with it, he thought and broke the branch right off. It gave him enough clearance that he could dig into the spot that had recently been excavated.

He dug gently, using the edge of the spade to scrape off layers of black earth. On his fifth sweep, the shovel hit something hard. The earth around it was loose enough that Spracklin was able to pull it out. Spracklin found himself holding an industrial garbage bag that seemed to contain a human head. He felt around it and was sure he could feel the stem of the neck. He set the bag to one side, and used the shovel to probe further. It took a few pokes to locate another bag. He shoveled the dirt away and pulled the bag from the hole in the ground. It could have contained a human head, but it seemed like there was something like a canvas bag inside the garbage bag. He left the shovel stuck in the dirt to mark the spot, and backtracked around the rhododendron bush.

Marie grimaced as she looked at the two garbage bags, knowing what they contained.

"What are we going to do with those?" she asked, obviously dreading the answer.

"I'm going to have to open them up. I'm pretty sure they're human heads but I have to make sure they're Byrne and Menendes."

"You mean they may belong to someone else?"

"If he killed anyone else, he may have stashed their heads here. I may have to dig more to be sure."

They went to the nearest picnic table and Spracklin laid the bags on the surface. Dark dirt fell from them. Spracklin felt through the plastic and was sure the first bag contained a head, a man's head, with the grizzled beginnings of a beard. He turned his attention to the second bag, which puzzled him. He decided to open it.

"Please look away, Marie," he said. She sat across from him facing the far woods and leaning against the picnic table.

Spracklin carefully untied the knot of the garbage bag and pulled it down to reveal a rucksack coated in slime. As he fumbled with the buckle, he realized the slime was blood. He got it open and peered inside. "Don't turn around, please," he said to Marie.

"Oh God," she said. "The smell is bad enough."

Spracklin wished he had something as simple as Vicks VapoRub to put under his nose to prevent himself from retching. But he didn't and he had to move on. He pulled down the canvas rucksack to expose the head. The matted hair was caked with blood, but in life it could have been strawberry blonde. Her blue eyes were open, wide-eyed in fact. The thing that seemed to confirm that it was Sarah Byrne was the nose stud in her left nostril, which glimmered green against the grey skin. There were no bruises or abrasions Spracklin could see, other than the jagged flesh where the killer had hacked her head off. There was only one thing he hadn't expected: the garrote wrapped around her throat that cut into the skin about an inch above the place where the neck was cut from the body.

Spracklin looked at the head and asked himself: *Is this garrote the only thing the killer did not want us to see?*

He examined all the surfaces of the head and pried open her mouth with his naked fingers, wishing he had gloves with him. He could see no other wounds. No articles left that might identify the killer. The only new piece of information was the garrote. He pulled a pen from his pocket and used it to loosen the cord. About three inches of the line was still embedded in her throat. He stretched out both ends of the garrote, and then tried to pry the embedded part of the line out of her neck. He tried again, then again, but it wouldn't budge. He knew there could be fingerprints on the wooden handles, so he couldn't touch them, but there wouldn't be prints on the wire itself. So, he pinched the wire on either side of the neck and tried to shake it out. He tugged hard enough that the head came up off the table, but he was unable to shake it loose.

"I guess we now know why he cut her head off," Marie said.

Spracklin looked up and saw his daughter had turned around and was watching him trying to disengage the garrote. "Huh?" he asked.

"You'd been wondering why he cut the head off. Obviously, the wire was jammed into her neck bones so he couldn't get it out. So, he cut the head off."

Spracklin wanted to tell her to turn around again. But she was sitting right there looking at the gruesome head and coping with it. He'd tried not to baby her since she came home, and he wasn't going to start now. "Couldn't he have cut the wires?"

She got up and walked over. She reached out and pinched the wire between her fingers. "That wire is pretty thick. Cutting through it with a knife would be tough. It might have been easier to cut between the bones of the neck."

In the distance, they could hear an electric guitar riff, and then drums and a bass coming in. The concert was ramping up. Spracklin lowered the wire and nodded. He was about to pull the bag up over the head when he decided to examine the handles of the garrote. He pinched the wire just beside the handle and held it up to examine it. It looked like the handle of some sort of specialist tool. There was a hole drilled through the middle that the wire passed through, but the wooden handle itself was puzzling. There was a broken piece of metal stuck in one end — it had broken off so it didn't even stick out. And at the other there was some sort of a logo. Spracklin couldn't read it for the blood. He put that handle down and picked up the other one, again pinching the wire to lift it. He could read the logo on this one. It was a simple circle with "A&J" on the inside.

"Ever heard of A and J?" he asked his daughter, who was again facing away from him.

"Nope," she said.

Spracklin drew the bag up over the head and tied a loose knot at the top. He untied the knot on the other bag and peered inside. He could see it was a male head and the back of the head was missing. He adjusted the bag and saw there was an exit wound through the left eye. It was consistent with their belief that one bullet remained in the head. He was about to pull the sides of the bag down when he was deafened by the crack of a gun. Marie shrieked and dove behind the table. Spracklin turned toward the sound of the report, puzzled as much as anything. As he withdrew his revolver from its holster, he wondered why he hadn't sensed any bullets flying by. In the shadowy trees he saw two flashes to the left of the path, then heard two cracks of a hand gun. Someone was trying to kill them.

CHAPTER 45

"Take cover," Spracklin shouted at his daughter. He stood by the picnic table, his revolver trained on the bushes where he thought the shots originated. He sensed his daughter moving below him, lying flat. Then it came: the flash and report of two more shots, followed by a bullet ripping into the turf about ten yards in front of the picnic table. Spracklin got a mark on the point where he'd seen the flash, by an oak tree within the wooden patch. He squeezed off three shots and saw bark and splinters fly around the oak tree.

"Get to the bushes," he yelled to Marie. She should have known a picnic table couldn't protect her. He glanced at her, expecting to see his daughter cowering. But she was on all fours, her eyes trained on the bushes where the shots were coming from.

"Go, run," he said. "I'll cover you."

Marie waited a beat, then grabbed one of the bags and galloped about thirty yards to the nearest trees. Spracklin didn't think he had to tell her that he'd worry about the heads, but she understood how important they were. Just before she reached the tree line, there were two more flashes, just uphill from the previous ones. Spracklin heard the trees around Marie crackle and twigs fall to the ground. He returned the fire, grabbed the last bag and ran toward his daughter, grabbing the shovel as he passed it.

He crouched beside her and surveyed the field. Across from them, he saw something, a sudden movement as the branch of a tree jostled. The shooter was at the east end of the field, and someone was moving around the field to the rear. He wondered how many there were, and how heavily armed they were.

"We gotta get out of here," he said.

"Where?"

"There's more than one of them." He nodded to the branches being moved across the field. "They'll reach the far end of the dell before we will. They're trying to cut us off, setting a trap."

Spracklin wedged his handgun back into its holster and glanced through the trees at the spot where he thought the shooter was hiding. The guy hadn't fired in more than a minute. Spracklin quickly undid the garbage bags so both were open, then he moved Menendes' head to the bag with the soiled backpack. He tied up the bag with the two heads in it.

"What are you doing?" Marie said. "Let's move."

"He wants to make sure we don't leave with the heads," said Spracklin as he took the shovel and began to tip dirt into the empty garbage bag. It was almost dark now, and Spracklin hoped he could fool the shooter into thinking they were leaving the heads behind. He shoveled five scoops of dirt and leaves into the plastic bag and tied it tight so it was round, sort of oblong. He glanced again toward the east end of the dell.

He tossed the bag of dirt out of the trees. It landed with a thud between the tree line and the picnic tables. Could it be mistaken for the heads in the dim light? Spracklin could only hope so. "You can have the heads," he called out. "Just let me get out of here with my daughter."

He grabbed the garbage bag with the two heads and led Marie up the wooded hill. They would cut back toward the east, toward the concert so they could mingle with the crowd and lose their pursuers. The ground was even but Spracklin was soon out of breath due to the steep slope. He paused and pushed Marie past him. He surveyed the forest and wondered if the guy was following them or trying to get to the decoy garbage bag. Every instinct Spracklin had been born with told him to double back and go after the guy. But he knew he had to stay with Marie and protect the evidence. He didn't know for sure the shooter had fallen for the ploy with the garbage bag. He had to get them both to safety.

They scrambled up the hill, and Marie slipped. While she stood and caught her breath, Spracklin scanned the woods but could see little in the falling dusk. "We have to get out of here," he whispered. "We don't know how many of them there are."

They continued pushing on. The ground was starting to level out, and suddenly there was a fence in front of them. It was the back of the compound.

"We're going that way," Spracklin said, nodding left toward Sharon Meadow and Hippie Hill. He took his gun out and led Marie on. The sound of electric guitars grew louder. If anyone was approaching through the woods, Spracklin wouldn't be able to hear them. He and Marie were on a trail, a fairly level thoroughfare, but he was worried about falling in the deepening dark. Spracklin stumbled on a root, but Marie steadied him. They crouched and moved on down the narrow trail. Spracklin wished the vegetation all around wasn't so thick. The music got louder, and Spracklin felt sure they were within a hundred yards of the concrete path. There would be people there, and he felt sure they could disappear into the crowd.

They heard the crack of a branch and the report of a gun, and they hit the dirt. Spracklin checked Marie. With bullets flying overhead, she looked at him, scared but in control, and nodded. Spracklin crawled to the trunk of a tree and looked around. The shooter must have been reloading or moving. It was quiet. Spracklin could see only the mingled branches fading into the blackness. Then he saw two flashes and heard the shots. He returned fire and ducked.

"Bad news," he said as he crawled back to Marie. "He's near the trail. We can't go forward."

They had to retrace their steps and hope that whoever had been across the dell wouldn't cut off their escape. Spracklin grabbed Marie's hand and dragged her along. He wondered if they should head downhill, back toward the dell, but the tree-lined gorge would be a deathtrap. They were gaining speed when Spracklin felt a bullet fly by his ear. Instinctively, he squeezed off a single shot into the darkness in front of them then cursed himself—he might have just given away clues to their location. He turned, grabbed Marie and dragged her to the ground as two more bullets flew past where they'd been standing. His worst fears were realized. The shooter had them covered from behind and his accomplice was armed and had cut off their escape route.

Spracklin had to think fast. The second shooter seemed to be a sharper shot than the first, better at shooting from cover to shield his position. They had to move east again, back toward Hippie Hill, back toward the novice who'd been shooting at them from the beginning. Spracklin liked his chances best against that guy.

He motioned for Marie to turn again, then edged behind her. He didn't want her to be the one closest to the second shooter. Spracklin didn't have to urge her on now—he gasped for breath as he tried to keep up with his daughter. He was worried she was moving too quickly. Somewhere ahead of them was a killer with a gun, and they were running right toward him.

He saw something move ahead and pulled Marie down into a bed of ferns as a bullet tore through the branches above them. The first shooter was closing in. Spracklin resisted the urge to shoot back. He grabbed Marie's wrist and together they belly-crawled away from the path to the foot of an oak tree. The shooter ahead fired three more shots toward where they'd been a few seconds earlier. It told Spracklin where the guy was, and that he didn't know where the Spracklins were.

Spracklin placed his mouth near his daughter's ear, speaking just loud enough to be heard above the guitar music. He put the garbage bag in her hands.

"I'm going to return their fire and hopefully take them out," he said. "You take these, go that way." He pointed in a direction parallel to the trail that skirted where he figured the first shooter was hiding.

"I won't leave you," she said.

"You need to get out of—"

"I won't leave you."

"You need to get the heads out. Take them to Park Station. Drop them at the desk and run."

"We have to stick together."

He scanned the woods again, then glanced behind them. The two shooters would have them pinned in minutes. "I can't protect myself if I'm worried about you." Spracklin opened his revolver and began plugging bullets into the barrel.

"And if they kill you, they'll come for me."

"I can cover you as you retreat."

"I need you to protect me and my baby."

Spracklin paused. Marie paused. They looked at each other.

Spracklin nodded. He knew Marie and he knew Marie wasn't going to leave him. He snapped the barrel shut and looked into her eyes again. He took the bulky garbage bag from her. As they rose, he waved the gun across the spot where the first shooter had been. He fired once, then again. The muzzle flashes revealed Spacklin's position, and he drew fire from the second assailant, who was now coming up behind them.

Spracklin twisted and fired to the rear. Then he fired again toward where the first shooter was. He had to keep firing at the guy. As long as the first shooter was taking cover, they could get around him and get to the paved path full of concert-goers. He and Marie sped toward the trail again. He wondered whether the first shooter had moved location, but another flash revealed his position. Spracklin and Marie ducked as they moved. Spracklin fired again, and they ran on. Spracklin shot in both directions as they sprinted toward the sound of the concert.

In seconds, they were beyond both shooters, and then they were on the dirt trail again. Move. They had to keep moving. After a few paces, Spracklin wheeled, dropped to one knee and caught a glimpse of someone pursuing them along the trail. Spracklin fired twice and the guy hit the ground. Spracklin didn't think he'd struck him, but he'd slowed him. He rose and followed his daughter out of the woods.

As they merged into the stream of hippies heading for the rock festival, Spracklin holstered his pistol again and looked at his daughter. He nodded. She nodded. And they walked on to the street with the hippies heading to the concert. He tried to be casual as he looked around, checking to see if there was anyone, cop or killer, who he recognized. But it was just an assortment of young people, their bell-bottoms swishing together as they strode along. Spracklin and Marie both knew what they had to do: just fit in and get to a place where they could get rid of the heads. They fell into step with the motley horde, adopting the role of a groundskeeper and his daughter strolling to the compound with a muddy garbage bag. No one could have suspected they were toting two human heads that had been severed from corpses.

It was in that surreal scene that Spracklin took on board the most bizarre thing that had happened to him that week. Marie was pregnant. His sweet little girl, not yet seventeen, was carrying a child. And whose child? It had to be Andy Fox's baby. His grandchild would be Andy Fox's offspring. The knowledge was sickening, but he had to set the news aside and concentrate on getting the heads to an inspector and getting Marie to safety.

The hippies began to veer east toward Sharon Meadow but Spracklin guided Marie along the winding road, back toward the phone booth he'd visited before. The booth was in the open but the sooner he got rid of the heads, the sooner he could turn his attention to solving the case and getting Marie out of the park.

Marie was looking around nervously. "Shouldn't we take cover?" she asked.

"Soon," he said. "I have to call someone, someone I trust. We'll get rid of the bag." He thought about getting her to hide in the bushes, but they may have been followed. He wanted Marie by him at all times. The phone booth came into view and Spracklin realized how much he wanted to get rid of that disgusting garbage bag. Marie must have felt it as well. They both picked up their pace. He found a place to stash the heads that he could describe to a colleague—a tall bush with yellow flowers. It stood out. He checked again to make sure no one was watching them, then he stole to the edge of the garden and stashed the bag under the branches. "Keep your eyes peeled," he said as he stepped into the booth. He plugged in his last quarter and dialed the Bureau of Inspectors. "It's Lieutenant Spracklin," he said, wondering if the dispatcher would now alert IA. "Put me through to Ed Burwell."

The phone was picked up quickly.

"Burwell."

"Ed, it's Jimmy. I got the heads."

"Where?"

"I'm in the park." He looked at the nearby shrubs. "They'll be behind the bushes at the south corner of the lawn bowling club. There's a phone booth there. They'll be under a shrub with yellow flowers, near the phone booth. We found them under a bush in de Laveaga Dell. There's a shovel by the spot where we found them, and there is at least one of the killer's bullets in the turf, about twenty yards east of the picnic tables."

"Got it," said Burwell. "Now, get the hell out of there. Fast"

"What do you mean?"

"Your buddy Ray Handell put out an APB for you. You and your daughter. Claims she's an accomplice in a drug-smuggling operation and possible murderer. The announcement went out about an hour ago. Every cop in the city is looking for you."

Burwell kept talking but Spracklin didn't hear anything more. He gazed at the trees, half expecting an army of cops to emerge. He had to move. "Ed," he interrupted the sergeant. "The two heads are in an industrial garbage bag. Make sure someone from the Bureau gets them. Fast."

"One more thing, Jimmy—"

"I got to go. Get the garbage bag to Ernie Swanson, or someone in the medical examiner's office."

"I will, but you know that photo of the young Byrne kid getting into a Mustang outside Compton's"

"The gay bar. Yeah."

"You can make out the plates. I ran a search on the car. Guess who owns it?"

"Just fucking tell me."

"It's Elias Wong's vehicle."

"Who cares?" he said. And then he began to work through the implications "Okay, okay," he said. "I get it. I gotta go."

He hung up, grabbed Marie's hand and dashed across the street. They were at an intersection so he had to check up and down four roads. He saw no one and prayed there was no longer anyone tailing them. They would camp out in the clump of trees opposite the phone booth for a while.

"What are we doing?" asked Marie as they crouched in the bushes.

"I have to make sure no one other than police get those heads."

She looked at the spot where they'd stashed the heads. Spracklin reached in his pocket and took out his notebook. Dusk was falling but it was light enough to take down some notes.

"What if someone else grabs them?" she asked.

"I have a gun." He began to jot things in the notebook.

"You'd shoot someone if they went after the heads?"

"In a heartbeat." He kept writing, holding his notebook. He knew she was curious, so he explained what he was writing. "I told you about Sarah's brother getting into a car outside a gay bar, right? Well, Sergeant Burwell just noticed that the car the kid was getting into belongs to Elias Wong. The private dick working for the Byrne family, the guy talking to the media about the case, he's the homosexual lover of one of the suspects."

"So what?"

Spracklin looked up from his notebook. "So what? He's been sowing confusion in the investigation from the word go—that's what." Spracklin began to wonder if Wong was motivated by more than just trying to get back at the SFPD. "Those homos could have hatched the murder together."

"Why would they have had the set list for the concert?" asked Marie. "What's their motive for killing Menendes? And if Wong has a car, he could have got rid of the heads a lot farther away than the park. I think you're letting your prejudice against gays cloud your judgment." They both let the comment hang in the air, then Marie said, "If he's working with the family, maybe he was just picking William Byrne up."

Spracklin shook his head and began to jot down notes again. "Wong was first hired to investigate a theft at the container terminal, and those photos were taken before the theft. Sarah Byrne and Menendes took the photos so they could blackmail William Byrne, long before the family hired Wong." He glanced out at the phone booth again. "Wong and William Byrne hang out together at gay bars. Elias isn't quite the dashing playboy we all thought he was."

"So, what does it mean?"

They were interrupted as headlight beams swept across the bushes. A police cruiser came rushing along the curved road and pulled up by the phone booth. A uniformed officer jumped out of the car and scanned the intersection. "It means someone was double-crossing someone," said Spracklin. The cop across the street was doing a three-sixty with the flashlight—obviously less interested in finding the two severed heads than in the renegade cop who'd dropped them off. "Menendes was working with Wong. Wong was in tight with young Byrne. Byrne was being blackmailed by Menendes and Sarah. Someone was knifing their partner in the back."

A second cop got out of the cruiser and joined his partner. They were almost at the bush when another set of headlines illuminated the scene, these ones coming from the direction of Park Station. A red Mustang pulled up under the streetlight.

"Well, speak of the devil," muttered Spracklin.

Elias Wong stepped out of the driver's door and paced toward the two uniforms. Spracklin felt anger heat his face. How had Wong found out so quickly that Spracklin had phoned in where the heads were? Had Burwell leaked it to him? Then the passenger door opened and out stepped a muscular form that joined the others. He had his back to Spracklin but it didn't matter.

"Is that brick shithouse William Byrne?" asked Marie.

"No," said Spracklin. "Will Byrne is getting out of the car now." He pointed and she could see the bucket seat had been pushed forward and Will Byrne was stepping out on to the grassy verge of the road. "The brick shithouse is Mickie O'Neill, the IA thug who wants to interview you."

CHAPTER 46

Spracklin still couldn't figure it out. As darkness fell, he and Marie had sat in the bushes and watched the police drama unfold across the street from them. The shrub with yellow flowers was lit by the headlights of three squad cars, whose red beams swirled around a scene of forensic scientists, medical examiners, cops, and the three men in street clothes who'd driven up in a red Mustang. The men with scientific training peered into the garbage bag and pored over the bush. *The sons of bitches want to find evidence against me*, thought Spracklin.

Through it all, O'Neill, Wong and Byrne hung around the Mustang, watching the proceedings and conferring among themselves. O'Neill was their emissary, the policeman who could legitimately discuss the operations with the other police officers. The body language of the patrolmen spoke volumes. From his hideout in the bushes, Spracklin could tell they were terse with the IA officer, and many glanced uneasily at Wong and Byrne as they spoke. By late afternoon, Ed Burwell showed up, spending most of his time with the medical examiner, and an assistant Spracklin recognized but didn't know, looking into the garbage bag. Burwell didn't say a word to O'Neill or his chums.

It was about nine o'clock when the officers began to clear out. Spracklin was relieved to see it was the ME's assistant who lugged the garbage bag off to his van. The evidence would be protected and analyzed. By 9:30, O'Neill, Wong and Byrne got back in the sports car and pulled slowly off toward the Pacific coast. They moved at a speed that suggested they were patrolling the park, and Spracklin felt sure they were looking for him.

He and Marie were unsure where to go, but they felt drawn back to Hippie Hill and Sharon Meadow. They took their time getting there and noticed two members of the Diggers entering the field. Marie was the one who saw the hippies, a girl and man, both with shoulder-length hair and threadbare clothes, carrying baskets full of loaves of bread. Marie asked for two, and Spracklin reached for his wallet. The young man, a jowly kid with huge sideburns, smiled and waved off the payment. The Spracklins hadn't eaten since breakfast and Marie bit into her bread. Spracklin was hungry but he studied the tall loaf. It was an extraordinary shape, cylindrical with a puffed crown.

"Coffee can loaves," said Marie with a wad of bread wedged into one cheek. "The Diggers have found the best way to produce a lot of bread for crowds of people is to pack it in coffee cans."

Spracklin nodded and bit in. It was fresh. They pulled apart the loaves and shoved them in their mouths as they wandered on to Sharon Meadow. The concert was now in full swing, and the crowd stood shoulder to shoulder for a hundred yards up Sharon Meadow. Spracklin took Marie's hand and they wandered into the back of the crowd, where they hoped they could disappear among the tangle of swaying forms. A four-man electric band was on the stage now, blazing away in the glow of the orange lights projected from across the field.

Spracklin could see no one he recognized on the field, though it would have been hard to pick people out in the dark. No sign of the bikers or cops, or any musicians he knew. The only figure he recognized was J.D. Ehler up by the stage, his face illuminated by the light of the soundboard. He still had the sound system blaring away as the clock approached midnight. The figures on the stage looked blurred to Spracklin in the intense light. He could make out the lead guitarist coming out of a solo and stepping to a microphone to belt out his song.

Spracklin saw someone he recognized, one of Ehler's lackeys, at the rear of the crowd, and he remembered what Ehler had told him: he was bootlegging during the festival. Spracklin wandered up to the kid, who recognized him and nodded a hello.

"Any scotch?" asked Spracklin. He felt a tug at his elbow. Marie tried to drag him away.

"Rum or gin?" asked the kid.

"Rum," said Spracklin, once again drawing his wallet from the overalls.

"You don't need that, Daddy," Marie yelled in his ear.

"No, but I want it."

He paid five bucks for the mickey, took a shot and tucked it into his overall pocket. He wandered into the dark crowd. Spracklin didn't know where he was going—he just needed to find some place to conceal himself, to be safe, to sort through all he'd seen. He led Marie through the clutches of hippies, wedging their way past three women who were dancing naked to the song, and zigzagging toward a lighting standard at the left of the field. A huge god's eye, about five feet by five feet on a ten-foot staff, was positioned just to the left of it. They huddled down beside the scaffolding. Spracklin sat on the platform the light technician was standing on, while Marie craned her neck to see the stage around the god's eye.

As he took the pen and notebook from his pocket, he realized his hands were shaking. He had no order for his thoughts. He only wrote down what he had learned.

> Wong, W. Byrne and O'Neill are working together.
> Wong was working with Menendes.
> Menendes is a victim.
> We think Menendes was working with Sarah in
>   blackmailing Will Byrne.
> Marie is pregnant.
> Will Byrne gave his sister info to help with a stereo heist.
> Sarah and Menendes were using stereo gear to launder
>   money from their drug smuggling.
> Marie is pregnant.
> Marie is pregnant – who's the father, could it be someone
>   other than Fox?

He took another swig of the rum. Mediocre drink but it was better than beer. If he ran out, he might be able to buy some scotch from another of Ehler's people. He took one final shot and closed his eyes as it slid down his throat. With the beat of the music pounding at his eardrums, he tried to shut out all distractions and ask himself one question: Who killed Sarah Byrne and Pete Menendes?

In his mind he repeated the question. Who killed Sarah Byrne and Pete Menendes?

He opened his eyes to write the question down, and realized Marie was standing beside him. In the ambient light from the spotlight above him, she could read what he had written down. She settled in beside him, and took the pen from his hand. She leaned over and above the sound of the rock band said, "The father is Andrew Fox."

She crossed off the final line of his list of issues.

"That's why you were in court on Monday?"

She nodded and leaned to his ear again. "I had to tell him. I mean, you know, I may not have another chance. After the judge finished with him, I mouthed the words to him. Then he was distracted. Then he punched that sheriff. The whole thing was surreal."

In the next second, there was no music on Sharon Meadow. The band finished its set and bowed as the crowd roared their applause. On stage, they began to change up for the next band.

"Fox didn't punch the sheriff because you said you were pregnant," said Spracklin, relieved that he no longer had to yell above the band. "He saw one of Bogdan Polgar's guys sitting near you. He knew Polgar was tracking him and could get to him in prison—so he had to do something to get thrown into solitary. He decked a sheriff."

There was enough light that he could see Marie nodding. She might have been hurt that Fox's outburst in court was strategic rather than passionate.

"You're going to keep it?" asked Spracklin.

"I think so." She took a deep breath and said, "Unless I'm in prison." She said it quickly, as if she was worried that she wouldn't finish the words if she slowed down.

Spracklin had to laugh. "The kid's father, grandfather, and mother would all be inside—the baby might as well join us."

He laughed again, but Marie looked puzzled. "Grandfather? You?"

Spracklin shrugged and nodded. "It's not looking good, honey. I have to emerge from the bushes at some point, and they're going to have some questions."

Marie laughed now. "You can outsmart them."

"Maybe."

"You said it yourself: finding Sarah's killer would be enough to redeem yourself."

"But the case is a dog's breakfast." He pulled out his pack of Chesterfields. He noticed he only had three left.

"So, what do we know about the killer?"

"We know that Sarah—probably with the help of Menendes—blackmailed her brother into handing over information that helped with a stereo heist, and she laundered the proceeds and stashed them in her bank account. And now her homosexual brother is working with Elias Wong and Mickie O'Neill, ostensibly to try to solve the case."

"OK, what do we know about this O'Neill guy?"

"He was one of Wong's guys in the Bureau of Inspectors when I joined. He hated me because he thought I stabbed Wong in the back. So, he moved to IA."

"And he's after me, using me to get back at you?"

Spracklin thought for a moment. "Yes."

"Is he gay?"

Spracklin paused. He'd never considered the question. He lit his cigarette. "Dunno. I think O'Neill has a wife."

"So, let's say the three of them, Wong, William, and O'Neill, are close, all gay. Maybe two of them are lovers. William was being blackmailed, so the other two helped him kill Sarah and—"

"There are three problems with that theory." Before she could ask, he listed them. "One, Wong wouldn't do it. I know the guy. He's an asshole, but he's not a hired gun. Two, I don't think William knew his sister was blackmailing him. And three, we have no evidence tying them to it. We have a motive, but no evidence." He lit his cigarette, then pulled it from his mouth. "We've got to focus on the evidence."

Marie took his notebook and again flicked to the list of suspects. "The little girl said it was a male. He carried a big knife. In the first killing he used a...." She motioned with her hands as if she were looping a chord around someone's neck. "What's that thing called?"

"A garrote."

"A garrote. He used it in the first killing. Then a gun in the second, and a knife in the third. And we think he has something to do with the concert."

"And he's a shitty shot." Spracklin took a drag on his cigarette. "He missed us by a mile down in the dell. He could have braced his arm against that tree. Wong would have made those shots. Maybe O'Neill as well. They weren't the ones shooting at us down there." He took a long enough pull on his cigarette that he could see it burning down. He needed more cigarettes. The case was driving him nuts.

"We have nothing…." Marie was speaking slowly, gazing out at the crowd that was dissolving before them. Several spectators were drifting away from Sharon Meadow, figuring the exciting part of the concert had finished. "Nothing that connects those three guys to the murders."

They watched a young woman, probably twenty, lead her two filthy toddlers out by the hands.

"Maybe that's because they weren't involved with the murder," said Marie. "Will Byrne was being blackmailed, and his company was robbed so he brought in his friend Elias Wong. When Sarah went missing, Wong was given the job of looking for her, and Menendes became his second. Menendes steered him away from the girl. Neither Wong, Byrne nor their friend O'Neill knew Sarah was the blackmailer." She closed the book. "That's all we know."

Spracklin pulled out his bottle and took a swig.

"Do you disagree with any of that?" asked Marie.

"Nothing."

"Let's think of it from the point of view of the killer," she said. "The guy stalks Sarah, finds out she goes out at night and…." She paused, and thought for a moment. "He used a garrote. I mean, like, what is that?"

"A garrote? It's a choke wire, with wooden holders at either end. Legend has it they're popular with the mafia on the East Coast."

They looked at each other. They both thought the same thing.

"The newspaper story," said Spracklin.

"It said there were rumors the mafia was one of the parties moving into the void left in Andy's patch in Haight-Ashbury," said Marie. "And the garrote we found on Sarah's head, it was wedged into the neckbones. The guy couldn't get it out."

"What are you getting at?"

"Let's say he didn't want you to see the garrote. Maybe the initials A&J mean something that has a clue. Or maybe the fact that it was a garrote tells you something. What would you usually think if you found a garrote with a body?"

"Italian mafia."

"Then maybe that's it. The mafia murdered Sarah. Then cut off her head because they didn't want the cops to think it was a mob hit. Or to see the A&J logo."

Spracklin wondered if he should have thought more about the mafia. The Italian crime organizations were never as prominent on the West Coast as they were in the big Eastern cities.

Marie was thinking in lock-step with him. "Are Italian mobsters even active in San Francisco?"

"Last one was Al Capone when they shipped him to Alcatraz," said Spracklin. He couldn't remember ever having to investigate a mob hit in San Francisco. But he knew that the mob had become active in Las Vegas, and there were worries about them in Los Angeles.

"Okay, let's say you're right," he said. "The guy didn't want us to know it was a mob hit so he decapitated Sarah Byrne. The next day, the media reports were all over the bike gang that decapitated its victims. So, when they killed Menendes, they cut his head off too so it would look like the bike gang was on a rampage."

Spracklin was thinking back through the case now. It was falling into place. There was a turf war in Haight-Ashbury. The bikers were at war with Polgar's gang. Polgar was showing up, feeding information to him and Elias Wong. And someone wanted to get rid of all vestiges of Fox's gang. And that, he thought, was why the guy in the bushes seemed to be shooting at Marie. She was part of the Fox gang. What they had to do now was find someone, individual or individuals, who had connections to the Eastern crime families.

Marie mumbled something he couldn't hear, so she repeated it. "Luigi Prodi." Spracklin shook his head, but his daughter persisted. "He's the only Italian I know of who's been hanging around the concert."

Spracklin thought of the flabby gallery owner and again shook his head. "Maybe I shouldn't rule it out so quickly, but he doesn't fit the bill. Every indication we have says this guy is athletic, physically very strong."

"So, are we looking for goombahs in suits and fedoras?"

"He'd sort of stand out on Haight Street, wouldn't he?" he asked.

"Anyone can hide on Haight Street. And these guys are probably smart enough to send in someone who looks like a hippie."

"Who's a lousy marksman." Spracklin checked his watch. It was past 1 a.m. That meant it was already past four on the East Coast. He couldn't use the phone by the bowling green. He knew there was a phone booth on Stanyan, but he would be a sitting duck going anywhere near it. He had to get to a phone, but he had to protect himself and Marie.

"We're making a move soon, Marie."

"Where to?"

Spracklin pointed to the west, at the Sharon Art Studio.

CHAPTER 47

Sometime after two, the lights went off and the ringing electric instruments fell silent. The city had cut the power to the festival, at long last. The silence was broken by the booing of the crowd, and seconds later the field was lit with flashlights and cigarette lighters. Spracklin heard Ehler say through a bullhorn: "We'll have a fifteen-minute intermission then proceed with our acoustic set." The response from the crowd was muted until he added: "Featuring Jasmine." That got a bit of approval.

Spracklin stood and looked around. Seeing no one menacing, he said to Marie, "Let's head off."

Marie stood and stretched. He could tell she was weary. A flickering orange light grabbed their attention. At the bottom of Hippie Hill, Ehler's crew had pushed back the crowd and had lit bonfires in two trash barrels. In the light of the flames, Spracklin could see the volunteers laying down palettes for a little makeshift stage amid the people. "Draft cards?" asked Ehler into the bullhorn. "Anyone want to add their draft cards to the blaze?" Two long-haired men stumbled forward from different directions, and tossed something into the fires, to cheers from the crowd.

Marie and Spracklin joined the tired, the bored, the stoned, the people who had to report to work in a few hours, now wandering to the back of the field. The Lieutenant noticed a guy in his forties who'd brought two teens to the concert. He'd stayed a lot later than Spracklin would have stayed if he'd brought Marie as a dad. Spracklin and Marie veered away from the others as they reached the rear of the field. They tried to look natural as they stepped on to the little patio in front of the Sharon Art Studio, a two-story stone structure tucked into a patch of shrubs.

Spracklin stepped beside some bushes and glanced back, trying to catch any sign of someone following them. Nothing. After a quick survey of the bushes, he saw only a pair of Flash running shoes sticking out from under a forsythia bush. Spracklin hoped it was just some kid sleeping off a night at a concert. There was a light over the main door to the arts building, but he had to risk it. He took out his keychain, and used the two picks to go to work on the deadlock bolt on the door.

"Hurry," said Marie.

"It's coming," he said. Seconds later, he pushed the door open, stepped inside and closed the door behind them. The room smelled of plasticine and crayons—smells from Marie's childhood when she'd spend afternoons coloring and making things. It seemed a reprieve from the stench of marijuana that hung over the concert-go-ers outside.

"What's the grand plan?" asked Marie.

"A supervisor's office," he responded as they climbed the stairs. "A supervisor would have long-distance privileges."

They were in a hall and could see just enough light coming through the frosted glass doors and transoms to find their way. He assumed that the guy in charge would want a corner office above everyone else, even in a two-story outfit like this. Spracklin went to work again with his picks, and a minute later they were in the sec-retary's suite. Sitting in the secretary's chair, he took out his address book, checked a number and dialed. It started ringing on the other end, and Spracklin knew he'd found a phone that could dial New York direct. Now he just had to hope his old friend was in.

"Hello, the Sanchez residence," said a deep voice.

"Iggie," said Spracklin. He had to keep his voice down, but he didn't want his old colleague Ignatius Sanchez to know he was up to no good. When they'd worked together at Justice in Washington, Sanchez had been one of the straighter arrows in the department. Now he was a field officer with the FBI in New York, specializing in organized crime, and Spracklin doubted he would have learned to tolerate cops who broke the rules. "It's Jimmy Spracklin. How the hell are you?"

"Jimmy Spracklin," came back the baritone response. You could hear the big smile in his voice. "You in town?"

"No. Still in San Francisco. I needed to call you with a favor."

"What is it—three o'clock there? And you're calling me at home before work. Must be a hell of a favor."

"Information."

"I figured as much. I'll see what I can do."

"We have a turf war going on here. We busted up a heroin ring and now there's a scramble to fill the void. We're hearing that one of the East Coast families, the mafia, is moving in. I'm wondering if you've heard anything."

Sanchez thought for a moment. "I doubt it's New York. We've had relative calm here for the past year. The economy is strong, and everyone is making money. There's a truce over expansion in Las Vegas. The impression I get is that everyone is just hunkering down and focusing on their business. It makes it harder for us to crack down, but there's relative peace in the underworld."

"Any thoughts on who might be interested in San Francisco?"

"Yeah. The Lucchese family in Boston. That's L-U-C-C-H-E-S-E." He answered quickly and decisively.

"Never heard of them."

"They're north Italian, not Sicilian, like most of the families here. So, they're kind of looked down on in New York. They tried to put a stake in the ground in Las Vegas about two years ago, and it got messy. It's known they want to move west but I haven't heard where. But I do know who would know. Max Atherton. Know him?"

"Nope."

"He's a field officer in Boston. He does commercial and organized crime." Sanchez excused himself for a moment and came back with home and office phone numbers, which he read out to Spracklin. "Tell Max I told you to call his home number because I knew the lazy shit would still be in bed."

They laughed and Spracklin was about to say goodbye when Sanchez stopped him. "Hey, Jimmy," he said. "It's a shame about Bobby, eh?"

Spracklin had not been in touch with anyone he'd worked with at Justice to commiserate about the death of Bobby Kennedy. He knew that Iggie Sanchez had admired the AG as much as he had.

"It was awful, Iggie. Just awful. We'll toast to his memory the next time I'm in Manhattan."

They said their goodbyes, and Spracklin filled Marie in on what he'd learned. He was already dialing the number as he wrapped up his recitation of it.

"Ath-ah-ton," said the guy who picked up the phone. Spracklin had to smile at the unmistakable Boston accent, which reminded him again of the Kennedys. The guy sounded groggy, like the phone had woken him. Spracklin explained who he was, that he was a friend of Iggie Sanchez and that he wanted information on the Lucchese family.

"I know them," said Atherton. "I know them well. I might be able to help you." He paused and added. "I can talk about them all day. I've got about fifteen minutes now."

"Iggie said they're interested in expanding to the West Coast."

"Word on the street is it's still part of their plan. They got the shit kicked out of 'em in Vegas." Spracklin thought he heard mattress springs squeaking, like the guy had settled in to tell the story. "But yeah, they're restless and ambitious. The family kingpin is Marco, who started their leather business forty years ago—imports, custom designs. It's the front for their narcotics and gambling business. Marco comes from around Lake Como in the north."

"Yeah, Iggie mentioned that."

"The Sicilians look down on them, think they're not as tough and disciplined as the southern wops. The Luccheses are out to prove them wrong. Marco and his three sons—they're taking over the business—they try to be as brutal as anyone. The sons—Tom, Jim and Lou—they're cruel, even by the standards of *Cosa Nostra*."

"And they're all in Boston, the sons?"

"Yup. No question they're here. We've got their phones tapped at their company, Anderson and Jones. And all three of them—"

"Anderson and Jones?"

"Yeah, they wanted their company to have an American name. That's what they came up with. Anyway, the three oldest sons have been in the office in the last seventy-two hours."

"You said the three *oldest* sons?"

"Well there's Francis, the youngest son. But he's not in the business. He's a hippie."

Spracklin sat up in the chair. Marie couldn't hear both ends of the conversation, but she could tell her father had heard something interesting. Marie squeezed in so she could hear Atherton as well. "You said the youngest son is a hippie?"

"Every family's got one these days. Kids who want to rebel against Pop and find peace, love, and harmony instead of make money. The Luccheses are no different. This Francis kid is a musician, a folk singer. Better with a guitar than a garrote."

"Max, why did you mention a garrote?"

"It's the Lucchese weapon of choice. They pride themselves on it. They even make their own garrotes out of old leather-making tools.

They use the wooden handles from broken tools to make the handles of the garrotes. Like, it's what the boys did together as kids—made their own garrotes. How sick is that? The family claims that their guys with garrotes can whoop other guys with guns. It didn't play out that way in Vegas, but that's what they say. Listen, Jimmy, I gotta run."

"Sure, sure. Just one more thing. Can you give me a description of Francis?"

"Sure. Charming guy. Medium build. Brown hair. Doesn't really look like a wop at all. Like I said, they're northern Italian—more German blood than Italian, I think." He shifted and said uncomfortably: "One thing I can tell you, Lieutenant, before you ask, is we don't have a recent photo of Francis Lucchese. I mean, we might have a grainy image of him as a kid, but nothing recent and nothing good. He's never been busted. And I doubt he's in the business. Too busy being free."

Spracklin was about to say something, when Atherton let out a laugh. "'Bout the only fun I have with my job is reminding Marco Lucchese that his youngest boy's a flower child. It ruins a mafioso's whole day."

Spracklin laughed audibly and thanked him and replaced the receiver. He looked at Marie—she was looking at him wide-eyed.

"You think this is the lead you need?" she asked.

"I don't know, honey. Certainty in a homicide detective is a dangerous thing." He needed a drink to help him digest all the information, and for the first time he was annoyed that Marie was with him

"But it's a lead. We can run a search and see if there's a Francis Lucchese in the area. It will probably come up blank—if he came here to kill, he'd be traveling incognito. But it will be a start. I can get word to Burwell that the guy's a made mafioso and we need an APB on him." He stood and stretched. "It's a lead," he repeated.

CHAPTER 48

Spracklin wanted to celebrate with a drink as they walked back across Sharon Meadow, toward the twin bonfires. He knew he should be cautious but his gut told him they were closing in on the killer. What he wanted to do was sit with a bottle of scotch and a sheet of paper and string together all the evidence they'd collected. But he knew that his daughter—just like her mother—would nag him if he pulled out his flask now.

"So, A&J—Anderson and Jones—make leather goods," said Marie. She was slowing down. They were heading back to the hard-core fans who were hanging on until sunlight, maybe five-hundred people huddled around the stage lit by the two bonfires. Spracklin could see the flickering of cigarettes and joints in the audience clustered around the makeshift stage.

"That's right," he said. "If we can find this Lucchese guy, we have the garotte tying the family to this killing at least." He shook his last cigarette out of the pack and tossed the pack away. Eventually, they would have to track down this Francis, even if it meant extraditing him from Boston. But he wanted to find the prick now. That night. Before dawn.

Most of the crowd was seated on the ground, listening intently to Jasmine. She looked minute on stage, but Spracklin had to smile as he gazed at her. Her growing celebrity made her appearance at the local festival endearing. J.D. Ehler was on the stage at the crest of Hippie Hill, looking with pride down on his creation. Luigi Prodi appeared to be asleep behind the stage and Ralph May was off to the side. Spracklin had to search to find Martha. It turned out she was just in front of them, huddled in a Hudson's Bay blanket. In the middle of them all, Jasmine sang as absent-mindedly as if she were still singing alone in the Victorian house where Spracklin had first seen her up on Masonic Avenue.

Azure eyes tempt strangers
They're zombied by her lips
And her skirt stirs up dust clouds
With the swaying of her hips

She shares a house on Page Street
With a dealer called Mac Raffie
She spray paints poems on sidewalks
by the Gnostic Toad Café

Marie rested her head against her father's chest and he wrapped his arm around her. "This will end, won't it?" she said. "We will get through this night, this case, get out of this park?"

Although worn to the bone, Spracklin knew it was time for strength, for kindness. "We need to get you somewhere you can sleep." He patted her shoulder and tried not to choke on his next words. "You have a baby to think about."

"Please don't mention it."

"You don't want it?"

"I don't know. I know that one day I want to be a mother, but this is not the time. I hope one day to have a daughter." She smiled. "I hope she's spirited and troublesome. And I hope that I can show her all the love and support when she gets in trouble that you've shown me."

Spracklin squeezed her shoulder and Jasmine introduced her next song as she tuned her guitar.

"Like, there's this cat up here and he really wants me to play his song, dig?" She tuned the guitar a bit more. "No, I mean it. He taught me his song last night and…." She laughed. "I don't know where the dude went but he's been telling me all night I have to play his song." She laughed, and Spracklin thought she was looking over toward the soundboard. "He told me it means a lot to him, so here goes."

It's a brand new da-a-a-a-ay
The world is unfoldin'
It's streamlined and golden
And what today shows is
It's all coming up roses
'Cause I'm made, made, made — in the shade.

The crowd responded with a wave of applause. Spracklin almost forgot himself and applauded as well. It was a nice song, one he thought he'd heard before, and her voice was divine. He glanced over to Marie to see what she thought. She was frozen with a look of horror on her face. It wasn't just that she was exhausted — she looked absolutely petrified. She grabbed her father's upper arm to steady herself.

"It's him," she said.

"What?"

"It's Ralph, Ralph May. 'I'm made.' Holy fuck. He was playing with us all the time."

"Who — what are you talking about?"

"Ralph May sang that song yesterday, maybe the day before. 'I'm Made in the Shade.' The chorus was him singing over and over again 'I'm made.' He said he'd just written it. He was playing with us." Spracklin could feel her grip tightening. "Didn't you say the killer is a *made* mafia guy? You used the word made."

"Yeah. Made — it means he's carried out a hit, killed someone."

"Ralph wrote a song saying he was 'made.' Maybe he was confessing to a mafia hit?"

Spracklin turned toward her. It made sense. Ralph May was a young man with enough strength to do the job. He was musical. Spracklin didn't know if he had Italian heritage. But once they had him in custody, the police could check his identity. They would learn, he was sure, that Ralph May's real name was Francis Lucchese.

Marie was wide awake now. "He was always watching me but I felt he was just coming on to me. And that belt he gave me — he knew all about leather works."

"You said Prodi gave it to you."

She blushed. "I said it was made by someone in Luigi's circle. Ralph made it."

"She always was a smart one, wasn't she, Jimmy?" said a voice behind him. Spracklin glanced over his shoulder, and saw Ralph May, the man he now knew was Francis Lucchese. May's hand gripped Marie's arm, and he was holding a knife in the small of her back. He was crowded in close to her so no one but Spracklin could see the knife. Spracklin then felt something stick into his own ribs. Turning, he saw a silver-haired man behind him. Spracklin couldn't quite place the guy, but he looked familiar. The silver-haired guy reached inside Spracklin's coveralls and took his revolver out of the holster. Spracklin assumed Lucchese was also armed with the gun he'd used to kill Pete Menendes. Right now, Spracklin was worried about the knife in Marie's back. He couldn't try anything while Marie was in danger.

"So, we're going to stand here and enjoy the rest of my song," said Lucchese. "It's a great song, isn't it? Then, when people start leaving, we're going to go with them. We'll tell you where to go after that. Any problems, the girl gets it first."

"Let her go, May," said Spracklin. He said it just loud enough that a few people nearby could hear. He raised his hands slightly so he looked like a hostage.

"Save it." Spracklin was about to say something but Lucchese silenced him. "Lester isn't afraid to finish you off right here and now." *Lester Fredericks*, thought Spracklin. It was Bogdan Polgar's bodyguard. Fredericks jammed the gun into Spracklin's ribs, and the Lieutenant was silent. The pieces fit together. The Lucchese family wanted a West Coast base and had a son who would fit right into the Haight-Ashbury scene. Polgar needed someone to clean out the remnants of the Fox gang. They'd teamed up and initiated the youngest Lucchese brother with contracts on Fox's people.

"Are you taking us to the dell to finish the job?" asked Spracklin. He was sure Lucchese wouldn't kill them in the crowd if he could help it. He had to keep talking, at least until he thought of something. "That's pretty close to Park Station."

Marie winced, and Spracklin knew Lucchese was pressing the knife harder.

"Shut your fucking mouth, Spracklin," Lucchese whispered. He looked around and seemed to be changing his mind. "Okay, we're going now. Off to the left. Any trouble, we won't hesitate."

He pulled at Marie's shoulder, moving too urgently, Spracklin thought. Even in the darkness, people noticed the jerking motion. Spracklin saw people in front of them turn around. "Easy Fredericks," said Spracklin in an audible voice. He knew the thug wanted to belt him, but he couldn't with all the witnesses around. Fredericks led Spracklin out of the park behind Marie and Lucchese. Spracklin noticed for the first time that Lucchese had a backpack slung over his shoulder.

Behind them, Jasmine had somehow moved out of Ralph May's song and gone back into the ballad she had been singing before. Her voice soared with the last verse of her reprisal.

She smiles with springtime promise
Shrouding torture slowly bled
And whispers prayers to Jesus Christ
In the shadow of her bed

There was a wave of applause as an em-cee came on stage to thank her. Then he pointed off toward Haight-Ashbury. "And if you look over there you can just notice the first beams of sunlight reaching out over Buena Vista." The crowd seemed roused by the thought of greeting the sun. Spracklin looked over and it was true. He could just see a light greying the horizon through the trees.

CHAPTER 49

Lucchese and his partner guided Marie and Spracklin west of Hippie Hill. They were in the shade of the great trees, so they had trouble seeing where they were going. Marie stumbled once, and sobbed as she caught her balance. Spracklin wanted to help her but knew he couldn't move. He had to stay alive to save Marie.

"You know this is useless, Francis," Spracklin said. "We've got the garrote, the A&J logo on it. It's already in the Hall of Justice and it will be analyzed today. You're making things—"

"Shut up, Spracklin," Francis said. "The cops are looking for you more than me."

"It's going to look more natural if we're talking," said the Lieutenant. Behind them they could hear the crowd welcoming the dawn. There was a new wave of revelers coming in—people who'd woken up early to catch the end of the concert. A trickle of hippies was coming toward them, some excited, others fighting off exhaustion, all scurrying to Sharon Meadow so they could greet the dawn with others.

"So, talk," said Lucchese. He seemed to agree that it caused less suspicion.

"The Lucchese family and Bogdan Polgar are teaming up to take over the drug trade in Haight-Ashbury," said Spracklin.

"We needed a local partner."

"You found redemption within your family. You're finally made and you get in on the ground floor of a big operation."

"Bogdan said you're sharp. He's been tailing you, studying you for months. He wanted to get something on you. He finally got it when he learned that your daughter was working with Fox."

"Fox told him?"

"Fox didn't have to. Bogdan knows your family and he caught wind that she was hanging around with Fox. He knew what Fox would ask her to do. He had me follow her. We told Internal Affairs anonymously that a dark-haired girl, about sixteen, picked up Sarah Byrne at the airport. IA started asking airport employees and someone confirmed it. She remembered the girl with the nose stud getting in a car."

Their footfalls resounded as they moved along the asphalt path. The birds were in full chorus now that the sun was rising, and beyond the park they could hear the traffic beginning to grind along the streets.

"Why did you have to kill Sarah Byrne?"

"We had to remove any trace of the Fox gang. It was small, but it had powerful allies in the Far East. We got rid of Byrne and Menendes. Marie is next. You're a bonus. We haven't been able to get to Fox yet. Bogdan will get him soon." The kid sounded so relaxed, so proud of himself and his part in the plan.

"You were embedded in Haight-Ashbury. You tracked down Sarah. You killed her in the park. And when you couldn't retract the garrote you cut her head off." Spracklin strode along and kept going. "And when young Bloom started following you, you killed him as well."

"All correct." Lucchese's voice swelled with pride. "The media started to blame these bikers from LA and we decided to behead Menendes as well. I hadn't got around to burying Sarah's head, so I buried them both during the rainstorm a few nights ago. You know where, I guess." He steered Marie to the left and pushed her on. "In fact, we're heading there now."

They began to wend down the winding trail into the de Laveaga Dell. It was quieter than on the main path. There was no sound of traffic, no cheers from the concert, only the morning song of the birds. They came out to the glade, and Spracklin could see the handle of the shovel he'd driven into the earth the afternoon before.

"Hold up," said Lucchese. He pushed Marie forward and his associate did likewise with Spracklin. The assailants stood, holding guns on the prisoners. Spracklin estimated they were at least thirty yards from the nearest woods. Too far to run. Lucchese tucked the knife into the back of his blue jeans and took a revolver from his knapsack. He looked at the brightening sky and said, "Don't try to run. Bogdan's people know I was bringing you here. They're surrounding the dell."

Spracklin gave a half-hearted laugh. "I thought it was only cops who told that whopper." It was a lame joke but Lucchese gave an exaggerated laugh. It told Spracklin the boy was far more nervous than he was letting on. Spracklin had to play him. With Marie shivering and crying beside him, he had to use his cunning to find the kid's weak spot and exploit it.

"One question, Lucchese," said Spracklin. "What reason did Bogdan give you for putting a contract out on me?"

"We decided that—"

"He decided. I'm as good as dead, Francis. I don't have time for your bullshit. Why did Bogdan want me dead?"

"We planned this. It was a partnership. We needed you out of the way."

Spracklin laughed for real this time. "And he gave you the gun to whack Menendes with, right?"

"Shut up, Spracklin."

"Did you ask yourself why he gave you the gun? We've got the slugs now from Menendes' head. We can trace it."

"I said shut up."

"And Lester here—was it your idea or Bogdan's to have him help you out?" Spracklin thought he noticed the kid's gun shaking. He thought about telling the kid that Fredericks would kill him once he and Marie were dead, but he knew that would prompt Fredericks to kill them all immediately. "Bogdan's played you," said Spracklin. "You kill me or Marie, there won't be any sanctuary for you or your family. The SFPD will hound you to the gates of hell. I just got off the phone with FBI Agent Max Atherton in Boston. He knows I'm on to you."

The boy's eyes widened at the mention of Atherton's name. He held his gun straight-arm, pointing it at Spracklin's head. "I said shut the fuck up," he yelled.

"He gave me the dirt on you, Francis. You're here to prove to your dad you're more than just a flower child. Once I'm gone, they're coming for you. And we have nothing linking any of this to Polgar. You know Bogdan Polgar doesn't care if you go down. And you're the low man on your family's totem pole."

"I said that's enough."

"That's why they sent you out here. Another fuckup like the one in Vegas and the Luccheses are dead. Boston will be as wide open as Haight-Ashbury."

Lucchese cocked the gun. Spracklin thought the next sound he heard—if he lived to hear it—would be the report of a gun. But it was the bellow of a gruff voice.

"Drop that gun."

Lucchese looked around, but kept his gun trained on Spracklin. In the dawn light, they could just make out several figures coming down the path and spreading out to take cover. Mickey O'Neill was standing at the front of them, yelling. Spracklin could make out Elias Wong beside him and William Byrne back in the trees. Two patrolmen, their weapons drawn, were spreading out on the periphery.

"Put down your weapons," said O'Neill. He was about one hundred yards away, pacing toward them. "This grove is surrounded. You can't escape."

Lucchese stepped behind Spracklin and held his gun to the Lieutenant's head. Spracklin realized now it was an old service pistol, the type he'd carried on his hip all through the Second World War. The young mafioso cocked the gun. Fredericks now felt exposed, so he stepped toward Marie, training his gun on the girl's head.

"Can you take him?" Lucchese asked Fredericks, keeping his own gun trained on Spracklin. The old Russian was nervous. He frowned as he looked at O'Neill marching toward them then nodded. Lucchese watched the other cops fanning out. Spracklin knew what Francis Lucchese was thinking: within seconds these cops would have them covered on all sides.

Fredericks took a shot at O'Neill, and the IA officer and one patrolman opened fire. It was then that Marie collapsed. Fredericks couldn't support her weight and aim at the cops. He let her drop.

"Do it," yelled Lucchese.

O'Neill, about eighty yards away, fell to one knee and grasped his pistol with two hands. The Russian shot once more and then kept pulling the trigger, but was hitting empty chambers. Two shots hit him at once. One in the knee, one in the head. He tumbled on to Marie, blood gushing from his forehead.

Lucchese pushed Spracklin down and dashed for the nearest trees, firing at the closest cop with the ancient pistol. He swiveled and shot twice at O'Neill, who was now moving again toward Fredericks. Spracklin ran after the young Italian. He intended to get the kid and kill him. He didn't know whether Marie was dead or alive. But he knew he had to kill Francis Lucchese. The bastard would have killed Marie, and now he would die — either to protect Marie if she were still alive, or in revenge if she were dead.

Lucchese made it to the tree line, turned and fired at Spracklin. The guy had missed him several times just one day earlier, and Spracklin felt sure he was a poor marksman on the run. Spracklin continued after him, and he began to recall he himself had lost his weapon to the Russian. He was closer to Francis than the armed cops, who were also in pursuit, and he was vulnerable. As he reached the bushes, Spracklin saw something. The spade that he had left stuck in the ground. He grabbed it. It was useless against a gun. But just having a weapon gave him the confidence he needed to pursue Francis Lucchese.

The woods were dark. He could make out patches of light above him. He stumbled over the uneven ground and up the hill. He grew winded quickly as he moved upwards. He couldn't see the boy, and he knew the young guy would be faster than him. But Spracklin was determined. He kept climbing, poised to bash the young hood at the first sight of him.

Trying to catch his breath, he burst out of the woods and entered a clear patch. There was an asphalt path with woods on either side. Spracklin tried to get his bearings and figure out where he was and where the young hood might have escaped to. He had the shovel up. He looked left and right but could see no sign of Francis Lucchese. He lowered the shovel as he searched around and tried to figure out where the made mafioso could have gone.

He heard two steps behind him and felt the killer's arms go over his head. As the arms descended, Spracklin reached and grabbed the wire that was falling in front of his face. The boy had been just awkward enough that Spracklin got a hand between the garrote and his throat. As he struggled, he felt the wire tighten and felt a sharp, burning pain radiate across the palm of his hand and around his neck. Lucchese was behind him pulling at the garrote with all his might.

He pulled hard enough to lift Spracklin off his feet. The wire dug into his neck and hand, and Spracklin screamed at the pain. It was agonizing but his hand was protecting the wire from severing his windpipe. Spracklin was powerless, and he knew it would just be seconds until the cord cut into his jugular. He would bleed to death. Spracklin's eyes bulged as his own knuckles began to block his throat and he had trouble breathing.

But he still had the shovel in his left hand and he flailed away with it trying to clobber Lucchese. The kid was able to duck the blows. He was young and strong and Spracklin was losing strength. He could feel his grip on the shovel loosening. He felt the unbelievable pain in his right hand.

A huge explosion shattered the silence, and the pressure on Spracklin's neck and hand eased. The Lieutenant fell to the ground and Lucchese's body collapsed on top of him. Spracklin gasped for breath as he clawed at the wire. He wanted to rip it off instantly, but he knew he'd rip his own flesh if he was too hasty. He fumbled to tug it out of the groove it had cut into his hand. He dropped the wire to the ground and rolled over on to his back. Ed Burwell was standing above him, his face smiling and his pistol smoking.

"You okay, Jimmy?" he asked. He glanced around to make sure there were no more gunmen around then turned his attention to Spracklin's neck, inspecting the wounds. He pried Spracklin's left hand away from the right, and looked at the bloody palm and fingers. "You may need stitches on that," he said as he withdrew a handkerchief from his pocket and pressed it into Spracklin's palm. "The neck wounds are superficial. Lucky you got that hand up."

Spracklin pressed the cloth against the back of his right hand. The pain subsided, and he struggled to understand what had happened.

"After your call, I came to the park to make sure we got those heads. I got them from the patrolmen, and found that prick O'Neill hanging around. I didn't like it so I went on patrol with two of my buddies...."

"How did you, O'Neill....?" Spracklin had almost blacked out and was having trouble finding his words.

"We were patrolling the park all night, we were one group and O'Neill was leading another. Looking for you and the killer. A minute ago, a redhead with big tits came running up to us, said a kid called Ralph led you and your daughter out of the concert to the west. Other kids said they saw them leading you down into de Laveaga Dell." Burwell holstered his pistol and looked at the dead man beside Spracklin. "O'Neill went after you. I stayed back in case they made a break for it. I heard your yell and came to help."

Spracklin looked back to his left. He could just see the body of Francis Lucchese lying beside him. His torso extended toward the trees, his arms lay akimbo. His head wasn't visible.

"Dead?" asked Spracklin.

"As a doornail," said Burwell. "Did he kill Sarah Byrne?"

"Yeah," said Spracklin. He used his left hand to push himself into a sitting position. He noticed the handkerchief was already showing red blotches. "And Pete Menendes and…." His voice tapered off. He pushed himself up, standing unsteadily.

"My daughter?" said Spracklin. "She was caught in the crossfire."

CHAPTER 50

Spracklin had the kerchief tied into a bandage around his hand by the time he broke through the trees into the dell again. He had stumbled but not fallen as he and Burwell scrambled down the wooded hill. Now he was once again in the enclosed field, surrounded by woods. Five men stood over the two figures on the ground. None said anything. Spracklin knew the look on their faces. He struggled to contain his grief.

Elias Wong caught sight of him first and said, "We've called for an ambulance, Sprack." The others turned to him.

By this time Spracklin was in a sprint. He pushed Mickey O'Neill out of the way as he arrived, and the big guy collided with William Byrne, who stabilized him.

"Woah, there," said O'Neill. Spracklin crouched down beside his daughter. Ed Burwell joined him. Spracklin knew his partner wanted to be with him during this ordeal.

Lester Fredericks was staring wide-eyed at the sky. He lay across Marie's lower half, pinning her legs and lower torso to the ground. Marie was covered with blood — it soaked through to her blue jeans and had splattered across her face. She lay on her back. Her eyes were closed, her mouth slightly open.

Spracklin pushed the dead man off Marie.

"Don't touch him, Jimmy," said O'Neill.

"My fucking daughter has to breathe, asshole," yelled Spracklin. He tugged at the Russian's arm again and dragged him off Marie's legs. Spracklin crouched beside his daughter and took her hand in his. "Marie, honey," he moaned. With the clean portion of the kerchief, he tried to wipe the blood off her face. He nudged the hair from her cheeks.

He put his mouth near her ear and said, "Marie, my darling, you're going to be all right." He hoped she couldn't hear the desperation in his voice. Behind him, Burwell was updating the others on the shooting on the other side of the woods. Spracklin gazed at Marie, searching for a pulse in her neck, trying to find signs that she was alive. She was cold and wasn't moving. "Marie," he said. "Always know I love you. Just remember that. I've always loved you."

He stood and tried to control himself. "Congratulations, O'Neill," he said. "You killed my daughter."

Looking over, he saw the hefty Internal Affairs officer staring back at him in disbelief. "Look, Jimmy," he said. "I feel for you about your girl. Seriously, man."

Spracklin stood and faced him. "You and Handell hounded her, persecuted her. Of course, she ran away last night. You guys coming to the house for her."

"Jimmy, you're emotional. It's understandable. But you can't pin this on Ray and me." Spracklin stepped over the dead man and reached out to where the pistol had fallen. He picked it up and put it in his holster.

"Jimmy, don't do anything you'll regret," said Wong.

"It's my gun and it's empty," said Spracklin. He stepped over the Russian's body again and walked toward O'Neill. Spracklin pushed O'Neill hard so he stumbled backward a couple of steps.

"Stand down, Spracklin," said O'Neill.

"I've lost my daughter, asshole." He shoved the IA officer again. He had to keep this going. He had to make sure the cops and Wong didn't try to break up the fight. He had to mix it up with O'Neill. He shoved O'Neill again, but the big man was resisting now. He only took one step back and cocked his fist.

"Lay off me, Sprack."

"I should put a beating on you just for fucking up my case." He could tell it registered with the other cops. "Patrolling with a suspect, colluding with—"

"What the hell are you talking about?" O'Neill was sounding defensive. He glanced once at the patrolmen, but Spracklin knew it was enough. The common men on the beat were witnessing a drag-em-out battle between a homicide detective and Internal Affairs— between a cop who punished murderers and a cop who punished cops. They were inclined to side with Spracklin, and Spracklin was going to use it to his advantage.

"For Chrissakes, O'Neill, my daughter and I risked our lives digging up those heads, protecting them. We get them to the cops and you show up with Wong and William Byrne." He pushed O'Neill again, challenging the big man to tangle.

O'Neill pointed at Spracklin and struggled to find the right words to respond. Wong stepped forward, as if he were the diplomat in the group. "Look, Jimmy, the important thing right now is we get your daughter the medical attention she needs." He stepped in between Spracklin and O'Neill.

"It's too late, asshole," yelled Spracklin. He grabbed Wong by the lapels and threw him to the ground. "You bastard," he shouted at the PI. "You screwed up the investigation from the word go. The murderer told me he decapitated Menendes because of what you leaked to the press about the bikers. He would have done the same to Marie and me. And you were feeding lies about me and Marie to your fag buddy here." He pointed to O'Neill. "And he was stupid enough to believe them."

"Watch it, Spracklin," said O'Neill.

Spracklin laughed. "I showed you yesterday who the tougher man was." Spracklin thought someone might come between them, but the cops were going to let them have it out. "Jesus Christ, O'Neill, I've got the photos Sarah Byrne was blackmailing her brother with." He gestured to William Byrne. "They show you guys outside Compton's. He was a suspect in my investigation but you chauffeured him around the crime scene."

"It's not true," yelled William. "He's lying."

"Your secret's out, sonny. We have the evidence." He turned again to O'Neill. "Not that I cared. What I care about was you and Wong here fucked up my case because of a grudge against me. And getting my daughter shot."

"I didn't get your daughter shot."

"She ran away from home to get away from you guys. That's how vile you are."

"Shut up, Spracklin. I'm warning you."

"Stick to bullying teenage girls, homo."

O'Neill took the bait. He lunged at Spracklin and the Lieutenant responded with a stiff left jab to his eye. Spracklin knew that O'Neill was younger and stronger and would win the fight. Spracklin's right hand was killing him, but he had to use it. He stepped into O'Neill and stung him with another left. He tried to follow up with a right cross, but O'Neill blocked it.

Spracklin backed up before O'Neill could grab him. Spracklin knew he was finished if it became a wrestling match. He circled O'Neill and backpedaled, drawing him and the cops farther from the two bloody bodies on the ground. Spracklin feinted with his right and landed another left. O'Neill's right eye was beginning to swell shut.

"I get that you like persecuting cops, O'Neill," he said. "But how long have you been shielding suspects because they're your queer friends?"

O'Neill took a lunge with his right, swinging it in a wide arc. Spracklin should have been able to duck it, but he was worn down. The punch caught him on the side of the head and dazed him. He struggled to retain his balance. Spracklin managed to get in three punches with his left before O'Neill grabbed his wrist. Spracklin got in one punch with his right before O'Neill hammered him again with another hook. Spracklin fell to the ground, and patrolmen moved in and grabbed O'Neill before he could pummel the prostrate Lieutenant. O'Neill struggled but he too was wearing out.

"You're going down, Spracklin," he yelled. "We got witnesses."

"You corrupted a murder investigation, you bastard."

They kept yelling at each other. Spracklin knew he had one victory. Burwell and the cops had heard the exchange. He'd turned the tables on O'Neill—actually he had turned them on Handell and the whole Internal Affairs division. Burwell and the patrolmen could all testify that O'Neill had been working with a suspect in a murder case and a former cop who was trying to sabotage the case. IA would be on the defensive now. Burwell, the only man there as strong as O'Neill was now bracing him, making sure the IA officer couldn't get to Spracklin.

One of the patrolmen said something, but it was drowned out by O'Neill yelling. "I'll wipe the floor with you, Spracklin. We've got so much shit on you and your daughter."

The patrolman waved an arm and started yelling. "The girl," he called. "The girl, the girl."

The others looked at him and he pointed to the spot where Marie had lain. All they could see was the flattened grass within the outline of her body. Fredericks' crumpled body was lying alone on the ground. In the distance, they could hear the wail of an ambulance siren. Spracklin realized it was the only sound they heard. The concert had ended.

"The girl's gone," said Wong.

"You did this, Spracklin. You created a diversion."

Spracklin had to play his advantage. "You are so full of shit, O'Neill."

"Barnes, Cooper, go after her," O'Neill told the patrolmen.

The patrolmen didn't move. Jimmy Wong shook his head and glared at them. He knew Spracklin had won. Burwell waved to the ambulance, which appeared in the glade. He pointed to the body on the ground, then told one of the patrolmen that they'd have to go reclaim another dead man lying by the roadside on the other side of the woody hill.

Spracklin and O'Neill stared at each other. O'Neill's right eye was swollen shut and his left eye burned with hatred. Spracklin did his best to return his glare. But in his mind, all he could think about was Marie. He knew she was moving into a crowd of sleepy hippies who were moving away from the all-night concert. He prayed with all his heart that the girl would be all right, that she'd be safe and sound. He turned away from O'Neill and joined Burwell in doing police work.

END

ENJOY THE FIRST CHAPTERS OF
THE PRODI SYNDICATE:
BOOK 3 OF THE HAIGHT CRIME SERIES

CHAPTER 1

Standing in the turret of his new office, Bogdan Polgar gazed through the five windows encircling him and realized he'd made a mistake. The windows offered a panoramic view of the intersection of Divisadero and Page, and occasional glimpses of the vestiges of the Summer of Love—teenaged girls in hot-pants, a rusted VW Bug with some message painted in white on its hood. When he'd decided in August to move his headquarters from a laundromat off Fillmore to the edge of Haight-Ashbury, Polgar had liked the idea of so many vistas. If he was ever forced to flee the building, he could check escape routes in four directions.

He'd chosen the old living room with the turret as his office because it was sunny and had that view. He'd be like the hipsters—the Grateful Dead, Country Joe McDonald—who had their pads in the Victorian homes in The Haight. His office would be on the second floor and, above it, a little apartment for himself. Now he understood how foolish he'd been. He wasn't a hipster. He was forty years old, as far as he knew. (He'd fled Poland in 1945 without any papers, but believed he'd been born in 1928.) He was a businessman with powerful enemies. He'd let his vanity overcome his innate caution.

As he looked around, he identified several places where an assassin could position himself for a clean shot at the turret. The Queen Anne home across Page Street was boarded up, and a sniper could take aim at Polgar in his new office from any of its empty rooms. There were parked cars offering a marksman cover. The broad boulevard of Divisadero could allow a hitman to launch volleys into the building from a passing car and be gone within seconds. In his mind's eye, Polgar envisioned Marcus Symmonds positioned behind the Chevy Caprice across the street, with a rifle aimed right at him.

"What's wrong, Bogdan?" asked Marcus Symmonds from behind him. He was sitting in one of the new plush chairs, flipping through the November issue of *Popular Mechanics*. The other guys in the gang always reached for *Playboy* or *Sports Illustrated*. Polgar had subscribed to *Popular Mechanics* for Symmonds.

"I don't like it," said Polgar. He turned back and walked across the living room, through the antique sliding doors into the dim dining room. It was a smaller, more humble space. There were two windows with frosted glass high above the wainscoting. "Here," said Polgar to the three men seated in the living room. "My office will be here."

"I thought the whole idea was for you to have a nice office," said Symmonds. "With a view."

Polgar gestured around the dining room. "It *is* a nice office — a step up from the laundromat."

Symmonds looked out the turret windows, which he could see from his seat. "There's no view."

"There's privacy," said Polgar. Symmonds, his lieutenant in Haight-Ashbury, seemed anxious for the boss to locate his desk in the turret, and Polgar didn't like it. "The dining room's perfect," said Polgar. "The meeting room will be here." He gestured to the living room, where his three underlings were sitting. Addressing two of them he said, "Edgar, Javarius, you guys will be in here. When I need privacy, I'll slide these doors shut. And Alex will be right across the hall from me."

Alex Hiltz, an accountant, had left Arthur Anderson two months earlier to become the Chief Financial Officer of the Fillmore Development Group, Polgar's new holding company.

Symmonds returned to his magazine, and once again Polgar noted his dissatisfaction. Polgar had always been able to read Symmonds — a ruthless streetfighter with more ambition than brains. If he had to name one of his men likely to murder him, Polgar would put money on Marcus Symmonds. He was an overweight black fella, born and raised in the Fillmore district. His mother, a bear of a woman, had worked as a mechanic at Hunters Point during the war and trained her sons in the field. Neither Marcus nor his brothers had reached high school, but could take apart and assemble any Ford engine blindfolded. Polgar had never cared about his abilities with engines, only his ability to lead men and beat them senseless when necessary. Symmonds' unusual strength had helped Polgar before, but now the crime boss worried that he had too much power.

Polgar trusted no one, except possibly his personal bodyguards Edgar Helmanis, an overly cautious Latvian, and Javarius Banks, a former welterweight Golden Gloves runner up. The organization's success in recent months had only heightened Polgar's paranoia.

Since July, everything had fallen in line for Bogdan Polgar. After spending a decade heading an organization in the Fillmore segment of the Western Addition, he'd realized he could only make so much money in a black district the city was intent on destroying. After a brief turf war, he'd expanded his patch so he now controlled the heroin trade in Haight-Ashbury. Though the Summer of Love was a distant memory, a steady flow of drug-hungry hippies kept coming into Haight-Ashbury. Polgar had to expand to keep up with demand.

Polgar heard a door open and close in the corner store below his office, which he planned to turn into a liquor store. Two heavy feet pounded up the back steps. He and his henchmen turned to the dining room door as Benny Delano burst into the room, the look on his jowly face told Polgar something had gone wrong.

"What?" asked Polgar.

Delano blew his cheeks out and threw himself into one of the chairs. He was a muscular guy with a permanent five o'clock shadow. He'd been with Hell's Angels up on Haight Street until developing some degenerative nerve disorder. Delano said he didn't know what the illness was—wouldn't go see a doctor. But he couldn't ride a chopper anymore and he'd left the Angels two years earlier to join Bogdan Polgar's gang. Polgar had bought him a cheap suit and some gel for his hair and he passed for muscle in an Italian mob.

"Luigi Prodi," Delano said, his cheek twitching. "He's dead."

"What?"

"Prodi. The gallery owner. He died." The twitch was worse than usual, a sign he was nervous.

"Did you kill him?" Polgar stepped into the sunny living room and stood before Delano.

"I never touched him. Let me—"

"What about the papers?"

"Jesus Bogdan, let me explain." Delano shook a cigarette out of a pack and stuck it in his fat lips. "I was up at Haight, meeting the boys near Buena Vista, and Jackie Pettis comes up to me. He'd been standing on the corner of Haight and Clayton, doing business. He hears a scream down the street and this woman came barreling out of Prodi's gallery. She runs to a payphone and two, three minutes later two cops show up. Patrol car. Roof-lights flashing."

"Cops on Haight Street?" said Symmonds. "No way."

Polgar had to admit it was rare these days. The beat cops avoided the place.

"Oh yeah," said Delano. "Pettis figures it's something big to bring the cops around so I go do a look-see. I find a crowd building up outside the gallery. I ask someone what's going on and she says the gallery owner is dead. I ask around and find out the cleaning lady went in to get back pay from Prodi and she found him dead at the back of the shop."

"What about the papers?" Polgar said.

"I don't know nothing about the papers, Bogdan," Delano said, the cigarette jiggling from his twitching. "The cops were in the gallery. I couldn't go in. That's the thing—it's not like they went in and called an ambulance. They were sticking around, like to investigate."

"Foul play?"

"Looks that way."

"No sign of the artist?"

Delano shook his head.

Polgar walked back into the dining room, grabbed a straight-back chair and dragged it into the living room. He sat facing his men. He couldn't believe what he'd heard. "So, we've got a dead gallery owner and no idea where the papers are." He glared at his men. "Do we know where Prodi lives?" None of his men said anything. "Find out. And find out fast."

"Take it easy, Bogdan," said Symmonds. "Once the cops leave the gallery, we'll check it out."

Polgar could feel anger welling inside him, but he knew his power over these men came from never letting his fury show. He would take action if needed, but he'd never lose his temper. All he had to do was let them understand the stakes.

"Gentlemen," he said. "We have to find those papers." He looked at each man in turn. "Everything we've been working toward requires those papers. We'll get the papers and track down the artist." He scanned the four men again. "Where's the body now?"

"In the back room. At the gallery up on Haight."

"Just two cops guarding it?"

Delano took another drag of his cigarette. He shrugged his shoulders again. "I think they called in homicide. One cop kept coming out to the black and white parked on the sidewalk, kept calling stuff in."

"They won't ignore a murder," said Polgar. He'd been surprised lately at the things the police were ignoring in Haight-Ashbury — muggings, armed robbery, rape. But they would come for a murder. "We don't need Spracklin or anyone like him coming back."

"Spracklin," snorted Delano with a laugh. "I thought he was on patrol in Skid Row."

Symmonds turned to Delano and said: "Bogdan's worried Spracklin will be so plastered he'll be seeing double and find two dead gallery owners. He'll call it a double homicide." He burst out laughing at his own joke.

Standing, Polgar turned to Edgar Helmanis, who he trusted to carry out instructions to the letter. "Edgar, take three guys and go to Prodi's gallery. Don't go near the police but if they leave, go inside and check it out. If you find the papers, grab them." As the small Latvian moved to the door, Polgar held up a hand to stop him, and said: "The attacker was probably a member of the syndicate."

Helmanis looked at him in confusion. "I know we don't know who they are," Polgar said. "But it makes sense. Keep an eye open for Europeans — French, Spanish, Eastern Europeans."

Helmanis nodded and left the room.

"And if Spracklin's there, buy him a drink," yelled Symmonds. He chuckled, and noticed again no one else found it funny. His friend Benny Delano sucked on the stub of a cigarette before tossing it in a Coke bottle a workman had left.

Polgar scowled and looked away. He wondered if Jimmy Spracklin would investigate Prodi's death, and if so, how much the liquor had got to the former head of the Bureau of Inspectors. Symmonds was right: word on the street said Spracklin was little better than a wino these days. Polgar didn't know. He believed that a down-and-out Spracklin would still prove a formidable foe. *And if he ever sobers up*, Polgar thought, *God help us.*

CHAPTER 2

Handsome Hank O'Dell was in his element. In his vest and shirt-sleeves, his ass on the edge of Ed Burwell's desk, he was shooting the shit with the Inspectors. They were seated at their desks and slouched against the square white pillars that made the Hall of Justice such a maze. Jimmy Spracklin sat at his new desk in the corner, so he had to peer around a post to see the man who'd replaced him as the head of the Bureau of Inspectors.

"It was a win for the team, the whole damn team," said O'Dell. In spite of everything, Spracklin liked him, with his easy-going manner and jockish charisma. O'Dell was a good cop—that's why Spracklin had brought him into the Bureau of Inspectors two years earlier. And it was why Chief Mark Patterson had hand-picked O'Dell as Spracklin's replacement earlier in the fall, promoting him to Captain.

"And the MVP of the team was Jake Jansen—who traced Marjory Haddon's phone records back to David LeBlanc," crowed O'Dell, waving a hand to Jansen. "He assembled all the evidence before bringing LeBlanc in and methodically got a confession—a confession!"

Jansen smiled and nodded at the applause. His face wore a natural frown, but he managed a smile. It was hard to guess Jansen's age but Spracklin pegged it at about thirty-five. His reddish-blond hair was longer than most SFPD personnel, but his stout build said he was out of his twenties. He stood to one side, his arms crossed, accentuating his powerful forearms. He gave a wave with his right hand, which had been missing the pointer and middle fingers since his stint in Korea.

"And I'll tell you one thing, the fellas on the fifth floor have taken note of Jake's performance," said O'Dell. As he said it, he gazed at the ceiling and crossed himself, jokingly deifying Chief Patterson and his gang.

Nice touch, thought Spracklin as the room erupted into laughter. Make fun of the powers that be. Remind the rank and file that Handsome Hank is still one of them. If Spracklin and Mark Patterson had one thing in common, it was that they'd both believed Hank O'Dell should be the head of the Bureau of Inspectors. Spracklin's plan had been to become Police Chief himself and name O'Dell as his replacement in the Bureau of Inspectors. Instead, Spracklin had run afoul of Internal Affairs and got demoted. Now he was back on the detective's rotation and O'Dell was heading the Bureau.

Spracklin wished Hank would wrap it up. The Lieutenant had come into work determined to investigate an unsolved case that had haunted him for years — the murders of Jacques Landry and Emmett Jason, two of Bogdan Polgar's henchmen. Polgar had recently moved from Fillmore up to Haight-Ashbury, and Spracklin wondered if he was loosening his grip on his old neighborhood. Spracklin was going through the interviews he'd conducted two years before, wondering if there was anyone around Fillmore he should revisit. What he wanted was to fetch his Thermos from his desk drawer so he could really get down to work. The mixture of coffee and Red Label it contained would be lukewarm by now, but he needed a little something to settle him down.

"Of course, there's enough glory to go around," said O'Dell in his booming voice. Beneath his Brylcreamed pompadour, his chiseled face beamed his Hollywood smile. "Sergeant Hastings ably backed up Jansen and Sergeant Burwell provided the shoe leather in tracking down witnesses." The inspectors clapped again, but with less enthusiasm. George Hastings was the first black man named to the Bureau of Inspectors, and some felt it was a political appointment for the sake of appearances.

"And last but not least," hollered Handsome Hank. "The maestro himself!" The few men Spracklin could see looked his way. "Jansen was smart enough to take the case to the best damn detective in California and ask how to work it," said O'Dell, pointing to Spracklin.

Spracklin looked at the men, the team he'd led until seventy-two days earlier. Their applause was robust — no, overwhelming — and for a moment he forgot about the work he had to do. He cared only about the kindness of the Inspectors. He mimed the doff of a hat, and knew that he was getting more credit than he deserved. Jansen had only asked him who to approach for phone records.

"This is our strength, gents," O'Dell said, looking around the room. "The guys in this room, the inspectors. We're going to back each other up and rely on each other." Spracklin leaned back, wondering when he could reach into his desk drawer for the Thermos. It didn't matter how cold the concoction in it was—he could feel heat radiating from the Thermos. It was calling to him.

O'Dell was about to say something, but was distracted by the receptionist waving from the elevator lobby. "Captain, I'm sorry to bother you," she said. "It's Lieutenant Shelton, at Park Station. He says it can't wait."

"We're just wrapping up here anyway," said O'Dell. "Back to work, gents." He strode to his office—the office Spracklin still considered his own. Every day he had to remind himself his demotion wasn't O'Dell's fault. It was the fault of that smarmy little shit Mark Patterson. Spracklin sighed. He needed a sip of Irish coffee—just a sip—to calm his resentment. He began to plot how he could get his Thermos to a quiet corner of the office—the kitchen, or maybe the men's room.

Before he could open the drawer, Spracklin's phone rang.

"Lieutenant, it's a woman called Mrs. Morgan," said the receptionist, some dimwit Spracklin had hired the previous spring. For some reason, the Bureau could never find a dependable receptionist. "It's the third time she's called this morning."

Spracklin sucked in his breath. "Put her through." He heard a click and said: "Lieutenant Spracklin." He'd previously answered the phone just with his surname. He now used the honorific "Lieutenant" almost as a defensive measure, as if his superiors couldn't strip him of his rank if he said it often enough.

"Lieutenant, it's Lucy Morgan, resident services at the YMCA. I'm sure you've seen the messages I left for you."

Bitch, thought Spracklin. "Yes, and I thought I'd cleared everything up when I spoke with Mrs. Rosetti on Monday."

"I spoke with Mrs. Rosetti. She said that she'd raised the matter with you but nothing's been resolved yet. And our records show that you're in arears by $37.24. We need that deficit cleared immediately."

Spracklin couldn't raise his voice. He suspected the receptionist hadn't disconnected her line and was listening, so it would be around the office soon no matter what he did. He faced the corner and whispered, "I think you should check your records again. I paid last Friday for the whole week."

"Our records don't show—"

"Look, I explained that to Mrs. Rosetti. I came in from work last Friday night, and I paid my balance due for last week, and my rent for this week."

"I'm sorry, Mr. Spracklin, but you leave us no choice. We have no alternative but to bar you from the premises until the balance is—"

Spracklin hung up. *Fucking YMCA.* He was certain he'd paid the guy at the desk Friday night. Spracklin had got forty dollars from the bank on Friday at noon—he had the receipt to show it. He had nothing but change when he woke up Saturday morning. There was no way he could have spent forty bucks at the bar in one night. He had to have paid his board for the next week at the Y. *Bastards.* He would have to find somewhere else to sleep.

He heard his name called. It was Handsome Hank standing at his office door. "Jansen, Spracklin," he called. "Into the Dugout."

He and Jansen looked at each other across the room, rose and walked into the office with the glass walls—"The Dugout", as Handsome Hank called it. It had changed in the past two months. The blackboard across from the window had been replaced with O'Dell's degree from University of Nebraska, and framed glossies of him playing outfield on the university's baseball team—Handsome Hank sliding into home plate in a cloud of dust, Handsome Hank reaching his right arm over the fence to capture a for-sure home run in his glove.

"You ever hear of Luigi Prodi?" O'Dell asked the two inspectors, as he held the receiver to his chest. His gaze shifted from Spracklin to Jansen and back.

"Yeah, he owns an art gallery up on Haight Street," said Spracklin. He was almost surprised by the question. Luigi Prodi was a gregarious guy, loved by the hippies and artists who hung out at the intersection of Haight and Ashbury. Everyone up there knew him. "Why?"

"Dead," said O'Dell. He spoke into the phone: "Yeah Joey. Sprack says he owns the gallery."

"What's going on?" asked Spracklin.

O'Dell excused himself and said to his inspectors: "Shelton at Park Station. Says they just got a call. A cleaner went into the gallery, needed to talk to the owner about payment. She found a body in the back of the gallery. Beat up and not breathing."

"Make sure they secure the crime scene," said Spracklin.

"They know what to do."

"It's Park Station and it's Haight-Ashbury," said Spracklin. "Tell them."

Hank O'Dell held Spracklin's gaze for a second, then told Joey Shelton to make sure his people sealed the scene. Spracklin could hear the angry tone but not the precise words in Shelton's reply. "I get it, Joey, but it's a crime scene," said O'Dell. "Make sure it's secure. Keep your people there till we arrive."

O'Dell hung up and faced his two detectives. "I want—"

"Will there be any backup from Park Station?" Spracklin interrupted. "We need uniforms to canvas the neighbors, seal the scene…"

O'Dell flopped down in his chair and shrugged his shoulders. "Christ knows, Sprack." He gestured for them to sit as well. "What do you know about this guy?"

"Luigi Prodi. Italian. Grew up in London—his family fled Mussolini's Fascists. Pudgy, artistic guy, maybe forty." He thought, trying to remember the gallery owner. "Nice fella. I guess he moved to the U.S. a few years ago and set up an art gallery in San Francisco. The hippies like him." He thought a moment longer and said, "Can't imagine who'd want to kill him."

O'Dell nodded. "Dunno if it was murder with intent," he said as he lit a cigarette. "What I heard from Joey, the guy was beat up but no signs of a weapon."

"Could have been a junkie after cash," said Spracklin.

"Could be. Anyway…" He turned to Jansen, who'd been sitting uneasily beside Spracklin. "Jake, you're up in the rotation. Jimmy knows the turf. I want the two of you working on this—"

"I'm good going solo," said Jansen.

O'Dell paused, taken aback. "You're lead investigator, Jake, but Jimmy knows the turf."

"As I said, I'm good on my own." Jansen held his boss with a stare.

"You need a partner."

"Gimme Hastings." Jansen obviously liked working with the black Sergeant.

O'Dell's face flushed. "I said the two of you work together."

"I don't work with drunks," said Jansen.

O'Dell's window was open, and in the chilly silence of the office they could hear sheriffs yelling at prisoners to get into a transport in the parking lot below. "Detective," said O'Dell slowly. "Lieutenant Spracklin is one of the best, if not the best, homicide investigator in

California. You can learn a lot from him. Together, you two will find and prosecute the person who killed this man."

Jansen looked ready to explode but thought better of it. Spracklin said nothing. As they left the office, Spracklin wondered if he could nip to the men's room with the Thermos before they left. He needed something to lift his spirits.

"We'll take my car," said Jansen as he put on his jacket. "And leave your Thermos in your desk drawer."

THE COMPLETE NOVEL
THE PRODI SYNDICATE WILL BE PUBLISHED SOON.

ACKNOWLEDGMENTS

I'm constantly overwhelmed by the kindness of friends and readers, and feel embarrassed that I can never thank all of them. Even when I do thank them, the words seem insufficient. There are so many people I owe and I hope they know how much I appreciate their help.

I've recently been working with the team at Post Hill's Permuted Press division, led by Managing Editor Kate Monahan, and they are a joy to work with. They include Roger Williams, a true gent who I've been working with since his days with New England Publishing Associates. I owe a huge debt of gratitude to this whole group.

I'd also like to thank my agent, Andy Ross, for representing me. Teddy Lapierre produced a great cover for the book, and Mike Hayes and the team at Charcoal Marketing helped immeasurably with social media and IT. Connor Kirby was also invaluable in providing graphics for my marketing effort.

One of the joys of writing is getting to know booksellers, and I've been lucky to meet some great ones. Two stand out, and they're at opposite ends of the continent. Mike Hamm of Bookmark in Halifax, N.S., is a great champion of all writers. And Jude Feldman, General Manager of Borderlands Books in San Francisco, is peerless in her kindness and encouragement. I really look forward to seeing Borderlands' new store on Haight Street.

Here are just a few of the people who helped me out along the way: Ken McGoogan, Pamela Callow, Rose Behar, Colleen Tapp, Joyce Howard Moreira, Sabina Wex, Stephen Patrick Clare, Stannous Flouride, Jamie Moreira, Stephen Bagworth, Dave Nodwell, Paul Nodwell, Ron Mitchell, and Tom and Sue Omstead. A huge thanks to all of them.

My children Cat and Scott deserve my thanks for their support and advice. And finally, to my collaborator, travel companion, business partner, and endless love Carol—thank you so much for everything.